The world of racing is, after all, a matter of many delights, at the same time a spectacle containing the thrill of seeing in action and on the stretch one of the most beautiful of creatures, the thoroughbred racehorse; a medium for the heightened excitement of the wager, of the pitting of wits against the imponderables; a matter of endless discussion of the merits and faults of man and horse. It is even an opportunity for the upwardly mobile to acquire prestige and social advancement, for was it not the Duke of Windsor in his riding days who advised those anxious for social preferment: "If you can't get in by the front door, try the stable door."

There we leave it in the hope that our selection will at least have provided a few hours of what, after all, despite its ups and downs, racing aims to be all about—entertainment and enjoyment.

DICK FRANCIS
From the Introduction

THE
DICK FRANCIS
TREASURY OF
GREAT RACING
STORIES

Edited and Introduced by
Dick Francis
and
John Welcome

FAWCETT CREST • NEW YORK

A Fawcett Crest Book
Published by Ballantine Books
Collection copyright © 1989 by Dick Francis and John Welcome

Library of Congress Catalog Card Number: 89-72151

ISBN 0-449-22049-4

This edition published by arrangement with W.W. Norton & Company, Inc.

Manufactured in the United States of America

First Ballantine Books Edition: May 1992

Cover photo © (Michael Coyne)/The Image Bank

Acknowledgements

Grateful acknowlegement is made to Mrs. R. Findlay for permission to reprint the story *The Dream*; to the authors and Messrs. John Johnson Ltd. for the stories *A Glass of Port with the Proctor* and *A Carrot for a Chestnut*; to the author and Mr. Murray Pollinger for the story *Prime Rogues* from *Conversation Piece*, published in Virago Modern Classics in the Commonwealth and in the same series distributed by Penguin in the USA; to Mary Lovell for the story *The Splendid Outcast*; to Messrs. Harold Ober Associates, acting on behalf of the Sherwood Anderson Estate, for the story *I'm a Fool* (copyright 1922 by Dial Publishing Co. Inc., copyright renewed 1949 by Eleanor Copenhaver Anderson); to the author and Messrs. Faber & Faber Ltd. for the story *The Major* from the *Faber Anthology*; to the Estate of J. P. Marquand for the story *What's It Get You?*; to Messrs. Curtis Brown Ltd., acting on behalf of the William Fain Estate, for the story *Harmony* (copyright © 1955, 83 by Nicholas Fain); and to Messrs. John Farquharson Ltd., acting on behalf of the Somerville and Ross Estate, for the story *The Bagman's Pony*.

CONTENTS

INTRODUCTION

THE late D.W.E. Brock, a charming and authoritative sporting writer and anthologist who wrote between the wars, stated in one of his prefaces that racing literature was neither so plentiful nor of such a high standard as that of fox-hunting. He was incorrect on both counts, as we trust we have been able to show in this collection. A sport which can command the pens and claim the attention of such writers as George Moore, Siegfried Sassoon and John Galsworthy has little need to apologize for its lack of literary quality, and as to the plenitude of its material, the collection will, we trust, speak for itself.

Moore and Sassoon produced no short stories so the races and racing of which they wrote cannot, alas, be included here, but Galsworthy did. Patrician that he was, it might have seemed more likely that Galsworthy would, when writing of racing, have turned his attention to the pillars of society and the Establishment to whose exclusive circles his birth and education (Harrow and New College, Oxford) gave him en-trée. But his sympathies, as displayed in all his writings, were always with the outsider, the little man, the human being against whom the odds are stacked, and he has written of him perceptively in *Had A Horse*, his tale of the timid and exploited man who for once turns the tables on his oppressors.

Kings, as we know from the oft-repeated saying, once

made the sport their own. Charles II rode the Rowley Mile at Newmarket and gave it his name; more recently the Duke of Windsor, when he was Prince of Wales and the Prince Charming of the world, rode the best against the best in steeplechases and point-to-points, until a nervous court put a stop to his race-riding; in the present day The Princess Royal carries on the race-riding tradition, while Her Majesty The Queen maintains her string and her stud, and The Queen Mother is the best-loved patron of steeplechasing. These notables are a far cry from some of the owners, trainers and riders depicted in this collection, but all are bound by the same threads that have captured hearts and minds from time immemorial—the thrill of the race and the roar of the ring. Romance and ruin, they say, stalk in double harness beside all who tread the Turf, but that only adds to its excitement and appeal. Whether, even in this egalitarian age, it remains true that all men are equal on the Turf, or under it, is open to doubt. Certainly Edgar Wallace's little cockney tipster, Educated Evans, had small reason to think so.

Wallace gained his knowledge of racing and experience of the Turf by the simple method of paying for it, since he maintained at enormous expense a large string of useless horses. "Hair trunks" his friend Jack Leach, trainer, jockey and journalist, called them. Against all advice Wallace believed each and every one of them to be a potential classic winner, and he backed them accordingly. "He fought," Jack Leach went on to say, "a continual battle against the bookmakers and scarcely won a round." At least his experiences gave him the material to write several racing thrillers, of which *The Flying Fifty Five* is probably the best, and a racing play, *The Calendar*, which even Jack Leach, who liked him at the same time as he laughed at him, conceded to be the only good racing play he ever saw.

The idea of writing about the exploits of Educated Evans came to Wallace from a chance acquaintanceship struck up on the racecourse with an engaging rogue called Peter Christian Barrie, who had already done time—three years hard labour—as a result of running "ringers" (horses running under false names and identities at various racecourses). This proved to be a profitable enterprise until overconfidence betrayed him and allowed the fraud to be discovered. Barrie's specialty was painting the lookalike so as to resemble more closely the switched horse, but on one occasion the paint came off at an inconvenient moment and alerted the authorities.

Though he was easily the most audacious, Barrie was far from the first to employ this ruse. Conan Doyle heard of a case in the eighties and used it as part of the plot in *Silver Blaze*. However, not all aspects of this famous story will commend themselves to purists in racing. It is unlikely, for instance, that Colonel Ross, who had been in racing and concerned with horses all his life, would have failed to recognize Silver Blaze, however camouflaged. But the story is redeemed for all time by what is probably the most famous of all Holmesian pronouncements when he expounds to Watson the significance of the curious incident of the dog in the night-time.

Barrie, for his part, coined a phrase which deserves, even if it has not received, almost equal fame. When asked by the judge at his trial what he considered to be a good thing in racing, ''a useful three-year-old in a moderate two-year-old race, my lord,'' was his reply. After his release from prison, Barrie, henceforth known on the racecourse and elsewhere as ''Ringer Barrie,'' went into the tipping business, circulating his selections to a wide range of clients from every walk of life, from parsons to peers of the realm. Wallace, captivated by Barrie's cheek and charm, first wrote his life story for *John Bull*, a tabloid of the time, and then adapted him as a character for his prolific pen. Not only that, but, still bemused by his self-assessed abilities as a tipster and expert on form, Wallace invested in the business, became a partner, and took over the tipping. Inevitably it failed. To quote Jack Leach again: ''I believe he did tip a winner once when the office boy got fed up with all the losers and changed the selection.''

The losses incurred by this failure and his own gambling

must to some extent at least have been offset for Wallace by the royalties earned by the Educated Evans stories which throw a lively and humorous light on one of the gamier aspects of the racing scene.

Wallace himself never rode a race in his life, nor for that matter did Richard Findlay, who wrote *The Dream*, concerned as it is with the pre-race nerves and anticipations of an amateur jockey. Findlay was a serving officer in the R.A.F. when he wrote the story, and it must have been his understanding of what went on in the minds of men in action that enabled him to enter into the hopes and fears of his protagonist Bobby Coplow.

Colin Davy, one of the few who rode and wrote fiction, is, unfairly, all but forgotten now. He was an amateur soldier-rider in the great days of soldier-riding between the wars, though his career in the saddle was dogged by ill-luck and injury which may have prevented him from reaching the very top. He saw, as many did in those days of wine and roses (in fact, it was mostly champagne—the great racing drink held by its apologists to be so because it does not put on weight), the humour and the fun of it all, and he recorded it with a light touch which concealed the insider's knowledge that came from his experiences in riding and running a stable, both at home and in India and Egypt. Some of those experiences in the latter countries, when in partnership with a present pillar of the Turf, did not exactly commend themselves to the colonel of the exclusive regiment in which they were then young officers, but to the reader they certainly add to the enjoyment and serve to spice the brew—even if the battle cry "twenty to one and not a pal on" was scarcely designed to attract favourable comment from their seniors. In *Ups and Downs* Davy wrote one of the best of all racing autobiographies, which he published when his career in the saddle was coming to a close. Unfortunately it came out in 1939 and was overshadowed by the outbreak of the war and it has not been reprinted. It remains a fascinating record of the true spirit of steeplechasing in its time, written by one who had lived it and loved it, and who knew and had experienced its many set-backs and the few triumphs that make it all worthwhile.

After the war, Davy continued to write novels and short stories. All of them, but especially the short stories, are full of life, fun and enjoyment. His characters, however, and the milieu in which they mixed, looked back to a vanished world. Fun, enjoyment and the copious consumption of champagne had little in common with the post-war austerities of the Attlee-Cripps regime. As he had not been a lucky rider so he was not a lucky writer and, as anyone who has had experience of both knows only too well, luck has a major part to play in both racing and writing; as a matter of fact, Davy called his first racing novel *Luck's Pendulum*. But he was felt to be out of touch with his times, his sales fell off and he put away his pen. However, at his best, Davy was splendid and his best is probably seen in his short humorous stories, an example of which we have included here.

The Americans J. P. Marquand and Sherwood Anderson came from very different backgrounds, both of them light years away from that of Colin Davy and the British cavalry. Marquand had impeccable New England ancestry which he put to good use in his slyly humorous social studies and conversation pieces, such as *The Late George Apley* and *Wickford Point* which, with others like them, became best-sellers making his name universally known and critically appreciated. Blessed with unflagging invention and a wide range of interests, Marquand was one of the most prolific of American writers, both before and just after the last war. Detective novels, historical and American civil war serials, *Saturday Evening Post* short stories, all flowed unceasingly from his pen. Many of the latter concerned racing and its characters, for racing and the racetrack and the raffish types who gathered there never ceased to fascinate him.

Although he earned a substantial income from writing, once he became established, Marquand's inbred New England caution precluded him from ever venturing into ownership, but he was delighted when a friend named a racehorse after him. The horse proved a dismal failure and disappeared from the track. Shortly afterwards Marquand was dining with the horse's owner at their Boston club when the waiter placed before them two steaks which proved uncommonly tough. "I wonder," Marquand said, sadly contemplating his plate, "if by any chance this could be J. P. Marquand?"

Anderson, unlike Marquand, was the boy from the wrong side of the tracks. He began his restless and roving career at the age of fourteen, drifting into occupations and out of them, gathering material which he was later to transmute into some of the earliest, small town, realistic American writing. It was this drifting which led him into racing and it was of the drifters and the under-privileged that he wrote, having been one himself. "His characters," one critic said of him, "are puzzled, groping, baffled," as indeed is the "big, lumbering fellow of nineteen" who "promised mother I'd give up racing for good." Like many another he failed to keep that promise with the results shown in *I'm a Fool*.

Anderson's big lumbering fellow has little in common with the neat and stylish John Stephens of whom William Fain writes in *Harmony*, his sensitive study of an ageing top jockey with an appreciation of his own abilities and an independent cast of mind. This story is a little gem which first appeared in the pages of *The New York Magazine*. It provides not only a background glance at Lamorlaye and Longchamp, but also brief sketches of owners, trainers, the occasional bitchiness of the weighing room and the riding of the race, which anyone acquainted with them will immediately recognize as authentic.

John Stephens, remote, reserved, determined to preserve his own inner integrity, would nevertheless have felt an affinity with Somerville and Ross's reluctant owner of *The Bagman's Pony*, who let himself in for rather more than he bargained for after a mess dinner, and with Molly Keane's innocent Englishman exposed in *Prime Rogues* to the wiles and machinations of upper class Irish ladies with a taste for devilment.

Much has been written about Somerville and Ross, for in sporting literature they stand second only to Surtees, who, incidentally, hated racing, especially steeplechasing, and had some hard words to say about those who took part in it. But no one, not even Surtees, has written better of the secret that exists between the sympathetic hands of the horseman and his mount than these two marvellous ladies.

The Bagman's Pony, the story we have included here, is less well known than those concerning that "stable boy among gentlemen and gentleman among stable boys," Flurry Knox M.F.H., and his chronicler and frequent victim, Major Sinclair Yeates R.M., but it is nevertheless well qualified in its own right to stand alongside the earlier and more famous "Experiences" of those two worthies, telling us as it does of a different type of racing, and revealing a glimpse of a long vanished India in the middle years of the Raj. It stems, as Miss Somerville candidly admits in her reminiscences, from a tale told by her uncle Colonel Kendall Coghill, a hero of the Mutiny and a veteran of Tel-El-kebir and "one of the most delightful raconteurs in the world with a memory of steel for names and events."

Molly Keane, a member of an illustrious Irish sporting family, commenced her writing career not long after the First World War. It was then considered not quite the thing for a young lady such as she to produce slightly racy sporting novels and, at a loss for a *nom de plume*, she adopted the pseudonym M. J. Farrell from a name glimpsed on a public house on the way home from hunting. Several novels set in the hunting country of County Wexford, which was lovingly described, followed in quick succession, of which *Mad Puppetstown* is outstanding.

This portrait of Irish country-house living in the troubled times and after is a magical evocation of the Irish sporting scene when, as she recalls, hunting and racing were almost a religion to those living there. To quote one of her own phrases, "the blood and bones" of both sports were bred in her, for her father and brothers were brilliant across country and between the flags, and she, though she does not say it, was not far behind. That she put that inheritance to good use can be seen in the story *Prime Rogues*, taken from a collec-

tion called *Conversation Piece* can well stand beside *Mad
Puppetstown* and indeed *The Irish R.M.* not only as a record
of another age but as a landmark in sporting literature.

The use of the word "landmark," though deserved, is
perhaps to predicate a heavy hand and a solemn approach
which is far from the case. These were young books full of
life and fire, full of a passion for houses and horses and for
that "fierce beauty," as she once so well described it, of the
Irish countryside.

Beryl Markham knew all about the hardships that a life
with horses can bring. A singularly beautiful woman brought
up in the wilds, she achieved worldwide fame in the thirties
when she became the first person to fly solo from England
to America. But, brilliant aviatrix though she was, it was
with horses that her real genius lay. Not only did she train
them successfully in England and South Africa, but from
girlhood she knew, understood and loved them. She could
also write, when she put her mind and her pen to it, although
there is still argument whether she or her third husband, Raoul
Schumacher, wrote her now best-selling memoirs *West With
The Night*. There can be little doubt, however, that it was she
who wrote *The Splendid Outcast*, the story which we have
included here, since it came from her own experience.

A colt, cast out as unmanageable from a powerful English
stable, came into the ring at Tattersalls when she was there.
In real life she was able, her biographer tells us, to buy him
cheaply. She renamed him "Messenger Boy," took him to
Kenya and won races with him. But the sight of him in the
sales ring, handsome, splendid and in chains, and the longing look of a little ex-jockey standing nearby inspired the
story.

All these writers in their very differing ways understood
racing people and what motivated them—be they punters,
owners, riders or those who just come for the spectacle and
the thrill. John Taintor Foote, whose story *The Look of Eagles* is a minor classic of the genre, also understood them
and, what is even more important and a fact that is sometimes overlooked, he understood those on whom the entire

lifeblood of the sport depends—the horses. Born in Leadville, Colorado, in 1891, he was a racing man through and through, having haunted the local tracks—and all others if he could get to them—from his early youth. He had grown up with racing in his blood. He died in 1950, at the comparatively early age of fifty-nine, leaving behind him a body of stories on racing and his other love, fishing, all of which bear the stamp of insight, authority and affection.

The phrase "The Look of Eagles" has now passed into current usage to describe that commanding presence which denotes a true champion and which only true champions have. But it was John Taintor Foote who coined the phrase and put it into print. He placed the making of the phrase into the mind and mouth of Old Man Sanford who, with his unfailing courtesy, old-world manners and all-seeing eye, is well worthy of taking his place amongst the finest delineations of real racing men, and the other characters in the story also ring true. The story first saw light in 1915, and, although its trappings may have dated somewhat, its main core and its characters remain ageless.

"Any damned fool knows that one horse can run faster than another," is the dismissive comment said to have been made to him by his father when Paul Mellon, one of the most successful of modern owners, bought his first racehorse. But there is rather more to it than that, as we hope these stories show. If that were all, why is it that so many, from peers, prime ministers, priests and parsons to newly enriched entrepreneurs and the man on the Clapham omnibus, whoever he may be, have all sought solace and success on the racecourse, and why have so many differing authors made it their subject?

It is, after all, a matter of many delights, at the same time a spectacle containing the thrill of seeing in action and on the stretch one of the most beautiful of creatures, the thoroughbred racehorse; a medium for the heightened excitement of the wager, of the pitting of wits against the imponderables; a matter of endless discussion of the merits and faults of man and horse. It is even an opportunity for the upwardly mobile to acquire prestige and social advancement, for was it not the Duke of Windsor in his riding days who advised those anxious for social preferment: "If you can't get in by the front door, try the stable door."

There we leave it in the hope that our selection will at least have provided a few hours of what, after all, despite its ups and downs, racing aims to be all about—entertainment and enjoyment.

THE DREAM

Richard Findlay

USUALLY when Bobby Coplow awoke he got out of bed at once and began to shave, feeling pleased with the prospect of the day's work. But on this cold February morning he lay for several minutes without moving. He was queerly perturbed, and could not at first discover the cause. And then he remembered his dream. It was a dream which he had had once before in the same week, down to the tiniest detail. He was riding his horse October Miracle in the Covertcoat Steeplechase at Lutterton. It was raining hard, and the going was very heavy. On both occasions his dream had commenced as they were approaching the worst fence on the course, and Bobby could remember nothing of the earlier part of the race, nor did he know whether they were on the first or second circuit. October Miracle was striding out easily, running well within himself, and Bobby was holding him on a tight rein, keeping him three lengths behind the two leaders. One of the two leading horses was Grey Marvel, with the stocky, broad-shouldered figure of Billy Sprott up. The other horse, who was almost level with Grey Marvel, but on the extreme outside of the course, was Battleaxe, a notoriously uncertain jumper. The fence they were approaching was a plain fence, but it was four feet nine inches high, and was set on a sharp bend in such a way that one came at it at an awkward angle. The ground rose slightly towards it, and then fell away so that there was a seven-foot

1

drop on the landing side. And like all the fences on the Lutterton course, it was as stiff as timber.

Bobby was thinking that Battleaxe might be a nuisance at this fence. You never knew what that horse was going to do. He would have to watch him very closely, he thought. He glanced quickly backwards over his left shoulder to see how much he was leading the nearest horse. He disliked looking back in a race because the action was apt to make one's horse unbalanced, but in this case the knowledge thus gained would make a difference to the way in which he would jump the fence. He was a good three lengths ahead of the field. He moved his hands forward a little on his horse's neck. October Miracle pricked his intelligent ears, and lengthened his stride appreciably to gain on the two leaders. Bobby kept him in the middle of the course as they began to round the bend. Twenty yards from the fence he pulled him in slightly to meet it squarely close to the inner wing. He moved his hands still farther forward, and sat very still. He saw Grey Marvel's forehand rise as he rose at the fence. A moment later he saw something else which made his heart leap sickeningly in his chest. Battleaxe had refused, and had swerved towards the inside of the fence. His jockey was fighting him desperately, but seemed unable to pull him up. October Miracle had seen what was happening, too, and made a gigantic effort to avert disaster. A full fifteen feet from the fence he took off with a tremendous spring. As he left the ground Battleaxe's shoulder struck him hard in the quarters, causing him to twist in the air so that he went over the fence back-first, on his side. God! thought Bobby. This is going to be a *hell* of a fall! Instinctively he withdrew his feet from the stirrup-irons and tried to push himself away from the falling horse, who otherwise must crush him beneath his weight. As the ground rushed up to meet him he tucked his head into his chest and raised his arms to shield his face, bracing himself for the impact. But the impact never came. Instead he found himself standing beside the fence, looking down at a figure which lay face downwards on the sodden turf, inert and still where it had fallen. He saw the black cap, the black woollen jersey

with the saxe-blue chevrons, and knew that it was himself.
A few feet away October Miracle lay on his side, his mud-
streaked flanks heaving spasmodically. Bobby felt strangely
light and detached. Suddenly, with a shock that was both
pain and fear, he knew that he was dead. And then, almost
in the same moment, it seemed, he found himself wide awake
in his own bed. The sequence of events was exactly the same
as on that other night when he had dreamed this dream.

As Bobby lay in his bed now he was thinking that the
Lutterton Meeting was to be held this afternoon. He was
riding his horse October Miracle in the Covertcoat Steeplechase at three o'clock. And underneath the emotions which
those thoughts engendered was the odd excitement which he
always felt on the day of a race. This excitement, which was
partly fear and partly joy, invariably increased as the time of
the race drew nearer. But as soon as he had the reins in his
hand to mount, it vanished completely. Suddenly, as he stared
through the window at the bleak daylight of the winter day,
he remembered that recurring dreams of this sort were believed to be an omen of disaster. Oh, what the hell, he
thought.

There was a knock at the door, and his servant came in
carrying a tray. On the tray were a cup and saucer, a teapot,
a milk-jug, a sugar-bowl and a plate containing two digestive
biscuits. The man looked surprised to find Bobby still in bed.
"Good morning, sir," he said. "It's seven o'clock."

"I know, Renton," said Bobby. "I've been thinking about
the race this afternoon. The going'll be pretty heavy."

Renton put the tray down on the table by the bedside. "It
will that, sir," he replied. " 'Ock deep, as the saying is. But
the Miracle won't mind," he added confidently. He poured
out a cup of tea, and began to lay out some clothes on an
armchair near the window.

Sipping his tea, and watching Renton's neat, methodical
movements, Bobby thought what an excellent fellow he was,
and wondered, with a sudden pang, if this was the last morning when he would do these things for him. The idea per-
sisted, in spite of all his efforts to drive it from his mind. He

got out of bed, and looked out of the window across the rolling grassland of the Leicestershire Wolds. Even under the dull grey sky, with the leafless trees dripping in the still, damp air, it seemed to him the loveliest countryside in all the world. Bobby thought again that the going would be very deep today. But, as Renton had said, October Miracle would not mind. Whether the ground was a rolling bog, or iron hard, it was all one to him. He was a hell of a horse.

Bobby crossed the room, and looked into the mirror above the wash-basin in the corner. The mirror reflected a narrow brown face, tousled dark hair, and a pair of large and rather wide-apart blue eyes. It was a strong face, but the expression just now, as always in repose, was a little sad. It was the face of a sensitive man who spent much time alone.

He shaved and washed quickly, pulled on a pair of jodhpurs and a dark-blue polo jersey, and went downstairs. In the hall he put on a cap, picked up his whip and gloves, and went out into the stable-yard. It was a little after half-past seven. Three racehorses, saddled and bridled, and with rugs under their saddles, were being led up and down the gravelled yard. Two of them were 'chasers, good performers up to three miles over park courses. The third was a hunter who, after a regular season's hunting, was now in training for point-to-point races. The stable-lads who were leading the three horses touched their caps as Bobby approached. He was smiling, but rather sadly, they thought. "Good morning," he said. "A rotten day. How's October Miracle?" he went on to Hogan, the head-lad.

"Oh, he's fine, sir," answered Hogan, who was leading one of the fencers, a chestnut mare. "Always quiet, never fusses at all. I never did see the likes," he added, with a puzzled expression on his weather-beaten face.

"Go on up to Throxton Park with this lot, Tom," said Bobby, patting the mare's sleek neck. "I want you and Arthur to take Annabel Lee and The Bowman a mile over fences. Jack," he said to the lad who was holding the point-to-point horse, "walk Torchlight about until I come up. If I'm not there by eight o'clock, canter him seven furlongs and bring him home." He waited until the three horses had passed up the drive into the road, until the dip in the road hid them from view. Then he crossed the stable-yard, passed through an opening on its farther side, and reached a post and rails enclosing a small paddock. He rested his foot upon the lowest rail, and, his arms upon the topmost, gazed across the paddock at the horse who was being led round the gravel path encircling it. October Miracle was a bay, with black points and tail. He was nine years old. Little could be seen of him at the moment because of the rug which protected him from the cold, damp air, but Bobby well knew what he would see if he rug was removed. The horse was sixteen hands two inches high, but his make and shape were so nearly perfect that he looked smaller at first glance. His shoulders were strong and well placed, and he had great depth of girth. The line from hip to hock was long and straight, and his second thighs were wide and fully developed. When you stood behind him and watched him move, you realized the immense power of his hind-limbs and quarters. He had a lot of bone and stood over a lot of ground. But perhaps the thing which struck you most about him was his proud and honest outlook. He was a beautiful horse.

When he saw Bobby, October Miracle pricked his ears and whinnied softly. Bobby climbed the fence and made much of the horse, whose cool dark muzzle was thrust into his hand. As he looked at those large brown eyes, October Miracle seemed to him the very embodiment of loyalty and splendid courage, of a woman's tenderness and a lion's heart. Neither as a hunter, nor in point-to-point races, nor in his two victorious seasons under Rules, had this beloved horse of his ever given him a fall. He seemed always to feel a deep responsibility for the man upon his back, and in the old hunting days, even when he had been tired at the end of a long run, he had jumped his fences carefully without rush or blunder. Watching him now as the stable-lad led him on around the paddock, Bobby thought of the wonderful ride he had given him at Liverpool in the previous November, when, gaining yards on his opponents with every leap over "those rasping five-foot fences," he had won the Grand Sefton Steeplechase in a canter. But the climax of his brilliant career lay still in the future, he thought. He would win the Grand National next month, if class meant anything at all. Thus would he join the ranks of the immortals. It was his due, the inalienable right of his great quality. He was a superhorse.

As he stood there, hearing once more the thunderous music of hoofs on grass, rapt in his dreams of glory, the shadow of that other, vivid dream, a dream of disaster, fell again across Bobby Coplow's mind. It made the dull day duller, changed the tenor of his thoughts to a minor key. But it could not quench the glory.

At eight o'clock the stable-lad brought October Miracle back to his box and gave him his morning feed. Bobby watched him with loving eyes as he fed, finding in the horse's quiet unconcern a sort of peace and comfort. After a few minutes he went back into the house. As he was having his bath he heard the other horses returning. "How did they go, Tom?" he called out of the window.

"Annabel Lee went very well, sir," Hogan called back. "The Bowman stopped at the ditch again," he added after a moment's pause, with a melancholy shake of his head.

"Oh, hell, he seems to be making a regular habit of that," said Bobby. "We must get him out of it somehow before Sandown next week. We'll give him a good school tomorrow." No doubt about it, he thought as he dressed, The Bowman had completely lost confidence in himself since he had had that nasty fall at the second open ditch at Leicester in January. He would have to nurse him along very carefully, or he would never recover his old form. Whatever happened, he should have a good school tomorrow.

After breakfast Bobby went out to the stable-yard and watched October Miracle being boxed for his forty-mile journey to Lutterton. The horse walked up the ramp at the back of the box with a quick, springy step, like a conqueror eager for fresh victories. Bobby followed him into the box. "See you soon, old man," he said. The horse nuzzled his cheek. Bobby walked down the ramp, and round to the front of the box. "Take it easy, Knocker," he said to the chauffeur, who was sitting at the wheel with Hogan at his side. "You've got plenty of time."

The man touched his cap. "Yes, sir," he said. He was very fond of horses, and particularly of October Miracle, and would never in any circumstances have driven in such a way as to endanger his safety, or even to cause him discomfort. Moreover, he knew that Bobby was quite aware of these facts. But he always expected some such remark as Bobby had just made, and would have been disappointed if it had not been forthcoming. It was an essential part of the ritual. He let in the clutch, and the horse-box moved slowly up the drive. "Bring Simon round to the front door at half-past ten." Bobby said to one of the stable-lads. He went into the house, and looked in the paper at the list of runners in the Covertcoat Steeplechase at Lutterton. It was a four-mile steeplechase, and was worth four hundred pounds to the winner. There were fifteen probable starters, with several National candidates amongst them. But October Miracle would win all right. Grey Marvel, and Ramadan, who had been second in the National in the previous year, and who, like October Miracle, was set to carry twelve stone, were the two horses most to be feared. But, barring accidents, October Miracle would certainly win all right. He was invincible.

When Simon was brought round to the door Bobby got up on him and rode out through the village to Throxton Park. Between the village and the first gate into the park he met Tom Green, the trainer, coming back from exercising his second string. He was on his old brown hack, leading the string of about twenty horses. He trained Grey Marvel.

"Hullo, squire," he said. "How's the champion this morning?"

"Fine," said Bobby.

"Grey Marvel's all right, too," said Tom Green. "Never been better. You won't see him this afternoon," he added with absolute conviction. He was always optimistic, and usually with good reason. He was a good trainer, and had good horses to train.

"No, I'll be in front," Bobby answered.

"Oh, yeah, wisecracker?" Tom Green said. He was a great cinema fan, and was always full of Americanisms. He was grinning. Oh, hell, do we have to go on talking bilge? thought Bobby. He could not help feeling depressed, and wanted to be alone. "So long, Tom," he said. "See you at Lutterton." He rode on. Eleven o'clock was striking from the church clock in the village as he passed through the last of the four gates and came out into the park. He shortened the reins, and dug his heels into Simon's flanks. The old horse started off in a fast gallop, his feet squelching on the sodden ground. On the far side of the park Bobby reined him in. Looking over the boundary wall, he saw the wide grass country stretching out to the misty horizon. It looked desolate under the lowering sky, but he knew every inch of it, and loved it all. Every detail seemed to stand out very clear. A mile away the bare trees of Sandon Spinney made a black smudge against the surrounding greyness. The whole world seemed drained of colour, lifeless. Bobby turned in his saddle and gazed back across the park. He saw the schooling gallops, the brush fences stretching away to the gate by which he had come in. Nearer to him were the remains of the old grandstand, relic of the days when Throxton Park had been a racecourse. In his imagination he saw it in its hey-day, women in crinolines, heavily whiskered men in swallow-tailed coats, moving leisurely in the sunshine of long ago. The jockeys were whiskered too, and rode with very long leathers horses with very long necks and very small heads, like the ones in the old sporting prints. Bobby knew, of course, that the horses were not really like that, but he always pictured them so. He had often laughed at himself for being so foolish. Departed glories! he thought. Those lovely yesterdays! he said to himself. And suddenly he realized that the world around him was not lifeless. It was alive with the lives of the men and women, yes by God, and horses too, who had passed that way once or twice or many times and now had gone. He could hear echoes of their laughter and of their sorrow and of the thud of horses' hoofs. Many of them had

had their dreams of glory and they had all had to go from this place and no doubt most of them had gone bravely and gallantly. Horses in the main were brave and splendid animals and there was this to be said for the men and women who loved and rode them that, though they might have many faults, most of them were brave and some were splendid. They had built up a tradition that if they had to die it was a fine thing to die on horseback, perhaps in battle, perhaps with the music of hounds or the rattle of guard-rails in their ears. Horsemen and warriors! he thought with a sudden fierce joy. That was their tradition, and if he had to die and to go from this place, he would be loyal to it. But he hoped that he would not have to go yet, to leave all this beauty. He did not want to go yet. Dear God, he prayed, let me go on staying here for a bit. Please dear God don't make me go from here yet. He looked at his watch. "Heavens!" he exclaimed. It was half-past eleven. "Come up, Simon," he said. The old hunter raised his head from the short, wet, brown grass. They did not take very long to get back to the house.

On the way to Lutterton, a solitary magpie flew quite low along the road in front of Bobby Coplow's car. It stayed there for so long that he thought it would never go away. It was very unlucky to see a single magpie. In the past it had always meant serious trouble of one sort or another. The bird would not go away. "Get to hell out of here," Bobby said. Eventually the magpie flew over a hedge and disappeared. Bobby was glad when it had gone. But he was worried, too. It was a bad omen, like his dream. He drove fast all the way, but the road was not very good. It was ten minutes past one when he arrived at the course. The first race, a two-mile selling hurdle race, was over, and the bookmakers were starting to pay out. The indefinable racecourse atmosphere stirred Bobby Coplow's blood. He looked through his glasses at the board by the judge's box, then at his card. Assurance had won by a head from Sussex Melody, with Kremlin third. There was a large crowd round the totalizator stand. Bobby saw several people whom he knew, but he did not want to talk to them. He walked round the back of the stand towards the stables. Tom Hogan was talking to Lord and Lady Cairngorm outside one of the boxes. Bobby took off his hat and shook hands with them both. "How are you, Bobby?" old Lord Cairngorm murmured. He always spoke very quietly, and when his wife was with him he hardly spoke at all. It was not necessary, and in fact was almost impossible. Bobby liked him very much, and was rather sorry for him, too. But Lady Cairngorm had a lot of money.

"I'm so glad to see you, Bobby," she said. "Hogan tells me you've only got one ride this afternoon. October Miracle *is* a lovely horse, isn't he? I wish he were mine. Will you ride Bright Angel for me in the third race?" she asked.

"Why, what's happened to Croppy?" said Bobby.

"Didn't you see the first race?" asked Lady Cairngorm. "Oh, you've only just arrived. That brute Stevedore fell three hurdles from home, and poor Croppy hurt his back rather badly. I've just come from the hospital. He won't be able to ride any more today, the doctor says. Such bad luck for the poor man. But there it is. You will ride Bright Angel, won't you?" she asked anxiously.

"Thanks very much, but I won't if you don't mind. I'm not feeling too good, and I think one ride will be enough for me today," Bobby answered. "You'll get a jockey all right, I expect," he added after a moment's pause.

"Oh, how beastly of you!" said Lady Cairngorm plaintively. "Bright Angel is just your affair. You couldn't look better, either. Still, I suppose you know best. But I do think it's beastly of you. Well, I must go and find somebody else, that's all. Come along, Angus," she said, moving off with long strides towards the weighing-room.

"The best of luck, Bobby," said old Lord Cairngorm, as he started to follow his wife. Most of his time was spent in following his wife. But that is neither here nor there, as they say.

Bobby and Hogan went into October Miracle's box. The horse rubbed his lean head against Bobby's shoulder, expelling air noisily through his expanded nostrils. Bobby did not want to watch the second race, and stayed looking at October

Miracle and talking to Hogan for about twenty minutes. Then he went out, crossed the course by the gate above the grandstand, and walked along to the water jump. Reggie Hope was there with two of the Valentine girls and several other people. They were all very gay.

"I'm going to win a packet today, Bobby. I've got my camisole on you at threes," Anne Valentine said.

"Listen, Anne, you're a damn fool," said Bobby, "Anything can happen in a 'chase, and I don't believe I'm going to win today. Go and hedge like hell on Grey Marvel; you'll get fours, I should think," he said. He was very serious.

Anne Valentine looked at him. "All right, I will after this race," she said. She took Bobby by the arm and led him away a few yards from the others. "What's the matter, old boy?" she asked.

"Oh, nothing much; I don't think I shall win, that's all," Bobby answered.

Anne Valentine looked at him very hard. She had grey eyes with long black lashes, set in a small, rather pointed face. Her skin was a pale golden colour, and her hair was thick and tawny. "Oh, don't ride," she said. Bobby smiled at her. Anne Valentine thought that she had never seen anything so sad as the smile on Bobby Coplow's face.

"I've got to ride," he said.

The twelve runners were coming out for the third race, a three-mile steeplechase. They watched them through their glasses as they went down to the start. Gerry Gilson was riding Bright Angel.

"I've got a bit on him each way," Anne Valentine told Bobby.

"He's no good. He'll blow up in the third mile; he always does," Reggie Hope said.

"He'd have won a lot of races if they hadn't always used him too much at the start. He runs himself out when he's in front," said Bobby. "Gerry Gilson'll wait on him all right," he went on.

"They're off now!" exclaimed Reggie Hope.

Bobby watched the race without much interest. But he

hoped that Bright Angel would win, because Anne Valentine had backed him. She was a fine girl. The field had been reduced to ten by the time the water was reached. Bright Angel was lying fifth. All the jockeys were already spattered from head to foot with mud. Several of the horses slithered badly on landing, but none fell. "Blooming awful going," Reggie Hope exclaimed. He did not like swearing in front of women, although they often swore in front of him. He was very old-fashioned. The second ditch brought down another of the runners. The next fence was the fence of Bobby's dreams. Prioress, who was in the lead, fell heavily, bringing down Bombardier, and leaving Gorcock to go on from Bright Angel, with the rest of the field some lengths behind. Coplow felt quite sick when he saw the two horses fall. Both of them were on their feet again in a few moments, and one of the jockeys too. Bobby could not see what had happened to the other jockey, but he saw two ambulance men running across in front of the fence. He lowered his glasses, and took his cigarette-case out of his pocket. He saw that Anne Valentine was looking at him intently, her enormous grey eyes very wide. She was rather pale, he noticed. He held out his case, and she took a cigarette. But she did not say anything. Just before the last ditch Bright Angel began to go up. Two fences from home he was level with Gorcock's girths, and coming over the last fence he had his head in front. Gerry Gilson had his whip out, but he did not need to use it. Bright Angel held off Gorcock's challenge on the flat and went away to win the race by a length, running on strongly at the finish. "Well, that's that," said Reggie Hope.

The whole party began to move along towards the gate opposite the paddock. Bobby and Anne Valentine walked side by side a few yards in front of the others, not saying anything. The "All Right" went up as they reached the paddock.

"I don't want to stay here; let's go and look at October Miracle," Anne Valentine said.

On the way to the stables they met several people whom they knew, and had to stop and talk to them for a few minutes. It was nearly half-past two when they reached October Miracle's box. Tom Hogan was watching the lad sponging out his nostrils. He threw back his rug, so that Anne Valentine could see him properly.

"I've never seen him look fitter; he'll walk that race," she said.

They did not stay very long in the box. When they got back to the gate which led to the dressing-room they stopped.

"I'll have to go in here now. You'd better hurry or you won't see the next race," said Bobby.

"I don't want to see it," Anne Valentine said.

"Yes, you'd better go and watch it," said Bobby. "You won't forget to back Grey Marvel, will you?" he asked anxiously.

Anne Valentine did not say anything for a moment or two. Her eyes were very bright. "No, I won't forget," she answered. She gripped his arm suddenly. "All the luck in the world," she said.

"That's sweet of you, Anne; you're a grand girl," Bobby told her.

"I'll see you after the race," said Anne Valentine.

Bobby watched her as she walked away towards the paddock. She was small and straight and very slender. At the corner of the stand she turned and waved her hand to him and he waved back. The next moment she was out of sight.

Bobby went into the dressing-room and started to change his clothes. The valet who always looked after him brought him the small bag containing his kit. His name was Sullivan and he was about sixty years old. Many years before he had been a successful steeplechase jockey and had made a lot of money. But unfortunately, like a good many jockeys before and since, he had spent it all as he earned it, so that instead of being able to set up as a trainer or perhaps retire altogether from racing he had had to go on working. Actually the drink was his trouble and when he got jobs with horses after he gave up riding races he lost them all through the drink. Now he was a jockeys' valet and on the whole he seemed quite happy. But sometimes he was silent for days at a time and his blue eyes were sombre and melancholy. He was never tired of talking about his racing days and he began now to tell Bobby of an experience that he had once had in Ireland. It appeared that he was riding in a hurdle race a horse who was inclined to be difficult at the post. So he arranged with the starter, who was a friend of his, that he should wait in the paddock until all the other runners were lined up, and that as soon as he was level with them the race should be started. None of the other jockeys knew of this arrangement and when they saw him cantering down behind them they naturally expected him to get into line in the ordinary way. Some of them were not even facing in the right direction. But when he was almost abreast of them the starter dropped his flag. "Begob, I was over the first hurdle before they had the reins in their hands!" he said.

When Bobby laughed at this story it made the hollow feeling in his stomach seem more hollow. So he did not laugh very much. He pulled on his boots and put on his cap and picked up his whip and saddle, weight-cloth and number-cloth, and went along to weigh out. There was a lot of noise in the weighing-room and he had to wait for some time while the jockeys from the previous race weighed in. When he got off the scales he gave the saddle and weight-cloth and number-cloth to Hogan, and put on his overcoat. He went out to the parade ring. The numbers went up almost immediately. Bobby looked all round for Anne Valentine. He could not see her anywhere. Hogan and the lad came into the ring with October Miracle and the lad began to lead him round in the parade with the other horses. Hogan came over to the corner where Bobby was and stood beside him. "Three to one bar one! Two to one the field!" shouted the bookmakers. There was no sign of Anne Valentine. It was a hell of a lonely business waiting about like this. At last the bell went. The lad brought October Miracle over and stripped off his rug and held his head while Hogan took Bobby's coat and gave him a leg up. "Good luck, sir," they said. The lad slipped off the leading strings and Bobby touched October Miracle with his heels and they walked out of the enclosure and through the gate on to the course. He touched him again and they cantered down to the start, Bobby feeling better than he had felt all day with October Miracle snorting and tossing his lovely head and moving under him with his beautiful easy action. It began to rain before they reached the post.

There was a certain amount of delay at the starting-gate because Battleaxe as usual gave a lot of trouble. He was a liver chestnut with one white stocking, and he was a proper handful. He fought his bit and nearly bucked Denton off and lashed out with his heels so that all the other horses were cannoning into one another to keep out of his way. There was a good deal of cursing, particularly from Captain Fitz-Gerald, the starter, but at last Battleaxe gave up and moved into the centre of the line next to Idolatry. "Come up there on Ramadan and Valiant Dust. Back on the grey; up on Starlight," Captain FitzGerald called out. "Steady now; easy," he said. The line of horses moved forward slowly. The gate went up.

The fifteen runners thundered down at the black line of fence in a bunched mass. Bobby let October Miracle go and the horse took hold of his bit and a hundred yards from the start he was clear of the field. Fifty yards from the fence he began as usual to measure his take-off. He jumped perfectly, and went away after landing without checking at all. It was raining hard now, and Bobby lowered his head so that the visor of his cap should keep the rain out of his eyes. Halfway to the second fence he took a pull at the reins. After a moment October Miracle came back to him like a well-trained show-ring hack. He was mad keen to race, but he had perfect confidence in Bobby and was quite content to go at the pace he wanted. Grey Marvel, Battleaxe and Ramadan shot out in front. Bobby watched Battleaxe carefully over the next two fences. He over-jumped at the first, and pitched badly on landing, but he recovered all right. At the second, an open ditch, Denton had to use his whip on him. It looked as though he might fall or run out before very long. But Bobby knew, somehow, that he would not. They were approaching that sinister fence now. As they started to round the sharp bend towards it Bobby had a fleeting moment's fear. It passed at once and he felt quite normal again. Valiant Dust was close up on his inside, so he could not jump the fence as he wanted to. He let October Miracle increase his pace a little. Two lengths ahead of him Battleaxe was showing signs of wanting to run out. But Denton kept him at it and he got over safely. Bobby sat well forward as October Miracle took off and the fence fairly whistled under and then he lay back because of the big drop and slipped the reins and they landed yards out. He got forward again in a couple of strides, hearing a crash and a thud behind him and knowing that Valiant Dust was down. He pulled October Miracle back to his original pace and they galloped on behind the leaders. Well, he thought, we're over that fence all right and perhaps after all there was nothing in that dream. But then he thought: we've got to jump it again you fool and what about that? "I'll go on watching Battleaxe," he said, "and forget the dream." He went on watching Battleaxe. Three of the fifteen starters had fallen now. The remainder galloped on, through the rain and mud. Battleaxe was running in his usual uncertain manner. At one fence he was over-jumping and pitching and at the next he was trying to run out. And then he would hit one hard and Bobby would feel certain that he was going to fall, but he never did. Denton was having a hell of a ride, and it was amazing how he kept his seat at some of the fences. Grey Marvel was making all the running, and setting a hot pace, too. Going into the water jump he was a length in front of Battleaxe, with Ramadan two lengths behind. October Miracle shortened his stride a little as they approached the water. He took off half a length behind Ramadan and landed a length in front, a colossal leap. He did not mind the rain or the heavy going or anything else. He was only half-extended and jumping like a stag and pulling double. By God, thought Bobby, there never was such a horse as October Miracle.

They were going out into the country again for the second circuit. There were three plain fences now and then the third open ditch, and then the fence of dreams and nightmares.

After the ditch, Bobby glanced quickly backwards over his left shoulder. He was a good three lengths in front of Ramadan, with the rest of the field some distance away. He moved his hands forward a little and October Miracle pricked his intelligent ears and lengthened his stride and began to go up to the two leaders. Bobby kept him in the middle of the course as they started to round the bend. He was very afraid. He had done all this twice before that week and something had happened both times and it was going to happen now. He clenched his teeth and twenty yards from the fence he pulled October Miracle in slightly to meet it squarely close to the inner wing. He moved his hands still farther forward, and sat very still. He saw Grey Marvel's forehand rise as he rose at the fence. A moment later he saw something else which made his heart leap sickeningly in his chest. Battleaxe had refused, and had swerved towards the inside of the fence. Denton was fighting him desperately, but seemed unable to pull him up. October Miracle had seen what was happening, too, and made a gigantic effort to avert disaster. A full fifteen feet from the fence he took off with a tremendous spring. As he left the ground Battleaxe's shoulder struck him hard in the quarters, causing him to twist in the air so that he went over the fence back-first, on his side. God, thought Bobby, it's happened all right! Instinctively he withdrew his feet from the stirrup irons and tried to push himself away from the falling horse, who otherwise must crush him beneath his weight. As the ground rushed up to meet him, he tucked his head into his chest and raised his arms to shield his face, bracing himself for the impact. He felt his body strike the ground with numbing force. There was a roaring in his ears and a sudden sharp pain in his head and then a great darkness enveloped him. But almost at once the darkness cleared and the pain and the roaring ceased and he found himself standing beside the fence, looking down at a figure which lay face downwards on the sodden turf, inert and still where it had fallen. He saw the black cap, the black woollen jersey with the saxe-blue chevrons, and knew that it was himself. A few feet away October Miracle lay on his side, his mud-streaked flanks heaving spasmodically. Bobby felt strangely light and detached. Suddenly, with a shock that was both pain and fear, he knew that he was dead. He felt himself falling endlessly through outer space. And then he was wide awake. But he was not in his own bed. He was lying on his back in the open air, with the rain beating in his face. Denton and two ambulance men were bending over him, looking strained and anxious. Denton's lips were trembling, and he was very white.

"Lie still; the ambulance will be here in a minute," one of the Red Cross men said.

"Help me up; I must get up," said Bobby.

"No, you lie still, sir," the other Red Cross man said.

Bobby struggled to his knees. Something warm was trickling down his forehead. He put up his hand, and brought it away covered with blood. There was a deep cut in his forehead. He felt very sick and giddy, and he could not think clearly. One of the Red Cross men was unrolling a lint bandage. "You must lie still, sir," he said. He took Bobby by the arm. "Help me up," said Bobby. The man helped him up. A few feet from the fence October Miracle lay on his side, muddy, glistening with wet, unnaturally huddled. He would never win the Grand National now. His back was broken. Everything dropped inside Bobby. "Oh, God, so it was you!" he said. He stumbled forward, and knelt down beside his horse. He put out his hand and touched the soft muzzle. October Miracle neighed feebly, and his muzzle stirred faintly in Bobby's hand. Suddenly he quivered, stretched his limbs, and was still. Bobby knelt beside him. The rain poured down. He felt a hand on his shoulder, and looked up. It was Denton.

"I don't know what to say, Mister Coplow," he said. He was nearly crying.

"You mustn't worry; it wasn't your fault," said Bobby. Blood and tears mingled in his mouth with a salty tang. He knelt beside his dead horse, in the rain.

SILVER BLAZE

A. Conan Doyle

"**I** AM afraid, Watson, that I shall have to go," said Holmes, as we sat down together to our breakfast one morning.

"Go! Where to?"

"To Dartmoor—to King's Pyland."

I was not surprised. Indeed, my only wonder was that he had not already been mixed up in this extraordinary case, which was the one topic of conversation through the length and breadth of England. For a whole day my companion had rambled about the room with his chin upon his chest and his brows knitted, charging and re-charging his pipe with the strongest black tobacco, and absolutely deaf to any of my questions or remarks. Fresh editions of every paper had been sent up by our newsagent only to be glanced over and tossed down into a corner. Yet, silent as he was, I knew perfectly well what it was over which he was brooding. There was but one problem before the public which could challenge his powers of analysis, and that was the singular disappearance of the favourite for the Wessex Cup, and the tragic murder of its trainer. When, therefore, he suddenly announced his intention of setting out for the scene of the drama, it was only what I had both expected and hoped for.

"I should be most happy to go down with you if I should not be in the way," said I.

"My dear Watson, you would confer a great favour upon

me by coming. And I think that your time will not be mis-spent, for there are points about this case which promise to make it an absolutely unique one. We have, I think, just time to catch our train at Paddington, and I will go further into the matter upon our journey. You would oblige me by bring-ing with you your very excellent field-glass.''

And so it happened that an hour or so later I found myself in the corner of a first-class carriage, flying along, *en route* for Exeter, while Sherlock Holmes, with his sharp, eager face framed in his ear-flapped travelling-cap, dipped rapidly into the bundle of fresh papers which he had procured at Paddington. We had left Reading far behind us before he thrust the last of them under the seat, and offered me his cigar-case.

''We are going well,'' said he, looking out of the window, and glancing at his watch. ''Our rate at present is fifty-three and a half miles an hour.''

''I have not observed the quarter-mile posts,'' said I.

''Nor have I. But the telegraph posts upon this line are sixty yards apart, and the calculation is a simple one. I presume that you have already looked into this matter of the murder of John Straker and the disappearance of Silver Blaze?''

''I have seen what the *Telegraph* and the *Chronicle* have to say.''

''It is one of those cases where the art of the reasoner should be used rather for the sifting of details than for the acquiring of fresh evidence. The tragedy has been so uncom-mon, so complete, and of such personal importance to so many people that we are suffering from a plethora of sur-mise, conjecture, and hypothesis. The difficulty is to detach the framework of fact—of absolute, undeniable fact—from the embellishments of theorists and reporters. Then, having established ourselves upon this sound basis, it is our duty to see what inferences may be drawn, and which are the special points upon which the whole mystery turns. On Tuesday eve-ning I received telegrams, both from Colonel Ross, the owner of the horse, and from Inspector Gregory, who is looking after the case, inviting my co-operation.''

"Tuesday evening!" I exclaimed. "And this is Thursday morning. Why did you not go down yesterday?"

"Because I made a blunder, my dear Watson—which is, I am afraid, a more common occurrence than anyone would think who only knew me through your memoirs. The fact is that I could not believe it possible that the most remarkable horse in England could long remain concealed, especially in so sparsely inhabited a place as the north of Dartmoor. From hour to hour yesterday I expected to hear that he had been found, and that his abductor was the murderer of John Straker. When, however, another morning had come and I found that, beyond the arrest of young Fitzroy Simpson, nothing had been done, I felt that it was time for me to take action. Yet in some ways I feel that yesterday has not been wasted."

"You have formed a theory then?"

"At least I have a grip of the essential facts of the case. I shall enumerate them to you, for nothing clears up a case so much as stating it to another person, and I can hardly expect your cooperation if I do not show you the position from which we start."

I lay back against the cushions, puffing at my cigar, while Holmes, leaning forward, with his long thin forefinger checking off the points upon the palm of his left hand, gave me a sketch of the events which had led to our journey.

"Silver Blaze," said he, "is from the Isonomy stock, and holds as brilliant a record as his famous ancestor. He is now in his fifth year, and has brought in turn each of the prizes of the turf to Colonel Ross, his fortunate owner. Up to the time of the catastrophe he was first favourite for the Wessex Cup, the betting being three to one on. He has always, however, been a prime favourite with the racing public, and has never yet disappointed them, so that even at short odds enormous sums of money have been laid upon him. It is obvious, therefore, that there were many people who had the strongest interest in preventing Silver Blaze from being there at the fall of the flag next Tuesday.

"This fact was, of course, appreciated at King's Pyland, where the Colonel's training stable is situated. Every precaution was taken to guard the favourite. The trainer, John Straker, is a retired jockey, who rode in Colonel Ross's colours before he became too heavy for the weighing-chair. He has served the Colonel for five years as jockey, and for seven as trainer, and has always shown himself to be a zealous and honest servant. Under him were three lads, for the establishment was a small one, containing only four horses in all. One of these lads sat up each night in the stable, while the others slept in the loft. All three bore excellent characters. John Straker, who is a married man, lived in a small villa about two hundred yards from the stables. He has no children, keeps one maid-servant, and is comfortably off. The country round is very lonely, but about half a mile to the north there is a small cluster of villas which have been built by a Tavistock contractor for the use of invalids and others who may wish to enjoy the pure Dartmoor air. Tavistock itself lies two miles to the west, while across the moor, also about two miles distant, is the larger training establishment of Capleton, which belongs to Lord Backwater, and is managed by Silas Brown. In every other direction the moor is a complete wilderness, inhabited only by a few roaming gipsies. Such was the general situation last Monday night, when the catastrophe occurred.

''On that evening the horses had been exercised and watered as usual, and the stables were locked up at nine o'clock. Two of the lads walked up to the trainer's house, where they had supper in the kitchen, while the third, Ned Hunter, remained on guard. At a few minutes after nine the maid, Edith Baxter, carried down to the stables his supper, which consisted of a dish of curried mutton. She took no liquid, as there was a water-tap in the stables, and it was the rule that the lad on duty should drink nothing else. The maid carried a lantern with her, as it was very dark, and the path ran across the open moor.

''Edith Baxter was within thirty yards of the stables when a man appeared out of the darkness and called to her to stop. As he stepped into the circle of yellow light thrown by the lantern she saw that he was a person of gentlemanly bearing, dressed in a grey suit of tweed with a cloth cap. He wore gaiters, and carried a heavy stick with a knob to it. She was most impressed, however, by the extreme pallor of his face and by the nervousness of his manner. His age, she thought, would be rather over thirty than under it.

" 'Can you tell me where I am?' he asked. 'I had almost made up my mind to sleep on the moor when I saw the light of your lantern.'

" 'You are close to the King's Pyland training stables,' she said.

" 'Oh, indeed! What a stroke of luck!' he cried. 'I understand that a stable-boy sleeps there alone every night. Perhaps that is his supper which you are carrying to him. Now I am sure that you would not be too proud to earn the price of a new dress, would you?' He took a piece of white paper folded up out of his waistcoat pocket. 'See that the boy has this tonight, and you shall have the prettiest frock that money can buy.'

"She was frightened by the earnestness of his manner, and ran past him to the window through which she was accustomed to hand the meals. It was already open, and Hunter was seated at the small table inside. She began to tell him of what had happened, when the stranger came up again.

" 'Good evening,' said he, looking through the window, 'I wanted to have a word with you.' The girl has sworn that as he spoke she noticed the corner of the little paper packet protruding from his closed hand.

" 'What business have you here?' asked the lad.

" 'It's business that may put something into your pocket,' said the other. 'You've two horses in for the Wessex Cup—Silver Blaze and Bayard. Let me have the straight tip, and you won't be a loser. Is it a fact that at the weights Bayard could give the other a hundred yards in five furlongs, and that the stable have put their money on him?'

" 'So you're one of those damned touts,' cried the lad. 'I'll show you how we serve them in King's Pyland.' He sprang up and rushed across the stable to unloose the dog. The girl fled away to the house, but as she ran she looked back, and saw that the stranger was leaning through the window. A minute later, however, when Hunter rushed out with the hound he was gone, and though the lad ran all round the buildings he failed to find any trace of him.''

"One moment!" I asked. "Did the stable-boy, when he ran out with the dog, leave the door unlocked behind him?"

"Excellent, Watson; excellent!" murmured my companion. "The importance of the point struck me so forcibly, that I sent a special wire to Dartmoor yesterday to clear the matter up. The boy locked the door before he left it. The window, I may add, was not large enough for a man to get through.

"Hunter waited until his fellow grooms had returned, when he sent a message up to the trainer and told him what had occurred. Straker was excited at hearing the account, although he does not seem to have quite realized its true significance. It left him, however, vaguely uneasy, and Mrs. Straker, waking at one in the morning, found that he was dressing. In reply to her inquiries, he said that he could not sleep on account of his anxiety about the horses, and that he intended to walk down to the stables to see that all was well. She begged him to remain at home, as she could hear the rain pattering against the windows, but in spite of her entreaties he pulled on his large mackintosh and left the house.

"Mrs. Straker awoke at seven in the morning, to find that her husband had not yet returned. She dressed herself hastily, called the maid, and set off for the stables. The door was open; inside, huddled together upon a chair, Hunter was sunk in a state of absolute stupor, the favourite's stall was empty, and there were no signs of his trainer.

"The two lads who slept in the chaff-cutting loft above the harnessroom were quickly roused. They had heard nothing during the night, for they are both sound sleepers. Hunter was obviously under the influence of some powerful drug; and, as no sense could be got out of him, he was left to sleep it off while the two lads and the two women ran out in search of the absentees. They still had hopes that the trainer had for some reason taken out the horse for early exercise, but on ascending the knoll near the house, from which all the neighbouring moors were visible, they not only could see no signs of the favourite, but they perceived something which warned them that they were in the presence of a tragedy.

"About a quarter of a mile from the stables, John Straker's overcoat was flapping from a furze bush. Immediately beyond there was a bowl-shaped depression in the moor, and at the bottom of this was found the dead body of the unfortunate trainer. His head had been shattered by a savage blow from some heavy weapon, and he was wounded in the thigh, where there was a long, clean cut, inflicted evidently by some very sharp instrument. It was clear, however, that Straker had defended himself vigorously against his assailants, for in his right hand he held a small knife, which was clotted with blood up to the handle, while in his left he grasped a red and black silk cravat, which was recognized by the maid as having been worn on the preceding evening by the stranger who had visited the stables.

"Hunter, on recovering from his stupor, was also quite positive as to the ownership of the cravat. He was equally certain that the same stranger had, while standing at the window, drugged his curried mutton, and so deprived the stables of their watchman.

"As to the missing horse, there were abundant proofs in the mud which lay at the bottom of the fatal hollow, that he had been there at the time of the struggle. But from that morning he has disappeared; and although a large reward has been offered, and all the gipsies of Dartmoor are on the alert, no news has come of him. Finally an analysis has shown that the remains of his supper, left by the stable lad, contain an appreciable quantity of powdered opium, while the people of the house partook of the same dish on the same night without any ill effect.

"Those are the main facts of the case stripped of all surmise and stated as baldly as possible. I shall now recapitulate what the police have done in the matter.

"Inspector Gregory, to whom the case has been committed, is an extremely competent officer. Were he but gifted with imagination he might rise to great heights in his profession. On his arrival he promptly found and arrested the man upon whom suspicion naturally rested. There was little difficulty in finding him, for he was thoroughly well known in the neighbourhood. His name, it appears, was Fitzroy Simpson. He was a man of excellent birth and education, who had squandered a fortune upon the turf, and who lived now by doing a little quiet and genteel bookmaking in the sporting clubs of London. An examination of his betting-book shows that bets to the amount of five thousand pounds had been registered by him against the favourite.

"On being arrested he volunteered the statement that he had come down to Dartmoor in the hope of getting some information about the King's Pyland horses, and also about Desborough, the second favourite, which was in the charge of Silas Brown, at the Capleton stables. He did not attempt to deny that he had acted as ascribed upon the evening before, but declared that he had no sinister designs, and had simply wished to obtain first-hand information. When confronted with the cravat he turned very pale, and was utterly unable to account for its presence in the hand of the murdered man. His wet clothing showed that he had been out in the storm of the night before, and his stick, which was a Penang lawyer, weighed with lead, was just such a weapon as might, by repeated blows, have inflicted the terrible injuries to which the trainer had succumbed.

"On the other hand, there was no wound upon his person, while the state of Straker's knife would show that one, at least, of his assailants must bear his mark upon him. There you have it all in a nutshell, Watson, and if you can give me any light I shall be infinitely obliged to you."

I had listened with the greatest interest to the statement which Holmes, with characteristic clearness, had laid before me. Though most of the facts were familiar to me, I had not sufficiently appreciated their relative importance, nor their connection with each other.

"Is it not possible," I suggested, "that the incised wound upon Straker may have been caused by his own knife in the convulsive struggles which follow any brain injury?"

"It is more than possible; it is probable," said Holmes.

"In that case, one of the main points in favour of the accused disappears."

"And yet," said I, "even now I fail to understand what the theory of the police can be."

"I am afraid that whatever theory we state has very grave objections to it," returned my companion. "The police imagine, I take it, that this Fitzroy Simpson, having drugged the lad, and having in some way obtained a duplicate key, opened the stable door, and took out the horse, with the intention, apparently, of kidnapping him altogether. His bridle is missing, so that Simpson must have put it on. Then, having left the door open behind him, he was leading the horse away over the moor, when he was either met or overtaken by the trainer. A row naturally ensued, Simpson beat out the trainer's brains with his heavy stick without receiving any injury from the small knife which Straker used in self-defence, and then the thief either led the horse on to some secret hiding-place, or else it may have bolted during the struggle, and be now wandering out on the moors. That is the case as it appears to the police, and improbable as it is, all other explanations are more improbable still. However, I shall very quickly test the matter when I am once upon the spot, and until then I really cannot see how we can get much further than our present position."

It was evening before we reached the little town of Tavistock, which lies, like the boss of a shield, in the middle of the huge circle of Dartmoor. Two gentlemen were awaiting us at the station; the one a tall fair man with lion-like hair and beard, and curiously penetrating light blue eyes, the other a small alert person, very neat and dapper, in a frock-coat and gaiters, with trim little side-whiskers and an eyeglass. The latter was Colonel Ross, the well-known sportsman, the other Inspector Gregory, a man who was rapidly making his name in the English detective service.

"I am delighted that you have come down, Mr. Holmes," said the Colonel. "The Inspector here has done all that could possibly be suggested; but I wish to leave no stone unturned in trying to avenge poor Straker, and in recovering my horse.''

''Have there been any fresh developments?'' asked Holmes.

''I am sorry to say that we have made very little progress,'' said the Inspector. ''We have an open carriage outside, and as you would no doubt like to see the place before the light fails, we might talk it over as we drive.''

A minute later we were all seated in a comfortable landau and were rattling through the quaint old Devonshire town. Inspector Gregory was full of his case, and poured out a stream of remarks, while Holmes threw in an occasional question or interjection. Colonel Ross leaned back with his arms folded and his hat tilted over his eyes, while I listened with interest to the dialogue of the two detectives. Gregory was formulating his theory, which was almost exactly what Holmes had foretold in the train.

''The net is drawn pretty close round Fitzroy Simpson,'' he remarked, ''and I believe myself that he is our man. At the same time, I recognize that the evidence is purely circumstantial, and that some new development may upset it.''

''How about Straker's knife?''

''We have quite come to the conclusion that he wounded himself in his fall.''

''My friend Dr. Watson made that suggestion to me as we came down. If so, it would tell against this man Simpson.''

''Undoubtedly. He has neither a knife nor any sign of a wound. The evidence against him is certainly very strong. He had a great interest in the disappearance of the favourite, he lies under the suspicion of having poisoned the stableboy, he was undoubtedly out in the storm, he was armed with a heavy stick, and his cravat was found in the dead man's hand. I really think we have enough to go before a jury.''

Holmes shook his head. ''A clever counsel would tear it all to rags,'' said he. ''Why should he take the horse out of the stable? If he wished to injure it, why could he not do it there? Has a duplicate key been found in his possession? What chemist sold him the powdered opium? Above all, where could he, a stranger to the district, hide a horse, and such a horse as this? What is his own explanation as to the paper which he wished the maid to give to the stable-boy?''

''He says that it was a ten-pound note. One was found in his purse. But your other difficulties are not so formidable as they seem. He is not a stranger to the district. He has twice lodged at Tavistock in the summer. The opium was probably brought from London. The key, having served its purpose, would be hurled away. The horse may lie at the bottom of one of the pits or old mines upon the moor.''

''What does he says about the cravat?''

''He acknowledges that it is his, and declares that he had lost it. But a new element has been introduced into the case which may account for his leading the horse from the stable.''

Holmes pricked up his ears.

''We have found traces which show that a party of gipsies encamped on Monday night within a mile of the spot where the murder took place. On Tuesday they were gone. Now, presuming that there was some understanding between Simpson and these gipsies, might he not have been leading the horse to them when he was overtaken, and may they not have him now?''

''It is certainly possible.''

''The moor is being scoured for these gipsies. I have also examined every stable and outhouse in Tavistock, and for a radius of ten miles.''

''There is another training stable quite close, I understand?''

''Yes, and that is a factor which we must certainly not neglect. As Desborough, their horse, was second in the betting, they had an interest in the disappearance of the favourite. Silas Brown, the trainer, is known to have had large bets upon the event, and he was no friend to poor Straker. We have, however, examined the stables, and there is nothing to connect him with the affair.''

''And nothing to connect this man Simpson with the interests of the Capleton stable?''

''Nothing at all.''

Holmes leaned back in the carriage and the conversation ceased. A few minutes later our driver pulled up at a neat little red-brick villa with overhanging eaves, which stood by the road. Some distance off, across a paddock, lay a long grey-tiled outbuilding. In every other direction the low curves of the moor, bronze-coloured from the fading ferns, stretched away to the skyline, broken only by the steeples of Tavistock, and by a cluster of houses away to the westward, which marked the Capleton stables. We all sprang out with the exception of Holmes, who continued to lean back with his eyes fixed upon the sky in front of him, entirely absorbed in his own thoughts. It was only when I touched his arm that he roused himself with a violent start and stepped out of the carriage.

"Excuse me," said he, turning to Colonel Ross, who had looked at him in some surprise. "I was day-dreaming." There was a gleam in his eyes and a suppressed excitement in his manner which convinced me, used as I was to his ways, that his hand was upon a clue, though I could not imagine where he had found it.

"Perhaps you would prefer at once to go on to the scene of the crime, Mr. Holmes?" said Gregory.

"I think that I should prefer to stay here a little and go into one or two questions of detail. Straker was brought back here, I presume?"

"Yes, he lies upstairs. The inquest is tomorrow."

"He has been in your service some years, Colonel Ross?"

"I have always found him an excellent servant."

"I presume that you made an inventory of what he had in his pockets at the time of his death, Inspector?"

"I have the things themselves in the sitting-room, if you would care to see them."

"I should be very glad."

We all filed into the front room, and sat around the central table, where the Inspector unlocked a square tin box and laid a small heap of things before us. There was a box of vestas, two inches of tallow candle, an A.D.P. briar-root pipe, a pouch of sealskin with half an ounce of long-cut cavendish, a silver watch with a gold chain, five sovereigns in gold, an aluminium pencil-case, a few papers, and an ivory-handle knife with a very delicate inflexible blade marked Weiss & Co., London.

"This is a very singular knife," said Holmes, lifting it up and examining it minutely. "I presume, as I see bloodstains upon it, that it is the one which was found in the dead man's grasp. Watson, this knife is surely in your line."

"It is what we call a cataract knife," said I.

"I thought so. A very delicate blade devised for very delicate work. A strange thing for a man to carry with him upon a rough expedition, especially as it would not shut in his pocket."

"The tip was guarded by a disc of cork which we found beside his body," said the Inspector. "His wife tells us that the knife had lain for some days upon the dressing-table, and that he had picked it up as he left the room. It was a poor weapon, but perhaps the best that he could lay his hand on at the moment."

"Very possible. How about these papers?"

"Three of them are receipted hay-dealers' accounts. One of them is a letter of instructions from Colonel Ross. This other is a milliner's account for thirty-seven pounds fifteen, made out by Madame Lesurier, of Bond Street, to William Darbyshire. Mrs. Straker tells us that Darbyshire was a friend of her husband's, and that occasionally his letters were addressed here."

"Madame Darbyshire had somewhat expensive tastes," remarked Holmes, glancing down the account. "Twenty-two guineas is rather heavy for a single costume. However, there appears to be nothing more to learn, and we may now go down to the scene of the crime."

As we emerged from the sitting-room a woman who had been waiting in the passage took a step forward and laid her hand upon the Inspector's sleeve. Her face was haggard, and thin, and eager; stamped with the print of a recent horror.

"Have you got them? Have you found them?" she panted.

"No, Mrs. Straker; but Mr. Holmes, here, has come from London to help us, and we shall do all that is possible."

"Surely I met you in Plymouth, at a garden-party, some little time ago, Mrs. Straker," said Holmes.

"No, sir; you are mistaken."

"Dear me; why, I could have sworn to it. You wore a costume of dove-coloured silk with ostrich feather trimming."

"I never had such a dress, sir," answered the lady.

"Ah; that quite settles it," said Holmes; and, with an apology, he followed the Inspector outside. A short walk across the moor took us to the hollow in which the body had been found. At the brink of it was the furze bush upon which the coat had been hung.

"There was no wind that night, I understand," said Holmes.

"None; but very heavy rain."

"In that case the overcoat was not blown against the furze bushes, but placed there."

"Yes, it was laid across the bush."

"You fill me with interest. I perceive that the ground has been trampled up a good deal. No doubt many feet have been there since Monday night."

"A piece of matting has been laid here at the side, and we have all stood upon that."

"Excellent."

"In this bag I have one of the boots which Straker wore, one of Fitzroy Simpson's shoes, and a cast horseshoe of Silver Blaze."

"My dear Inspector, you surpass yourself!"

Holmes took the bag, and descending into the hollow he pushed the matting into a more central position. Then stretching himself upon his face and leaning his chin upon his hands he made a careful study of the trampled mud in front of him.

"Halloa!" said he, suddenly, "what's this?"

It was a wax vesta, half burned, which was so coated with mud that it looked at first like a chip of wood.

"I cannot think how I came to overlook it," said the Inspector, with an expression of annoyance.

"It was invisible, buried in the mud. I only saw it because I was looking for it."

"What! You expected to find it?"

"I thought it not unlikely." He took the boots from the bag and compared the impressions of each of them with marks upon the ground. Then he clambered up to the rim of the hollow and crawled about among the ferns and bushes.

"I am afraid that there are no more tracks," said the Inspector. "I have examined the ground very carefully for a hundred yards in each direction."

"Indeed!" said Holmes, rising, "I should not have the impertinence to do it again after what you say. But I should like to take a little walk over the moors before it grows dark, that I may know my ground tomorrow, and I think that I shall put this horseshoe into my pocket for luck."

Colonel Ross, who had shown some signs of impatience at my companion's quiet and systematic method of work, glanced at his watch.

"I wish you would come back with me, Inspector," said he. "There are several points on which I should like your advice, and especially as to whether we do not owe it to the public to remove our horse's name from the entries for the Cup."

"Certainly not," cried Holmes, with decision; "I should let the name stand."

The Colonel bowed. "I am very glad to have had your opinion, sir," said he. "You will find us at poor Straker's house when you have finished your walk, and we can drive together into Tavistock."

He turned back with the Inspector, while Holmes and I walked slowly across the moor. The sun was beginning to sink behind the stables of Capleton, and the long sloping plain in front of us was tinged with gold, deepening into rich, ruddy brown where the faded ferns and brambles caught the evening light. But the glories of the landscape were all wasted upon my companion, who was sunk in the deepest thought.

"It's this way, Watson," he said, at last. "We may leave

the question of who killed John Straker for the instant, and confine ourselves to finding out what has become of the horse. Now, supposing that he broke away during or after the tragedy, where could he have gone to? The horse is a very gregarious creature. If left to himself, his instincts would have been either to return to King's Pyland or go over to Capleton. Why should he run wild upon the moor? He would surely have been seen by now. And why should gipsies kidnap him? These people always clear out when they hear of trouble, for they do not wish to be pestered by the police. They could not hope to sell such a horse. They would run a great risk and gain nothing by taking him. Surely that is clear.''

''Where is he, then?''

''I have already said that he must have gone to King's Pyland or to Capleton. He is not at King's Pyland, therefore he is at Capleton. Let us take that as a working hypothesis, and see what it leads us to. This part of the moor, as the Inspector remarked, is very hard and dry. But it falls away towards Capleton, and you can see from here that there is a long hollow over yonder, which must have been very wet on Monday night. If our supposition is correct, then the horse must have crossed that, and there is the point where we should look for his tracks.''

We had been walking briskly during this conversation, and a few more minutes brought us to the hollow in question. At Holmes' request I walked down the bank to the right, and he to the left, but I had not taken fifty paces before I heard him give a shout, and saw him waving his hand to me. The track of a horse was plainly outlined in the soft earth in front of him, and the shoe which he took from his pocket exactly fitted the impression.

''See the value of imagination,'' said Holmes. ''It is the one quality which Gregory lacks. We imagined what might have happened, acted upon the supposition, and find ourselves justified. Let us proceed.''

We crossed the marshy bottom and passed over a quarter of a mile of dry, hard turf. Again the ground sloped and again we came on the tracks. Then we lost them for half a mile, but only to pick them up once more quite close to Capleton. It was Holmes who saw them first, and he stood pointing with a look of triumph upon his face. A man's track was visible beside the horse's.

"The horse was alone before," I cried.

"Quite so. It was alone before. Halloa! what is this?"

The double track turned sharp off and took the direction of King's Pyland. Holmes whistled, and we both followed along after it. His eyes were on the trail, but I happened to look a little to one side, and saw to my surprise the same tracks coming back again in the opposite direction.

"One for you, Watson," said Holmes, when I pointed it out; "you have saved us a long walk which would have brought us back on our own traces. Let us follow the return track."

We had not to go far. It ended at the paving of asphalt which led up to the gates of the Capleton stables. As we approached a groom ran out from them.

"We don't want any loiterers about here," said he.

"I only wished to ask a question," said Holmes, with his finger and thumb in his waistcoat pocket. "Should I be too early to see your master, Mr. Silas Brown, if I were to call at five o'clock tomorrow morning?"

"Bless you, sir, if any one is about he will be, for he is always the first stirring. But here he is, sir, to answer your questions for himself. No, sir, no; it's as much as my place is worth to let him see me touch your money. Afterwards, if you like."

As Sherlock Holmes replaced the half-crown which he had drawn from his pocket, a fierce-looking elderly man strode out from the gate with a hunting-crop swinging in his hand.

"What's this, Dawson?" he cried. "No gossiping! Go about your business! And you—what the devil do you want here?"

"Ten minutes' talk with you, my good sir," said Holmes, in the sweetest of voices.

"I've no time to talk to every gadabout. We want no strangers here. Be off, or you may find a dog at your heels."

Holmes leaned forward and whispered something in the trainer's ear. He started violently and flushed to the temples.

"It's a lie!" he shouted. "An infernal lie!"

"Very good! Shall we argue about it here in public, or talk it over in your parlour?"

"Oh, come in if you wish to."

Holmes smiled. "I shall not keep you more than a few minutes, Watson," he said. "Now, Mr. Brown, I am quite at your disposal."

It was quite twenty minutes, and the reds had all faded into greys before Holmes and the trainer reappeared. Never have I seen such a change as had been brought about in Silas Brown in that short time. His face was ashy pale, beads of perspiration shone upon his brow, and his hands shook until the hunting-crop wagged like a branch in the wind. His bullying, overbearing manner was all gone too, and he cringed along at my companion's side like a dog with its master.

"Your instructions will be done. It shall be done," said he.

"There must be no mistake," said Holmes, looking round at him. The other winced as he read the menace in his eyes.

"Oh, no, there shall be no mistake. It shall be there. Should I change it first or not?"

Holmes thought a little and then burst out laughing. "No, don't," said he. "I shall write to you about it. No tricks now or—"

"Oh, you can trust me, you can trust me!"

"You must see to it on the day as if it were your own."

"You can rely upon me."

"Yes, I think I can. Well, you shall hear from me tomorrow." He turned upon his heel, disregarding the trembling hand which the other held out to him, and we set off for King's Pyland.

"A more perfect compound of the bully, coward and sneak than Master Silas Brown I have seldom met with," remarked Holmes, as we trudged along together.

"He has the horse, then?"

"He tried to bluster out of it, but I described to him so

exactly what his actions had been upon that morning, that he is convinced that I was watching him. Of course, you observed the peculiarly square toes in the impressions, and that his own boots exactly corresponded to them. Again, of course, no subordinate would have dared to have done such a thing. I described to him how when, according to his custom, he was the first down, he perceived a strange horse wandering over the moor; how he went out to it, and his astonishment at recognizing from the white forehead which has given the favourite its name that chance had put in his power the only horse which could beat the one upon which he had put his money. Then I described how his first impulse had been to lead him back to King's Pyland, and how the devil had shown him how he could hide the horse until the race was over, and how he had led it back and concealed it at Capleton. When I told him every detail he gave it up, and thought only of saving his own skin.''

''But his stables had been searched.''

''Oh, an old horse-faker like him has many a dodge.''

''But are you not afraid to leave the horse in his power now, since he has every interest in injuring it?''

''My dear fellow, he will guard it as the apple of his eye. He knows that his only hope of mercy is to produce it safe.''

''Colonel Ross did not impress me as a man who would be likely to show much mercy in any case.''

''The matter does not rest with Colonel Ross. I follow my own methods, and tell as much or as little as I choose. That is the advantage of being unofficial. I don't know whether you observed it, Watson, but the Colonel's manner has been just a trifle cavalier to me. I am inclined now to have a little amusement at his expense. Say nothing to him about the horse.''

''Certainly not, without your permission.''

''And, of course, this is all quite a minor case compared with the question of who killed John Straker.''

''And you will devote yourself to that?''

''On the contrary, we both go back to London by the night train.''

I was thunderstruck by my friend's words. We had only been a few hours in Devonshire, and that he should give up an investigation which he had begun so brilliantly was quite incomprehensible to me. Not a word more could I draw from him until we were back at the trainer's house. The Colonel and the Inspector were awaiting us in the parlour.

"My friend and I return to town by the midnight express," said Holmes. "We have had a charming little breath of your beautiful Dartmoor air."

The Inspector opened his eyes, and the Colonel's lips curled in a sneer.

"So you despair of arresting the murderer of poor Straker," said he.

Holmes shrugged his shoulders. "There are certainly grave difficulties in the way," said he. "I have every hope, however, that your horse will start upon Tuesday, and I beg that you will have your jockey in readiness. Might I ask for a photograph of Mr. John Straker?"

The Inspector took one from an envelope in his pocket and handed it to him.

"My dear Gregory, you anticipate all my wants. If I might ask you to wait here for an instant, I have a question which I should like to put to the maid."

"I must say that I am rather disappointed in our London consultant," said Colonel Ross, bluntly, as my friend left the room. "I do not see that we are any further than when he came."

"At least, you have his assurance that your horse will run," said I.

"Yes, I have his assurance," said the Colonel, with a shrug of his shoulders. "I should prefer to have the horse."

I was about to make some reply in defence of my friend, when he entered the room again.

"Now, gentlemen," said he, "I am quite ready for Tavistock."

As we stepped into the carriage one of the stable-lads held the door open for us. A sudden idea seemed to occur to

Holmes, for he leaned forward and touched the lad upon the sleeve.

"You have a few sheep in the paddock," he said. "Who attends to them?"

"I do, sir."

"Have you noticed anything amiss with them of late?"

"Well, sir, not of much account; but three of them have gone lame, sir."

I could see that Holmes was extremely pleased, for he chuckled and rubbed his hands together.

"A long shot, Watson; a very long shot!" said he, pinching my arm. "Gregory, let me recommend to your attention this singular epidemic among the sheep. Drive on, coachman!"

Colonel Ross still wore an expression which showed the poor opinion which he had formed of my companion's ability, but I saw by the Inspector's face that his attention had been keenly aroused.

"You consider that to be important?" he asked.

"Exceedingly so."

"Is there any other point to which you would wish to draw my attention?"

"To the curious incident of the dog in the night-time."

"The dog did nothing in the night-time."

"That was the curious incident," remarked Sherlock Holmes.

Four days later Holmes and I were again in the train bound for Winchester, to see the race for the Wessex Cup. Colonel Ross met us, by appointment, outside the station, and we drove in his drag to the course beyond the town. His face was grave and his manner was cold in the extreme.

"I have seen nothing of my horse," said he.

"I suppose that you would know him when you saw him?" asked Holmes.

The Colonel was very angry. "I have been on the turf for twenty years, and never was asked such a question as that before,'' said he. ''A child would know Silver Blaze with his white forehead and his mottled off foreleg.''

''How is the betting?''

''Well, that is the curious part of it. You could have got fifteen to one yesterday, but the price has become shorter and shorter, until you can hardly get three to one now.''

''Hum!'' said Holmes. ''Somebody knows something, that is clear!''

As the drag drew up in the enclosure near the grandstand, I glanced at the card to see the entries. It ran:

Wessex Plate. 50 sovs. each, h ft, with 1,000 sovs. added, for four- and five-year olds. Second £300. Third £200. New course (one mile and five furlongs).

1. Mr. Heath Newton's The Negro (red cap, cinnamon jacket).
2. Colonel Wardlaw's Pugilist (pink cap, blue and black jacket).
3. Lord Backwater's Desborough (yellow cap and sleeves).
4. Colonel Ross's Silver Blaze (black cap, red jacket).
5. Duke of Balmoral's Iris (yellow and black stripes).
6. Lord Singleford's Rasper (purple cap, black sleeves).

''We scratched our other one and put all hopes on your word,'' said the Colonel. ''Why, what is that? Silver Blaze favourite?''

''Five to four against Silver Blaze!'' roared the ring. ''Five to four against Silver Blaze! Fifteen to five against Desborough! Five to four on the field!''

''There are the numbers up,'' I cried. ''They are all six there.''

''All six there! Then my horse is running,'' cried the Colonel, in great agitation. ''But I don't see him. My colours have not passed.''

''Only five have passed. This must be he.''

As I spoke a powerful bay horse swept out from the weighing enclosure and cantered past us, bearing on its back the well-known black and red of the Colonel.

"That's not my horse," cried the owner. "That beast has not a white hair upon its body. What is this that you have done, Mr. Holmes?"

"Well, well, let us see how he gets on," said my friend, imperturbably. For a few minutes he gazed through my field-glass. "Capital! An excellent start!" he cried suddenly. "There they are, coming round the curve!"

From our drag we had a superb view as they came up the straight. The six horses were so close together that a carpet could have covered them, but half-way up the yellow of the Capleton stable showed to the front. Before they reached us, however, Desborough's bolt was shot, and the Colonel's horse, coming away with a rush, passed the post a good six lengths before its rival, the Duke of Balmoral's Iris making a bad third.

"It's my race anyhow," gasped the Colonel, passing his hand over his eyes. "I confess that I can make neither head nor tail of it. Don't you think that you have kept up your mystery long enough, Mr. Holmes?"

"Certainly, Colonel. You shall know everything. Let us all go round and have a look at the horse together. Here he is," he continued, as we made our way into the weighing enclosure where only owners and their friends find admittance. "You have only to wash his face and his leg in spirits of wine and you will find that he is the same old Silver Blaze as ever."

"You take my breath away!"

"I found him in the hands of a faker, and took the liberty of running him just as he was sent over."

"My dear sir, you have done wonders. The horse looks very fit and well. It never went better in its life. I owe you a thousand apologies for having doubted your ability. You have done me a great service by recovering my horse. You would do me a greater still if you could lay your hands on the murderer of John Straker."

"I have done so," said Holmes, quietly.

The Colonel and I stared at him in amazement. "You have got him! Where is he, then?"

"He is here."

"Here! Where?"

"In my company at the present moment."

The Colonel flushed angrily. "I quite recognize that I am under obligations to you, Mr. Holmes," said he, "but I must regard what you have just said as either a very bad joke or an insult."

Sherlock Holmes laughed. "I assure you that I have not associated you with the crime, Colonel," said he; "the real murderer is standing immediately behind you!"

He stepped past and laid his hand upon the glossy neck of the thoroughbred.

"The horse!" cried both the Colonel and myself.

"Yes, the horse. And it may lessen his guilt if I say that it was done in self-defence, and that John Straker was a man who was entirely unworthy of your confidence. But there goes the bell; and as I stand to win a little on this next race, I shall defer a more lengthy explanation until a more fitting time."

We had the corner of the Pullman car to ourselves that evening as we whirled back to London, and I fancy that the journey was a short one to Colonel Ross as well as to myself, as we listened to our companion's narrative of the events which had occurred at the Dartmoor training stables upon that Monday night, and the means by which he had unravelled them.

"I confess," said he, "that any theories which I had formed from the newspaper reports were entirely erroneous. And yet there were indications there, had they not been overlaid by other details which concealed their true import. I went to Devonshire with the conviction that Fitzroy Simpson was the true culprit, although, of course, I saw that the evidence against him was by no means complete.

"It was while I was in the carriage, just as we reached the trainer's house, that the immense significance of the curried mutton occurred to me. You may remember that I was distrait, and remained sitting after you had all alighted. I was marvelling in my own mind how I could possibly have overlooked so obvious a clue.''

''I confess,'' said the Colonel, ''that even now I cannot see how it helps us.''

''It was the first link in my chain of reasoning. Powdered opium is by no means tasteless. The flavour is not disagreeable, but it is perceptible. Were it mixed with any ordinary dish, the eater would undoubtedly detect it, and would probably eat no more. A curry was exactly the medium which would disguise this taste. By no possible supposition could this stranger, Fitzroy Simpson, have caused curry to be served in the trainer's family that night, and it is surely too monstrous a coincidence to suppose that he happened to come along with powdered opium upon the very night when a dish happened to be served which would disguise the flavour. That is unthinkable. Therefore Simpson becomes eliminated from the case, and our attention centres upon Straker and his wife, the only two people who could have chosen curried mutton for supper that night. The opium was added after the dish was set aside for the stable-boy, for the others had the same for supper with no ill effects. Which of them, then, had access to that dish without the maid seeing them?

''Before deciding that question I had grasped the significance of the silence of the dog, for one true inference invariably suggests others. The Simpson incident had shown me that a dog was kept in the stables, and yet, though someone had been in and had fetched out a horse, he had not barked enough to arouse the two lads in the loft. Obviously the midnight visitor was someone whom the dog knew well.

''I was already convinced, or almost convinced, that John Straker went down to the stables in the dead of the night and took out Silver Blaze. For what purpose? For a dishonest one, obviously, or why should he drug his own stable-boy? And yet I was at a loss to know why. There have been cases before now where trainers have made sure of great sums of money by laying against their own horses, through agents, and then prevented them from winning by fraud. Sometimes it is a pulling jockey. Sometimes it is some surer and subtler means. What was it here? I hoped that the contents of his pocket might help me to form a conclusion.

"And they did so. You cannot have forgotten the singular knife which was found in the dead man's hand, a knife which certainly no sane man would choose for a weapon. It was, as Dr. Watson told us, a form of knife which is used for the most delicate operations known in surgery. And it was to be used for a delicate operation that night. You must know, with your wide experience of turf matters, Colonel Ross, that it is possible to make a slight nick upon the tendons of a horse's ham, and to do it subcutaneously so as to leave absolutely no trace. A horse so treated would develop a slight lameness which would be put down to a strain in exercise or a touch of rheumatism, but never to foul play."

"Villain! Scoundrel!" cried the Colonel.

"We have here the explanation of why John Straker wished to take the horse out on to the moor. So spirited a creature would have certainly roused the soundest of sleepers when it felt the prick of the knife. It was absolutely necessary to do it in the open air."

"I have been blind!" cried the Colonel. "Of course, that was why he needed the candle, and struck the match."

"Undoubtedly. But in examining his belongings, I was fortunate enough to discover, not only the method of the crime, but even its motives. As a man of the world, Colonel, you know that men do not carry other people's bills about in their pockets. We have most of us quite enough to do to settle our own. I at once concluded that Straker was leading a double life, and keeping a second establishment. The nature of the bill showed that there was a lady in the case, and one who had expensive tastes: liberal as you are with your servants, one hardly expects that they can buy twenty-guinea walking dresses for their women. I questioned Mrs. Straker as to the dress without her knowing it, and having satisfied myself that it had never reached her, I made a note of the milliner's address, and felt that by calling there with Straker's photograph, I could easily dispose of the mythical Darbyshire.

"From that time on all was plain. Straker had led out the horse to a hollow where his light would be invisible. Simpson, in his flight, had dropped his cravat, and Straker had picked it up with some idea, perhaps, that he might use it in securing the horse's leg. Once in the hollow he had got behind the horse, and had struck a light, but the creature, frightened at the sudden glare, and with the strange instinct of animals feeling that some mischief was intended, had lashed out, and the steel shoe had struck Straker full on the forehead. He had already, in spite of the rain, taken off his overcoat in order to do his delicate task, and so, as he fell, his knife gashed his thigh. Do I make it clear?"

"Wonderful!" cried the Colonel. "Wonderful! You might have been there."

"My final shot was, I confess, a very long one. It struck me that so astute a man as Straker would not undertake this delicate tendon-nicking without a little practice. What could he practise on? My eyes fell upon the sheep, and I asked a question which, rather to my surprise, showed that my surmise was correct."

"You have made it perfectly clear, Mr. Holmes."

"When I returned to London I called upon the milliner, who at once recognized Straker as an excellent customer, of the name of Darbyshire, who had a very dashing wife with a strong partiality for expensive dresses. I have no doubt that this woman had plunged him over head and ears in debt, and so led him into this miserable plot."

"You have explained all but one thing," cried the Colonel. "Where was the horse?"

"Ah, it bolted and was cared for by one of your neighbours. We must have an amnesty in that direction, I think. This is Clapham Junction, if I am not mistaken, and we shall be in Victoria in less than ten minutes. If you care to smoke a cigar in our rooms, Colonel, I shall be happy to give you any other details which might interest you."

A GLASS OF PORT
WITH THE PROCTOR

John Welcome

B Y the time my third year at the long-ago Oxford of the
1930s had come round, I had acquired some small—
very small—proficiency in the business of sitting a horse at
racing pace over fences and making a pretence of staying on
him if things went wrong. This had not been achieved without a considerable amount of bruising and breaking, hard
work, dedication, disappointment, toil and sweat but as a
result I had been permitted to become a sort of associate
member in the unholy alliance between my best friend, Brian
Manson, and his trainer, Mr. Alfred Kerrell, who ran a racing stable of sorts out Headington way.

Brian was a tough, hard-bitten, rich young man with no
interests in life beyond hunting and racing; Mr. Kerrell was
middle-aged—at least we thought he was; I imagine he was
about forty—impecunious and every bit as tough and hard-
bitten as Brian with the added cunning and experience which
the years had given him. When the two of them were not
combining to defeat a third party, they waged between themselves a bitter and unremitting battle of wits. In this power-
game I acted as a pawn pushed hither and thither, now the
ally of one, then of the other in their schemes, connivances,
disasters and occasional triumphs.

It was, however, an accolade of sorts to be allowed to act
as a most minor member of what was then a triumvirate and
I had recently shared in a lucky touch when Brian and Kerrell

brought one up at a long price in a hurdle at Stratford. This had enabled me to buy a point-to-point horse or, rather, Kerrell to buy one for me. He was a big rangy bay who had been given at some stage of his career the extraordinary name of The Circus probably because on his near side he bore a large circular white mark rather like an aircraft roundel. As his markings were individual so was his character. He liked his own way and I was only too anxious to give it to him.

Kerrell, as happens with some exceptional dealers and trainers, had the gift of matching horse and man. He knew that so far as I was concerned all that I could do in a race was to sit still and try to stay on, and that this was exactly the sort of rider the old horse needed to get the best out of him. Once you left him alone he was a superb conveyance only needing a hiss and a squeeze to change into top gear at the end of a race and display, as we all discovered to our astonishment, a surprising turn of foot.

Brian spoke scathingly about passengers on horseback as he watched us in action and when he was told by Kerrell to sit up on The Circus and ride him in a school he caught hold of his head and sent him along in real racing fashion. As a result he was promptly deposited into the bottom of the first fence they met, and I noticed that he did not appear unduly anxious to ride him again.

Anyway I won three open point-to-points on the trot with him and then began to get ideas above my station. After consultation with Kerrell I entered him in a Hunters' Chase at a meeting in Kent.

Brian just then had been having a run of bad luck but he had a point-to-pointer that could go more than a bit and which he had been saving up for something. Never anything other than contemptuous of my abilities, he entered this horse called, as far as I can remember, Jack Go Nimble, in the same Hunters' Chase. Having done so, he made open fun at my temerity in taking him on and Kerrell's foolishness in allowing me to do so. But as The Circus began to go better and better on the gallops he could be seen to be wearing a slightly pensive look. This was an expression that I knew well and had reason to fear for it invariably meant he was searching in his mind, in order, to use his own phrase, "to think something up."

Kerrell noticed it too. A day or two before the race he took me aside. "You'll be all right, sir, you'll find," he said. "I haven't told him but yours is a stone better than his. I think we'll have a bet."

"I wish I knew what was going on inside his head," I said.

"Nobody, unless it's the Archangel Gabriel, knows that," Kerrell said, "and even he isn't going to help him much."

"I don't suppose he'll call him in anyway," I said. "He'd be a bit conspicuous on a racecourse with all those wings. It'd more likely be Lucifer."

"Ha," said Kerrell, "They'd be well-matched those two." He spoke feelingly. A bloodlike brown horse with all the stamp of a Leicestershire hunter on him had recently passed from his ownership to Brian's. I didn't know the details of the transaction but from what I had gathered the sale or transfer had not been an entirely willing one and it was evident that its circumstances still rankled.

Brian and I had arranged to meet in the Mitre tavern for a drink the evening before the race. I was walking along The Turl when he caught me up. He appeared to have been running and was slightly out of breath. "Go on in and order," he said. "I've got to see a man in B.N.C. I'll be along in a minute or two."

I was sitting on a bench with a glass of beer on the table in front of me, waiting for him, when I felt my shoulder touched. Turning round I saw a large man in a bowler hat and a blue suit looking down at me. He was a proctor's bull-dog. The proctorial procession was formed by a member of the disciplinary staff of the University attended by an escort of ex-N.C.O.s who were called bulldogs or, more familiarly "bullers." This procession wound its solemn way around the public houses of the city summoning undergraduates found on their premises to appear before the proctors and suffer a fine, since drinking in a public house was, by some absurd survival of the old days of town and gown violence, forbidden to undergraduates by University decree. I believe this ridiculous ban has been long since abolished.

"Excuse me, sir, are you a member of the University?" the bulldog enquired courteously.

"Yes," I said. "I am."

"Ah," said the proctor. "Your name and college then, please."

When I had given these to him he wrote them down in a little book. "Kindly attend at the proctor's office at ten thirty tomorrow morning," he said. The procession then left the public house and, a minute or two later, Brian came in. The full enormity of what had happened was only just beginning to become clear to me when he sat down opposite me.

"I've been progged," I said.

"Bad luck, I saw them coming out."

"Yes, but look, that means I won't be able to ride in the Hunters' Chase tomorrow. What time are you leaving?"

"Nine o'clock. It's a long way. No, you won't will you? We're all going on with the horses. Drink's an evil, isn't it? Have another?"

"Wait a bit," I said, as something struck me. "There's no rule against undergraduates riding in steeplechases, at least I don't think there is."

"Isn't there? Of course there is. There must be."

"I don't care. I'm going after him to see if he'll change the date. They're supposed to send a note around anyway."

"Don't be a fool. He'll gate you for a month and then where'll you be?"

But I was already out of the door and running up the slope to the Turl. I caught up with the proctorial procession just as it was turning into the High.

"Excuse me, sir," I said to the proctor.

He turned round and I noticed that he was rather older than the usual run of young dons who performed their duties. I was also aware of a pair of very bright, sardonic eyes which regarded me steadily. "Yes, well, what is it? And speak up Mr.—Er—. I'm a little deaf from a—"

"I wonder, sir, could you change the time of that appointment tomorrow morning?" I blurted out. "You see I'm riding in a Hunters' Chase tomorrow and I won't be able to if—"

"God bless my soul. *What* did you say?"

"I'm riding in a Hunters' Chase tomorrow," I shouted desperately at him.

"There is no need to raise the dead. I am not quite stone deaf. Mr—er—Welcome, I think it is, are you aware that this University is supposedly a seat of learning? Might I be informed what school you grace with your studies?"

"I'm reading law, sir."

"Jurisprudence and steeplechasing. A strange juxtaposition."

The conversation was rapidly taking on a sort of Alice in Wonderland quality. I think that was what made me say next: "F. E. Smith used to ride in point-to-points, sir."

"Scarcely a recommendation for a steady career at the bar. He also earned the name of 'Galloper' as I recall. Am I to understand you wish to follow in his footsteps? Perhaps in one respect you may in view of where we have just met."

"But its awfully important to me," I said, miserably. "It's my first chase and I think I have a chance."

"Indeed. Mr. Welcome, don't you think a racing stable would be a more suitable home for your talents?"

"Well, no, sir. It's difficult to explain if you sort of don't know about it, but I don't think I could go on as an amateur if I went to a racing stable and anyway I doubt if any racing stable would have me!"

"So this University which, may I remind you, was originally started as a home for poor scholars has to house you instead. But not, I fancy, for very long."

"But you see, sir," I said desperately, "it is usual, I think, to send a note around. It's such short notice and it means so much to me—"

He looked at me sternly. Then a quirk appeared at the

corners of his mouth. "Mr. Welcome," he said. "You have at least one essential of successful advocacy which you appear to share with that great man you have just mentioned—audacity. On this occasion it has served you well. I accept your arguments and I hold in your favour though with the greatest reluctance. Very well then. Call on me at ten-thirty on Monday instead." He turned to go. Then suddenly he stopped. "Mr. Welcome!"

"Yes, sir."

"At what time do you propose to return from this field of battle tomorrow?"

"I'm going to dine in hall, sir."

"I see. Then perhaps you'd do me the pleasure of having a glass of port with me after dinner in my rooms. I have long wanted to know the exact meaning and derivation of those strange racing animals a pony and a monkey. Perhaps you can explain these and other arcane mysteries to me."

"Yes, sir, I'll try, sir. And, I say, sir, thank you, sir."

"My pleasure, Mr. Welcome. And, Mr. Welcome, may I also wish you good luck?" With a swirl of his gown he was gone down the High and I was left to try to collect my scattered wits.

As they came back to me, I began to see one or two things very clearly. Brian had been in a hurry when he met me in the Turl, in fact he had been running. When we had arranged to meet he had said nothing about seeing someone in B.N.C. I doubted very much if he knew anyone in that College which was then crammed to bursting with bruisers who played Rugby Football. However much he decried my abilities, it was obviously to his advantage if The Circus and I should not compete tomorrow. Might it not very well be that he had encountered the progs on their way and then made sure that I was in the Mitre and he was not when they came along the Turl? I resolved to say nothing at all to him about my success with the proctor.

Back in the pub my suspicions were more or less confirmed. Brian had an evening paper open at the racing page in front of him, but he was not reading it. He was sipping his beer with the expression on his face of a cat who has just stolen a jug of cream and got away with it. I had seen him looking like that before when he had just taken advantage of an unexpected stroke of luck. "Well, how did that go?" he said.

"More or less what you thought. He threatened to fine me double tomorrow for impertinence."

"Well, what did you expect? You took the hell of a chance." He picked up the paper. "I see," he said, "that I am quoted at 10-1 tomorrow. That's quite a nice price."

"Just as a matter of interest what is The Circus?"

"50-1 others. Let's have the other half. Don't look so glum. At least you won't fall off and break your neck."

When we had finished our drinks I made my way back to my College and went into the telephone booth in the porter's lodge. There I rang up Kerrell and told him what had happened and my suspicions.

"I knew he'd be up to something," Kerrell observed with satisfaction. "Don't worry, sir, we'll do him properly this time. I'll send the horse on and tell him I advised you to get a race into him. I won't go with them at all. I can say I have something urgent to do in Oxford. Then I'll pick you up outside your digs in my car and bring you on myself."

"That sounds just the job," I said. "Thanks, Mr. Kerrell."

"Wait till he sees us turn up together at the meeting. He'll have something to think about then, I shouldn't wonder."

Kerrell drove an Essex coupé with an English fabric body which he had bought somewhere for twenty-five pounds or had taken in a partial swop for a horse, I forget which. Punctually to the minute he was there waiting for me the following morning parked at the pavement outside my digs. I put my bag containing my racing clothes in the back and away we went along the empty roads of that forgotten time on our long cold drive to the races.

When we approached the course, Kerrell pulled the car to the side of the road and stopped. He opened the door and got out. "No need to tell Mr. Manson we've arrived, until we have to," he said, "We can walk the course from here."

After crossing a couple of fields, we climbed a very insecure boundary fence and were on the track. It was roughly circular in shape and beyond the winning post the ground sloped down to a dip and climbed fairly steeply on the far side. It was, as Kerrell said, rather like "a bloomin' bicycle track" and we had to go three times round it to complete the three miles two furlongs of the Hunter's Chase. The turf, however, was firm and sound and the fences were well made. Kerrell, like most of his kind, was not a believer in tying down a rider with a great deal of advice and instructions. As we tramped around, he confined himself to saying it was not a track on which to give away distance, not to make up ground going up the hill, and to be there or thereabouts after the third last.

I was in my usual state of jelly-like cowardice by this time but I did absorb something of what he said. When we returned to the Essex, he muttered something about having a bet. "A fiver, I think," he said. "That'll do nicely at the price."

I put my hand into my trouser pocket and pulled out five single pound notes. That left about fifteen shillings in cash between me and my bank manager if The Circus did not oblige. I handed them over silently. After all, Kerrell's training bills would be the first casualty if we failed to touch.

Outside the weighing-room we met Brian. When he saw me a heavy scowl appeared on his face. "What the devil are you doing here?" he asked.

"I cut the progs," I said.

"Did you then. You'll be sent down."

"Change of plan. There's been a change of plan, sir," Kerrell said.

"So I gather. I asked Bill Johnson to ride The Circus. Now I'll have to tell him he's not wanted."

"That's right, sir. Lucky, isn't it? You know the old horse goes better for Mr. Welcome than anyone else."

Somehow, as usual, I got through the preliminaries without being sick. In the parade ring Kerrell materialized beside me. "I've got the money on," he said.

"What price are we?" I asked him. Though just at this moment it didn't seem to matter much. I was far too busy wondering if I'd fall off at the first and thinking it was highly likely.

"100-8," Kerrell said.

That did wake some response in me. I thought I'd risked my fiver at fifties and said so.

"You never get these prices in a Hunters' Chase here," was the answer. "It's a small market. Even a tenner knocks it down."

"What's Brian at?"

"Fives. Now, watch him, sir. He wants to win this one and he'll be up to something, mark my words. Not that it matters," he added hastily, to cheer me up. "You'll be all right, you'll find. Remember, you've a stone in hand." Then his hand was under my leg and I was whisked into the saddle.

The start was to the left of the stands just at the beginning of the dip. I remembered to go up past the judge's box and then turned round to canter down. There were seven other runners most of them inexperienced bumpers like myself who were cheerfully or glumly apprehensive. Brian and, I think, one other, were the only hard-faced toughs who had lost the right to claim and who knew exactly what they were about.

At first all went well. I left The Circus severely alone and he swung along, pulling himself to the front at the beginning of the second circuit. He was jumping the fences easily and effortlessly out of his stride. There had been one or two fallers to thin the field and just after what would be the second last fence Brian joined me. He was sitting tight and looking grim. About half way between the two fences to my astonishment I saw him appear to begin to shake up his horse. Then he looked at me. "What the hell are you doing sitting there like a traffic policeman?" he called across to me. "Don't you know we finish this time?"

Up till then I'd been relaxed and comfortable on the old

horse, delighted we were going on so well and not, I fear, concentrating very much on anything. When I heard those words all sorts of thoughts and fears sprang alive in my mind. Could Kerrell have made a mistake in his instructions to me? I hadn't read the article carefully. Maybe they'd changed it and altered the distance. Brian, after all, had forgotten more about racing then I'd ever learn. This was my first chase and here I was making a mess of it.

"Come on, you fool," Brian shouted again. "Don't hang about or you'll be in trouble."

God! I would, too, if I didn't make some show of riding my horse at the finish and was up before the stewards for not trying. That decided me. I squeezed The Circus with my legs and went after Brian.

The Circus took the next fence like a rocket. I shook the reins at him. Away we went down the straight with myself giving the best imitation I could of riding a finish. No challenge came. The judge's box flashed. It all seemed too easy. It was.

As I commenced to pull up the first doubts came to me. The noises from the crowd on my left did not exactly sound like cheering. Soon I realized they were the very opposite. Boos, catcalls, jeers and lurid remarks about my ancestry were coming from the cheaper rings. At that moment Brian came past me with a satisfied grin on his face. I knew then just what had happened. I had fallen right into his trap. I had won my race a mile too soon.

By this time he was four lengths in front and going away from me. Two of the other runners came and caught me, their riders' faces adorned with wide grins.

Then I did what I should have done some time ago. I began to concentrate. I remembered that Kerrell had said I had a stone in hand. Steadying the old horse, I set off down the hill trying to give him what time I could to get his breath back.

The Circus was by now of course thoroughly unsettled. He got too near the fence at the bottom of the hill and nearly jumped me off. When I had climbed back into the saddle, I saw the two in front going hell for leather after Brian. I thought to myself that they were doing exactly what I had been warned not to and might soon run out of steam. I let Circus lope along. He jumped the ditch at the top of the hill perfectly. By now he seemed to be settled once more into his stride, and to my delight, I saw that the others were beginning to come back to me. At the third last he jumped past them, and then there was only Brian to beat.

I was alongside him at the next and when we landed I knew I was going the better. Brian began to kick and scrub. He gave me a sideways glance and then shouted. "You don't want to make a damn fool of yourself again, do you? Don't you know we go round again?"

Despite myself I hesitated. Could he be right? At that moment a stentorian voice rang out from the rails beside me: "Take no notice, sir! I heard him! He's up to his games again. Go on! Go on!" It was Kerrell come to the rescue once more.

I wondered how much The Circus had left in him. I was beginning to roll about a bit myself. It was all up to him now. I squeezed at him as best I could and he answered like the gallant old devil he was.

Jack Go Nimble was visibly tiring. Brian got out his whip. I couldn't do anything about that. I couldn't use a whip. The Circus stood back at the last and leaped. So did Jack Go Nimble, but the crash I heard as I landed told me that at least he had hit the top and gone through it. For the second time in five minutes, I sat down to try to ride a finish. This time it was all right. We came home alone and as I pulled up I saw Brian, who had sat on like a leech, passing the post in second place.

It was all even more dreamlike after that. I had actually won a steeplechase. I sat on a bench in the changing room in a happy trance with Brian glowering and muttering beside me. Then a man in a tweed suit came in. "The stewards want a word with you, Mr. Welcome," he said.

"Me?" I said. "Why me?"

"They want you to explain why you won your race halfway round,'' Brian said with a crow of laughter. ''They'll probably take it away from you.''

''They want you, too, Mr. Manson,'' the man said.

''I can't think what they want me for,'' Brian said as we stood outside the stewards' room.

''Probably they think you can tell them what happened,'' I said to him sourly. I was feeling much the same as I had felt outside my headmaster's study not so long ago. ''You bloody well know, anyway.''

''Me? You must be mad or dreaming. And they're not likely to believe any cock and bull story from you, let me tell you.''

The door opened and we were ushered inside. The stewards' room at that meeting was as primitive as the rest of the appointments. It was draughty and bare and its walls were of unsheeted corrugated iron. Behind a plain deal table, the three of them were sitting. Another man, who had a heavy military moustache, was at the end of the table slightly away from them. The man in the middle was, I supposed, the senior steward. He had a long humorous face. I recognized him. He was a chap called Hugh Clumber, a well-known amateur from a year or two back who had won the National on his own horse as a serving cavalryman. We were in good hands anyway. He'd know what he was about.

''Now, then, Welcome,'' he said. ''Can you give any explanation of that interesting display you gave and why you rode a finish a mile from home?''

''No, sir. I can't.''

''None at all?'' His tone was more friendly than frightening.

''No, sir, except I think I must have lost my head.''

''Did you walk the course?''

''Yes, I did.''

''Well,'' Clumber said slowly. ''You lost your head, you say. Not a very sensible thing to do in a steeplechase. You were beside him, Manson. Can you give us any help?''

''No, sir, I'm afraid I can't.'' Brian stared ahead of him, po-faced as they say nowadays.

"Are you *quite* sure, Manson?"

"Yes, sir. Quite, sure." Brian, who was no fool, shuffled his feet slightly. Something was afoot and both of us knew it.

"Major Warburton, I wonder if you would mind telling us what you saw—and heard," Clumber said to the man at the end of the table. "Major Warburton," he explained to us, "is the stewards' secretary."

The man with the moustache leaned forward and spoke. "I was standing down the course between the last two fences the second time round," he said.

"Yes. And did you hear anything?"

"I heard Manson call across to Welcome to get on—that they finished this time."

"I see. Manson has ridden quite a bit, hasn't he?"

"Yes. He lost the allowance six months ago."

"Do you want to ask Major Warburton any questions, Manson?"

"No, sir."

"I don't think I'll ask you any questions, either," Clumber said aimably to him. "I don't want to make you out a bigger liar than you've already made yourself."

The three of them then put their heads together. After a minute or two, Clumber took a piece of paper from the table in front of him and wrote on it. He showed it to the others who nodded their heads. Then he looked at us. "We've now considered the matter," he said. "As for you, Welcome, we've heard your explanation and we caution you against being such a bloody fool as to listen to what someone shouts at you in a race about where you finish. And we advise you not to do it again. That will be put into rather more Parliamentary language by the time it appears in the Calendar. Now, then, Manson—"

For the first time in our acquaintanceship, I thought Brian appeared apprehensive. He couldn't guess what was coming. Neither could I.

"The stewards," Clumber went on and I noticed his lips twitching slightly, "find you guilty of conduct unbecoming a gentleman rider. That won't appear in the Calendar, either, but this will." He picked up the piece of paper and read from it: " 'The stewards enquired into the riding of Mr. B. Manson in The Tallyho Hunters' Steeplechase, and not being satisfied with his explanation, they fined him ten sovereigns!' You can both go now, and don't let me see either of you in here again—ever."

"Ten pounds! Ten bloomin' pounds! You bloody man!" Brian said, turning on me when we got outside.

"Sovereigns," I said, savouring the word. "Sovereigns. But why blame me. You tried it on once too often, that's all."

"If you hadn't cut the progs—"

"Oh, but I didn't cut them at all. I only told you that. As a matter of fact, I'm going to have a glass of port with the prog and tell him something about racing. An arcane mystery, he called it. He may be right."

Just then Kerrell came up with a bundle of notes in his hand. "Your winnings, sir," he said, holding them out to me. Then, turning to Brian: "You'll be taking the horses home, sir. Mr. Welcome is coming with me in the car. He has an appointment, I understand."

The expression on Brian's face at that moment is one of the racing recollections I shall treasure to the end of my life.

Kerrell and I stopped on the way home to split a bottle of champagne. "I knew he was up to something, sir," Kerrell said as he buried his big nose in a pewter tankard brimming with bubbles. "And when I saw what had happened first time, I thought he might try it again. Never gives up, does Mr. Manson."

"I wish I could ride like him," I said, remembering how he had driven a tired horse, whip swinging, into the last and sat on him when he blundered.

"Ah," said Mr. Kerrell. "They don't make 'em that way every day and that's a fact."

* * *

I had time for a bath before dinner. Afterwards I walked towards the proctor's college through the mellow Oxford night. The stars were out, the old walls gleamed almost white in the pale light of the moon. I was tired and happy but a little apprehensive as to what I would find when I arrived and what sort of a don this would turn out to be.

I climbed his staircase and knocked on the door. A voice told me to come in. It was a long room running from window to window, panelled in dark oak and softly lighted. A large and ruby-red decanter with two glasses beside it stood on a salver. My host rose from his chair and reached out a hand towards it.

"Come in, Welcome," he said. "I expect you're tired. This should do you good."

But I was looking past him to a portrait over the mantel-piece. It showed a man in racing colours sitting a big bay horse with a background of stands and paddock. Below it in a long glass case was a racing whip.

"You must speak up to me when you recount the events of the day," he said. "As I was about to mention to you last night when you so rudely interrupted me, I'm a little deaf from a fall at Cheltenham ten years ago. After that I'm afraid I couldn't resist having some amusement at your expense. Well, what happened?"

"I hacked it," I said happily. "At a hundred to eight."

"Indeed. Then you will be able to pay your fine at all events. Now tell me about it."

So I did. And we finished the port.

CARROT FOR
A CHESTNUT

Dick Francis

C HICK stood and sweated with the carrot in his hand.
His head seemed to be floating and he couldn't feel
his feet on the ground, and the pulse thudded massively
in his ear. A clammy green pain shivered in his gut.

Treachery was making him sick.

The time: fifty minutes before sunrise. The morning: cold.
The raw swirling wind was clearing its throat for a fiercer
blow, and a heavy layer of nimbostratus was fighting every
inch of the way against the hint of light. In the neat box stalls
round the stable-yard the dozing horses struck a random hoof
against a wooden wall, rattled a tethering chain, sneezed the
hay dust out of a moist black nostril.

Chick was late. Two hours late. He'd been told to give the
carrot to the lanky chestnut at four o'clock in the morning,
but at four o'clock in the morning it had been pouring with
rain—hard, slanting rain that soaked a man to the skin in one
minute flat, and Chick had reckoned it would be too difficult
explaining away a soaking at four o'clock in the morning.
Chick had reckoned it would be better to wait until the rain
stopped, it couldn't make any difference. Four o'clock, six
o'clock, what the hell, Chick always knew better than anyone
else.

Chick was a thin, disgruntled nineteen-year-old who always felt the world owed him more than he got. He had been a bad-tempered, argumentative child and an aggressively rebellious adolescent. The resulting snarling habit of mind was precisely what was now hindering his success as an adult. Not that Chick would have agreed, of course. Chick never agreed with anyone if he could help it. Always knew better, did Chick.

He was unprepared for the severity of the physical symptoms of fear. His usual attitude toward any form of authority was scorn (and authority had not so far actually belted him one across his sulky mouth). Horses had never scared him because he had been born to the saddle and had grown up mastering everything on four legs with contemptuous ease. He believed in his heart that no one could really ride better than he could. He was wrong.

He looked apprehensively over his shoulder, and the shifting pain in his stomach sharply intensified. That simply couldn't happen, he thought wildly. He'd heard about people getting sick with fear. He hadn't believed it. It couldn't happen. Now, all of a sudden, he feared it could. He tightened all his muscles desperately, and the spasm slowly passed. It left fresh sweat standing out all over his skin and no saliva in his mouth.

The house was dark. Upstairs, behind the black open window with the pale curtain flapping in the spartan air, slept Arthur Morrison, trainer of the forty-three racehorses in the stables below. Morrison habitually slept lightly. His ears were sharper than half a dozen guard dogs', his stable-hands said.

Chick forced himself to turn his head away, to walk in view of that window, to take the ten exposed steps down to the chestnut's stall.

If the guvernor woke up and saw him. . . . Gawd, he thought furiously, he hadn't expected it to be like this. Just a lousy walk down the yard to give a carrot to the gangly chestnut. Guilt and fear and treachery. They bypassed his sneering mind and erupted through his nerves instead.

He couldn't see anything wrong with the carrot. It hadn't been cut in half and hollowed out and packed with drugs and tied together again. He'd tried pulling the thick end out like a plug, and that hadn't worked either. The carrot just looked like any old carrot, any old carrot you'd watch your ma chop up to put in a stew. Any old carrot you'd give to any old horse. Not a very young, succulent carrot or a very aged carrot, knotted and woody. Just any old ordinary *carrot*.

But strangers didn't proposition you to give any old carrot to one special horse in the middle of the night. They didn't give you more than you earned in half a year when you said you'd do it. Any old carrot didn't come wrapped carefully alone in a polythene bag inside an empty cheese-cracker packet, given to you by a stranger in a car park after dark in a town six miles from the stables. You didn't give any old carrot in the middle of the night to a chestnut who was due to start favourite in a high-class steeplechase eleven hours later.

Chick was getting dizzy with holding his breath by the time he'd completed the ten tiptoed steps to the chestnut's stall. Trying not to cough, not to groan, not to let out the strangling tension in a sob, he curled his sweating fingers around the bolt and began the job of easing it out, inch by frightening inch, from its socket.

By day he slammed the bolts open and shut with a smart practiced flick. His body shook in the darkness with the strain of moving by fractions.

The bolt came free with the tiniest of grating noises, and the top half of the split door swung slowly outward. No squeaks from the hinges, only the whisper of metal on metal. Chick drew in a long breath like a painful, trickling, smothered gasp and let it out between his clenched teeth. His stomach lurched again, threateningly. He took another quick, appalled grip on himself and thrust his arm in a panic through the dark, open space.

Inside the stall, the chestnut was asleep, dozing on his feet. The changing swirl of air from the opening door moved the sensitive hairs around his muzzle and raised his mental state from semi-consciousness to inquisitiveness. He could smell the carrot. He could also smell the man: smell the fear in the man's sweat.

"Come on," Chick whispered desperately. "Come on, then, boy."

The horse moved his nose around toward the carrot and finally, reluctantly, his feet. He took it indifferently from the man's trembling palm, whiffling it in with his black mobile lips, scrunching it languidly with large rotations of his jaw. When he had swallowed all the pulped-up bits he poked his muzzle forward for more. But there was no more, just the lighter square of sky darkening again as the door swung shut, just the faint sounds of the bolt going back, just the fading smell of the man and the passing taste of carrot. Presently he forgot about it and turned slowly round again so that his hindquarters were toward the door, because he usually stood that way, and after a minute or two he blinked slowly, rested his near hind leg lazily on the point of the hoof and lapsed back into twilight mindlessness.

Down in his stomach the liquid narcotic compound with which the carrot had been injected to saturation gradually filtered out of the digesting carrot cells and began to be absorbed into the bloodstream. The process was slow and progressive. And it had started two hours late.

Arthur Morrison stood in his stable-yard watching his men load the chestnut into the motor horse-box that was to take him to the races. He was eyeing the proceedings with an expression that was critical from habit and bore little relation to the satisfaction in his mind. The chestnut was the best horse in his stable: a frequent winner, popular with the public, a source of prestige as well as revenue. The big steeplechase at Cheltenham had been tailor-made for him from the day its conditions had been published, and Morrison was adept at producing a horse in peak condition for a particular race. No one seriously considered that the chestnut would be beaten. The newspapers had tipped it to a man and the bookmakers were fighting shy at 6-4 on. Morrison allowed himself a glimmer of warmth in the eyes and a twitch of smile to the lips as the men clipped shut the heavy doors of the horse van and drove it out of the yard.

These physical signs were unusual. The face he normally wore was a compound of concentration and disapproval in roughly equal proportions. Both qualities contributed considerably to his success as a racehorse trainer and to his unpopularity as a person, a fact Morrison himself was well aware of. He didn't in the least care that almost no one liked him. He valued success and respect much more highly than love and held in incredulous contempt all those who did not.

Across the yard Chick was watching the horse van drive away, his usual scowl in place. Morrison frowned irritably. The boy was a pest, he thought. Always grousing, always impertinent, always trying to scrounge up more money. Morrison didn't believe in boys having life made too easy: a little hardship was good for the soul. Where Morrison and Chick radically differed was the point at which each thought hardship began.

Chick spotted the frown and watched Morrison fearfully, his guilt pressing on him like a rock. He couldn't know, he thought frantically. He couldn't even suspect there was anything wrong with the horse or he wouldn't have let him go off to the races. The horse had looked all right, too. Absolutely his normal self. Perhaps there had been nothing wrong with the carrot. . . . Perhaps it had been the wrong carrot, even. . . . Chick glanced around uneasily and knew very well he was fooling himself. The horse might look all right but he wasn't.

Arthur Morrison saddled up his horse at the races, and Chick watched him from ten nervous paces away, trying to hide in the eager crowd that pushed forward for a close view of the favourite. There was a larger admiring crowd outside the chestnut's saddling stall than for any of the other seven runners, and the bookmakers had shortened their odds. Behind Morrison's concentrated expression an itch of worry was growing insistent. He pulled the girth tight and adjusted the buckles automatically, acknowledging to himself that his former satisfaction had changed to anxiety. The horse was not himself. There were no lively stamping feet, no playful nips from the teeth, no response to the crowd; this was a horse that usually played to the public like a film star. He couldn't be feeling well, and if he wasn't feeling well he wouldn't win. Morrison tightened his mouth. If the horse were not well enough to win, he would prefer him not to run at all. To be beaten at odds-on would be a disgrace. A defeat on too large a scale. A loss of face. Particularly as Morrison's own eldest son Toddy was to be the jockey. The newspapers would tear them both to pieces.

Morrison came to a decision and sent for the vet.

The rules of jump racing in England stated quite clearly that if a horse had been declared a runner in a race, only the say-so of a veterinarian was sufficient grounds for withdrawing him during the last three-quarters of an hour before post time. The Cheltenham racecourse veterinarian came and looked at the chestnut and, after consulting with Morrison, led it off to a more private stall and took its temperature.

"His temperature's normal," the veterinarian assured Morrison.

"I don't like the look of him."

"I can't find anything wrong."

"He's not well," Morrison insisted.

The veterinarian pursed his lips and shook his head. There was nothing obviously wrong with the horse, and he knew he would be in trouble himself if he allowed Morrison to withdraw so hot a favourite on such slender grounds. Not only that, this was the third application for withdrawal he'd had to consider that afternoon. He had refused both the others, and the chestnut was certainly in no worse a state.

"He'll have to run," the veterinarian said positively, making up his mind.

Morrison was furious and went raging off to find a steward, who came and looked at the chestnut and listened to the vet and confirmed that the horse would have to run whether Morrison liked it or not. Unless, that was, Morrison cared to involve the horse's absent owner in paying a heavy fine?

With the face of granite Morrison resaddled the chestnut, and a stable-lad led him out into the parade ring, where most of the waiting public cheered and a few wiser ones looked closely and hurried off to hedge their bets.

With a shiver of dismay, Chick saw the horse reappear and for the first time regretted what he'd done. That stupid vet, he thought violently. He can't see what's under his bloody nose, he couldn't see a barn at ten paces. Anything that happened from then on was the vet's fault, Chick thought. The vet's responsibility, absolutely. The man was a criminal menace, letting a horse run in a steeplechase with dope coming out of its eyeballs.

Toddy Morrison had joined his father in the parade ring and together they were watching with worried expressions as the chestnut plodded lethargically around the oval walking track. Toddy was a strong, stocky professional jockey in his late twenties with an infectious grin and a generous view of life that represented a direct rejection of his father's. He had inherited the same strength of mind but had used it to leave home at eighteen to ride races for other trainers, and had only consented to ride for his father when he could dictate his own terms. Arthur Morrison, in consequence, respected him deeply. Between them they had won a lot of races.

Chick didn't actually dislike Toddy Morrison, even though, as he saw it, Toddy stood in his way. Occasionally Arthur let Chick ride a race if Toddy had something better or couldn't make the weight. Chick had to share these scraps from Toddy's table with two or three other lads in the yard who were, though he didn't believe it, as good as he was in the saddle. But though the envy curdled around inside him and the snide remarks came out sharp and sour as vinegar, he had never actually come to hate Toddy. There was something about Toddy that you couldn't hate, however good the reason. Chick hadn't given a thought to the fact that it would be Toddy who would have to deal with the effects of the carrot. He had seen no further than his own pocket. He wished now that it had been some other jockey. Anyone but Toddy.

The conviction suddenly crystalized in Chick's mind as he

looked at Toddy and Morrison standing there worried in the parade ring that he had never believed the chestnut would actually start in the race. The stranger, Chick said to himself, had distinctly told him the horse would be too sick to start. I wouldn't have done it, else, Chick thought virtuously. I wouldn't have done it. It's bloody dangerous, riding a doped steeplechaser. I wouldn't have done that to Toddy. It's not my fault he's going to ride a doped steeplechaser, it's that vet's fault for not seeing. It's that stranger's fault, he told me distinctly the horse wouldn't be fit to start. . . .

Chick remembered with an unpleasant jerk that he'd been two hours late with the carrot. Maybe if he'd been on time the drug would have come out more and the vet would have seen. . . .

Chick jettisoned this unbearable theory instantly on the grounds that no one can tell how seriously any particular horse will react to a drug or how quickly it will work, and he repeated to himself the comforting self-delusion that the stranger had promised him the horse wouldn't ever start— though the stranger had not in fact said any such thing. The stranger, who was at the races, was entirely satisfied with the way things were going and was on the point of making a great deal of money.

The bell rang for the jockeys to mount. Chick clenched his hands in his pockets and tried not to visualize what could happen to a rider going over jumps at thirty miles an hour on a doped horse. Chick's body began playing him tricks again: he could feel the sweat trickling down his back and the pulse had come back in his ears.

Supposing he told them, he thought. Supposing he just ran out there into the ring and told Toddy not to ride the horse, it hadn't a chance of jumping properly, it was certain to fall, it could kill him bloody easily because its reactions would be all shot to bits.

Supposing he did. The way they'd look at him. His imagination blew a fuse and blanked out on that picture because such a blast of contempt didn't fit in with his overgrown self-esteem. He could not, could *not* face the fury they would feel. And it might not end there. Even if he told them and saved Toddy's life, they might tell the police. He wouldn't put it past them. And he could end up in the dock. Even in jail. They weren't going to do that to him, not to *him*. He wasn't going to give them the chance. He should have been paid more. Paid more because he was worth more. If he'd been paid more, he wouldn't have needed to take the stranger's money. Arthur Morrison had only himself to blame.

Toddy would have to risk it. After all, the horse didn't look too bad, and the vet had passed it, hadn't he, and maybe the carrot being two hours late was all to the good and it wouldn't have done its work properly yet, and in fact it was really thanks to Chick if it hadn't; only thanks to him that the drug was two hours late and that nothing much would happen, really, anyway. Nothing much would happen. Maybe the chestnut wouldn't actually *win*, but Toddy would come through all right. Of course he would.

The jockeys swung up into their saddles, Toddy among them. He saw Chick in the crowd, watching, and sketched an acknowledging wave. The urge to tell and the fear of telling tore Chick apart like the Chinese trees.

Toddy gathered up the reins and clicked his tongue and steered the chestnut indecisively out on to the track. He was disappointed that the horse wasn't feeling well but not in the least apprehensive. It hadn't occurred to him, or to Arthur Morrison, that the horse might be doped. He cantered down to the post standing in his stirrups, replanning his tactics mentally now that he couldn't rely on reserves in his mount. It would be a difficult race now to win. Pity.

Chick watched him go. He hadn't come to his decision, to tell or not to tell. The moment simply passed him by. When Toddy had gone he unstuck his leaden feet and plodded off to the stands to watch the race, and in every corner of his mind little self-justifications sprang up like nettles. A feeling of shame tried to creep in round the edges, but he kicked it out smartly. They should have paid him more. It was their fault, not his.

He thought about the wad of notes the stranger had given

him with the carrot. Money in advance. The stranger had trusted him, which was more than most people seemed to. He'd locked himself into the bathroom and counted the notes, counted them twice, and they were all there, £300 just as the stranger had promised. He had never had so much money all at once in his life before. . . . Perhaps he never would again, he thought. And if he'd told Arthur Morrison and Toddy about the dope, he would have to give up that money, give up the money and more. . . .

Finding somewhere to hide the money had given him difficulty. Three hundred used £1 notes had turned out to be quite bulky, and he didn't want to risk his ma poking around among his things, like she did, and coming across them. He'd solved the problem temporarily by rolling them up and putting them in a brightly coloured round tin which once held toffees but which he used for years for storing brushes and polish for cleaning his shoes. He had covered the money with a duster and jammed the brushes back on the shelf in his bedroom where it always stood. He thought he would probably have to find somewhere safer, in the end. And he'd have to be careful how he spent the money—there would be too many questions asked if he just went out and bought a car. He'd always wanted a car . . . and now he had the money for one . . . and he still couldn't get the car. It wasn't fair. Not fair at all. If they'd paid him more. . . . Enough for a car. . . .

Up on the well-positioned area of stands set aside for trainers and jockeys, a small man with hot dark eyes put his hand on Chick's arm and spoke to him, though it was several seconds before Chick started to listen.

" . . . I see you are here, and you're free, will you ride it?"

"What?" said Chick vaguely.

"My horse in the Novice Hurdle," said the little man impatiently. "Of course, if you don't want to. . . ."

"Didn't say that," Chick mumbled. "Ask the guvnor. If he says I can, well, I can."

The small trainer walked across the stand to where Arthur

Morrison was watching the chestnut intently through the race glasses and asked the same question he'd put to Chick.

"Chick? Yes, he can ride it for you, if you want him." Morrison gave the other trainer two full seconds of his attention and glued himself back on his race glasses.

"My jockey was hurt in a fall in the first race," explained the small man. "There are so many runners in the Novice Hurdle that there's a shortage of jockeys. I just saw that boy of yours, so I asked him on the spur of the moment, see?"

"Yes, yes," said Morrison, ninety per cent uninterested. "He's moderately capable, but don't expect too much of him." There was no spring in the chestnut's stride. Morrison wondered in depression if he was sickening for the cough.

"My horse won't win. Just out for experience you might say."

"Yes. Well, fix it with Chick." Several other stables had the coughing epidemic, Morrison thought. The chestnut couldn't have picked a worse day to catch it.

Chick, who would normally have welcomed the offer of a ride with condescending complacency, was so preoccupied that the small trainer regretted having asked him. Chick's whole attention was riveted on the chestnut, who seemed to be lining up satisfactorily at the starting tape. Nothing wrong, Chick assured himself. Everything was going to be all right. Of course it was. Stupid getting into such a state.

The start was down the track to the left, with two fences to be jumped before the horses came past the stands and swung away again on the left-hand circuit. As it was a jumping race, they were using tapes instead of stalls, and as there was no draw either, Toddy had lined up against the inside rails, ready to take the shortest way home.

Down in the bookmakers' enclosure they were offering more generous odds now and some had gone boldly to evens. The chestnut had cantered past them on his way to the start looking not his brightest and best. The bookmakers in consequence were feeling more hopeful. They had expected a bad day, but if the chestnut lost, they would profit. One of them would profit terrifically—just as he would lose terrifically if the chestnut won.

Alexander McGrant (Est. 1898), real name Harry Buskins, had done this sort of thing once or twice before. He spread out his fingers and looked at them admiringly. Not a tremble in sight. And there was always a risk in these things that the boy he'd bribed would get cold feet at the last minute and not go through with the job. Always a gamble, it was. But this time, this boy, he was pretty sure of. You couldn't go wrong if you sorted out a vain little so-and-so with a big grudge. Knockovers, that sort were. Every time.

Harry Buskins was a shrewd middle-aged East End Londoner for whom there had never been any clear demarcation between right and wrong and a man who thought that if you could rig a nice little swindle now and then, well, why not? The turnover tax was killing betting . . . you had to make a quick buck where you could . . . and there was nothing quite so sure or quick as raking in the dough on a red-hot favourite and knowing for certain that you weren't going to have to pay out.

Down at the post the starter put his hand on the lever and the tapes went up with a rush. Toddy kicked his chestnut smartly in the ribs. From his aerie on top of the stand the commentator moved smartly into his spiel, ''They're off, and the first to show is the grey. . . .'' Arthur Morrison and Chick watched with hearts thumping from different sorts of anxiety, and Harry Buskins shut his eyes and prayed.

Toddy drove forward at once into the first three, the chestnut beneath him galloping strongly, pulling at the bit, thudding his hoofs into the ground. He seemed to be going well enough, Toddy thought. Strong. Like a train.

The first fence lay only one hundred yards ahead now, coming nearer. With a practiced eye Toddy measured the distance, knew the chestnut's stride would meet it right, collected himself for the spring and gave the horse the signal to take off. There was no response. Nothing. The chestnut made no attempt to bunch his muscles, no attempt to gather himself on to his haunches, no attempt to waver or slow down or take any avoiding action whatsoever. For one incredulous second Toddy knew he was facing complete and imminent disaster.

The chestnut galloped straight into the three-foot-thick, chest-high solid birch fence with an impact that brought a groan of horror from the stands. He turned a somersault over the fence with a flurry of thrashing legs, threw Toddy off in front of him and fell down on top and rolled over him.

Chick felt as if the world were turning grey. The colours drained out of everything and he was halfway to fainting. Oh God, he thought. Oh God. *Toddy.*

The chestnut scrambled to his feet and galloped away. He followed the other horses toward the second fence, stretching out into a relentless stride, into a full-fledged thundering racing pace.

He hit the second fence as straight and hard as the first. The crowd gasped and cried out. Again the somersault, the spread-eagled legs, and crashing fall, the instant recovery. The chestnut surged up again and galloped on.

He came up past the stands, moving inexorably, the stir-rups swinging out from the empty saddle, flecks of foam flying back now from his mouth, great dark patches of sweat staining his flanks. Where the track curved round to the left, the chestnut raced straight on. Straight on across the curve, to crash into the rail around the outside of the track. He took the solid timber across the chest and broke it in two. Again he fell in a thrashing heap and again he rocketed to his feet. But this time not to gallop away. This time he took three painful limping steps and stood still.

Back at the fence Toddy lay on the ground with first-aid men bending over him anxiously. Arthur Morrison ran down from the stands toward the track and didn't know which way to turn first, to his son or his horse. Chick's legs gave way and he sagged down in a daze on to the concrete steps. And down in the bookmakers' enclosure Harry Buskins' first re-action of delight was soured by wondering whether, if Toddy Morrison were badly injured, that stupid boy Chick would be scared enough to keep his mouth shut.

Arthur Morrison turned toward his son. Toddy had been knocked unconscious by the fall and had had all the breath squeezed out of him by the chestnut's weight, but by the time his father was within 100 yards he was beginning to come round. As soon as Arthur saw the supine figure move, he turned brusquely round and hurried off toward the horse: it would never do to show Toddy the concern he felt. Toddy would not respect him for it, he thought.

The chestnut stood patiently by the smashed rail, only dimly aware of the dull discomfort in the foreleg that wouldn't take his weight. Arthur Morrison and the veterinarian arrived beside him at the same time, and Arthur Morrison glared at the vet.

"You said he was fit to run. The owner is going to hit the roof when he hears about it." Morrison tried to keep a grip on a growing internal fury at the injustice of fate. The chestnut wasn't just any horse—it was the best he'd ever trained, had hoisted him higher up the stakes-won list then he was ever likely to go again.

"Well, he seemed all right," said the vet defensively.

"I want a dope test done," Morrison said truculently.

"He's broken his shoulder. He'll have to be put down."

"I know. I've got eyes. All the same, I want a dope test first. Just being ill wouldn't have made him act like that."

The veterinarian reluctantly agreed do take a blood sample, and after he fitted the bolt into the humane killer and shot it into the chestnut's drug-crazed brain. The best horse in Arthur Morrison's stable became only a name in the record books. The digested carrot was dragged away with the carcass but its damage was by no means spent.

It took Chick fifteen minutes to realize that it was Toddy who was alive and the horse that was dead, during which time he felt physically ill and mentally pulverized. It had seemed so small a thing, in the beginning, to give a carrot to the chestnut. He hadn't thought of it affecting him much. He'd never dreamed anything like that could make you really sick.

Once he found that Toddy had broken no bones, had re-

covered consciousness and would be on his feet in an hour
or two, the bulk of his physical symptoms receded. When
the small trainer appeared at his elbow to remind him sharply
that he should be inside changing into colours to ride in the
Novice Hurdle race, he felt fit enough to go and do it, though
he wished in a way that he hadn't said he would.

In the changing room he forgot to tell his valet he needed
a lightweight saddle and that the trainer had asked for a breast
girth. He forgot to tie the stock round his neck and would
have gone out to ride with the ends flapping. He forgot to
take his watch off. His valet pointed out everything and
thought that the jockey looked drunk.

The novice hurdler Chick was to ride wouldn't have finished within a mile of the chestnut if he'd started the day
before. Young, green, sketchily schooled he hadn't even the
virtue of a gold streak waiting to be mined: this was one
destined to run in the ruck until the owner tired of trying.
Chick hadn't bothered to find out. He'd been much too preoccupied to look in the form book, where a consistent row
of noughts might have made him cautious. As it was, he
mounted the horse without attention and didn't listen to the
riding orders the small trainer insistently gave him. As usual,
he thought he knew better. Play it off the cuff, he thought
scrappily. Play it off the cuff. How could he listen to fussy
little instructions with all that he had on his mind?

On his way out from the weighing-room he passed Arthur
Morrison, who cast an inattentive eye over his racing colours
and said, "Oh yes . . . well, don't make too much of a mess
of it. . . ."

Morrison was still thinking about the difference the chestnut's death was going to make to his fortunes and he didn't
notice the spasm of irritation that twisted Chick's petulant
face.

There he goes, Chick thought. That's typical. *Typical.*
Never thinks I can do a bloody thing. If he'd given me more
chances . . . and more money . . . I wouldn't have
given. . . . Well, I wouldn't have. He cantered down to the
post, concentrating on resenting that remark, "don't make

too much of a mess of it,'' because it made him feel justified, obscurely, for having done what he'd done. The abyss of remorse opening beneath him was too painful. He clutched at every lie to keep himself out.

Harry Buskins had noticed that Chick had an unexpected mount in the Novice Hurdle and concluded that he himself was safe, the boy wasn't going to crack. All the same, he had shut his bag over its swollen takings and left his pitch for the day and gone home, explaining to his colleagues that he didn't feel well. And in truth he didn't. He couldn't get out of his mind the sight of the chestnut charging at those fences as if he couldn't see. Blind, the horse had been. A great racer who knew he was on a racetrack starting a race. Didn't understand there was anything wrong with him. Galloped because he was asked to gallop, because he knew it was the right place for it. A great horse, with a great racing heart.

Harry Buskins mopped the sweat off his forehead. They were bound to have tested the horse for dope, he thought, after something like that. None of the others he'd done in the past had reacted that way. Maybe he'd got the dose wrong or the timing wrong. You never knew how individual horses would be affected. Doping was always a bit unpredictable.

He poured himself half a tumbler of whiskey with fingers that were shaking after all, and when he felt calmer he decided that if he got away with it this time he would be satisfied with the cleanup he'd made, and he wouldn't fool around with any more carrots. He just wouldn't risk it again.

Chick lined up at the starting post in the centre of the field, even though the trainer had advised him to start on the outside to give the inexperienced horse an easy passage over the first few hurdles. Chick didn't remember this instruction because he hadn't listened, and even if he had listened he would have done the same, driven by his habitual compulsion to disagree. He was thinking about Toddy lining up on this spot an hour ago, not knowing that his horse wouldn't see the jumps. Chick hadn't known dope could make a horse blind. How could anyone expect that? It didn't make sense. Perhaps it was just that the dope had confused the chestnut so much that, although its eyes saw the fence, the message didn't get through that he was supposed to jump over it. The chestnut couldn't have been really blind.

Chick sweated at the thought and forgot to check that the girths were still tight after cantering down to the post. His mind was still on the inward horror when the starter let the tapes up, so that he was caught unawares and flat-footed and got away slowly. The small trainer on the stand clicked his mouth in annoyance, and Arthur Morrison raised his eyes to heaven.

The first hurdle lay side-by-side with the first fence, and all the way to it Chick was illogically scared that his horse wouldn't rise to it. He spent the attention he should have given to setting his horse right in desperately trying to convince himself that no one could have given it a carrot. He couldn't be riding a doped horse himself . . . it wouldn't be fair. Why wouldn't it be fair? Because . . . because . . .

The hurdler scrambled over the jump, knocked himself hard on the timber frame, and landed almost at a standstill. The small trainer began to curse.

Chick tightened one loose rein and the other, and the hurdler swung to and fro in wavering indecision. He needed to be ridden with care and confidence and to be taught balance and rhythm. He needed to be set right before the jumps and to be quickly collected afterwards. He lacked experience, he lacked judgment and he badly needed a jockey who could contribute both.

Chick could have made a reasonable job of it if he'd been trying. Instead, with nausea and mental exhaustion draining what skill he had out of his muscles, he was busy proving that he'd never be much good.

At the second fence he saw in his mind's eye the chestnut somersaulting through the air, and going round the bend his gaze wavered across to the broken rail and the scuffed-up patches of turf in front of it. The chestnut had died there. Everyone in the stable would be poorer for it. He had killed the chestnut, there was no avoiding it anymore, he'd killed it with that carrot as surely as if he'd shot the bolt himself. Chick sobbed suddenly, and his eyes filled with tears.

He didn't see the next two hurdles. They passed beneath him in a flying blurr. He stayed on his horse by instinct, and the tears ran down and were swept away as they trickled under the edge of his jockey's goggles.

The green hurdler was frightened and rudderless. Another jump lay close ahead, and the horses in front went clattering through it, knocking one section half over and leaving it there at an angle. The hurdler waited until the last minute for help or instructions from the man on his back and then in a muddled way dived for the leaning section, which looked lower to him and easier to jump than the other end.

From the stands it was clear to both the small trainer and Arthur Morrison that Chick had made no attempt to keep straight or to tell the horse when to take off. It landed with its forefeet tangled up in the sloping hurdle and catapulted Chick off over its head.

The instinct of self-preservation which should have made Chick curl into a rolling ball wasn't working. He fell through the air flat and straight, and his last thought before he hit was that that stupid little sod of a trainer hadn't schooled his horse properly. The animal hadn't a clue how to jump.

He woke up a long time later in a high bed in a small room. There was a dim light burning somewhere. He could feel no pain. He could feel nothing at all. His mind seemed to be floating in his head and his head was floating in space.

After a long time he began to believe that he was dead. He took the thought calmly and was proud of himself for his calm. A long time after that he began to realize that he wasn't dead. There was some sort of casing round his head, holding it cushioned. He couldn't move.

He blinked his eyes consciously and licked his lips to make sure that they at least were working. He couldn't think what had happened. His thoughts were a confused but peaceful fog.

Finally he remembered the carrot, and the whole complicated agony washed back into his consciousness. He cried out in protest and tried to move, to get up and away, to escape the impossible, unbearable guilt. People heard his voice and came into the room and stood around him. He looked at them uncomprehendingly. They were dressed in white.

"You're all right, now," they said. "Don't worry, young man, you're going to be all right."

"I can't move," he protested.

"You will," they said soothingly.

"I can't feel . . . anything. I can't feel my feet." The panic rose suddenly in his voice. "I can't feel my hands. I can't . . . move . . . my hands." He was shouting, frightened, his eyes wide and stretched.

"Don't worry," they said. "You will in time. You're going to be all right. You're going to be all right."

He didn't believe them, and they pumped a sedative into his arm to quiet him. He couldn't feel the prick of the needle. He heard himself screaming because he could feel no pain.

When he woke up again he knew for certain that he'd broken his neck.

After four days Arthur Morrison came to see him, bringing six new-laid eggs and a bottle of fresh orange juice. He stood looking down at the immobile body with the plaster cast round its shoulders and head.

"Well, Chick," he said awkwardly. "It's not as bad as it could have been, eh?"

Chick said rudely, "I'm glad you think so."

"They say your spinal cord isn't severed, it's just crushed. They say in a year or so you'll get a lot of movement back. And they say you'll begin to feel things any day now."

"They say," said Chick sneeringly. "I don't believe them."

"You'll have to, in time," said Morrison impatiently.

Chick didn't answer, and Arthur Morrison cast uncomfortably around in his mind for something to say to pass away the minutes until he could decently leave. He couldn't visit the boy and just stand there in silence. He had to say *some-*

thing. So he began to talk about what was uppermost in his mind.

"We had the result of the dope test this morning. Did you know we had the chestnut tested? Well, you know we had to have it put down anyway. The results came in this morning. They were positive. . . . *Positive*. The chestnut was full of some sort of narcotic drug, some long name. The owner is kicking up hell about it and so is the insurance company. They're trying to say it's my fault. My security arrangements aren't tight enough. It's ridiculous. And all this on top of losing the horse itself, losing that really great horse. I questioned everyone in the stable this morning as soon as I knew about the dope, but of course no one knew anything. God, if I knew who did it I'd strangle him myself." His voice shook with the fury which had been consuming him all day.

It occurred to him at this point that Chick being Chick, he would be exclusively concerned with his own state and wouldn't care a damn for anyone else's troubles. Arthur Morrison sighed deeply. Chick did have his own troubles now, right enough. He couldn't be expected to care all that much about the chestnut. And he was looking very weak, very pale.

The doctor who checked on Chick's condition ten times a day came quietly into the small room and shook hands with Morrison.

"He's doing well," he said. "Getting on splendidly."

"Nuts," Chick said.

The doctor twisted his lips. He didn't say he had found Chick the worst-tempered patient in the hospital. He said, "Of course, it's hard on him. But it could have been worse. It'll take time, he'll need to learn everything again, you see. It'll take time."

"Like a bloody baby," Chick said violently.

Arthur Morrison thought, a baby again. Well, perhaps second time around they could make a better job of him.

"He's lucky he's got good parents to look after him once he goes home," the doctor said.

Chick thought of his mother, forever chopping up carrots

to put in the stew. He'd have to eat them. His throat closed convulsively. He knew he couldn't.

And then there was the money, rolled up in the shoe-cleaning tin on the shelf in his bedroom. He would be able to see the tin all the time when he was lying in his own bed. He would never be able to forget. Never. And there was always the danger his ma would look inside it. He couldn't face going home. He couldn't face it. And he knew he would have to. He had no choice. He wished he were dead.

Arthur Morrison sighed heavily and shouldered his new burden with his accustomed strength of mind. "Yes, he can come home to his mother and me as soon as he's well enough. He'll always have us to rely on."

Chick Morrison winced with despair and shut his eyes. His father tried to stifle a surge of irritation, and the doctor thought the boy an ungrateful little beast.

THE LOOK OF EAGLES

John Taintor Foote

I HAD waited ten minutes on that corner. At last I ventured out from the curb and peered down the street, hoping for the sight of a red and white sign that read: THIS CAR FOR THE RACES. Then a motor horn bellowed, too close for comfort. I stepped back hastily in favour of the purring giant that bore it, and looked up into the smiling eyes of the master of Thistle Ridge. The big car slid its length and stopped. Its flanks were white with dust. Its little stint that morning had been to sweep away the miles between Lexington and Louisville.

"Early, aren't you?" asked Judge Dillon as I settled back contentedly at his side.

"Thought I'd spend a few hours with our mutual friend," I explained.

I felt an amused glance.

"Diverting and—er—profitable, eh? What does the victim say about it?"

"He never reads them," I confessed; and Judge Dillon chuckled.

"I've come over to see our Derby candidate in particular," he informed me. "I haven't heard from him for a month. Your friend is a poor correspondent."

The gateman at Churchill Downs shouted directions at us a few moments later and the car swung to the left, past a city of stables. As we wheeled through a gap in a line of white-washed stalls we heard the raised voice of Blister Jones. He was confronting the hapless Chick and a steaming bucket.

"Fur the brown stud, eh?" we heard. "Let's look at it."

Chick presented the bucket in silence. Blister peered at its contents.

"Soup!" he sniffed. "I thought so. Go rub it in your hair."

"You tells me to throw the wet feed into him, didn't you?" Chick inquired defensively.

"Last week—yes," said Blister. "Not all summer. Someday a thought'll get in your nut 'n' bust it!" His eyes caught the motor and his frown was instantly blotted out.

"Why, how-de-do, Judge!" he said. "I didn't see you."

"Don't mind us," Judge Dillon told him as we alighted. "How's the colt?"

Blister turned and glanced at a shining bay head protruding from an upper door.

"Well, I'll tell you," he said deliberately. "He ain't such a bad sort of a colt in some ways. Fur a while I liked him; but here lately I get to thinkin' he won't do. He's got a lot of step. He shows me a couple o' nice works; but if he makes a stake hoss I'm fooled bad."

"Huh!" grunted Judge Dillon. "What's the matter? Is he sluggish?"

"That wouldn't worry me so much if he was," said Blister. "They don't have to go speed crazy all at once." He hesitated for a moment, looking up into the owner's face. Then, as one breaking terrible news: "Judge," he said, "he ain't got the class."

There followed a silence. In it I became aware that the blue and gold of Thistle Ridge would not flash from the barrier on Derby Day.

"Well, ship him home," said Judge Dillon at last as he sat down rather heavily on a bale of hay. He glanced once at the slim bay head, then turned to us with a smile. "Better luck next year," he said.

I was tongue-tied before that smile, but Blister came to the rescue.

"You still like that Fire Fly cross don't you?" he asked with a challenge in his voice.

"I do," asserted Judge Dillon firmly. "It gives 'em bone like nothing else."

"Yep," agreed Blister, " 'n' a lot of it goes to the head. None of that Fire Fly blood fur mine. Nine out of ten of 'em sprawl. They don't gather up like they meant it. Now you take ole Torch Bearer—"

I found a chair and became busy with my own thoughts. I wondered if, after all, the breeding of speed horses was not too cruelly disappointing to those whose heart and soul were in it. The moments of triumph were wonderful, of course. The thrill of any other game was feeble in comparison; but oh, the many and bitter disappointments!

At last I became conscious of a little old man approaching down the line of stalls. His clothes were quite shabby; but he walked with crisp erectness, with something of an air. He carried his soft hat in his hand and his silky hair glistened like silver in the sunshine. As he stopped and addressed a stable boy, a dozen stalls from where we sat, the courteous tilt of his head was vaguely familiar.

"Who's that old man down there?" I asked, "I think I've seen him before."

Blister followed my eyes and sat up in his chair with a jerk. He looked about him as though contemplating flight.

"Oh, Lord!" he said. "Now I'll get mine!"

"Who is it?" I repeated.

"Ole Man Sanford," answered Blister. "I ain't seen him fur a year. I hopped a hoss fur him once. I guess I told you."

I nodded.

"What's he talking about?" asked Judge Dillon.

And I explained how Old Man Sanford, a big breeder in his day, was now in reduced circumstances; how he had, with a small legacy, purchased a horse and placed him in Blister's hands; how Blister had given the horse stimulants before a race, contrary to racing rules; and how Mr. Sanford had discovered it and had torn up his tickets when the horse won.

"Tore up his tickets!" exclaimed Judge Dillon. "How much?"

"Fifteen hundred dollars," I replied. "All he had in the world."

Judge Dillon whistled.

"I've met him," he said. "He won a Derby thirty years ago." He bent forward and examined the straight, white-haired little figure. "Tore up his tickets, eh?" he repeated. Then softly: "Blood will tell!"

"Here he comes," said Blister uneasily. "He'll give me the once-over 'n' brush by, I guess."

But Old Man Sanford did nothing of the sort. A radiant smile and two extended hands greeted Blister's awkward advance.

"My deah young friend, how is the world treatin' you these days?"

"Pretty good, Mr. Sanford," answered Blister and hesitated. "I kinda thought you'd be sore at me," he confessed. "While I didn't mean it that way, I give you a raw deal, didn't I?"

A hand rested on Blister's sleeve for an instant.

"When yoh hair," said Old Man Sanford, "has taken its colour from the many wintuhs whose stohms have bowed yoh head, you will have learned this: We act accohdin' to our lights. Some are brighter, some are dimmer, than others; but who shall be the judge?"

Whether or not Blister got the finer shadings of this, the sense of it was plain.

"I might have knowed you wouldn't be sore," he said relievedly. "Here's Chick. You remember Chick, Mr. Sanford."

Chick was greeted radiantly. Likewise "Petah."

"And the hawses? How are the hawses? Have you a nice string?" Blister turned and "made us acquainted" with Old Man Sanford.

"Chick," he called, "get a chair fur Mr. Sanford. Pete—you boys start in with the sorrel hoss 'n' bring 'em all out, one at a time!"

"Why, now," said Mr. Sanford, "I mustn't make a nuisance of myself. It would be a great pleasuh, suh, to see yoh hawses; but I do not wish to bothah you. Suppose I just walk from stall to stall?"

He tried to advance toward the stalls, but was confronted by Blister, who took him by the arms, smiled down into his face, and gave him a gentle shake.

"Now listen!" said Blister. "As long as we're here you treat this string like it's yours. They'll come out 'n' stand on their ears if you want to see it. You got me?"

I saw a dull red mount slowly to the wrinkled cheeks. The little figure became straighter, if possible, in its threadbare black suit. I saw an enormous silk handkerchief, embroidered and yellow with age, appear suddenly as Old Man Sanford blew his nose. He started to speak, faltered, and again was obliged to resort to the handkerchief.

"I thank you, suh," he said at last, and found a chair as Judge Dillon's eyes sought mine.

We left him out of our conversation for a time; but as the string was led before him one by one the horseman in Mr. Sanford triumphed. He passed loving judgment on one and all, his face keen and lighted. Of the colt I had just heard doomed he said:

"A well-made youngsteh, gentlemen; his blood speaks in every line of him. But as I look him oveh I have a feeling—it is, of cohse, no moh than that—that he lacks a certain quality essential to a great hawse."

"What quality?" asked Judge Dillon quickly.

"A racin' heart, suh," came the prompt reply.

"Oh, that's it, is it?" said Judge Dillon, and added dryly: "I own him."

Mr. Sanford gave one reproachful glance at Blister.

"I beg yoh pahdon, suh," he said earnestly to Judge Dillon. "A snap judgment in mattehs of this sawt is, of cohse, wo'thless. Do not give my words a thought, suh. They were spoken hastily, without due deliberation, with no real knowledge on which to base them. I sincerely hope I have not pained you, suh."

Judge Dillon's big hand swung over and covered one of the thin knees encased in shiny broadcloth.

"No sportsman," he said, "is hurt by the truth. That's just exactly what's the matter with him. But how did you know it?"

Mr. Sanford hesitated.

"I'm quite likely to be mistaken, suh," he said; "but if it would interest you I may say that I missed a certain look about his head, and moh pahticularly in his eyes, that is the hallmark—this is merely my opinion, suh—of a really great hawse."

"What kind of a look?" I asked.

Again Mr. Sanford hesitated.

"It is hard to define, suh," he explained. "It is not a matteh of skull structure—of confohmation. It is—" He sought for words. "Well, suh, about the head of a truly great hawse there is an air of freedom unconquerable. The eyes seem to look on heights beyond our gaze. It is the look of a spirit that can soar. It is not confined to hawses; even in his pictures you can see it in the eyes of the Bonaparte. It is the birthright of eagles. They all have it—But I express myself badly." He turned to Judge Dillon. "Yoh great mayeh has it, suh, to a marked degree."

"Très Jolie?" inquired Judge Dillon, and Mr. Sanford nodded.

I had heard of a power—psychic, perhaps—which comes to a few, a very few, who give their lives and their hearts to horses. I looked curiously at the little old man beside me. Did those faded watery eyes see something hidden from the rest of us? I wondered.

Blister interrupted my thoughts.

"Say, Mr. Sanford," he asked suddenly, "what did you ever do with Trampfast?"

"I disposed of him, suh, foh nine hundred dollahs."

Blister considered this for a moment.

"Look-a-here!" he said. "You don't like the way I handled that hoss fur you, 'n' I'd like a chance to make good. I know where I can buy a right good plater fur nine hundred dollars. I'll make him pay his way or no charge. What do you say?"

Mr. Sanford shook his head. "As a matteh of fact," he stated, "I have only six hundred dollahs now in hand. Aside from having learned that my racing methods are not those of today, I would not care to see the pu'ple and white on a six-hundred-dollah hawse."

"Why, look-a-here!" urged Blister. "All the big stables race platers. There's good money in it when it's handled right. Let a goat chew dust a few times till you can drop him in soft somewheres, 'n' then put a piece of change on him at nice juicy odds. The boy kicks a win out of him, maybe; 'n' right there he don't owe you nothin'."

Once more I saw a dull red flare up in Mr. Sanford's face; but now he favoured Blister with a bristling stare.

"I have difficulty in following you at times, suh," he said. "Am I justified in believing that the word 'goat' is applied to a thoroughbred race hawse?"

"Why, yes, Mr. Sanford," said Blister, "that's what I mean, I expect."

The old gentleman seemed to spend a moment in dismissing his wrath. When he spoke at last no trace of it was in his voice.

"I am fond of you, my young friend," he said. "Under a cynical exterior I have found you courteous, loyal, tender-hearted; but I deplore in you the shallow flippancy of this age. It is the fashion to sneer at the finer things; and so you call a racin' thoroughbred a goat. He is not of stake quality perhaps." Here the voice became quite gentle: "Are you?"

"I guess not, Mr. Sanford," admitted Blister.

"Never mind, my boy. If man breeds one genius to a decade it is enough. And so it goes with hawses. Foh thirty years, with love, with reverence, I tried to breed great hawses—hawses that would be a joy, an honoh to my state. In those days ninety colts were foaled each spring at Sanfo'd Hall. I have spent twenty thousand dollahs foh a single ma-tron. How many hawses—truly great hawses—did such brood mayehs as that produce? How many do you think?"

Judge Dillon gave Mr. Sanford the warm look of a brother.

"Not many," he murmured.

"Why, I dunno, Mr. Sanford," said Blister. "You tells me about one—the filly that copped the Derby fur you."

"Yes; she was one. And one moh, suh. Two in all."

"I never hear you mention but the one," said Blister.

"The other never raced," explained Mr. Sanford. "I'll tell you why."

He lapsed into silence, into a sort of reverie, while we waited. When he spoke it was totally without emotion. His voice was dull. It seemed somehow as though speech had been given to the dead past.

"It has been a long time," he said, more to himself than to us. "A long time!" he repeated, nodding thoughtfully, and again became silent.

"In those days," he began at last, "it was the custom of their mistress to go to the no'th pastuh with sugah, and call to the weanlin's. In flytime the youngstehs preferred the willow trees by the creek, and there was a qua'tah of a mile of level bluegrass from those willows to the pastuh gate. She would stand at the gate and call. As they heard her voice the colts would come oveh the creek bank as though it were a barrier—a fair start and no favohs asked. The rascals like sugah, to be sure; but an excuse to fight it out foh a qua'tah was the main point of the game.

"One year a blood bay colt, black to the hocks and knees, was foaled in January. In June he got his sugah fuhst by two open lengths. In August he made them hang their heads foh shame—five, six, seven lengths he beat them; and their siahs watchin' from the paddocks.

"In the spring of his two-year-old fohm he suffered with an attack of distempah. He had been galloped on the fahm track by then, and we knew just what he was. We nuhsed him through it, and by the following spring he was ready to go out and meet them all foh the honoh of the pu'ple and white.

"Then, one night, I was wakened to be told that a doctoh must be fetched and that each moment was precious. I sent my body sehvant to the bahns with the message that I wished a saddle on the best hawse in stable. When pahtially dressed I followed him, and was thrown up by a stable man. . . .

"There was a moon—a gracious moon, I remembah—the white road to Gawgetown, and a great fear at my heart. I did not know what was under me until I gave him his head on that white, straight road. Then I knew. I cannot say in what time we did those four miles; but this I can tell you—the colt ran the last mile as stanchly as the first, and one hour later he could barely walk. His terrific pace oveh that flinty road destroyed his tendons and broke the small bones in his legs. He gave his racin' life foh his lady, like the honest gentleman he was. His sacrifice, howeveh, was in vain. . . . Death had the heels of him that night. Death had the heels of him!'"

In a tense silence I seemed to hear a bell tolling. "Death had the heels of him!" it boomed over and over again.

Blister's eyes were starting from their sockets, but he did not hear the bell. He wet his parted lips.

"What become of him?" he breathed.

"When the place was sold he went with the rest. You have seen his descendants race on until his name has become a glory. The colt I rode that night was—Torch Bearer."

Blister drew in his breath with a whistling sound.

"Torch Bearer!" he gasped. "Did you own Torch Bearer?"

"I did, suh," came the quiet answer. "I bred and raised him. His blood flows in the veins of many—er—goats, I believe you call them."

"Man, oh, man!" said Blister, and became speechless.

I, too, was silent of necessity. There was something wrong with my throat.

And now Judge Dillon spoke, and it was apparent that he was afflicted like myself. Once more the big hand covered the thin knee.

"Mr. Sanford," I heard, "you can do me a favour if you will."

"My deah suh, name it!"

"Go to Lexington. Look over the colts at Thistle Ridge.

If you find one good enough for the purple and white, bring
him back here. . . . He's yours!''

I went along. Oh, yes; I went along. I should miss two days
of racing; but I would have missed more than that quite willingly. I was to see Old Man Sanford pick out one from a
hundred colts—and all ''bred clear to the clouds,'' as Blister
explained to us on the train. I wondered whether any one of
them would have that look—''the birthright of eagles''—and
hoped, I almost prayed, that we should find it.

That the colt was to be a purchase, not a gift, had made
our journey possible. Five hundred dollars cash and ''my
note, suh, for a like amount.''

Judge Dillon had broken the deadlock by accepting; then
offered his car for the trip to Lexington. At this a grin had
appeared on Blister's face.

''No chance, Judge,'' he said.

''I thank you, suh, foh youh generosity,'' apologized Mr.
Sanford. ''It gives me the deepest pleasuh, the deepest grat-
ification, suh; but, if you will pahdon me, I shall feel moh
at home on the train.''

''You couldn't get him in one of them things on a bet,''
Blister explained; and so a locomotive pulled us safely into
Lexington.

We spent the night at the hotel and drove to Thistle Ridge
early next morning behind a plodding pair. Even in Kentucky, livery horses are—livery horses.

A letter from Judge Dillon opened the big gates wide and
placed us in charge of one Wesley Washington—as I live by
bread, that was his name—suspicious by nature and black as
a buzzard. I reminded him of my previous visit to Thistle
Ridge. He acknowledged it with no sign of enthusiasm.

''What kinda colt you want?'' he asked Blister.

''A good one!'' answered Blister briefly.

Wesley rolled the whites of his eyes at him and sniffed.

''You ain' said nothin','' he stated. ''Dat's all we got.''

''You're lucky,'' Blister told him. ''Well, trot 'em out.''

Then Wesley waved his wand—it chanced to be a black

paw with a pinkish palm—and they were trotted out; or, rather, they came rearing through the doorway of the biggest of the big stables. Bays, browns, blacks, sorrels, chestnuts, roans—they bubbled out at us in an endless stream. Attached precariously to each of them—this was especially true when they reared—was a coloured boy. These Wesley addressed in sparkling and figuratively speech. His remarks, as a rule, were prefaced by the word "Niggah."

At last Blister shouted through the dust.

"Say," he said, "this ain't gettin' us nowhere. Holy fright! How many you got?"

"Dat ain' half," said Wesley ominously.

"Cut it out!" directed Blister. "You'll have me popeyed in a minute. We'll go through the stalls 'n' pick out the live ones. This stuff's too young anyway. We want a two-year-old broke to the barrier. Have you got any?"

I turned to Mr. Sanford. He was standing hat in hand, as was his custom, his face ablaze.

"The grandest spectacle I have witnessed in thirty yeahs, suh!" he informed me.

"Has we got a two-year-old broke to de barrieh?" I heard from Wesley, "Hush! Jus' ambulate oveh disaway." He led us to a smaller stable. It contained two rows of box stalls with a wide alley down the middle. Through the iron gratings in each stall I could see a snakelike head. The door at the opposite end of the stable looked out on the tawny oval of the farm track, and suddenly something flashed across the doorway so quickly that I only guessed it to be a thorough-bred with a boy crouching along his neck.

Wesley's eye swept up and down the two lines of box stalls. He looked at Blister with a prideful gleam.

"All two-yeah-olds," he said, "an' ready to race."

If this statement made any impression it was concealed. Blister yawned and sauntered to the first stall on the right.

"Well, there might be a plater among 'em," he said. "This all you got?"

"Ain' dat enough?" inquired Wesley with a snort.

"Not if they're the culls," said Blister. "You read that letter, didn't you? We're to see 'em all. Don't forget that."

"Hyar dey is," said Wesley. "Jus' use yoh eyes an' yoh han's."

"All right," said Blister as he opened the stall door—"but don't hold nothin' out on us. Mr. Sanford here is an old friend of the Judge."

Wesley rolled an inspecting eye over Mr. Sanford.

"I ain' neveh seen him roun' hyar," he stated, and honours were easy.

The battle was on in earnest a moment later. The colt in the first stall was haltered and led out into the runway. He was jet black with one white star, and wonderful to see.

"Nothing' finah on fo' laigs," said Wesley, and I mentally agreed with him; but Blister walked once round that glorious creature and waved him back into his stall.

"Yep," he said; "he's right good on four legs, but he'll be on three when that curb begins to talk to him."

"Shuh!" said Wesley in deep disgust. "You ain' goin' to call dat little fullness in de tendon a curb, is you? He'll die of ole aige an' neveh know he's got it."

"He dies of old age before I own him," said Blister, and walked to the second stall.

And so it went for an hour. Mr. Sanford was strangely silent. When he ventured an opinion at all it was to agree with Wesley, and I was disappointed. I had hoped for delightful dissertations, for superhuman judgments. I had expected to see a master at work with his chosen medium. Instead, he seemed a child in the hands of the skillful Wesley; and I felt that Blister was our only hope.

This opinion had become settled when the unexpected happened. After a more than careful inspection of a chestnut colt, Blister turned to Wesley.

"What's this colt done?" he asked.

"Half in fifty," Wesley stated, "Jus' play foh him."

"Put a boy on him 'n' let's see him move," said Blister.

Then Mr. Sanford spoke.

"It will be unnecessary," he said quietly. "I do not like him."

A puzzled expression spread itself over Blister's face.

"All right," he said with a shade of annoyance in his voice. "You're the doctor."

And then I noticed Wesley—Wesley, the adroit—and a look of amazement, almost of terror, was in his eyes as he stared at Mr. Sanford.

"Yessuh," he said with a gulp. "Yessuh." Then he pulled himself together. "Put him up, black boy," he directed magnificently, and moved to the next stall.

I stayed behind and displayed a quarter cautiously.

"Do you like this colt?" I asked, looking the boy straight in the face.

For a moment he hesitated. Then:

"No, suh," he whispered.

"Why not?" I inquired.

There was a flicker of contempt in the white eyeballs.

"He's a houn'," I barely heard as the quarter changed owners.

It was a well-spent quarter; it had purchased knowledge. I knew now that among our party was a pair of eyes that could look deep into the heart of things. Old they were and faded, those eyes; but I felt assured that a glistening flank could not deceive them.

We worked down one side of the stable and up the other. We had seen twenty colts when we arrived at the last stall. It contained a long-legged sorrel and Blister damned him with a grunt when he was led out.

"If he ever gets tangled up," was his comment, "you don't get his legs untied that year. This all you got?"

Wesley assured him it was. We seemed to have reached an *impasse*. Then, as Blister frowned absently at the sorrel colt, a voice began singing just outside the stable. It was a rich treble and it chanted in a minor key. I saw the absent look wiped slowly from Blister's face. It was supplanted by a dawning alertness as he listened intently.

Suddenly he disappeared through the doorway and there

came to me a regular scuff-scuff on the gravel outside, in time to the words of the song, which were these:

> *"Bay colt wuck in fo'ty-eight,*
> *Goin' to de races—goin' to de races;*
> *Bay colt wuck in fo'ty-eight,*
> *Goin' to de races now."*

I felt my jaw begin to drop, for Blister's voice had joined the unknown singer's.

> *"Bay colt wuck in fo'ty-eight,"*

sang the voice; and then a bellow from Blister:

> *"Goin to the races—goin' to the races."*

The voice repeated:

> *"Bay colt wuck in fo'ty-eight,"*

and resigned to Blister's:

> *"Goin' to the races now!"*

I went hastily through that doorway and arrived at the following phenomena:

Exhibit A—One chocolate-coloured boy, not more than three feet high. His shoes (I mention them first because they constituted one-half of the whole exhibit) were—But the words are feeble—*prodigious, Gargantuan*, are only mildly suggestive of those shoes. His stockings—and now I cross my heart and hope to die—were of the variety described commercially as ladies' hose, and they were pink and they were silk. Somewhere beneath their many folds two licorice sticks performed the miracle of moving those unbelievable shoes through an intricate clog dance.

Exhibit B—One Blister Jones, patting with feet and hands

an accompaniment to the wonders being performed by the marvellous shoes.

Both exhibits were entirely in earnest and completely absorbed. As has been already told, they were joined in song.

As I assured myself that the phenomena were real and not imaginary, the words of the song changed.

> *"Bay colt wuck in fo'ty-eight,"*

came steadfastly from the smaller singer; but Blister, instead of "Going to the races," sang:

> *"Where's he at? Where's he at?"*
> *"Bay colt wuck in fo'ty-eight,"*

insisted Exhibit A; and Exhibit B sang:

> *"Where's that bay colt now?"*

They learn early, in Kentucky, that track and farm secrets are sacred. A suspicion of all outsiders, though dulled by the excitement of white folks' appreciation, still flickered somewhere in the kinky dome of Exhibit A. The song was twice repeated without variation, and the "Where's he at?" became tragic in its pleading tone.

At last Exhibit A must have decided that his partner in song was a kindred spirit and worthy of trust. At any rate,

> *"Oveh in de coolin' shed—oveh in de coolin' shed,"*

I heard; and Blister brought the duet to a triumphant close with:

> *"Over in the coolin' shed now!"*

He swung round and grinned at Wesley, who was standing stupefied in the doorway.

"Why, Wes!" he said reproachfully. "I'm surprised at you!"

Wesley glowered at Exhibit A.

"You ramble!" he said and the marvellous shoes bore their owner swiftly from our sight.

So, through song, was the wily Wesley brought to confusion. We found four two-year-olds in the long, squatty cooling shed, and Wesley admitted, under pressure, that they were the pick of their year, kept for special training.

Three of them stood in straw to their knees, confined in three tremendous box stalls. One was being led under blankets up and down the runway. His sides lifted their covering regularly. His clean-cut velvet nostrils widened and contracted as he took his breath. His eyes were blazing jewels. To him went Blister, like iron filings to a magnet.

"Peel him fur a minute," he said, and the still dazed and somewhat chastened Wesley nodded his permission.

Then appeared the most perfect living creature I had ever seen. He was a rich bay—now dark mahogany because of a recent bath—and the sheer beauty of him produced in me a feeling of awe, almost of worship. I was moved as though I listened to the Seventh Symphony or viewed the Winged Victory; and this was fit and proper, for my eyes were drinking in a piece by the greatest of all masters.

Blister was cursing softly, reverently, as though he were at prayer.

"If he's only half as good as he looks!" he sighed at last. "How about *him*, Mr. Sanford?"

I had forgotten Old Man Sanford. I now discovered him standing before a stall and gazing raptly at what was within. At Blister's words he turned and surveyed the bay colt.

"The most superb piece of hawseflesh," he said, "I have eveh had the pleasuh of observing. I could not fault him with a microscope. He is nothing shawt of perfection, suh— nothing shawt of perfection." His eyes lingered for an instant on the wet flanks of the uncovered colt. "He's too wahm to be without his clothing," he suggested, and turned again to the stall before him.

Blister covered the colt with one dexterous swing. He glanced at the name embroidered on the blankets.

"Postman," he read aloud. "He'll be by Messenger, won't he?" The boy at the colt's head nodded. "Worked in forty-eight just now, eh?" said Blister to no one in particular. Again the boy nodded. "Well," decided Blister, "we'll take a chance on him. Train fur Looeyville at four o'clock—ain't they, Wes?"

Wesley gave a moan of anguish.

"My Gawd!" he said.

"What's bitin' you?" demanded Blister. "We're payin' fur him, ain't we?"

"Lemme have dat letter one moh time," said Wesley. He absorbed the letter's contents as though it were poison, and came at last to the fatal "John C. Dillon" at the end. This he read aloud and slowly shook his head. "He's los' his min'," he stated, and glared at Mr. Sanford. "What you payin' fo'' dis hyar colt?" he demanded.

Mr. Sanford glanced in our direction. His eyes had a far-away look.

"Were you addressing me?" he asked.

"Yessuh," replied Wesley. "I was inquirin' de price you aim to pay foh dis colt."

"That is a matteh," said Old Man Sanford, "that concerns only yoh mas—employeh and myself. Howeveh, I am not going to pu'chase the colt to which you refeh." He glanced dreamily into the stall before which he seemed rooted. "I have taken a fancy to my little friend in hyar. . . . Could you oblige me with a piece of sugah?"

As one man, Blister and I made a rush for that stall. We peered through the bars for a moment and our amazed eyes met. In Blister's an angry despair was dawning. He turned savagely on Mr. Sanford.

"You goin' to buy that shrimp?" he demanded.

"Yes, suh," said Old Man Sanford mildly. "I expect to pu'chase him. . . . Ah, here's the sugah!" He took some lumps of sugar from the now beaming Wesley and opened the stall door.

Blister stepped inside the stall and devoted some moments to vain pleadings. Mr. Sanford was unmoved by them.

Then the storm broke. Blister became a madman who raved. He cursed not only the small black two-year-old, standing knee-deep in golden straw, but the small, white-haired old gentleman who was placidly feeding him sugar. The storm raged on, but Mr. Sanford gave no sign.

At last I saw a hand that was extended to the colt's muzzle begin to tremble, and I took Blister by the arm and drew him forcefully away.

"Stop!" I said in an undertone. "You're doing no good and he's an old man."

Blister tore his arm from mine.

"He's an old fool!" he cried. "He's chuckin' away the chance of a lifetime!" Then his eye fell on the bay colt and his voice became a wail. "Ain't it hell?" he inquired of high heaven. "Ain't it just hell?"

At this point Wesley saw fit to emit a loud guffaw. Blister advanced on him like a tiger.

"Laugh, you black boob!" he shot out, and Wesley's joyous expression vanished.

I saw that I was doing no good and joined Mr. Sanford in the stall.

"Rather small, isn't he?" I suggested.

"He could be a little larger," Mr. Sanford admitted. "He could stand half a han' and fifty pounds moh at his aige; but then, he'll grow. He'll make a hawse some day."

And now came Blister, rather sheepish, and stood beside us.

"I got sore, Mr. Sanford," he said. "I oughta be kicked!"

Old Man Sanford proffered a lump of sugar to the slim black muzzle. It was accepted so eagerly that the sugar was knocked from the extended hand. Mr. Sanford pointed a reproving finger at the colt.

"Not quite so fast, young man!" he admonished. Then he turned to Blister with a gentle smile. "Youth is hasty," he said, "and sometimes—mistaken."

* * *

I returned to Cincinnati and work that night, filled with speculations about a small black colt and his new owner. The latter, I felt, had reached a stubborn dotage.

Two months rolled by; they crawled for me. . . . The powers above decreed that the paper should fight the Bull Moose to the death. I trained the guns of the editorial page on a dauntless smile and adored its dynamic owner in secret.

Those were full days, but I found time somehow for a daily glance at the racing news. One morning I read the following:

> Postman, a bay colt, bred and owned by John C. Dillon, captured the two-year-old event without apparent effort. It was the winner's first appearance under colors. He is a big, rangy youngster, as handsome as a picture. He appears to be a very high-class colt and should be heard from.

"Poor Blister!" I thought; and later, as I read again and again of smashing victories by a great and still greater Postman, I became quite venomous when I thought of Old Man Sanford. I referred to him mentally as "That old fool!" and imagined Blister in horrid depths of despair.

Then the bugle called for the last time that year at Lexington, and the thoroughbreds came to my very door to listen for it.

For days thereafter, as luck would have it, I was forced to pound my typewriter viciously, everlastingly, and was too tired when night came to do more than stagger to bed. At last there came a lull, and I fled incontinently to Latonia and the world of horse.

I approached Blister's stalls as one draws near a sepulchre. I felt that my voice, when I addressed him, should be pitched as though in the presence of a casket. I was shocked, therefore, at his lightness of mien.

"Hello, Four Eyes!" he said cheerfully. "How's the ole scout?"

I assured him that my scouting days were not yet over. And then: "I've been reading about Postman," I said.

"Some colt!" said Blister. "He's bowed 'em home five times now. They've made him favourite fur the Hammond against all them Eastern babies."

There was genuine enthusiasm in his voice and I was filled with admiration for a spirit that could take a blow so jauntily. His attitude was undoubtedly the correct one, but I could not accomplish it. I thought of the five thousand dollars that went, with the floral horseshoe, to the winner of the Hammond stake. I thought of a gentle, fine, threadbare old man who needed that five thousand—Oh, so desperately—and I was filled with bitter regrets, with malice and bad words.

"Of course he'll win it!" I burst out spitefully.

"Why, I dunno," drawled Blister, and added: "I thought Judge Dillon was a friend of yours."

"Oh, damn!" I said.

"Why, Four Eyes!" said Blister. " 'N' Chick listenin' to you too!"

Chick grinned appreciatively. "Don't let him kid ya," he advised. "He wasn't so gay hisself till—"

"Take a shot of grape juice," interrupted Blister, " 'n' hire a hall."

Chick's voice trailed off into unintelligible mutterings as he turned away.

"How about Mr. Sanford's colt?" I asked. "Have you still got him?"

To my astonishment Blister broke into one of his rare fits of laughter. He all but doubled up with unaccountable mirth.

"Say, Chick," he called when he could control his voice, "he wants to know if we still got the Sanford colt!"

Chick had turned a rather glum face our way; but at the words his expression became instantly joyous.

"Oh, say!" he said.

Then began a series of hilarious exchanges, entirely without meaning to me.

"He's hangin' round somewhere, ain't he, Chick?"

"Why, maybe he is," said Chick.

"You still throw a little rough feed into him occasionally, don't you, Chick?"

"When I got the time," said Chick; and the two imbeciles roared with laughter.

At last Blister began beating me between the shoulder blades.

"We got him, Four Eyes," he told me between thumps, "Yep—we got him."

"Stop!" I shouted. "What the devil's the matter with you?"

Blister became serious.

"Come here!" he said, and dragged me to a stall. He threw back the upper door and a shaft of sunlight streamed into the stall's interior, bathing a slim black head and neck until they glistened like a vein of coal. "Know him?" asked Blister.

"Yes," I said. "He's bigger though."

"Look at him good!" ordered Blister.

I peered at the relaxed inmate of the stall, who blinked sleepily at me through the shaft of sunlight. Blister pulled me back, closed the stall door, and tightened his grip on my arm.

"Now listen!" he said. "You just looked at the best two-year-old God ever put breath in!"

I took in this incredible information slowly. I exulted in it for a moment and then came doubts.

"How do you know?" I demanded.

"How do I know!" exclaimed Blister. "It 'ud take me a week to tell you. Man, he can fly! He makes his first start tomorrow—in the Hammond. Old Man Sanford'll get in to-night. Come out 'n' see a real colt run."

My brain was whirling.

"In the Hammond?" I gasped. "Does Mr. Sanford know all this?"

Blister gave me a slow, a thoughtful look.

"It sounds nutty," he said; "but I can't figger it no other way. As sure as you 'n' me are standin' here—he knowed it from the very first!"

Until I closed my eyes that night I wondered whether Blister's words were true. If so, what sort of judgment, instinct, intuition had been used that day at Thistle Ridge? I gave it up at last and slept, to dream of a colt that suddenly grew raven wings and soared over the grandstand while I nodded wisely and said: "Of course—the birthright of eagles!"

I got to Blister's stalls at one o'clock next day, and found Mr. Sanford clothed in a new dignity hard to describe. Perhaps he had donned it with the remarkable flowered waistcoat he wore—or was it due to his flowing double-breasted coat, a sprightly blue in colour and suggesting inevitably a leather trunk, dusty, attic-bound, which had yawned and spat it forth?

"Welcome, suh; thrice welcome!" he said to me. "I take the liberty of presuming that the pu'ple and white is honoured with yoh best wishes today."

I assured him that from the bottom of my heart this was so. He wrung my hand again and took out a gold watch the size of a bun.

"Three hours moh," he said, "before our hopes are realized or shattered."

"You think the colt will win?" I inquired.

Mr. Sanford turned to the southwest. I followed his eyes and saw a bank of evil-looking clouds creeping slowly up the sky.

"I like our chances, suh," he told me; "but it will depend on those clouds yondeh. We want a fast track foh the little chap. He is a swallow. Mud would break his heart."

"She's fast enough now," said Blister, who had joined us; and Mr. Sanford nodded.

So for three hours I watched the sky prayerfully and saw it become more and more ominous. When the bugle called for the Hammond at last, Latonia was shut off from the rest of the world by an inverted inky cup, its sides shot now and then with lightning flashes. We seemed to be in a great vacuum. I found my lungs snatching for each breath, while my racing card grew limp as I clutched it spasmodically in a sweating hand.

I had seen fit to take a vital interest in the next few moments; but I glanced at faces all about me in the grandstand

and found them strained and unnatural. Perhaps in the gloom they seemed whiter than they really were; perhaps my own nerves pricked my imagination until this packed humanity became one beating heart.

I do not think that this was so. The dramatic moment goes straight to the soul of a crowd, and this crowd was to see the Hammond staged in a breathless dark, with the lightning's flicker for an uncertain spotlight.

No rain would spoil our chances that day, for now, across the centre field at the half-mile post, a mass of colours boiled at the barrier. The purple and white was somewhere in the shifting, surging line, borne by a swallow, so I had been told. Well, even so, the blue and gold was there likewise—and carried by what? Perhaps an eagle!

Suddenly a sigh—not the customary roar, but a deep intaking of the grandstand's breath—told me they were on the wing. I strained my eyes at the blurred mass of them, which seemed to move slowly in the distance as it reached the far turn of the back stretch. Then a flash of lightning came and my heart skipped a beat and sank.

They were divided into two unequal parts. One was a crowded, indistinguishable mass. The other, far ahead in unassailable isolation, was a single spot of bay with a splash of colour clinging above.

A roar of "Postman!" shattered the quiet like a bombshell, for that splash of colour was blue and gold. The favourite was making a runaway race of it. He was coming home to twenty thousand joyful backers, who screamed and screamed his name.

Until that moment I had been the victim of a dream. I had come to believe that the little old man, standing silent at my side, possessed an insight more than human. Now I had wakened. He was an old fool in a preposterous coat and waistcoat, and I looked at him and laughed a mirthless laugh. He was squinting slightly as he peered with his washed-out eyes into the distance. His face was placid; and as I noticed this I told myself that he was positively witless. Then he spoke.

"The bay colt is better than I thought," he said.

"True," I agreed bitterly and noted, as the lightning flashed again, that the blue and gold was an amazing distance ahead of those struggling mediocre others.

"A pretty race," murmured Old Man Sanford; and now I thought him more than doddering—he was insane.

Some seconds passed in darkness, while the grandstand gave off a contented murmur. Then suddenly the murmur rose to a new note. It held fear and consternation in it. My eyes leaped up the track. The bay colt had rounded the curve into the stretch. He was coming down the straight like a bullet; but—miracle of miracles!—it was plain that he was not alone. . . .

In a flash it came to me: stride for stride, on the far side of him, one other had maintained a flight equal to his own. And then I went mad; for this other, unsuspected in the darkness until now, commenced to creep slowly, surely, into the lead. Above his stretching neck his colours nestled proudly. He was bringing the purple and white safe home to gold and glory.

Nearer and nearer he came, this small demon whose coat matched the heavens, and so shot past us, with the great Postman—under the whip—two lengths behind him!

I remember executing a sort of bear dance, with Mr. Sanford enfolded in my embrace. I desisted when a smothered voice informed me that my conduct was "unseemly, suh—most unseemly!"

A rush to the track followed, where we found Blister, quite pale, waiting with a blanket. Suddenly the grandstand, which had groaned once and become silent, broke into a roar that grew and grew.

"What is it?" I asked.

Blister whirled and stared at the figures on the timing board. I saw a look of awe come into his face.

"What is it?" I repeated. "Why are they cheering? Is it the time?"

"Oh, no!" said Blister with scornful sarcasm and a look of pity at my ignorance. "It ain't the time!" He nodded at the figures. "That's only the world's record fur the age 'n' distance."

And now there came, mincing back to us on slender, nervous legs, something wet and black and wonderful. It pawed and danced wildly in a growing ring of curious eyes.

Then, just above the grandstand, the inky cup of the sky was broken and there appeared the light of an unseen sun. It turned the piled white clouds in the break to marvels of rose and gold. They seemed like the ramparts of heaven, set there to guard from earthly eyes the abode of the immortals.

"Whoa, man! Whoa, hon!" said Blister, and covered the heaving sides.

As he heard Blister's voice and felt the touch of the blanket the colt grew quiet. His eyes became less fiery wild. He raised his head, with its dilated blood-red nostrils, and stared—not at the mortals standing reverently about him, but far beyond our gaze—through the lurid gap in the sky, straight into Valhalla.

I felt a hand on my arm.

"The look of eagles, suh!" said Old Man Sanford.

PRIME ROGUES

Molly Keane

"Y OU'VE walked the course, I suppose," Lady Honour asked me, and I nodded. Indeed, Dick and I
had but just completed the three miles in time for me to meet
her in the throng that seethed (quite irrespective of owner or
jockeyship) in the saddling enclosure before the horses went
out for the second race.

We had been late in starting from Pullinstown that morning. James, who was staying behind to minister to the wants
of a bedridden and sulking Willow, had not, I think, quite
put the spur on his underlings in the matter of lunch, or at
any rate not to the extent he would have done had he himself
been in a fever to see the start of the first race on the card.

"Ah, what matter the first race," he said in answer to
Dick's protests, "that confined race is no race. And for walking the course, Master Dick, that'll hardly delay ye any
length, for it's a course needs very little improvement."

I was still pondering on the true inwardness of this statement when the car, mercifully driven by Dick, got under
way. We had not, however, proceeded very far down the
avenue before our attention was attracted by a rook-like
squawking from James and steam-whistle yells from a young
member of Pullinstown's domestic staff, who at the same
time pursued the car at a pace that did equal credit to her legs
and lungs.

Dick reversed impatiently to meet her, wondering voluably as he did so what dire necessity of the day James had forgotten to pack into the car.

"A limon, Master Dick," she breathed in his ear, thrusting her empurpled face in at the window, "would ye bring a limon from the town, if ye please, and a couple o' round o' Beckett's Blue; and would ye leave the bets in with Miss Doyle." She handed several mysterious little packages through the window.

"If Bridgie Hogan," said Dick swiftly, "hadn't broken down the bicycle with the weight she is from taking no exercise, I'd say she could ride it into town herself for her lemons and put on her own bets. As it is, she can go in on Shank's mare and out again. You may tell her that from me."

"Oh great and merciful God—" The young messenger clapped a hand to her mouth and subsided in giggles, so we drove on and left her.

"Those divils," Sir Richard observed negligently; "how much work will they do today, I wonder."

"Drinking tea and passing rude remarks with the stable-boys," Dick commented. "By the way, father, did ye tell Johnny to put that blister on Goldenrod?"

"I did, I think. I think I did. I wonder, Dick, would it have been wiser to have had him fired?"

"I wonder, would it?" Dick was never very committal with his father, I had noticed.

"I have had nothing but worry with that horse since he came into the place," Sir Richard pondered grievously. "I was really *hurt* when Lady Duncannon sent him back to me. You know she's a suspicious sort of woman—*very*. She wouldn't believe my word it was only splints he was lame on—all the same I'll never buy a horse again that's back of his knees, they always go on their tendons. Mrs. Pheelan is out pretty smart to open the gate this morning, I notice. I think she kept Oliver and me waiting half an hour last night."

"I suppose she thought you and Oliver were stopping out the night at Templeshambo—I know we did." Dick shot a look at his father in which was as much censure as he dared combine with raillery.

"Ah," said Sir Richard, "we walked the soles off our boots looking for those young horses of your cousin Honour's. They might be anywhere in that place."

"So they might. It's a great range for young horses. I hear she has a very nice two-year-old—out of the old mare. Is that true, father?"

"She has a very nice foal there, and not a bad sort of a yearling at all. I didn't think much of the two-year-old—she's a leggy divil, but, of course, the old ladies are cracked about her."

"Out of their minds, I suppose." Dick let the subject drop. He had no more curiosity in it. At this, indeed, I did not wonder, for I had myself unfolded to him and Willow every circumstance of our doings at Templeshambo, not omitting Sir Richard's secret visit to Mycross Station.

"I don't know what he's at," Willow had commented. "He has me puzzled." And neither could Dick throw any light on Sir Richard's perplexing behaviour. "It might be nothing at all," Willow had said, "or it might be *a bit of a plan*"; and there was as much dark secrecy in the way she said this as to fill my mind with a hundred suppositions of possible roguery.

But today I could not think why anything should be wrong. I was glad to be having a ride round, and very glad that the ride should be Lady Honour's horse. Unlikely, I knew, that I would beat Dick on Romance, even though he was giving me a lot of weight. Still, they say Dick is worth a stone to any horse he rides. There were other good things in the race besides Romance, for this was the end of the point-to-pointing season, which meant a fairly hot class of horses in an open light-weight race. The possible stars that had crowded the fields earlier in the season had now waned in their owners' estimation. They ran them no longer. Lady Honour being, I suppose, an exception to this, as to most other rules.

"Tootle around and enjoy yourself," had been Willow's parting advice to me. "Try not to take a fall, because falls hurt. Barring accidents, Dick should win it, though I'm a bit frightened of that horse of old Colonel Power's. I think he'd have beaten me at Lisgarry if he hadn't fallen, and he's receiving 7 lb. from us today.''

"Ah, he'll tip up again—" Dick had been optimistic.

"Well, if he doesn't, Dick? It rained a lot last night and the going will be deep. Romance isn't too fond of the mud, and the 7 lb. might just beat her. D'you remember that awful day at Kylemore? Ah, that race went *through* the mare; absolutely went through her." Her voice was frail and vibrant at this suffering memory.

"I don't know. I'd be more afraid of something unknown in the field, such as Oliver's ride, for instance. D'you know, I think I'm giving him 21 lb.—it's a divil of a penalty."

"That, my dear? A four-year-old and I never liked her lack of guts. She was a good lepper, though, for a young horse. All Honour's horses lep like dogs. She has them following her round the country on strings like dogs—that's why. Well, I hope you enjoy yourself, Oliver, and collect all the chat for me." Willow had said.

And we had walked the course, Dick and I—three miles over a very fair country it was. Banks with ditches mostly to you, a few stone walls, and not a twisty course either. "All the same, mind you, this course walks a lot nicer than it rides, I always think," Dick told me. "I don't know what it is about these banks. They'd all meet you right if you were going the other way round. As it is there's always a lot of clouting and falling here."

In the shelter of a gorse-blown bank we lit our cigarettes, the loud, small flutter of a white flag in our ears. Far and away blue shadows were painted wet and heavy on the mountains, and nearer fields of young oats were square-cut tourmalines in the flowing bright air—thickened to honey and burdened by almonds this loving air. But beyond any loving, far and unto itself, the little flame of a lark's song burned against the sky.

Dick took a walk out across the field and came back to me. "I wonder how much ground you'd save if you did that,'' he said, and stood considering the matter, his head sunk, his hands in his breeches pockets. "You could jump the wall there instead of the bank, and not miss a flag at all. I do think that'd be the shortest course to go, Oliver. We'd better go back to the car and eat a sandwich now, I suppose. And you have to meet your owner." He grinned unkindly: "I'd rather ride for the devil himself," said he, "than ride a horse for Cousin Honour."

But I found her still enchanting. When we had struggled out of the throng in the enclosure and through the mob that surged about the bookies' stand, she went straight as a bird to the spot where her car was parked, and this was a position which had (in addition to being not too far away from the weighing tent) the advantages of combining an excellent view of the course and an easy exit from the car park; this she told me on our way thither. "And," she said, unfolding her shooting stick, spearing it into the ground and seating her person thereon immediately before the dirtiest and most demure of the old, blunt-nosed Morris cars, "Let me introduce you, Oliver, to Mr. Billy Morgan; Captain Pulleyns—Mr. Morgan."

"Very pleased to meet you," a preposterously good-looking young man shook me by the hand. He gave me his left hand because his right arm was in a sling, and he gave me three parts of a glance out of his navy-blue eyes that surprised me. He was tall, Mr. Morgan. Yes, and dark, and handsome. Only his legs were vulgar, although he had taken some pains about them, for his brown field boots were by an excellent maker. His voice, too, was as preposterous as his looks, and there hung about it the same rich comeliness. My cousins, Dick and Willow, frequently speak in a strange brogue, and indeed express their meaning more coarsely than did this young man; nevertheless their voices cannot be compared. Theirs never lack a certain quality. His never attained that certain quality.

"What bad luck about your collar bone," I said.

"Wasn't it—rotten! Lady Honour's very cross with me," there was a certain charm about him, "and Lady Eveleen won't speak to me at all."

It was only now that I perceived Lady Eveleen seated in the car—on the seat beside her was a vast blue roll of cotton wool, neatly rolled white bandages, a saddle and a weight cloth. She looked as important as any priestess at any other altar.

"Good morning," I said, taking off my hat. "Good morning," said she, and that was all. I could not help disliking her still evident displeasure in the prospect of my riding. After all, how did she know I would not give the horse a real good ride? Lady Honour, though very sweet, was a little strained, perhaps a little silent. I wondered if they could really be having a good bet on their horse, but thought it unlikely. Mr. Morgan only was happy, confident and friendly. He stood upon the step of the car, his glasses to his eyes, and kept up a running commentary on the horses going down to the start.

"God, that's a common divil of Hanlon's. Do you like that mare of Johnny Kehoe's, Lady Honour? You know she's bred fit to win races. I like the way she goes, too—near the ground and doesn't take too much out of herself, she would stay. Look at young O'Brien now, having a preliminary. What's that—black and a cerise cap—a chestnut horse. Is it Bonny Judy? They're all down there now, I think; twelve starters, that's not a bad field at all to go out in a Farmer's race. Johnny Kehoe can't get a pull on that mare; look at her shaking her head, she'll gallop into the bog-hole if he doesn't watch himself—that's a shocking soft bog there on your left, mind, as you go down to the start. Keep in beside the fence—They're off—they're not; false start. God, he could have let them go, this isn't five furlongs. Now they're off—there's some wicked riding the first mile in this race, I tell you. That thing of Johnny Kehoe's is jumping very ignorant—Johnny went out between her two ears. I thought he'd never meet the saddle again. Wait now, this is a straight one they're coming to. A horse very rarely meets it really right. I think there's not a big enough ditch to you for the height of it. They get under it somehow. Furlong's down! Well, the *welt* he hit it. Bonny Judy's down and there's another down. I can't see who it is.

Johnny Kehoe's taking them a good gallop. He may quieten himself now—this is a real soft field and so is the next. That thing of Hartigan's is going very easily—he's jumping well; I wouldn't wonder if he beat Johnny.''

"What's leading, Major?" An incredibly old man, balancing on the fence beside the car, grasped my hand to pull me up beside him.

"I'll tell you in a minute." I had found them again now. "Kehoe's horse is leading still; Vain Lady second; and a chestnut horse third."

"A chaistnut horse? Is it Tommy Hartigan is on him?"

"I couldn't tell you."

"It must be them spy-glasses is not great good so. God knows ye'd nearly see that much with the sight o' yer eyes."

I ventured after this to read the race aloud no more, and indeed the horses were but four fences from home, so we could see them plainly. The chestnut horse had gone up to the leaders now, and something of a contest was in progress.

"Come on, Hartigan! *Come* on, Hartigan!" The old man clung to me for his balance, and we swayed together on the bank in an ecstasy of excitement. "Aha! Aha! He have John Kehoe bestered. Look at he sweepin' home. *God, he's off*—" as the chestnut horse, in landing over the last fence, made a bad mistake and a grand recovery. "He's off! He's not! He's not, b'god! Only for he to be so great a jock and so constant he was gone—"

Tears streaming from his eyes, and the wind blowing his long hair and beard upwards and backwards, this ancient votary of sport clasped both my hands and would for very little, I think, have kissed me as a salute to speed and young courage, and to the emotion of dangerous endeavour.

"Bedam, he was as wise as a dog," he said, "I'd have to cry to see the poor bastard so courageous. 'Tis for a passion o' love I'd cry, or for the like of a horse race I'd rain tears from me two eyes. Did ye remark the way Hartigan did was to foster Johnny Kehoe always. Did he go nigh him at all till he come to win his race? He did not. Did he ever let him more than a couple o' perches out before him? He did not.

Ah, Johnny Kehoe puts great conceit out of himself to be a real up-to-date jock, but—be the Holy Seaman—young Hartigan have him bewitched, bothered and bewildered." He whipped round on a dreary young friend who up to the moment had simmered unnoticed beside him, and recommended his masterly analysis of the race. But the time now being more than come when I should struggle again towards the weighing tent, I picked up saddle and weight cloth and accompanied by Lady Honour (her hand-bag full of spare lead), regretfully parted from my old companion.

"See here, Oliver," said she to me as we clove our way through a party of young girls who had chosen the only gap in the fence as a suitable spot in which to drink pink lemonade and sport with their loves. "Don't pay *any* attention to *any*thing Beauty says to you about riding the mare." I looked down to see two deep triangles of carnation in her cheeks, and tears, I think, excited her eyes. "I don't like to say any one is a fool," said she, and the tears snapped back from her eyes, "but I think poor Beauty's *dull*."

"She's not far out in thinking me a very inexperienced jockey over banks," I put in guardedly.

"My dear boy," Lady Honour was indeed in earnest, "provided you don't actually fall off the mare the race is a gift to us. The mare's fit, she won't fall down and she has the legs of the lot of them; what more to you want?"

After which encomium of confidence I felt that any blame for defeat would more than certainly be laid at my door, which, since my mount was a four-year-old and this her first time out, I felt would be manifestly unfair. In fact, Lady Honour's unbridled expression of confidence in her horse depressed rather than cheered me. Almost I found myself at one with Lady Eveleen in wishing Mr. Billy Morgan and not myself had the honour of the ride.

But that was before I had seen Surprise, for such was the name of Lady Honour Dearmot's brown mare, four years old, to whom almost every other horse in the field of ten was giving a stone and some so much as 21 lb. I think only two of the entries on the card were at level weights with us, and

I knew one of these did not run. In my opinion Surprise looked like giving weight and a beating to any horse in the race, although as a four-year-old she was so justly entitled to receive both. That she was indeed, but four off I found it difficult to believe, such muscle and such condition are not often carried by a young horse. I have seldom seen anything fitter run in a point-to-point, or look more like winning one.

Lady Honour and Lady Eveleen quarrelled outrageously over the saddling of their horse, a task with which Mr. Billy Morgan and an astute-looking lad in a purple coat and trousers proceeded undeterred by the commands and suggestions of either lady.

"Put a pad under the saddle," Lady Eveleen insisted. "Can't any fool see it will cut the withers out of the mare the way it's down on her back?"

"Do no such thing; leave the saddle the way it is. Take up that girth, Jim. Willy, you put those bandages on beautifully in spite of your arm. I never saw bandages better put on, even by you."

Mr. Morgan, very quick and certain in his way of saddling a horse, accepted the compliment in silence.

"All the same," Lady Eveleen was almost in tears, "I can't bear the mare to go out with the saddle like that on her."

"It's not down on her, Lady Eveleen. Really, it's not," Mr. Morgan found patience to tell her.

"Are you sure? Oh, did you *see* that poor horse that came in after the first race. Did you *see* it's back?"

"No, but Beauty, did you see the jockey's boots?" Lady Honour included even the lad in her exasperated witticism, "they were oozing blood!"

"Now get mounted, please. Get mounted, please. Come on now, jockeys, get mounted, please." An impatient steward made his first effort to get the horses out of the saddling enclosure and down to the start.

"*Oliver,*" Lady Eveleen hissed in my ear, "you go up to the front and stay there. You'll keep out of trouble and interference."

"Do no such thing." Lady Honour's angrier hiss overrode her sister's whisper in my other ear. "Let young Dick make the pace. That mare of his won't stay two miles in this going. Goodness me, she's tied to the ground with that penalty on her. Come away from him the last mile, and don't go winning the race before that, mind."

All Mr. Morgan said, as the boy led my mount out of the enclosure and clove for us a path through the mob outside was: "You can fall and win the race. So don't let her go from you if you do fall." And with such instructions I set out on my lone (lone at last) adventure.

"Thanks, thanks very much. *Would* you mind letting us through? We *rather* want to ride our horses—" It was Dick in the crowd behind me; Dick sitting on top of a packet of lead and Romance shaking her game little head and laying the ears back at the crowd. And there were others; the lad with the ankle-length boots and spurs two inches long and his breeches worn over his stockings, riding a savage of a brown horse that had killed one man and frightened several so badly that they never wanted to ride again; an M.F.H. with a face like one of his own dog hounds had a very pretty sort of hunting seat on a horse. An old man of a curious brave fragility. "Many happy returns, Colonel Power," Dick said to him. He told me afterwards that this was a sixty-fourth birthday party.

But we were out of the crowd now and riding our horses down a series of three small, bare fields, their grass eaten low by sheep and geese, and through a gap where a wall had been summarily knocked down to let us out into a lane and back into the country again through another gap of the same nature. The mare fidgeted and pulled me as we went, her head carried low, her back up under the saddle, she was, I have no doubt, switching her tail in a way that would have frightened me worse could I have seen it. As it was I felt miserably nervous. A cold wind turned knifishly on my cheek and made fun of the jersey (royal blue and a yellow sash, Lady Honour's colours) which I wore. I was the strange victim of that unhappy lack of feeling, in which state one belongs neither to one's self nor to one's horse, but to a chill blankness in which habit and instinct take the place of reasoned action.

Dick, riding up beside me, looked as strained and as paper-thin and as anxious as he always does look when going out to ride a race; keyed to the moment so that should one but gently touch him one might think he would thrum like a fiddle-string. He looked at me now and at the mare. "Oliver," he said, "I'd say you'd beat me if you stand up. I never saw anything come on like that mare. I don't know her at all." He looked puzzled for a moment instead of strained. It was then, I think, that my feeling of blankness and nerves fell from me. I was warm again and knew what I was about. I felt the mare's mouth and sat forward to canter down to the start, and it was when she felt me take hold of her that she jumped off after a fashion which might have told a sillier man even than I am that she had been ridden in work at least. I wondered; and I dropped my hands to her, and she stopped like an old chaser who has had plenty of it might do. And then I think, had I been wise, was the moment for me to decide on a soft fall out in the country or such palpable missing of a flag as could not but be objected to. But I am seldom wise though often lucky. Besides I had felt the mare's low, powerful stride, and the strange lust that comes on men to ride a race was on me now. Which is an emotional way of stating that when the starter let us go I was quite as mad to win my race as though no feelings of doubt had ever plucked at my reason as to whether or not my horse was qualified to run at all, much less to win.

This course doesn't ride as nice as it walks, Dick had said. Neither, he had said, did the fences meet you kindly. But if the fences did not meet us right, we met them so well that I would not have faulted them in any respect.

Never shall I describe my ride on Surprise that day. I may say that in the matter of riding to instructions I obeyed Lady Eveleen's to the letter, for after we had jumped the first fence blinded, and saved a fall how I knew not—I thought there was something in keeping out of trouble, and sent the mare on with the first three. Before we had gone a mile I knew without any doubt that I had the legs of the lot of them and a couple of stone in hand. The course rode heavy enough, and a field of plough followed by two with pretty deep going, brought Dick and Romance back to us all right. It was then that I sent Surprise into the lead, for, I thought, Dick won't want to lose me altogether, and the going and the weight between them will beat him here. Four banks in a nice straight line from us, the last one jumped on the down-hill and I went on at them. Dick stuck to me; I think he was right, for he knew now my mount was unlikely to tip up, and he could see she was going very easily; it would be difficult for him to make up ground later. The course turned pretty sharp left after the fourth of these nice banks, and Dick as he landed in the field beyond fairly cut the nose off me. "*There's* a rudeness," I said to him as his sister Willow might have done, and terrified lest no nicer considerations should prevent his either pushing me off or tripping my horse up, I took a frightened look over my shoulder and went away from him like a scalded cat. We were less than a mile from home now, and I think Romance was stone-cold. How Dick sat still on her and held her together I do not know, but game and honest little bit that she is, Romance was giving us more weight than she could have done, even on top of the ground. We won very easily. Dick was not going to kill the mare when he saw he could not win. He finished third. The gentleman who was celebrating his sixty-fourth birthday second, and not a feather out of him. He was very fit.

It was Lady Eveleen (surprisingly enough) who detached herself from the crowd and beat her sister by a short head only for the honour of leading their horse in to unsaddle.

"My dear," she said, "you gave her a great ride and I'm so *delighted* we've beaten Richard." She was looking back at me and talking, her face very gently radiant, not minding at all where she was going or leading the horse. But I thought it unkind of Lady Honour to snatch the rein from her sister with a biting comment. But Lady Eveleen refused to be shaken off, and so conducted by them both I dismounted at last and departed with my saddle towards the scales, while they alternately assisted the boy to scrape lather off the mare, and turned from their task to receive the congratulations of their friends.

Any man who wins a race, whether point-to-point, steeplechase, or on the flat is, for that brief moment, a hero and a good jockey. Let him be beaten by a better horse and a short head when riding the race of his life, and his stock is down at once. No one but can put a finger then on some gross error in judgement on his part and there are few among the commentators unconvinced that they (or almost any one, indeed) could have ridden the race better. Today I was in the former and more enviable position, and enjoyed it to the full as I sat on the step of Lady Honour's car eating salmon sandwiches (Dick's salmon was all right in sandwiches, anyhow) with a whisky and soda, half a horn tumbler full of port and a rapidly cooling cup of coffee ranged on the grass beside me. The arrival of Mr. Billy Morgan interrupted the praises and the questions of my two owners, which I was enjoying almost as much as their food and drink.

"Well, didn't I tell you you'd enjoy yourself?" he said to me by way, I suppose, of congratulation. "But isn't she a great mare? A different class from the ordinary point-to-point horse, isn't she? I think indeed it's a pity for Lady Honour to knock her about in point-to-points at all. That mare should be winning chases this minute."

"Will you have a bun, Mr. Morgan?" Lady Eveleen asked him, and her manner was more than repressive.

"Thank you, but I don't care about sweet cakes." Mr. Morgan accepted a salmon sandwich and a cup of tea, and we all ate comfortably, our anxieties so happily over and the glow of success so close about us.

"Do you know anything, Lady Honour," Mr. Morgan inquired suddenly, "is good for the nerves?"

"Goodness knows you're not troubled with nerves, Billy," Lady Honour was both surprised and amused.

"Ah no, not in regard o' horses I wouldn't be," Mr. Morgan reassured us. "But," he went on seriously, "when

I'd be readin' a book—when I'd get to the excitin' part I'd
have to t'row it down. I'd accuse it," he added thoughtfully,
"on drinkin' tea." And swilling the dregs of his cup three
times round he aimed them with great precision at the nearest
gorse bush.

"Has the mare started for home?" Lady Honour asked,
fitting the lid on to a sandwich box with quick dexterity.

"Yes. I sent the boy off with her at once." Mr. Morgan
put his cup away in a basket and rose to his feet; whether or
not he had seen Dick and Sir Richard's approach, he took
his departure without undue delay.

"Well, Oliver, you brat, that was a noble victory," Dick
smiled at me. "Wait till Willow hears you defeated the
mare—she'll tear you. I must congratulate Cousin Honour,"
he said, and did so with all politeness. Sir Richard, too,
expressed himself delighted at the race if not his should then
be hers. "Were you satisfied with Oliver's riding, Beauty?"
he asked Lady Eveleen, but did not embarrass her by requir-
ing an answer. "I'm coming over to you tomorrow to look
at that filly again," he said to Lady Honour. "I must get the
car out now before the last race. Some of these cars will be
here tomorrow morning." He gathered Dick and myself to
him with a glance in which appeal and authority balanced
each other, and so we left the ladies of Templeshambo. But
before we had gone Lady Eveleen caught awkwardly at the
elbow of my coat and "come tomorrow with Richard, Oliver," she said. She was earnest and without charm, but there
was a steadfastness behind her nervous face like a light beyond lanternglass. When Lady Honour laughed and told me
not to waste my time visiting two old women, I said that I
would like to come, but would not trouble her since Lady
Eveleen had promised to look after me.

"You'll have Honour and Beauty at one another's throats,"
Sir Richard said to me a little later as we seated ourselves in
the car and proceeded to repulse the army of mendicant
guardians of its safety who swarmed for alms about our departure.

" 'Twas I minded the car, sir—"

"No, 'twas I, yer honour—any looked near it I belted hell out o' them, and the young lad of a son I have pasted them also."

I gave the young lad two shillings. Sir Richard disposed himself in the car beside Dick. "Be off, now, the lot of you."

"Sure, that's not my son, your honour—the lad with the locks is my son." But Sir Richard wound up his window, immovable to further petition.

In the back of the car I turned up the collar of my coat, an even simplicity of delight about me, the limber glow that succeeds striven effort, the level mind that follows on success were mine. I lit two cigarettes, one for Dick and one for myself, and handed him his when we had lurched, our engine racing, out of the field and down the rutted lane towards the main road.

"Thank you, Oliver." Dick leaned forward to set the windscreen wiper working, for a shower of rain lashed bitterly towards us from the mountains. The day was turned suddenly to indigo and silver, darkly changing behind the sloped spears of rain. I thought of the fire in Willow's room where Dick and I would sit making toast and telling of our doings. I thought of little rivers rushing low and dark beneath blackthorns and hazel, and the hewn wings of a gull brought a pale greyhound bitch to my mind, I had called her Sally. But Dick was talking:

"Twenty-one pounds was a cruel penalty to put on that little mare. She was tied to the floor. I couldn't stop you coming up on the inside, could I, Oliver? Ah, she was stone-cold going up the hill. I knew I couldn't do it, so I thought I'd finish without a fall. Would I have done it if we'd been on top of the ground, Father. I wouldn't?"

"You would not," said Sir Richard suddenly. "You did what five steeplechase jockeys out of ten can't do, and nine point-to-point jockeys out of ten can't do—you sat still on her and kept hold of her head. And I'll tell you another thing, Dick, you wouldn't have beaten Oliver today at level weights either."

"What? And that mare only four years old—well, five now. Oh, Sir Richard!''

"Four years old?" said Sir Richard. "A four-year-old— *She is*?''

"What d'you mean, father?" Dick asked him, but he would not tell us, switching into another topic with the disconcerting independence of mind that was particularly his own.

"That lad," he said, "that Honour had with the mare— do you know where I saw him last? In Tommy Redmond's stables. And as tough a place as Tommy's is—they didn't keep that beauty long in it.''

"Who is Tommy Redmond?" I asked.

"Tommy? Oh, he trains horses. He's a sort of relation of Honour's and Beauty's. Well, in a kind of way, he's one of the old Lords. And a horrible fellow. There's no villainy or trickery or roguery he's not up to it and he runs his horses about as straight as a ram's horn.''

"Oh," I said, and a lonely blankness settled now on my spirit. Coldly and slowly the pieces of a difficult and sorry business fitted their places in my mind. The memory of my ride was distant from me now, apart from its heat and effort it would seem to have been but a nasty ramp. But I had not known. How could I even now be sure? I must wait and see what would follow. There was no cohesion in this villainy. Any key there might be to the matter was in Sir Richard's canny grasp. Somehow I felt that there would be suffering yet over this, and it was not Honour who would suffer most for it but that poor Beauty, poor stricken goose.

And the weight of this doubt stayed with me heavily, disallowing Willow's generous congratulations and Dick's assurances that the Sir was never without a bee in his bonnet over any horse that was good enough to beat one of his own. I would have liked, I think, to talk the matter over with James, but since the neuralgia he said was stitching in and out through his poll like the devil's needle, I could not think the evening opportune for the discussion of my own trivial affairs.

The afternoon of the following day a strangely solemn and silent Sir Richard drove me over to Templeshambo. Sometimes, as we drove, I saw his lips move, and I knew he was rehearsing to himself the speeches of his part in whatever piece this was which presently he would stage. I wondered how my part was cast and I felt, indeed, a soured and unwilling puppet. The more so when I saw the airy nonchalance of manner which could not quite disguise the shifting anxiety in Lady Honour's eyes as she greeted us.

"To see you three days running, Richard, it makes us feel quite young and silly," Lady Honour was naughty, not sentimental, "and *Oliver*, my dear, Beauty will be mad with excitement"—here was malice.

She went on before us down the long narrow dark hall, her little head poised back, her narrow shoulder blades knife-sharp under her coat. She had a peculiar way of walking, sliding her feet very evenly past each other like a little fox. When she turned her head to smile round at us, I thought I saw again in her the vixen and forgot how yesterday her bird-like charm had ravished me.

"We are sitting in here today," she said, opening a door at the end of the hall, "because one of Beauty's puppies has the yellows and as she insisted on lighting a fire for it I thought we might as well have the good of it too."

"Well, after your win yesterday," Sir Richard said swiftly, "I should think you might light fires all over the house and hang the expense, eh, Honour?"

"Indeed, if we had only backed the mare we were right," Lady Honour answered regretfully. "But poor Beauty has no courage. She wouldn't let me do it. Well, I suppose she was right, really. What did we know about the mare except that she could lep and we *thought* she could gallop? But a four-year-old and running in such good company—wouldn't we have been very silly, Richard? Don't you think so? We would have been, wouldn't we?"

"Well," said Sir Richard, with undue weightiness, "circumstances, of course, alter cases." He sat himself down on a minor inquisition in the shape of a sofa and added, "My dear Honour.'' I sat down on a chair near the sick puppy's basket, wishing very much that I might be bidden to take myself off for a little walk in the garden, rain it never so hard; failing this I could only look about the room and pretend I was not there. As such a room, as different as it could be from that room of fragile adventure where yesterday we had drunk our tea in the glamour of a Perhaps that Never Was. Here was Time Past; and rightly so, I thought, my mind petrifying in its contemplation of case upon glass case of stuffed birds, gulls of every variety, their beauty betrayed forever to clumsiness: hawks primly hovering, jays and magpies perched forever; two white owls, in all the sulkiness of their unspread wings, squinted forbiddingly down their crooked parrot beaks. A stuffed fox was curled woodenly in a chair, and a badger lay for a footstool beneath a distant writing-table—his back was worn nearly bare by the feet that had rested on it so often. And there was (this started me) a little monkey stuffed, and for more ghastly realism chained to the corner of a bookcase. The curtains in the high windows and all the chair covers were dark red and every inch of woodwork had been painted dark brown. The rain lashed forbiddingly against the windows and the sick puppy rose waveringly from its basket. I wished very much that Lady Eveleen would come in.

''And so you see, Richard,'' Lady Honour was saying, ''as the filly's really as much Beauty's as mine, I have very little say in the matter. And you know Beauty is wickedly obstinate.''

''I see. And I suppose Tommy Redmond has a share in her too?''

''What do you mean?'' Poor sorry little fox! A thin, frightened shadow passed, it seemed, right through her. Now she was indeed beset.

''Well, the fact is, Honour,'' Sir Richard said, ''there's been a certain amount of talk about the running of your mare yesterday, which puts me in a very difficult position as a steward, because I happen to know what I would a lot rather I didn't know, and that is, the mare is not yours at all but Tommy Redmond's, and what's more, she's a winner under rules, and she's unqualified to run at any point-to-point meeting.''

''And may one ask how you came to that interesting conclusion?'' Lady Honour was game.

''Well, there *are* such things as consignments of the boxing of horses to be seen at railway stations, if a person has the wit to go and look for them, eh, Honour? That was a silly mistake you made, you know. She should have gone in your name from Killanna Station instead of being booked in Tommy's from Myross. It was only six miles farther to walk her to Killanna, that's where you should have ordered the box. No, if there is any fuss about it, I'm afraid—''

''If there is any fuss about it, the best thing *you* could do, Richard, would be to keep your mouth shut.'' Such complete and sudden acceptance of the matter on Lady Honour's part fairly surprised me, nor was I less taken aback by Sir Richard's answer.

''Now, Honour, if there is any inquiry, I don't see how I can help saying what I know. Some one might know I knew it, you never can tell.''

''You can't do that, Richard—a nice mess you'd get Oliver into. However satisfactory the explanation of his part of the business is, you know yourself that any one mixed up with Tommy must put up with the reputation of being fairly hot.''

''Too hot to touch.'' Sir Richard looked over at me sourly. I could feel that in his imagination he already saw me in the part of a willing accomplice to the ramp. ''What a lucky thing for you Billy Morgan laid himself up,'' he said. ''It looked a lot better for Oliver to have the ride. I suppose you thought I'd keep quiet about it all rather than see him in a scrape. B'God, Honour, you very nearly brought the thing off nicely. I'm sorry about Oliver; I wish now I'd never allowed you to give him the ride. I encouraged the idea in my innocence.'' He looked sadly from one to the other of us. ''Poor Beauty,'' he said, ''will be very upset,'' and as he said it I saw her going past the windows in a mackintosh, carrying a bucket of dogs' food and leaning towards its weight and into the rain.

"If you won't mind," I said, "I think I'll go out and help Lady Eveleen feed the dogs while you and Cousin Richard think of some way out of this difficulty. I really feel so shaken by all this—"

She was not with the dogs, Lady Eveleen, but I found her in the tower-foot room regulating the incubator. "I hope these eggs are all right," she said. "We forgot about them yesterday in our excitement over the point-to-point. I hope they'll be all right. Honour and I never seem to have any success with things like chickens. By the way, Oliver, I had a fiver on the mare for you yesterday." She said this so sadly as she pushed in a drawer of eggs that I wondered whether she knew what had brought Sir Richard here today. She would not look at me at all and then I saw why. She was crying, poor Beauty in distress—I saw her tears—they were helpless and foolish and how they grieved and shocked me I never can tell. Back and forth went her awkward hands over the tidy drawers of eggs. The light in the little room was almost none, the white sprouting of potatoes in a corner illuminated the darkness. Her pale, stooped neck another moony thing.

"What is it?" I was saying. I took her arm and sat her down on a dishevelled chair. I put my handkerchief in her hand, for hers, I observed, she had used to wipe tears from her eyes and from the eggs with indiscriminate carefulness for the latter's welfare.

"Honour and Richard are so *unkind*," she whimpered at last. "Honour is such a dreadful tease. She goes on and on and on, until—oh, *please* don't mind me, I'm a silly disgusting old woman to cry like this. It is very shameful."

"Why do they tease you?"

"Oh, for no reason—it's just my stupidity." She was incoherent; a cruel colour blazed down her long neck. And when I turned and saw Lady Honour laughing in the doorway and Sir Richard, blue and beaky in the rain behind her, I was almost staggered by the strength of my pity for my poor goose.

"Come in, Richard; come in out of the rain." Lady Honour would suckle him still to her with sweet, twisty ways, I thought. A turn in her voice and a light in her eye, alike they said, "Escape me, never!"

"See, Beauty," she addressed her poor sister, "Richard has bid me within twenty-five pounds of the price you put on the filly. Will you deal?"

"I will not," said Lady Eveleen. She was calm now and passionately determined. "I won't sell that mare for one penny less than I said I would."

Sir Richard from the doorway gave her a very dark look and said he: "Well, indeed, my dear Beauty, I came here to-day on a very different matter, but as Honour seemed anxious, and rightly so, to get out of the mare, I made her my outside bid for her, and neither will I go one penny beyond it."

"And what did you come for then?" Lady Eveleen held on to the seat of her chair and faced them both with the unanswerable gallantry of a goose at bay.

"Oh." Sir Richard jerked his head, the fine tilted bones of his face were drawn with sudden impressionistic beauty against the dreary light. "Honour has persuaded me to say no more about the matter I came for, and though I hate to tell a lie"—his hands on his stick before him crossed and knotted, Sir Richard appeared for the moment the very epitome of aristocratic impeccability—"though it really *hurts* me to tell a lie I think, b'God, it would put you all in a very uncomfortable position if I told the truth. And when I think of poor Oliver. You know I loved his father"—here he waited for a moment and I could feel that indeed he spoke the truth, without a doubt he had loved my father, and while that love would never straiten him in any present convenient betrayal, nevertheless it was a truthful emotion—"and more for his sake than any of your sakes I've agreed to keep quiet about this matter, do you see, Beauty?"

"*Well*, Beauty?" Lady Honour's voice slipped exasperatedly into the silence that fell when Sir Richard, having said his say, waited for some answer.

But Beauty made no answer. Her pale unfocused eyes sought blindly from one to the other of them. One saw her mind groping helpless in its stupidity for some telling weapon wherewith to strike at them, and finding none, I feared she would weep again. I was angry because they had made of me and of her sad memory of my father a twice-knotted stick with which to beat her to submission, angry and ashamed for their unkindness.

"I leave it entirely to you, Honour," she said at last, "whatever you think best—" She gave us all a queer, stricken look, grotesque in its youthfulness, and slipped out into the rain to feed her dogs.

"I'm too kindhearted," Sir Richard said, as down the avenue to Pullinstown young horses advanced swooping and stopping, upon us. "That's the worse of me. You know, Oliver, I should *never* have bought that mare from the old ladies. This place is rotten with horses as it is. And I'm not really fond of the mare, you know. There are several things I don't like about her."

"Then why did you buy her, Cousin Richard?" I asked curiously.

"Ah well, it's not a bad thing for Honour to have a good fright now and again. That was a shocking thing she did, you know—running that mare yesterday. I must say I was surprised at her. And she thought she had me nicely cornered if she gave you the ride; I couldn't say a word about anything then—she must think I have very little regard for the truth—that's what hurt me. That's what shocked me."

"Anyhow," I said, with the graven and crude condemnation of my age, "between you, you twisted poor Beauty's tail till you got the filly out of her for your own price."

"Oh, I gave Beauty her price in the end," Sir Richard's excellent manners entirely ignored my rather rude speech. "You see, I had a tenner on the mare when you won yesterday—I could afford to give her another twenty-five quid. But I gave Honour a good fright too." And he added, with almost sentimental satisfaction, "The prime little rogue!"

THE COOP

Edgar Wallace

SOMETIMES they referred to Mr. Yardley in the newspapers as "the Wizard of Stotford," sometimes his credit was diffused as the "Yardley Confederation"; occasionally he was spoken of as plain "Bert Yardley" but invariably his entries for any important handicaps were described as "The Stotford Mystery." For nobody quite knew what Mr. Yardley's intentions were until the day of the race. Usually after the race, for it is a distressing fact that the favourite from his stable was usually unplaced, and the winner—also from his stable—started amongst the "100 to 7 others."

After the event was all over and the "weighed in" had been called, people used to gather in the paddock in little groups and ask one another what this horse was doing at Nottingham, and where were the stewards and why Mr. Yardley was not jolly well warned off. And they didn't say "jolly" either.

For it is an understood thing in racing that, if an outsider wins, its trainer ought to be warned off. Yet neither Bert Yardley, nor Colonel Rogersman, nor Mr. Lewis Feltham—the two principal owners for whom he trained—were so much as asked by the stewards to explain the running of their horses. Thus proving that the Turf needed reform, and the stipendiary steward was an absolute necessity.

Mr. Bert Yardley was a youngish man of thirty-five, who spoke very little and did his betting by telegram. He had a suite at the Midland Hotel, and was a member of a sedate and respectable club in Pall Mall. He read extensively, mostly such classics as *Races to Come*, and the umpteenth volume of the Stud Book, and he leavened his studies with such lighter reading as the training reports from the daily sporting newspapers—he liked a good laugh.

His worst enemy could not complain of him that he refused information to anybody.

"I think mine have some sort of chance, and I'm backing them both. Tinpot? Well, of course, he may win; miracles happen, and I shouldn't be surprised if he made a good show. But I've had to ease him in his work and when I galloped him on Monday he simply wouldn't have it—couldn't get him to take hold of his bit. Possibly he runs better when he's a little above himself, but he's a horse of moods. If he'd only give his running, he'd trot in! Lampholder, on the other hand, is as game a horse as ever looked through a bridle. A battler! He'll be there or thereabouts."

What would you back on that perfectly candid, perfectly honest information straight, as it were, from the horse's mouth?

Lampholder, of course; and Tinpot would win. Even stipendiary stewards couldn't make Lampholder win, not if they got behind and shoved him. And that, of course, is no part of a stipendiary steward's duties.

Mr. Bert Yardley was dressing for dinner one March evening when he discovered that a gold watch had disappeared. He called his valet, who could offer no other information than that it had been there when they left Stotford for Sandown Park.

"Send for the police," said Mr. Yardley, and there came to him Detective-Sergeant Challoner.

Mr. Challoner listened, made a few notes, asked a few, a very few, questions of the valet and closed his book.

"I think I know the person," he said, and to the valet: "A big nose—you're sure of the big nose?"

The valet was emphatic.

"Very good," said The Miller. "I'll do my best, Mr.

Yardley. I hope I shall be as successful as Amboy will be in the London Handicap.''

Mr. Yardley smiled faintly.

''We'll talk about that later,'' he said.

The Miller made one or two inquiries and that night pulled in Nosey Boldin, whose hobby it was to pose as an inspector of telephones and who, in this capacity, had made many successful experiments. On the way to the station, Nosey, so-called because of a certain abnormality in that organ, delivered himself with great force and venom.

''This comes of betting on horse races and follering Educated Evans's perishin' five-pounds specials! Let this be a warning to you, Miller!''

''No so much lip,'' said The Miller.

''He gave me one winner in ten shots, and *that* started at 11 to 10 on,'' ruminated Nosey. ''Men like that drive men to crime. There ought to be a law so's to make the fifth loser a *felony*! And after the eighth loser he ought to 'ang! That'd stop 'em.''

The Miller saw his friend charged and lodged for the night and went home to bed. And in the morning, when he left his rooms to go to breakfast, the first person he saw was Educated Evans, and there was on that learned man's unhappy face a look of pain and anxiety.

''Good morning, Mr. Challoner. Excuse me if I'm taking a liberty, but I understand that a client of mine is in trouble?''

''If you mean Nosey, he is,'' agreed The Miller. ''And what's more, he attributes his shame and downfall to following your tips. I sympathize with him.''

Educated Evans made an impatient clicking sound, raised his eyebrows and spread out his hand.

''Bolsho,'' he said simply.

''Eh?'' The Miller frowned suspiciously. ''You didn't give Bolsho?''

''Every guaranteed client received 'Bolsho: fear nothing,' '' said Evans even more simply: ''following Mothegg (ten to one, beaten a neck, hard lines), Toffeetown (third, hundred to eight, very unlucky), Onesided (won, seven to two, what a beauty!), followin' Curds and Whey (won, eleven to ten—can't help the price). Is that fair?''

"The question is," said The Miller deliberately, "Did Nosey subscribe to your guarantee wire, your five pounds special, or your Overnight nap?''

"That," said Educated Evans diplomatically, "I can't tell till I've seen me books. The point is this: if Nosey wants bail, am I all right? I don't want any scandal, and you know Nosey. He ought to have been in advertisin'.''

The advertising propensities of Nosey were, indeed, well known to The Miller. He had the knack of introducing some startling feature into the very simplest case, and attracting to himself the amount of newspaper space usually given to scenes in the House and important murders.

It was Nosey who, by his startling statement that pickles were a greater incentive to crime than beer, initiated a press correspondence which lasted for months. It was Nosey who, when charged with hotel larceny—his favourite aberration— made the pronouncement that buses were a cause of insanity. Upon the peg of his frequent misfortunes, it was his practice to hang a showing up for somebody.

The case of Nosey was dealt with summarily. Long before the prosecutor had completed his evidence he realized that his doom was sealed.

"Anything known about this man?" asked the magistrate.

A jailer stepped briskly into the box and gave a brief sketch of Nosey's life, and Nosey, who knew it all before, looked bored.

"Anything to say?" asked the magistrate.

Nosey cleared his throat.

"I can only say, your worship, that I've fell into thieving ways owing to falling in the hands of unscrupulous racing tipsters. I'm ruined by tips, and if the law was just, there's a certain party who ought to be standing here by my side.''

Educated Evans, standing at the back of the court, squirmed.

"I've got a wife, as true a woman as ever drew the breath of life," Nosey went on. "I've got two dear little children, and I ask your worship to consider me temptation owing to horse-racing, and betting and this here tipster."

"Six months," said the magistrate, without looking up.

Outside the court Mr. Evans waited patiently for the appearance of The Miller.

"Nosey never had more than a shilling on a horse in his life," he said bitterly, "and he *owes*! Here's the bread being took out of my mouth by slander and misrepresentation; do you think they'll put it in the papers, Mr. Challoner?"

"Certain," said The Miller cheerfully, and Educated Evans groaned.

"That man's worse than Lucreature Burgia, the celebrated poisoner," he said, "that Shakespeare wrote a play about. He's a snake in the grass and viper in the bosom. And to think I gave him Penwiper for the Manchester November, and he never so much as asked me if I was thirsty! Mr. Challoner."

Challoner, turning away, stopped.

"Was that Yardley? I mean the trainer?"

The Miller looked at him reproachfully.

"Maybe I'm getting old and my memory is becoming defective," he said, "but I seem to remember that when you gave me Tellmark the other day, you said that you were a personal friend of Mr. Yardley's, and that the way he insisted on your coming down to spend the weekends was getting a public nuisance."

Educated Evans did not bat a lid.

"That was his brother," he said.

"He must have lied when he told me he had no brothers," said The Miller.

"They've quarrelled," replied Educated Evans frankly. "In fact, they never mention one another's names. It's tragic when brothers quarrel, Mr. Challoner. I've done my best to reconcile 'em—but what's the use? He didn't say anything about Amboy, did he?"

"He said nothing that I can tell you," was his unsatisfactory reply, and he left Mr. Evans to consider means and methods by which he might bring himself into closer contact with the Wizard of Stotford.

All that he feared in the matters of publicity was realized to the full. One evening paper said:

RUINED BY TIPSTERS
Once prosperous merchant goes to prison for theft.

And in the morning press one newspaper may be quoted as typical of the rest:

TIPSTER TO BLAME
Pest of the Turf wrecks a home.

Detective-Sergeant Challoner called by appointment at the Midland Hotel, and Mr. Yardley saw him.

"No, thank you, sir," The Miller was firm.

Mr. Yardley put back the fiver he had taken from his pocket.

"I'll put you a tenner on anything I fancy," he said. "Who's this tipster, by the way?—the man who was referred to by the prisoner?"

The Miller smiled.

"Educated Evans," he said, and when he had finished describing him Mr. Yardley nodded.

He was staying overnight in London *en route* for Lincoln and he was inclined to be bored. He had read the *Racing Calendar* from the list of the year's races to the last description of the last selling hurdle race on the back page. He had digested the surprising qualities of stallions and he could have almost recited the forfeit list from Aaron to Znosberg. And he was aching for diversion when the bell boy brought a card.

It was a large card, tastefully bordered with pink and green roses. Its edge was golden and in the centre were the words:

J. T. EVANS
(better known as "Educated Evans")!!)

The World's Foremost and Leading Turf
Adviser and Racing Cricit
c/o Jockey Club, Newmarket or direct:
92 Bayham Mews, N.W.1
"The Man Who Gave Braxted!!
What a beauty!"—*vide* Press.

Mr. Yardley read, lingering over the printer's errors.

"Show this gentleman up, page," he said.

Into his presence came Educated Evans, a solemn, purposeful man.

"I hope the intrusion will be amply excused by the important nature or character of my business," he said. This was the opening he had planned.

"Sit down, Mr. Evans," said Yardley, and Educated Evans put his hat under the chair and sat.

"I've been thinking matters over in the privacy of my den—" began Evans, after a preliminary cough.

"You're a lion tamer as well?" asked the Wizard of Stotford, interested.

"By 'den' I mean 'study,'" said Evans, gravely. "To come to the point without beating about the bush—to use a well-known expression—I've heard of a coop."

"A what?"

"A coop," said Evans.

"A chicken coop?" asked the puzzled Wizard.

"It's a French word, meaning 'ramp,'" said Evans.

"Oh yes, I see, 'Coup'—it's pronounced 'coo,' Mr. Evans."

Educated Evans frowned.

"It's years since I was in Paris," he said; "and I suppose they've altered it. It used to be 'coop' but these French people are always messing and mucking about with words."

"And who is working this coop?" asked the trainer, politely adopting the old French version.

"Higgson."

Educated Evans pronounced the word with great emphasis. Higgson was another mystery trainer. His horses also won when least expected. And after they won, little knots of men gathered in the paddock and asked one another if the Stewards had eyes, and why wasn't Higgson warned off?

"You interest me," said the trainer of Amboy. "Do you mean that he's winning with St. Kats?"

Evans nodded more gravely still.

"I think it's me duty to tell you," he said. "My information"—he lowered his voice and glanced round to the door to be sure that it was shut—"comes from the boy who does this horse!"

"Dear me!" said Mr. Yardley.

"I've got correspondents everywhere," said Educated Evans mysteriously. "My man at Stockbridge sent me a letter this morning—I daren't show it to you—about a horse in that two-year-old race that will win with his ears pricked."

Mr. Yardley was looking at him through half-closed eyes.

"With his ears pricked?" he repeated, impressed. "Have they trained his ears too? Extraordinary! But why have you come to tell me about Mr. Higgson's horse?"

Educated Evans bent forward confidentially.

"Because you've done me many a turn, sir," he said; "and I'd like to do you one. I've got the information. I could shut my mouth an' make millions. I've got nine thousand clients who'd pay me the odds to a pound—but what's money?"

"True," murmured Mr. Yardley, nodding. "Thank you, Mr. Evans. St. Kats, I think you said? Now, in return for your kindness, I'll give you a tip."

Educated Evans held his breath. His amazingly bold plan had succeeded.

"Change your printer," said Mr. Yardley, rising. "He can't spell. Good night."

Evans went forth with his heart turned to stone and his soul seared with bitter animosity.

Mr. Yardley came down after him and watched the shabby figure as it turned the corner, and his heart was touched. In two minutes he had overtaken the educated man.

"You're a bluff and a fake," he said, good humouredly, "but you can have a little, a very little, on Amboy."

Before Educated Evans could prostrate himself at the bene-factor's feet Mr. Yardley was gone.

The next day was a busy one for Educated Evans. All day Miss Higgs, the famous typist of Great College Street, turned her duplicator, and every revolution of the cylinder threw forth, with a rustle and a click, the passionate appeal which Educated Evans addressed to all clients, old and new. He was not above borrowing the terminology of other advertise-ment writers.

> You want the best winners—I've got them.
> Bet in Evans' way! Eventually, why not now?
> I've got the winner of the Lincoln!
>> What a beauty!
>> What a beauty!
>> What a beauty!
> Confidentially! From the trainer! This is the coop
> of the season! Help yourself! Defeat ignored!

To eight hundred and forty clients this moving appeal went forth.

On the afternoon of the race Educated Evans strolled with confidence to the end of the Tottenham Court Road to wait for the *Star*. And when it came he opened the paper with a quiet smile. He was still smiling, when he read:

> Tenpenny, 1
> St. Kats, 2
> Ella Glass, 3
> All probables ran.

"Tenpenny?—never heard of it," he repeated, dazed, and produced his noon edition. Tenpenny was starred as a doubt-ful runner.

It was trained by—Yardley.

For a moment his emotions almost mastered him.

"That man ought to be warned off," he said hollowly, and dragged his weary feet back to the stable-yard.

In the morning came a letter dated from Lincoln.

Dear Mr. Evans,—What do you think of my coop?—
                                   Yours, H. YARDLEY

There was a P.S. which ran:

I put a fiver on for you. Your enterprise deserved it.

Evans opened the cheque tenderly and shook his head.

"After all," he said subsequently to the quietly jubilant Miller, "clients can't expect to win *every* time—a Turf Adviser is entitled to his own coops."

Tenpenny started at 25 to 1.

THE SPLENDID OUTCAST

Beryl Markham

T HE stallion was named after a star, and when he fell
from his particular heaven, it was easy enough for people to say that he had been named too well. People like to
see stars fall, but in the case of Rigel, it was of greater importance to me. To me and to one other—to a little man with
shabby cuffs and a wilted cap that rested over eyes made mild
by something more than time.

It was at Newmarket, in England, where, since Charles I
instituted the first cup race, a kind of court has been held for
the royalty of the turf. Men of all classes come to Newmarket
for the races and for the December sales. They come from
everywhere—some to bet, some to buy or sell, and some
merely to offer homage to the resplendent peers of the Stud
Book, for the sport of kings may, after all, be the pleasure
of every man.

December can be bitterly cold in England, and this December was. There was frozen sleet on buildings and on
trees, and I remember that the huge Newmarket track lay on
the downs below the village like a noose of diamonds on a
tarnished mat. There was a festive spirit everywhere, but it
was somehow lost on me. I had come to buy new blood for
my stable in Kenya, and since my stable was my living, I
came as serious buyers do, with figures in my mind and
caution in my heart. Horses are hard to judge at best, and

139

the thought of putting your hoarded pounds behind that judgement makes it harder still.

I sat close on the edge of the auction ring and held my breath from time to time as the bidding soared. I held it because the casual mention of ten thousand guineas in payment for a horse or for anything else seemed to me wildly beyond the realm of probable things. For myself, I had five hundred pounds to spend and, as I waited for Rigel to be shown, I remember that I felt uncommonly maternal about each pound. I waited for Rigel because I had come six thousand miles to buy him, nor was I apprehensive lest anyone should take him from me; he was an outcast.

Rigel had a pedigree that looked backward and beyond the pedigrees of many Englishmen—and Rigel had a brilliant record. By all odds, he should have brought ten thousand guineas at the sale, but I knew he wouldn't, for he had killed a man.

He had killed a man—not fallen upon him, nor thrown him in a playful moment from the saddle, but killed him dead with his hoofs and with his teeth in a stable. And that was not all, though it was the greatest thing. Rigel had crippled other men and, so the story went, would cripple or kill still more, so long as he lived. He was savage, people said, and while he could not be hanged for his crimes, like a man, he could be shunned as criminals are. He could be offered for sale. And yet, under the implacable rules of racing, he had been warned off the turf for life—so who would buy?

Well, I for one—and I had supposed there would not be two. I would buy if the price were low enough, because I had youth then, and a corresponding contempt for failure. It seemed probably that in time and with luck and with skill, the stallion might be made manageable again, if only for breeding—especially for breeding. He could be gentled, I thought. But I found it hard to believe what I saw that day. I had not known that the mere touch of a hand, could in an instant, extinguish the long-burning anger of an angry heart.

I first noticed the little man when the sale was already well on its way, and he caught my attention at once, because he was incongruous there. He sat a few benches from me and held his lean, interwoven fingers upon his knees. He stared down upon the arena as each horse was led into it, and he listened to the dignified encomiums of the auctioneer with the humble attention of a parishioner at mass. He never moved. He was surrounded by men and women who, by their impeccable clothes and by their somewhat bored familiarity with pounds and guineas, made him conspicuous. He was like a stone of granite in a jeweller's window, motionless and grey against the glitter.

You could see in his face that he loved horses—just as you could see, in some of the faces of those around him, that they loved the idea of horses. They were the cultists, he the votary, and there were, in fact, about his grey eyes and his slender lips, the deep, tense lines so often etched in the faces of zealots and of lonely men. It was the cast of his shoulders, I think, the devotion of his manner that told me he had once been a jockey.

A yearling came into the ring and was bought, and then another, while the pages of catalogues were quietly turned. The auctioneer's voice, clear but scarcely lifted, intoned the virtues of his magnificent merchandise as other voices, responding to this magic, spoke reservedly of figures. "A thousand guineas . . . two thousand . . . three . . . four . . ."

The scene at the aution comes to me clearly now, as if once again it was happening before my eyes.

"Five, perhaps?" The auctioneer scans the audience expectantly as a groom parades a dancing colt around the arena. There is a moment of near silence, a burly voice calls, "Five!" and the colt is sold while a murmur of polite approval swells and dies.

And so they go, one after another, until the list is small, the audience thins and my finger traces the name, Rigel, on the last page of the catalogue. I straighten on my bench and hold my breath a little, forgetting the crowd, the little man, and a part of myself. I know this horse. I know he is by Hurry On out of Bounty—the sire unbeaten, the dam a great steeplechaser—and there is no better blood than that. Killer or not, Rigel has won races, and won them clean. If God and Barclays Bank stay with me, he will return to Africa when I do.

And there, at last, he stands. In the broad entrance to the ring, two powerful men appear with the stallion between them. The men are not grooms of ordinary size; they have been picked for strength, and in the clenched fist of each is the end of a chain. Between the chain and the bit there is on the near side a short rod of steel, close to the stallion's mouth—a rod of steel, easy to grasp, ease to use. Clenched around the great girth of the horse, and fitted with metal rings, there is a strap of thick leather that brings to mind the restraining harness of a madman.

Together, the two men edge the stallion forward. Tall as they are, they move like midgets beside his massive shoulders. He is the biggest thoroughbred I have ever seen. He is the most beautiful. His coat is chestnut, flecked with white, and his mane and tail are close to gold. There is a blaze on his face—wide and straight and forthright, as if by his marking he proclaims that he is none other than Rigel, for all his sins, for all the hush that falls over the crowd.

He is Rigel and he looks upon the men who hold his chains as a captured king may look upon his captors. He is not tamed. Nothing about him promises that he will be tamed. Stiffly, on reluctant hoofs, he enters the ring and flares his crimson nostrils at the crowd, and the crowd is still. The crowd whose pleasure is the docile beast of pretty paddocks, the gainly horse of cherished prints that hang upon the finest walls, the willing winner of the race—upon the rebel this crowd stares, and the rebel stares back.

His eyes are lit with anger or with hate. His head is held disdainfully and high, his neck an arc of arrogance. He prances now—impatient in the thudding of his hoofs upon the tanbark, defiance in his manner—and the chains jerk tight. The long stallion reins are tightly held—apprehensively held—and the men who hold them glance at the auctioneer, an urgent question in their eyes.

The auctioneer raises his arm for silence, but there is silence. No one speaks. The story of Rigel is known—his breeding, his brilliant victories, and finally his insurgence and his crimes. Who will buy the outcast? The auctioneer shakes his head as if to say that this is a trick beyond his magic. But he will try. He is an imposing man, an experienced man, and now he clears his throat and confronts the crowd, a kind of pleading in his face.

"This splendid animal—" he begins—and does not finish. He cannot finish.

Rigel has scanned the silent audience and smelled the unmoving air, and he—a creature of the wind—knows his indignity of this skyless temple. He seems aware at last of the chains that hold him, of the men who cling forlornly to the heavy reins. He rears from the tanbark, higher and higher still, until his golden mane is lifted like a flag unfurled and defiant. He beats the air. He trembles in his rising anger, and the crowd leans forward.

A groom clings like a monkey to the tightened chain. He is swept from his feet while his partner, a less tenacious man, sprawls ignobly below, and men—a dozen men—rush to the ring, some shouting, some waving their arms. They run and swear in lowered voices; they grasp reins, chains, rings, and swarm upon their towering Gulliver. And he subsides.

With something like contempt for this hysteria, Rigel touches his forehoofs to the tanbark once more. He has killed no one, hurt no one, but they are jabbing at his mouth now, they are surrounding him, adding fuel to his fiery reputation, and the auctioneer is a wilted man.

He sighs, and you can almost hear it. He raises both arms and forgoes his speech. "What," he asks with weariness, "am I offered?" And there is a ripple of laughter from the crowd. Smug in its wisdom, it offers nothing.

But I do, and my voice is like an echo in a cave. Still there is triumph in it. I will have what I have come so far to get— I will have Rigel.

"A hundred guineas!" I stand as I call my price, and the auctioneer is plainly shocked—not by the meagreness of the offer, but by the offer itself. He stares upward from the ring, incredulity in his eyes.

He lifts a hand and slowly repeats the price. "I am offered," he says, "one hundred guineas."

There is a hush, and I feel the eyes of the crowd and watch the hand of the auctioneer. When it goes down, the stallion will be mine.

But it does not go down. It is still poised in mid-air, white, expectant, compelling, when the soft voice, the gentle challenging voice is lifted. "Two hundred!" the voice says, and I do not have to turn to know that the little jockey has bid against me. But I do turn.

He has not risen from the bench, and he does not look at me. In his hand he holds a sheaf of bank notes. I can tell by their colour that they are of small denomination, by their rumpled condition that they have been hoarded long. People near him are staring—horrified, I think—at the vulgar spectacle of cash at a Newmarket auction.

I am not horrified, nor sympathetic. Suddenly I am aware that I have a competitor, and I am cautious. I am here for a purpose that has little to do with sentiment, and I will not be beaten. I think of my stable in Kenya, of the feed bills to come, of the syces to be paid, of the races that are yet to be won if I am to survive in this unpredictable business. No, I cannot now yield an inch. I have little money, but so has he. No more, I think, but perhaps as much.

I hesitate a moment and glance at the little man, and he returns my glance. We are like two gamblers bidding each against the other's unseen cards. Our eyes meet for a sharp instant—a cold instant.

I straighten and my catalogue is crumpled in my hand. I moisten my lips and call, "Three hundred!" I call it firmly, steadily, hoping to undo my opponent at a stroke. It is a wishful thought.

He looks directly at me now, but does not smile. He looks at me as a man might look at one who bears false witness against him, then soundlessly he counts his money and bids again, "Three fifty!"

The interest of the crowd is suddenly aroused. All these people are at once conscious of being witnesses, not only before an auction, but before a contest, a rivalry of wills. They shift in their seats and stare as they might stare at a pair of duelists, rapiers in hand.

But money is the weapon, Rigel the prize. And prize enough, I think, as does my adversary.

I ponder and think hard, then decide to bid a hundred more. Not twenty, not fifty, but a hundred. Perhaps by that I can take him in my stride. He need not know there is little more to follow. He may assume that I am one of the casual ones, impatient of small figures. He may hesitate, he may withdraw. He may be cowed.

Still standing, I utter, as indifferently as I can, the words, "Four fifty!" and the auctioneer, at ease in his element of contention, brightens visibly.

I am aware that the gathered people are now fascinated by this battle of pounds and shillings over a stallion that not one of them would care to own. I only hope that in the heat of it some third person does not begin to bid. But I need not worry; Rigel takes care of that.

The little jockey has listened to my last offer, and I can see that he is already beaten—or almost, at least. He has counted his money a dozen times, but now he counts it again, swiftly, with agile fingers, as if hoping his previous counts had been wrong.

I feel a momentary surge of sympathy, then smother it. Horse training is not my hobby. It is my living. I wait for what I am sure will be his last bid, and it comes. For the first time, he rises from his bench. He is small and alone in spirit, for the glances of the well-dressed people about him lend him nothing. He does not care. His eyes are on the stallion and I can see that there is a kind of passion in them. I have seen that expression before—in the eyes of sailors appraising a comely ship, in the eyes of pilots sweeping the clean, sweet contours of a plane. There is reverence in it, desire—and even hope.

The little man turns slightly to face the expectant auctioneer, then clears his throat and makes his bid. "Four eighty!" he calls, and the slight note of desperation in his voice is unmistakable, but I force myself to ignore it. Now, at last, I tell myself, the prize is mine.

The auctioneer receives the bid and looks at me, as do a hundred people. Some of them, no doubt, think I am quite mad or wholly inexperienced, but they watch while the words "Five hundred" form upon my lips. They are never uttered.

Throughout the bidding for Rigel, Rigel has been ignored. He has stood quietly enough after his first brief effort at freedom, he has scarcely moved. But now, at the climax of the sale, his impatience overflows, his spirit flares like fire, his anger bursts through the circle of men who guard him. Suddenly there are cries, shouts of warning, the ringing of chains and the cracking of leather, and the crowd leaps to its feet. Rigel is loose. Rigel has hurled his captors from him and he stands alone.

It is a beautiful thing to see, but there is terror in it. A thoroughbred stallion with anger in his eye is not a sight to entrance anyone but a novice. If you are aware of the power and the speed and the intelligence in that towering symmetrical body, you will hold your breath as you watch it. You will know that the teeth of a horse can crush a bone, that hoofs can crush a man. And Rigel's hoofs have crushed a man.

He stands alone, his neck curved, his golden tail a battle plume, and he turns, slowly, deliberately, and faces the men he has flung away. They are not without courage, but they are without resource. Horses are not tamed by whips or by blows. The strength of ten men is not so strong as a single stroke of a hoof; the experience of ten men is not enough, for this is the unexpected, the unpredictable. No one is prepared. No one is ready.

The words "Five hundred" die upon my lips as I watch, as I listen. For the stallion is not voiceless now. His challenging scream is shrill as the cry of winter wind. It is bleak and heartless. His forehoofs stir the tanbark. The auction is forgotten.

A man stands before him—a man braver than most. He holds nothing in his hands save an exercise bat; it looks a feeble thing, and is. It is a thin stick bound with leather—enough only to enrage Rigel, for he has seen such things in men's hands before. He knows their meaning. Such a thing as this bat, slight as it is, enrages him because it is a symbol that stands for other things. It stands, perhaps, for the confining walls of a darkened stable, for the bit of steel, foreign, but almost everpresent in his mouth, for the tightened girth, the command to gallop, to walk, to stop, to parade before the swelling crowd of gathered people, to accept the measured food gleaned from forbidden fields. It stands for life no closer to the earth than the sterile smell of satin on a jockey's back or the dead wreath hung upon a winner. It stands for servitude. And Rigel has broken with his overlords.

He lunges quickly, and the man with a bat is not so quick. He lifts the pathetic stick and waves it in desperation. He cries out, and the voice of the crowd drowns his cry. Rigel's neck is outstretched and straight as a sabre. There is dust and the shouting of men and the screaming of women, for the stallion's teeth have closed on the shoulder of his forlorn enemy.

The man struggles and drops his bat, and his eyes are sharp with terror, perhaps with pain. Blood leaves the flesh of his face, and it is a face grey and pleading, as must be the faces of those to whom retribution is unexpected and swift. He beats against the golden head while the excitement of the crowd mounts against the fury of Rigel. Then reason vanishes. Clubs, whips, and chains appear like magic in the ring, and a regiment of men advance upon the stallion. They are angry men, brave in their anger, righteous and justified in it. They advance, and the stallion drops the man he has attacked, and the man runs for cover, clutching his shoulder.

I am standing, as is everyone. It is a strange and unreal thing to see this trapped and frustrated creature, magnificent and alone, away from his kind, remote from the things he understands, face the punishment of his miniscule masters.

He is, of course, terrified, and the terror is a mounting mad-
ness. If he could run, he would leave this place, abandoning
his fear and his hatred to do it. But he cannot run. The walls
of the arena are high. The doors are shut, and the trap makes
him blind with anger. He will fight, and the blows will fall
with heaviness upon his spirit, for his body is a rock before
these petty weapons.

The men edge closer, ropes and chains and whips in determined hands. The whips are lifted, the chains are ready;
the battle line is formed, and Rigel does not retreat. He comes
forward, the whites of his eyes exposed and rimmed with
carnelian fire, his nostrils crimson.

There is a breathless silence, and the little jockey slips like
a ghost into the ring. His eyes are fixed on the embattled
stallion. He begins to run across the tanbark and breaks
through the circle of advancing men and does not stop.
Someone clutches at his coat, but he breaks loose without
turning, then slows to an almost casual walk and approaches
Rigel alone. The men do not follow him. He waves them
back. He goes forward, steadily, easily and happily, without
caution, without fear, and Rigel whirls angrily to face him.

Rigel stands close to the wall of the arena. He cannot
retreat. He does not propose to. Now he can focus his fury
on this insignificant David who has come to meet him, and
he does. He lunges at once as only a stallion can—swiftly,
invincibly, as if escape and freedom can be found only in the
destruction of all that is human, all that smells human, and
all that humans have made.

He lunges and the jockey stops. He does not turn or lift a
hand or otherwise move. He stops, he stands, and there is
silence everywhere. No one speaks; no one seems to breathe.
Only Rigel is motion. No special hypnotic power emanates
from the jockey's eyes; he has no magic. The stallion's teeth
are bared and close, his hoofs are a swelling sound when the
jockey turns. Like a matador of nerveless skill and studied
insolence, the jockey turns his back on Rigel and does not
walk away, and the stallion pauses.

Rigel rears high at the back of the little man, screaming

his defiant scream, but he does not strike. His hoofs are close to the jockey's head, but do not touch him. His teeth are sheathed. He hesitates, trembles, roars wind from his massive lungs. He shakes his head, his golden mane, and beats the ground. It is frustration—but of a new kind. It is a thing he does not know—a man who neither cringes in fear nor threatens with whips or chains. It is a thing beyond his memory perhaps—as far beyond it as the understanding of the mare that bore him.

Rigel is suddenly motionless, rigid, suspicious. He waits, and the grey-eyed jockey turns to face him. The little man is calm and smiling. We hear him speak, but cannot understand his words. They are low and they are lost to us—an incantation. But the stallion seems to understand at least the spirit if not the sense of them. He snorts, but does not move. And now the jockey's hand goes forward to the golden mane—neither hurriedly nor with hesitance, but unconcernedly, as if it had rested there a thousand times. And there it stays.

There is a murmur from the crowd, then silence. People look at one another and stir in their seats—a strange self-consciousness in their stirring, for people are uneasy before the proved worth of their inferiors, unbelieving of the virtue of simplicity. They watch with open mouths as the giant Rigel, the killer Rigel, with no harness save a head collar, follows his Lilliputian master, his new friend, across the ring.

All has happened in so little time—in moments. The audience begins to stand, to leave. But they pause at the lift of the auctioneer's hand. He waves it and they pause. It is all very well, his gestures say, but business is, after all, business, and Rigel has not been sold. He looks up at me, knowing that I have a bid to make—the last bid. And I look down into the ring at the stallion I have come so far to buy. His head is low and close to the shoulder of the man who would take him from me. He is not prancing now, not moving. For this hour, at least, he is changed.

I straighten, and then shake my head. I need only say, "Five hundred," but the words won't come. I can't get them out. I am angry with myself—a sentimental fool—and I am disappointed. But I cannot bid. It is too easy—twenty pounds too little, and yet too great an advantage.

No. I shake my head again, the auctioneer shrugs and turns to seal his bargain with the jockey.

On the way out, an old friend jostles me. "You didn't really want him then," he says.

"Want him? No. No, I didn't really want him."

"It was wise," he said. "What good is a horse that's warned off every course in the Empire? You wouldn't want a horse like that."

"That's right. I wouldn't want a horse like that."

We move to the exit, and when we are out in the bright cold air of Newmarket, I turn to my friend and mention the little jockey. "But he wanted Rigel," I say.

And my old friend laughs. "He would," he says. "That man has himself been barred from racing for fifteen years. Why, I can't remember. But it's two of a kind, you see— Rigel and Sparrow. Outlaws, both. He loves and knows horses as no man does, but that's what we call him around the tracks—the Fallen Sparrow."

I'M A FOOL

Sherwood Anderson

I T was a hard jolt for me, one of the bitterest I ever had to face. And it all came about through my own foolishness, too. Even yet sometimes, when I think of it, I want to cry or swear or kick myself. Perhaps, even now, after all this time, there will be a kind of satisfaction in making myself look cheap by telling of it.

It began at three o'clock one October afternoon as I sat in the grandstand at the fall trotting-and-pacing meet at Sandusky, Ohio.

To tell the truth, I felt a little foolish that I should be sitting in the grandstand at all. During the summer before I had left my hometown with Harry Whitehead and, with a nigger named Burt, had taken a job as swipe with one of the two horses Harry was campaigning through the fall race-meets that year. Mother cried and my sister Mildred, who wanted to get a job as a schoolteacher in our town that fall, stormed and scolded about the house all during the week before I left. They both thought it something disgraceful that one of our family should take a place as a swipe with racehorses. I've an idea Mildred thought my taking the place would stand in the way of her getting the job she'd been working so long for.

But after all I had to work, and there was no other work to be got. A big lumbering fellow of nineteen couldn't just hang around the house and I had got too big to mow people's lawns and sell newspapers. Little chaps who could get next

151

to people's sympathies by their sizes were always getting jobs away from me. There was one fellow who kept saying to everyone who wanted a lawn mowed or a cistern cleaned, that he was saving money to work his way through college, and I used to lay awake nights thinking up ways to injure him without being found out. I kept thinking of wagons running over him and bricks falling on his head as he walked along the street. But never mind him.

I got the place with Harry and I liked Burt fine. We got along splendid together. He was a big nigger with a lazy sprawling body and soft, kind eyes, and when it came to a fight he could hit like Jack Johnson. He had Bucephalus, a big black pacing stallion that could do 2.09 or 2.10, if he had to, and I had a little gelding named Doctor Fritz that never lost a race all fall when Harry wanted him to win.

We set out from home late in July in a box car with the two horses, and after that, until late November, we kept moving along to the race-meets and the fairs. It was a peachy time for me, I'll say that. Sometimes now I think that boys who are raised regular in houses, and never have a fine nigger like Burt for best friend, and go to high schools and college, and never steal anything, or get drunk a little, or learn to swear from fellows who know how, or come walking up in front of a grandstand in their shirt sleeves and with dirty horsy pants on when the races are going on and the grandstand is full of people all dressed up—What's the use of talking about it? Such fellows don't know nothing at all. They've never had no opportunity.

But I did. Burt taught me how to rub down a horse and put the bandages on after a race and steam a horse out and a lot of valuable things for any man to know. He could wrap a bandage on a horse's leg so smooth that if it had been the same colour you would think it was his skin, and I guess he'd have been a big driver, too, and got to the top like Murphy and Walter Cox and the others if he hadn't been black.

Gee whizz! it was fun. You got to a county seat town, maybe say on a Saturday or Sunday, and the fair began the next Tuesday and lasted until Friday afternoon. Doctor Fritz would be, say in the 2.25 trot on Tuesday afternoon, and on Thursday afternoon Bucephalus would knock 'em cold in the ''free-for-all'' pace. It left you a lot of time to hang around and listen to horse talk, and see Burt knock some yap cold that got too gay, and you'd find out about horses and men and pick up a lot of stuff you could use all the rest of your life, if you had some sense and salted down what you heard and felt and saw.

And then at the end of the week when the race-meet was over, and Harry had run home to tend up to his livery-stable business, you and Burt hitched the two horses to carts and drove slow and steady cross country, to the place for the next meeting, so as to not overheat the horses, etc., etc., you know.

Gee whizz! Gosh a'mighty! the nice hickory-nut and beech-nut and oaks and other kinds of trees along the roads, all brown and red, and the good smells, and Burt singing a song that was called Deep River, and the country girls at the windows of houses and everything. You can stick your colleges up your nose for all me. I guess I know where I got my education.

Why, one of those little burgs of towns you come to on the way, say now on a Saturday afternoon, and Burt says, ''Let's lay up here.'' And you did.

And you took the horses to a livery stable and fed them, and you got your good clothes out of a box and put them on.

And the town was full of farmers gaping, because they could see you were racehorse people, and the kids maybe never see a nigger before and was afraid and run away when the two of us walked down their main street.

And that was before prohibition and all that foolishness, and so you went into a saloon, the two of you, and all the yaps come and stood around, and there was always someone pretended he was horsy and knew things and spoke up and began asking questions, and all you did was to lie and lie all you could about what horses you had, and I said I owned them, and then some fellow said, ''Will you have a drink of whisky?'' and Burt knocked his eye out the way he could say, off-hand like, ''Oh well, all right, I'm agreeable to a little nip. I'll split a quart with you.'' Gee whizz!

* * *

But that isn't what I want to tell my story about. We got home late in November and I promised mother I'd quit the racehorses for good. There's a lot of things you've got to promise a mother because she don't know any better.

And so, there not being any work in our town any more than when I left there to go to the races, I went off to Sandusky and got a pretty good place taking care of horses for a man who owned a teaming and delivery and storage and coal and real-estate business there. It was a pretty good place with good eats, and a day off each week, and sleeping on a cot in a big barn, and mostly just shovelling in hay and oats to a lot of big good-enough skates of horses, that couldn't have trotted a race with a toad. I wasn't dissatisfied and I could send money home.

And then, as I started to tell you, the fall races came to Sandusky and I got the day off and I went. I left the job at noon and had on my good clothes and my new brown derby hat, I'd just bought the Saturday before, and a stand-up collar.

First of all I went down-town and walked about with the dudes. I've always thought to myself, "Put up a good front," and so I did it. I had forty dollars in my pocket, and so I went into the West House, a big hotel, and walked up to the cigar-stand. "Give me three twenty-five-cent cigars," I said. There was a lot of horsemen and strangers and dressed-up people from other towns standing around in the lobby and in the bar, and I mingled amongst them. In the bar there was a fellow with a cane and a Windsor tie on, that it made me sick to look at him. I like a man to be a man and dress up, but not to go put on that kind of airs. So I pushed him aside, kind of rough, and had me a drink of whisky. And then he looked at me, as though he thought maybe he'd get gay, but he changed his mind and didn't say anything. And then I had another drink of whisky, just to show him something, and went out and had a hack out to the races, all to myself, and when I got there I bought myself the best seat I could get up in the grandstand, but didn't go in for any of these boxes. That's putting on too many airs.

And so there I was, sitting up in the grandstand as gay as you please and looking down on the swipes coming out with their horses, and with their dirty horsy pants on and the horse blankets swung over their shoulders, same as I had been doing all the year before. I liked one thing about the same as the other, sitting up there and feeling grand and being down there and looking up at the yaps and feeling grander and more important, too. One thing's about as good as another, if you take it just right. I've often said that.

Well, right in front of me, in the grandstand that day, there was a fellow with a couple of girls and they was about my age. The young fellow was a nice guy all right. He was the kind maybe that goes to college and then comes to be a lawyer or maybe a newspaper editor or something like that, but he wasn't stuck on himself. There are some of that kind are all right and he was one of the ones.

He had his sister with him and another girl and the sister looked around over his shoulder, accidental at first, not intending to start anything—she wasn't that kind—and her eyes and mine happened to meet.

You know how it is. Gee, she was a peach! She had on a soft dress, kind of blue stuff and it looked carelessly made, but was well sewed and made and everything. I knew that much. I blushed when she looked right at me and so did she. She was the nicest girl I've ever seen in my life. She wasn't stuck on herself and she could talk proper grammar without being like a schoolteacher or something like that. What I mean is, she was O.K. I think maybe her father was well-to-do, but not rich enough to make her chesty because she was his daughter, as some are. Maybe he owned a drugstore or a dry-goods store in their home town, or something like that. She never told me and I never asked.

My own people are all O.K., too, when you come to that. My grandfather was Welsh and over in the old country, in Wales he was—But never mind that.

The first heat of the first race come off and the young fellow sitting there with the two girls left them and went down to make a bet. I knew what he was up to, but he didn't talk big and noisy and let everyone around know he was a sport, as some do. He wasn't that kind. Well, he come back and I heard him tell the two girls what horse he'd bet on, and when the heat was trotted they all half got to their feet and acted in the excited, sweaty way people do when they've got money down on a race, and the horse they bet on is up there pretty close at the end, and they think maybe he'll come on with a rush, but he never does because he hasn't got the old juice in him, come right down to it.

And then, pretty soon, the horses came out for the 2.18 pace and there was a horse in it I knew. He was a horse Bob French had in his string, but Bob didn't own him. He was a horse owned by a Mr. Mathers down at Marietta, Ohio.

This Mr. Mathers had a lot of money and owned some coal mines or something, and he had a swell place out in the country, and he was stuck on racehorses, but was a Presbyterian or something, and I think more than likely his wife was one, too, maybe a stiffer one than himself. So he never raced his horses hisself, and the story round the Ohio racetracks was that when one of his horses got ready to go to the races he turned him over to Bob French and pretended to his wife he was sold.

So Bob had the horses and he did pretty much as he pleased and you can't blame Bob, at least, I never did. Sometimes he was out to win and sometimes he wasn't. I never cared much about that when I was swiping a horse. What I did want to know was that my horse had the speed and could go out in front, if you wanted him to.

And, as I'm telling you, there was Bob in this race with one of Mr. Mathers' horses, which was named "About Ben Ahem" or something like that, and was fast as a streak. He was a gelding and had a mark of 2.21, but could step in .08 or .09.

Because when Burt and I were out, as I've told you, the year before there was a nigger, Burt knew, worked for Mr. Mathers and we went out there one day when we didn't have

no race on at the Marietta Fair and our boss Harry was gone
home.

And so everyone was gone to the fair but just this one
nigger and he took us all through Mr. Mathers' swell house
and he and Burt tapped a bottle of wine Mr. Mathers had hid
in his bedroom, back in a closet, without his wife knowing,
and he showed us this Ahem horse. Burt was always stuck
on being a driver but didn't have much chance to get to the
top, being a nigger; and he and the other nigger gulped that
whole bottle of wine and Burt got a little lit up.

So the nigger let Burt take this About Ben Ahem and step
him a mile in a track Mr. Mathers had all to himself, right
there on the farm. And Mr. Mathers had one child, a daughter, kinda sick and not very good looking, and she came
home and we had to hustle and get About Ben Ahem stuck
back in the barn.

I'm only telling you to get everything straight. At Sandusky,
that afternoon I was at the fair, this young fellow with the
two girls was fussed, being with the girls and losing his bet.
You know how a fellow is that way. One of them was his girl
and the other his sister. I had figured that out.

"Gee whizz!" I says to myself, "I'm going to give him
the dope."

He was mighty nice when I touched him on the shoulder.
He and the girls were nice to me right from the start and clear
to the end. I'm not blaming them.

And so he leaned back and I give him the dope on About
Ben Ahem. "Don't bet a cent on this first heat because he'll
go like an oxen hitched to a plough, but when the first heat
is over go right down and lay on your pile." That's what I
told him.

Well, I never saw a fellow treat anyone sweller. There was
a fat man sitting beside the little girl, that had looked at me
twice by this time, and I at her, and both blushing, and what
did he do but have the nerve to turn and ask the fat man to
get up and change places with me so I could sit with his
crowd.

Gee whizz, craps a'mighty! There I was. What a chump I was to go and get gay up there in the West House bar, and just because that dude was standing there with a cane and that kind of a necktie on, to go and get all balled up and drink that whisky, just to show off.

Of course she would know, me sitting right beside her and letting her smell of my breath. I could have kicked myself right down out of that grandstand and all around that race-track and made a faster record than most of the skates of horses they had there that year.

Because that girl wasn't any mutt of a girl. What wouldn't I have given right then for a stick of chewing-gum to chew, or a lozenger, or some liquorice, or most anything. I was glad I had those twenty-five-cent cigars in my pocket and right away I gave that fellow one and lit one myself. Then that fat man got up and we changed places and there I was, plunked right down beside her.

They introduced themselves and the fellow's best girl, he had with him, was named Miss Elinor Woodbury, and her father was a manufacturer of barrels from a place called Tiffin, Ohio. And the fellow himself was named Wilbur Wessen and his sister was Miss Lucy Wessen.

I suppose it was their having such swell names got me off my trolly. A fellow, just because he has been a swipe with a race-horse, and works taking care of horses for a man in the teaming, delivery, and storage business, isn't any better or worse than anyone else. I've often thought that, and said it, too.

But you know how a fellow is. There's something in that kind of nice clothes, and the kind of nice eyes she had, and the way she had looked at me, awhile before, over her brother's shoulder, and me looking back at her, and both of us blushing.

I couldn't show her up for a boob, could I?

I made a fool of myself, that's what I did. I said my name was Walter Mathers from Marietta, Ohio, and then I told all three of them the smashingest lie you ever heard. What I said was that my father owned the horse About Ben Ahem and that he had let him out to this Bob French for racing purposes, because our family was proud and had never gone into racing that way, in our own name, I mean. Then I had got started and they were all leaning over and listening, and Miss Lucy Wessen's eyes were shining, and I went the whole hog.

I told about our place down at Marietta, and about the big stables and the grand brick house we had on a hill, up above the Ohio River, but I knew enough not to do it in no bragging way. What I did was to start things and then let them drag the rest out of me. I acted just as reluctant to tell as I could. Our family hasn't got any barrel factory, and, since I've known us, we've always been pretty poor, but not asking anything of anyone at that, and my grandfather, over in Wales—but never mind that.

We sat there talking like we had known each other for years and years, and I went and told them that my father had been expecting maybe this Bob French wasn't on the square, and had sent me up to Sandusky on the sly to find out what I could.

And I bluffed it through I had found out all about the 2.18 pace, in which About Ben Ahem was to start.

I said he would lose the first heat by pacing like a lame cow and then he would come back and skin 'em alive after that. And to back up what I said I took thirty dollars out of my pocket and handed it to Mr. Wilbur Wessen and asked him, would he mind, after the first heat, to go down and place it on About Ben Ahem for whatever odds he could get. What I said was that I didn't want Bob French to see me and none of the swipes.

Sure enough the first heat come off and About Ben Ahem went off his stride, up the back stretch, and looked like a wooden horse or a sick one, and come in to be last. Then this Wilbur Wessen went down to the betting-place under the grandstand and there I was with the two girls, and when that Miss Woodbury was looking the other way once, Lucy Wessen kinda, with her shoulder you know, kinda touched me. Not just tucking down, I don't mean. You know how a woman can do. They get close, but not getting gay either. You know what they do. Gee whizz!

And then they give me a jolt. What they had done, when I didn't know, was to get together, and they had decided Wilbur Wessen would bet fifty dollars, and the two girls had gone and put in ten dollars each, of their own money, too. I was sick then, but I was sicker later.

About the gelding, About Ben Ahem, and their winning their money, I wasn't worried a lot about that. It come out O.K. Ahem stepped the next three heats like a bushel of spoiled eggs going to market before they could be found out, and Wilbur Wessen had got nine to two for the money. There was something else eating at me.

Because Wilbur come back, after he had bet the money, and after that he spent most of his time talking to that Miss Woodbury, and Lucy Wessen and I was left alone together like on a desert island. Gee, if I'd only been on the square, or if there had been any way of getting myself on the square. There ain't any Walter Mathers, like I said to her and them, and there hasn't ever been one, but if there was, I bet I'd go to Marietta, Ohio, and shoot him tomorrow.

There I was, big boob that I am. Pretty soon the race was over, and Wilbur had gone down and collected our money, and we had a hack down-town, and he stood us a swell supper at the West House, and a bottle of champagne beside.

And I was with that girl and she wasn't saying much, and I wasn't saying much either. One thing I know. She wasn't stuck on me because of the lie about my father being rich and all that. There's a way you know. . . . Craps a'mighty! There's a kind of girl, you see just once in your life, and if you don't get busy and make hay, then you're gone for good and all, and might as well go jump off a bridge. They give you a look from inside of them somewhere, and it ain't no vamping, and what it means is—you want that girl to be your wife, and you want nice things around her like flowers and swell clothes, and you want her to have the kids you're going to have, and you want good music played and no ragtime. Gee whizz!

There's a place over near Sandusky, across a kind of bay,

and it's called Cedar Point. And after we had supper we went over to it in a launch, all by ourselves. Wilbur and Miss Lucy and that Miss Woodbury had to catch a ten o'clock train back to Tiffin, Ohio, because, when you're out with the girls like that you can't get careless and miss any trains and stay out all night, like you can with some kinds of Janes.

And Wilbur blowed himself to the launch, and it cost him fifteen cold plunks, but I wouldn't never have knew if I hadn't listened. He wasn't no tin-horn kind of a sport.

Over at the Cedar Point place, we didn't say around where there was a gang of common kind of cattle at all.

There was big dance-halls and dining-places for yaps, and there was a beach you could walk along and get where it was dark, and we went there.

She didn't talk hardly at all and neither did I, and I was thinking how glad I was my mother was all right, and always made us kids learn to eat with a fork at table, and not swell soup, and be noisy and rough like a gang you see around a race-track that way.

Then Wilbur and his girl went away up the beach and Lucy and I sat down in a dark place, where there was some roots of old trees the water had washed up, and after that the time, till we had to go back in the launch and they had to catch their trains, wasn't nothing at all. It went like winking your eye.

Here's how it was. The place we were sitting in was dark, like I said, and there was the roots from that old stump sticking up like arms, and there was a watery smell, and the night was like—as if you could put your hand out and feel it—so warm and soft and dark and sweet like an orange.

I 'most cried and I 'most swore and I 'most jumped up and danced, I was so mad and happy and sad.

When Wilbur come back from being alone with his girl, and she saw him coming, Lucy she said, "We got to go to the train now," and she was 'most crying too, but she never knew nothing I knew, and she couldn't be so all busted up. And then, before Wilbur and Miss Woodbury got up to where we was, she put her face up and kissed me quick and put her head up against me and she was all quivering and—Gee whizz!

Sometimes I hope I have cancer and die. I guess you know what I mean. We went in the launch across the bay to the train like that, and it was dark, too. She whispered and said it was like she and I could get out of the boat and walk on the water, and it sounded foolish, but I knew what she meant.

And then quick we were right at the depot, and there was a big gang of yaps, the kind that goes to the fairs, and crowded and milling around like cattle, and how could I tell her? "It won't be long because you'll write and I'll write to you." That's all she said.

I got a chance like a hay-barn afire. A swell chance I got.

And maybe she would write me, down at Marietta that way, and the letter would come back, and stamped on the front of it by the U.S.A., "There ain't any such guy," or something like that, whatever they stamp on a letter that way.

And me trying to pass myself off for a big bug and a swell—to her, as decent a little body as God ever made. Craps a'mighty—a swell chance I got!

And then the train come in, and she got on it, and Wilbur Wessen he come and shook hands with me, and that Miss Woodbury was nice, too, and bowed to me, and I at her, and the train went and I busted out and cried like a kid.

Gee, I could have run after that train and made Dan Patch look like a freight train after a wreck but, sock a'mighty, what was the use? Did you ever see such a fool?

I'll bet you what—if I had an arm broke right now or a train had run over my foot—I wouldn't go to no doctor at all. I'd go sit down and let her hurt and hurt—that's what I'd do.

I'll bet you what—if I hadn't a drunk that booze I'd a never been such a boob as to go tell such a lie—that couldn't never be made straight to a lady like her.

I wish I had that fellow right here that had on a Windsor tie and carried a cane. I'd smash him for fair. Gosh darn his eyes. He's a big fool—that's what he is.

And if I'm not another you just go find me one and I'll quit working and be a bum and give him my job. I don't care nothing for working, and earning money, and saving it for no such boob as myself.

HAD A HORSE

John Galsworthy

SOME quarter of a century ago, there abode in Oxford a small bookmaker called James Shrewin—or more usually "Jimmy," a run-about and damped-down little man, who made a precarious living out of the effect of horses on undergraduates. He had a so-called office just off the "Corn," where he was always open to the patronage of the young bloods of Bullingdon, and other horse-loving coteries, who bestowed on him sufficient money to enable him to live. It was through the conspicuous smash of one of them—young Gardon Colquhoun—that he became the owner of a horse. He had been far from wanting what was in the nature of a white elephant to one of his underground habits, but had taken it in discharge of betting debts, to which, of course, in the event of bankruptcy, he would have no legal claim. She was a three-year-old chestnut filly, by Lopez out of Calendar, bore the name Calliope, and was trained out on the Downs near Wantage. On a Sunday afternoon, then, in late July Jimmy got his friend, George Pulcher, the publican, to drive him out there in his sort of dog-cart.

"Must 'ave a look at the blinkin' mare," he had said; "that young 'Cocoon' told me she was a corker; but what's third to Referee at Sandown, and never ran as a two-year-old? All I know is, she's eatin' 'er 'ead off!"

Beside the plethoric bulk of Pulcher, clad in a light-coloured box cloth coat with enormous whitish buttons and

163

a full-blown rose in the lapel, Jimmy's little, thin, dark-clothed form, withered by anxiety and gin, was, as it were, invisible; and compared with Pulcher's setting sun, his face, with shaven cheeks sucked-in, and smudged-in eyes, was like a ghost's under a grey bowler. He spoke off-handedly about his animal, but he was impressed, in a sense abashed, by his ownership. What the 'ell? was his constant thought. Was he going to race her, sell her—what? How, indeed, to get back out of her the sum he had been fool enough to let "young Cocoon" owe him, to say nothing of her trainer's bill? The notion, too, of having to confront that trainer with his ownership was oppressive to one whose whole life was passed in keeping out of the foreground of the picture. Owner! He had never owned even a white mouse, let alone a white elephant. And an 'orse would ruin him in no time if he didn't look alive about it!

The son of a small London baker, devoted to errandry at the age of fourteen, Jimmy Shrewin owed his profession to a certain smartness at sums, a dislike of baking, and an early habit of hanging about street corners with other boys, who had their daily pennies on an 'orse. He had a narrow calculating head, which pushed him towards street corner books before he was eighteen. From that time on he had been a surreptitious nomad, till he had silted up at Oxford, where, owing to Vice-Chancellors, an expert in underground life had greater scope than elsewhere. When he sat solitary at his narrow table in the back room near the "Corn"—for he had no clerk or associate—eyeing the door, with his lists in a drawer before him, and his black shiny betting book ready for young "bloods," he had a sharp, cold, furtive air, and but for a certain imitated tightness of trouser, and a collar standing up all round, gave no impression of ever having heard of the quadruped called horse. Indeed, for Jimmy "horse" was a newspaper quantity with figures against its various names. Even when, for a short spell, hanger-on to a firm of cheap-ring bookmakers, he had seen almost nothing of horse; his racecourse hours were spent ferreting among a bawling, perspiring crowd, or hanging round within earshot of tight-lipped nobs, trainers, jockeys, anyone who looked like having "information." Nowadays he never went near a race-meeting—his business, of betting on races, giving him no chance—yet his conversation seldom deviated for more than a minute at a time from that physically unknown animal the horse. The ways of making money out of it, infinite, intricate, variegated, occupied the mind in all his haunts, to the accompaniment of liquid and tobacco. Gin and bitters was Jimmy's drink; for choice he smoked cheroots; and he would cherish in his mouth the cold stump of one long after it had gone out, for the homely feeling it gave him, while he talked, or listened to talk on horses. He was of that vast number, town bred, who, like crows round a carcase, feed on that which to them is not alive. And now he had a horse!

The dog-cart travelled at a clinking pace behind Pulcher's bob-tail. Jimmy's cheroot burned well in the warm July air; the dust powdered his dark clothes and pinched, sallow face. He thought with malicious pleasure of that young spark "Co-coon's" collapse—high-'anded lot of young fools, thinking themselves so knowing; many were the grins, and not few the gritting of his blackened teeth he had to smother at their swagger. "Jimmy, you robber!" "Jimmy, you little black-guard!" Young sparks—gay and languid—well, one of 'em had gone out!

He looked round with his screwed-up eyes at his friend George Pulcher, who, man and licensed victualler, had his bally independence; lived remote from "the Quality" in his Paradise, The Green Dragon; had not to kow-tow to anyone; went to Newbury, Gatwick, Stockbridge, here and there, at will. Ah! George Pulcher had the ideal life—and looked it: crimson, square, full-bodied. Judge of a horse, too, in his own estimation; a leery bird—for whose judgement Jimmy had respect—who got "the office" of any clever work as quick as most men! And he said:

"What am I going to do with this blinkin' 'orse, George?"

Without moving its head the oracle spoke, in a voice rich and raw: "Let's 'ave a look at her first, Jimmy! Don't like her name—Calliope; but you can't change what's in the Stud-book. This Jenning that trains 'er is a crusty chap.''

Jimmy nervously sucked in his lips. The cart was mounting through the hedgeless fields which fringed the Downs; larks were singing, the wheat was very green, and patches of charlock brightened everything; it was lonely, few trees, few houses, no people, extreme peace, just a few rooks crossing under a blue sky.

''Wonder if he'll offer us a drink?'' said Jimmy.

''Not he; but help yourself, my son.''

Jimmy helped himself from a large wicker-covered flask.

''Good for you, George—here's how!''

The large man shifted the reins and drank, in turn, tilting up a face whose jaw still struggled to assert itself against chins and neck.

''Well, here's your bloomin' horse,'' he said. ''She can't win the Derby now, but she may do us a bit of good yet.''

The trainer, Jenning, coming from his Sunday afternoon round of the boxes, heard the sound of wheels. He was a thin man, neat in clothes and boots, medium in height, with a slight limp, narrow grey whiskers, thin shaven lips, eyes sharp and grey.

A dog-cart stopping at his yard-gate and a rum-looking couple of customers!

''Well, gentlemen?''

''Mr. Jenning? My name's Pulcher—George Pulcher. Brought a client of yours over to see his new mare. Mr. James Shrewin, Oxford city.''

Jimmy got down and stood before his trainer's uncompromising stare.

''What mare's that?'' said Jenning.

''Calliope.''

''Calliope—Mr. Colquhoun's?''

Jimmy held out a letter.

''Dear Jenning,

''I have sold Calliope to Jimmy Shrewin, the Oxford bookie. He takes her with all engagements and liabilities, including your training bill. I'm frightfully sick at having to part with her, but needs must when the devil drives.

"GARDON COLQUHOUN."

The trainer folded the letter.

"Got proof of registration?"

Jimmy drew out another paper.

The trainer inspected it, and called out; "Ben, bring out Calliope. Excuse me a minute," and he walked into his house.

Jimmy stood, shifting from leg to leg. Mortification had set in; the dry abruptness of the trainer had injured even a self-esteem starved from youth.

The voice of Pulcher boomed. "Told you he was a crusty devil. 'And 'im a bit of his own."

The trainer was coming back.

"My bill," he said. "When you've paid it you can have the mare. I train for gentlemen."

"The hell you do!" said Pulcher.

Jimmy said nothing, staring at the bill—seventy-eight pounds three shillings! A buzzing fly settled in the hollow of his cheek, and he did not even brush it off. Seventy-eight pounds!

The sound of hoofs roused him. Here came his horse, throwing up her head as if enquiring why she was being disturbed a second time on Sunday! In the movement of that small head and satin neck was something free and beyond present company.

"There she is," said the trainer. "That'll do, Ben. Stand, girl!"

Answering to a jerk or two of the halter, the mare stood kicking slightly with a white hind foot and whisking her tail. Her bright coat shone in the sunlight, and little shivers and wrinklings passed up and down its satin because of the flies. Then, for a moment, she stood still, ears pricked, eyes on the distance.

Jimmy approached her. She had resumed her twitchings,

swishings, and slight kicking, and at a respectful distance he circled, bending as if looking at crucial points. He knew what her sire and dam had done, and all the horses that had beaten, or been beaten by them; could have retailed by the half-hour the peculiar hearsay of their careers; and here was their offspring in flesh and blood, and he was dumb! He didn't know a thing about what she ought to look like, and he knew it; but he felt obscurely moved. She seemed to him "a picture."

Completing his circle, he approached her head, white-blazed, thrown up again in listening, or scenting, and gingerly he laid his hand on her neck, warm and smooth as a woman's shoulder. She paid no attention to his touch, and he took his hand away. Ought he to look at her teeth or feel her legs? No, he was not buying her, she was his already; but he must say something. He looked round. The trainer was watching him with a little smile. For almost the first time in his life the worm turned in Jimmy Shrewin; he spoke no word and walked back to the cart.

"Take her in," said Jenning.

From his seat beside Pulcher, Jimmy watched the mare returning to her box.

"When I've cashed your cheque," said the trainer, "you can send for her"; and, turning on his heel, he went towards his house. The voice of Pulcher followed him.

"Blast your impudence! Git on, bob-tail, we'll shake the dust off 'ere."

Among the fringing fields the dog-cart hurried away. The sun slanted, the heat grew less, the colour of young wheat and of the charlock brightened.

"The tyke! By Gawd, Jimmy, I'd 'ave hit him on the mug! But you've got one there. She's a bit o' blood, my boy, and I know the trainer for her, Polman—no blasted airs about 'im."

Jimmy sucked at his cheroot.

"I ain't had your advantages, George, and that's a fact. I got into it too young, and I'm a little chap. But I'll send the

. . . my cheque tomorrow. I got my pride, I 'ope!'' It was the first time that thought had ever come to him.

Though not quite the centre of the Turf, The Green Dragon had nursed a *coup* in its day, nor was it without a sense of veneration. The ownership of Calliope invested Jimmy Shrewin with the importance of those out of whom something can be had. It took time for one so long accustomed to beck and call, to mole-like procedure, and the demeanour of young bloods to realize that he had it. But slowly, with the marked increase in his unpaid-for cheroots, with the way in which glasses hung suspended when he came in, with the edgings up to him, and a certain tendency to accompany him along the street, it dawned on him that he was not only an out-of-bounds bookie, but a man. So long as he had remained unconscious of his double nature he had been content with laying the odds, as best he might, and getting what he could out of every situation, straight or crooked. Now that he was also a man, his complacency was ruffled. He suffered from a growing headiness connected with his horse. She was trained, now, by Polman, further along the Downs, too far for Pulcher's bob-tail; and through her public life was carried on at The Green Dragon, her private life required a train journey over night. Jimmy took it twice a week—touting his own horse in the August mornings up on the Downs, without drink or talk, or even cheroots. Early morning, larks singing, and the sound of galloping hoofs! In a moment of expansion he confided to Pulcher that it was ''bally 'olesome.''

There had been the slight difficulty of being mistaken for a tout by his new trainer Polman, a stoutish man with the look of one of those large sandy Cornish cats, not precisely furtive because reticence and craft are their nature. But, that once over, his personality swelled slowly. This month of August was one of those interludes, in fact, when nothing happens, but which shape the future by secret ripening.

An error to suppose that men conduct finance, high or low, from greed, or love of gambling; they do it out of self-esteem, out of an itch to prove their judgement superior to their neighbours', out of a longing for importance. George Pulcher did not despise the turning of a penny, but he valued much more the consciousness that men were saying: "Old George, what 'e says goes—knows a thing or two—George Pulcher!"

To pull the strings of Jimmy Shrewin's horse was a rich and subtle opportunity, absorbingly improvable. But first one had to study the animal's engagements, and, secondly, to gauge that unknown quality, her "form." To make anything of her this year they must "get about it." That young "toff," her previous owner, had of course flown high, entering her for classic races, high-class handicaps, neglecting the rich chances of lesser occasions.

Third to Reference in the three-year-old race at Sandown Spring—two heads—was all that was known of her, and now they have given her seven two in the Cambridgeshire. She might have a chance, and again she might not. He sat two long evenings with Jimmy in the little private room off the bar, deliberating this grave question.

Jimmy inclined to the bold course. He kept saying: "The mare's a flyer, George—she's the 'ell of a flyer!"

"Wait till she's been tried," said the oracle.

Had Polman anything that would give them a line?

Yes, he had The Shirker (named with that irony which appeals to the English), and one of the most honest four-year-olds that ever looked through bridle, who had run up against almost every animal of mark—the one horse that Polman never interfered with, for if interrupted in his training, he ran all the better; who seldom won, but was almost always placed—the sort of horse that handicappers pivot on.

"But," said Pulcher, "try her with The Shirker, and the first stable money will send her up to tens. That 'orse is so darned regular. We've got to throw a bit of dust first, Jimmy. I'll go over and see Polman."

In Jimmy's withered chest a faint resentment rose—it wasn't George's horse, but it sank again beneath his friend's bulk and reputation.

The "bit of dust" was thrown at the ordinary hour of

exercise over the Long Mile on the last day of August—the five-year-old Hangman carrying eight stone seven, the three-year-old Parrot seven stone five; what Calliope was carrying nobody but Polman knew. The forethought of George Pulcher had secured the unofficial presence of the Press. The instructions to the boy on Calliope were to be there at the finish if he could, but on no account to win. Jimmy and George Pulcher had come out over night. They sat together in the dog-cart by the clump of bushes which marked the winning-post, with Polman on his cob on the far side.

By a fine, warm light the three horses were visible to the naked eye in the slight dip down by the start. And, through the glasses, invested in now that he had a horse, Jimmy could see every movement of his mare with her blazed face—rather on her toes, like the bright chestnut and "bit o' blood" she was. He had a pit-patting in his heart, and his lips were tight pressed. Suppose she was no good after all, and that young "Cocoon" had palmed him off a pup! But mixed in with his financial fear was an anxiety more intimate, as if his own value were at stake.

From George Pulcher came an almost excited gurgle.

"See the tout! See 'im behind the bush. Thinks we don't know 'e's there, wot oh!"

Jimmy bit into his cheroot. "They're running," he said.

Rather wide, the black Hangman on the far side, Calliope in the middle, they came sweeping up the long mile. Jimmy held his tobaccoed breath. The mare was going freely—a length or two behind—making up her ground! Now for it!—

Ah! she 'ad the 'Angman beat, and ding-dong with this Parrot! It was all he could do to keep from calling out. With a rush and cludding of hoofs they passed—the blazed nose just behind the Parrot's bay nose—dead heat all but, with the Hangman beat a good length!

"There 'e goes, Jimmy! See the blank scuttlin' down the 'ill like a blinkin' rabbit. That'll be in tomorrow's paper, that trial will. Ah! but 'ow to read it—that's the point."

The horses had been wheeled and were sidling back; Polman was going forward on his cob.

Jimmy jumped down. Whatever that fellow had to say, he meant to hear. It was his horse! Narrowly avoiding the hoofs of his hot, fidgeting mare, he said sharply:

"What about it?"

Polman never looked you in the face; his speech came as if not intended to be heard by anyone:

"Tell Mr. Shrewin how she went."

"Had a bit up my sleeve. If I'd hit her a smart one, I could ha' landed by a length or more."

"That so?" said Jimmy with a hiss. "Well, *don't* you hit her; she don't want hittin'. You remember that."

The boy said sulkily: "All right!"

"Take her home," said Polman. Then, with that reflective averted air of his, he added: "She was carrying eight stone, Mr. Shrewin; you've got a good one there. She's the Hangman at level weights."

Something wild leaped up in Jimmy—the Hangman's form unrolled itself before him in the air—he had a horse—he dam' well had a horse!

But how delicate is the process of backing your fancy! The planting of a commission—what tender and efficient work before it will flower! That sixth sense of the racing man, which, like the senses of savages in great forests, seizes telepathically on what is not there, must be dulled, duped, deluded.

George Pulcher had the thing in hand. One might have thought the gross man incapable of such a fairy touch, such power of sowing with one hand and reaping with the other. He intimated rather than asserted that Calliope and the Parrot were one and the same thing. "The Parrot," he said, "couldn't win with seven stone—no use thinkin' of this Calliope."

Local opinion was the rock on which, like a great tactician, he built. So long as local opinion was adverse, he could dribble money on in London; the natural jump-up from every long shot taken was dragged back by the careful radiation of disparagement from the seat of knowledge.

Jimmy was the fly in his ointment of those balmy early weeks while snapping up every penny of long odds, before suspicion could begin to work from the persistence of enquiry. Half-a-dozen times he found the ''little cuss within an ace of blowing the gaff on his own blinkin' mare''; seemed unable to run his horse down; the little beggar's head was swellin'! Once Jimmy had even got up and gone out, leaving a gin and bitters untasted on the bar. Pulcher improved on his absence in the presence of a London tout.

''Saw the trial meself! Jimmy don't like to think he's got a stiff 'un.''

And next morning his London agent snapped up some thirty-threes again.

According to the trial the mare was the Hangman at seven stone two, and really hot stuff—a seven-to-one chance. It was none the less with a sense of outrage that, opening the *Sporting Life* on the last day of September, he found her quoted at 100–8. Whose work was this?

He reviewed the altered situation in disgust. He had invested about half the stable commission of three hundred pounds at an average of thirty-to-one, but, now that she had ''come'' in the betting, he would hardly average tens with the rest. What fool had put his oar in?

He learned the explanation two days later. The rash, the unknown backer, was Jimmy! He had acted, it appeared, from jealousy; a bookmaker—it took one's breath away!

''Backed her on your own just because that young 'Cocoon' told you he fancied her!''

Jimmy looked up from the table in his ''office,'' where he was sitting in wait for the scanty custom of the Long Vacation.

''She's not *his* horse,'' he said sullenly. ''I wasn't going to have *him* get the cream.''

''What did you put on?'' growled Pulcher.

''Took five hundred to thirty, and fifteen twenties.''

''An' see what it's done—knocked the bottom out of the commission. Am I to take that fifty as part of it?''

Jimmy nodded.

"That leaves an 'undred to invest," said Pulcher, somewhat mollified. He stood, with his mind twisting in this thick still body. "It's no good waitin' now," he said; "I'll work the rest of the money on today. If I can average tens on the balance, we'll 'ave six thousand three hundred to play with and the stakes. They tell me Jenning fancies this Diamond Stud of his. *He* ought to know the form with Calliope, blast him! We got to watch that."

They had! Diamond Stud, a four-year-old with eight stone two, was being backed as if the Cambridgeshire were over. From fifteens he advanced to sevens, thence to favouritism at fives. Pulcher bit on it. Jenning *must* know where he stood with Calliope! It meant—it meant she couldn't win! The tactician wasted no time in vain regret. Establish Calliope in the betting and lay off. The time had come to utilize The Shirker.

It was misty on the Downs—fine-weather mist of a bright October. The three horses became spectral on their way to the starting-point. Polman had thrown the Parrot in again, but this time he made no secret of the weights. The Shirker was carrying eight seven, Calliope eight, the Parrot seven stone.

Once more, in the cart, with his glasses sweeping the bright mist, Jimmy had that pit-patting in his heart. Here they came! His mare leading—all riding hard—a genuine finish! They passed—The Shirker beaten, a clear length, with the Parrot at his girth. Beside him in the cart, George Pulcher mumbled;

"She's The Shirker at eight stone four, Jimmy!"

A silent drive, big with thought, back to a river inn; a silent breakfast. Over a tankard at the close the Oracle spoke.

"The Shirker, at eight stone-four, is a good 'ot chance, but no cert, Jimmy. We'll let 'em know this trial quite open, weights and all. That'll bring her in the betting. And we'll watch Diamond Stud. If he drops back we'll know Jenning thinks he can't beat us now. If Diamond Stud stands up, we'll know Jenning thinks he's still got our mare safe. Then our line'll be clear: we lay off the lot, pick up a thousand or so, and 'ave the mare in at a nice weight at Liverpool.''

Jimmy's smudged-in eyes stared hungrily.

"How's that?'' he said. "Suppose she wins!''

"Wins! If we lay off the lot, she *won't* win.''

"Pull her!''

George Pulcher's voice sank half an octave with disgust.

"Pull her! Who's talked of pullin'? She'll run a bye, that's all. We shan't ever know whether she could 'a won or not.''

Jimmy sat silent; the situation was such as his life during sixteen years had waited for. They stood to win both ways with a bit of handling.

"Who's to ride?'' he said.

"Polman's got a call on Docker. He can just ride the weight. Either way he's good for us—strong finisher, and a rare judge of distance; knows how to time things to a T. Win or not, he's our man.''

Jimmy was deep in figures. Laying-off at sevens, they would still win four thousand and the stakes.

"I'd like a win,'' he said.

"Ah!'' said Pulcher. "But there'll be twenty in the field, my son; no more uncertain race than that bally Cambridgeshire. We could pick up a thou—as easy as I pick up this pot. Bird in the 'and, Jimmy, and a good 'andicap in the bush. If she wins, she's finished. Well, we'll put this trial about and see 'ow Jenning pops.''

Jenning popped amazingly. Diamond Stud receded a point, then re-established himself at nine to two. Jenning was clearly not dismayed.

George Pulcher shook his head, and waited, uncertain still which way to jump. Ironical circumstances decided him.

Term had begun; Jimmy was busy at his seat of custom. By some miracle of guardianly intervention, young Colquhoun had not gone broke. He was "up" again, eager to retrieve his reputation, and that little brute Jimmy would not lay against his horse! He merely sucked in his cheeks, and answered: "I'm not layin' my own 'orse.'' It was felt that he was not the man he had been; assertion had come into his manner, he was better dressed. Someone had seen him at the station looking quite a "toff" in a blue box-cloth coat standing well out from his wisp of a figure, and with a pair of brown race-glasses slung over the shoulder. Altogether the "little brute was getting too big for his boots."

And this strange improvement hardened the feeling that his horse was a real good thing. Patriotism began to burn in Oxford. Here was a "snip" that belonged to them, as it were, and the money in support of it, finding no outlet, began to ball.

A week before the race—with Calliope at nine to one, and very little doing—young Colquhoun went up to town, taking with him the accumulated support of betting Oxford. That evening she stood at sixes. Next day the public followed on.

George Pulcher took advantage. In this crisis of the proceedings he acted on his own initiative. The mare went back to eights, but the deed was done. He had laid off the whole bally lot, including the stake money. He put it to Jimmy that evening in a nutshell.

"We pick up a thousand, and the Liverpool as good as in our pocket. I've done worse."

Jimmy grunted out: "She could 'a won."

"Not she. Jenning knows—and there's others in the race. This Wasp is goin' to take a lot of catchin', and Deerstalker's not out of it. He's a hell of a horse, even with that weight."

Again Jimmy grunted, slowly sucking down his gin and bitters. Sullenly he said:

"Well, I don't want to put money in the pocket of young 'Cocoon' and his crowd. Like his impudence, backin' my horse as if it was his own."

"We'll 'ave to go and see her run, Jimmy."

"Not me," said Jimmy.

"What! First time she runs! It won't look natural."

"No," repeated Jimmy. "I don't want to see 'er beat."

George Pulcher laid his hand on a skinny shoulder.

"Nonsense, Jimmy. You've got to, for the sake of your reputation. You'll enjoy seein' your mare saddled. We'll go up over night. I shall 'ave a few pound on Deerstalker. I believe he can beat this Diamond Stud. And you leave Docker to me; I'll 'ave a word with him at Gatwick tomorrow. I've known 'im since he was that 'igh; an' 'e ain't much more now.''

"All right!" growled Jimmy.

The longer you can bet on a race the greater its fascination. Handicappers can properly enjoy the beauty of their work; clubmen and oracles of the course have due scope for reminiscence and prophecy; bookmakers in lovely leisure can indulge a little of their own calculated preferences, instead of being hurried to soulless conclusions by a half-hour's market on the course; the professional backer has the longer in which to dream of his fortune made at last by some hell of a horse—spotted somewhere as interfered with, left at the post, running green, too fat, not fancied, backward—now bound to win this hell of a race. And the general public has the chance to read the horses' names in the betting news for days and days; and what a comfort that is!

Jimmy Shrewin was not one of those philosophers who justify the great and growing game of betting on the ground that it improves the breed of an animal less and less in use. He justified it much more simply—he lived by it. And in the whole of his career of nearly twenty years since he made hole-and-corner books among the boys of London, he had never stood so utterly on velvet as that morning when his horse must win him five hundred pounds by merely losing. He had spent the night in London anticipating a fraction of his gains with George Pulcher at a music-hall. And, in a first-class carriage, as became an owner, he travelled down to Newmarket by an early special. An early special key turned in the lock of the carriage door, preserved their numbers at six, all professionals, with blank, rather rolling eyes, mouths shut or slightly fishy, ears to the ground; and the only natural talker, a red-faced man, who had "been at it thirty years." Intoning the pasts and futures of this hell of a horse or that, even he was silent on the race in hand; and the journey was half over before the beauty of their own judgements loosened tongues thereon. George Pulcher started it.

"I fancy Deerstalker," he said; "he's a hell of a horse."

"Too much weight," said the red-faced man. "What about this Calliope?"

"Ah!" said Pulcher. "D'you fancy your mare, Jimmy?"

With all eyes turned on him, lost in his blue box-cloth coat, brown bowler, and cheroot smoke, Jimmy experienced a subtle thrill. Addressing the space between the red-faced man and Pulcher, he said:

"If she runs up to 'er looks."

"Ah!" said Pulcher, "she's dark—nice mare, but a bit light and shelly."

"Lopez out o' Calendar," muttered the red-faced man. "Lopez didn't stay, but he was the hell of horse over seven furlongs. The Shirker ought to 'ave told you a bit."

Jimmy did not answer. It gave him pleasure to see the red-faced man's eye trying to get past, and failing.

"Nice race to pick up. Don't fancy the favourite meself; he'd nothin' to beat at Ascot."

"Jenning knows what he's about," said Pulcher.

Jenning! Before Jimmy's mind passed again that first sight of his horse, and the trainer's smile, as if he—Jimmy Shrewin, who owned her—had been dirt. Tyke! To have the mare beaten by one of his! A deep, subtle vexation had oppressed him at times all these last days since George Pulcher had decided in favour of the mare's running a bye. D—n George Pulcher! He took too much on himself! Thought he had Jimmy Shrewin in his pocket! He looked at the block of crimson opposite. Aunt Sally! If George Pulcher could tell what was passing in his mind!

But driving up to the Course he was not above sharing a sandwich and a flask. In fact, his feelings were unstable and gusty—sometimes resentment, sometimes the old respect of his friend's independent bulk. The dignity of ownership takes long to establish itself in those who have been kicked about.

"All right with Docker," murmured Pulcher, sucking at the wicker flask. "I gave him the office at Gatwick."

"She could 'a won," muttered Jimmy.

"Not she, my boy; there's two at least can beat 'er."

Like all oracles, George Pulcher could believe what he wanted to.

Arriving, they entered the grandstand enclosure, and over the dividing railings Jimmy gazed at the Cheap Ring, already filling up with its usual customers. Faces and umbrellas—the same old crowd. How often had he been in that Cheap Ring, with hardly room to move, seeing nothing, hearing nothing but "Two to one on the field!" "Two to one on the field!" "Threes Swordfish!" "Fives Alabaster!" "Two to one on the field!" Nothing but a sea of men like himself, and a sky overhead. He was not exactly conscious of criticism, only of a dull "Glad I'm shut of that lot" feeling.

Leaving George Pulcher deep in conversation with a crony, he lighted a cheroot and slipped out on to the Course. He passed the Jockey Club enclosure. Some early "toffs" were there in twos and threes, exchanging wisdom. He looked at them without envy or malice. He was an owner himself now, almost one of them in a manner of thinking. With a sort of relish he thought of how his past life had circled round those "toffs," slippery, shadowlike, kicked about; and now he could get up on the Downs away from "toffs," George Pulcher, all that crowd, and smell the grass, and hear the bally larks, and watch his own mare gallop!

They were putting the numbers up for the first race. Queer not to be betting, not to be touting round; queer to be giving it a rest! Utterly familiar with those names on the board, he was utterly unfamiliar with the shapes they stood for.

I'll go and see 'em come out of the paddock, he thought, and moved on, skimpy in his bell-shaped coat and billycock with flattened brim. The clamour of the Rings rose behind him while he was entering the paddock.

Very green, very peaceful, there; not many people, yet! Three horses in the second race were being led slowly in a sort of winding ring; and men were clustering round the further gate where the horses would come out. Jimmy joined them, sucking at his cheroot. They were a picture! Damn it!

He didn't know but that 'orses laid over men! Pretty creatures!

One by one they passed out of the gate, a round dozen. Selling platers, but pictures for all that!

He turned back towards the horses being led about; and the old instinct to listen took him close to little groups. Talk was all of the big race. From a tall "toff" he caught the word Calliope.

"Belongs to a bookie, they say."

Bookie! Why not? Wasn't a bookie as good as any other? Ah! and sometimes better than these young snobs with everything to their hand! A bookie—well, what chance had he ever had?

A big brown horse came by.

"That's Deerstalker," he heard the "toff" say.

Jimmy gazed at George Pulcher's fancy with a sort of hostility. Here came another—Wasp, six stone ten, and Deerstalker nine stone—top and bottom of the race!

My 'orse'd beat either o' them, he thought stubbornly. Don't like that Wasp.

The distant roar was hushed. They were running in the first race! He moved back to the gate. The quick clamour rose and dropped, and here they came—back into the paddock, darkened with sweat, flanks heaving a little!

Jimmy followed the winner, saw the jockey weigh in.

"What jockey's that?" he asked.

"That? Why, Docker!"

Jimmy stared. A short, square, bow-legged figure, with a hardwood face! Waiting his chance, he went up to him and said:

"Docker, you ride my 'orse in the big race."

"Mr. Shrewin?"

"The same," said Jimmy. The jockey's left eyelid drooped a little. Nothing responded in Jimmy's face. "I'll see you before the race," he said.

Again the jockey's eyelid wavered, he nodded and passed on.

Jimmy stared at his own boots; they struck him suddenly

as too yellow and not at the right angle. But why, he couldn't say.

More horses now—those of the first race being unsaddled, clothed, and led away. More men—three familiar figures: young "Cocoon" and two others of his Oxford customers.

Jimmy turned sharply from them. Stand their airs?—not he! He had a sudden sickish feeling. With a win, he'd have been a made man—on his own! Blast George Pulcher and his caution! To think of being back in Oxford with those young bloods jeering at his beaten horse! He bit deep into the stump of his cheroot, and suddenly came on Jenning standing by a horse with a star on its bay forehead. The trainer gave him no sign of recognition, but sighed to the boy to lead the horse into a stall, and followed, shutting the door. It was exactly as if he had said: "Vermin about!"

An evil little smile curled Jimmy's lips. The tyke!

The horses for the second race passed out of the paddock gate, and he turned to find his own. His ferreting eyes soon sighted Polman. What the cat-faced fellow knew, or was thinking, Jimmy could not tell. Nobody could tell.

"Where's the mare?" he said.

"Just coming round."

No mistaking her; fine as a star; shiny-coated, sinuous, her blazed face held rather high! Who said she was "shelly?" She was a picture! He walked a few paces close to the boy.

"That's Calliope. . . . H'm! . . . Nice filly! . . . Looks fit. . . . Who's this James Shrewin? . . . What's she at? . . . I like her looks."

His horse! Not a prettier filly in the world!

He followed Polman into her stall to see her saddled. In the twilight there he watched her toilet; the rub-over; the exact adjustments; the bottle of water to the mouth; the buckling of the bridle—watched her head high above the boy keeping her steady with gentle pulls of a rein in each hand held out a little wide, and now and then stroking her blazed nose; watched her pretence of nipping at his hand; he watched the beauty of her exaggerated in this half-lit isolation away from the others, the life and litheness in her satin body, the wilful expectancy in her bright soft eyes.

Run a bye! This bit o' blood—this bit o' fire! This horse of his! Deep within that shell of blue box-cloth against the stall partition a thought declared itself: I'm—if she shall! She can beat the lot! And she's—well going to!

The door was thrown open, and she led out. He moved alongside. They were staring at her, following her. No wonder! She was a picture, his horse—his! She had gone to Jimmy's head.

They passed Jenning with Diamond Stud waiting to be mounted. Jimmy shot him a look. Let the—wait!

His mare reached the palings and was halted. Jimmy saw the short square figure of her jockey, in the new magenta cap and jacket—*his* cap, *his* jacket! Beautiful they looked, and no mistake!

"A word with you," he said.

The jockey halted, looked quickly round.

"All right, Mr. Shrewin. I know."

Jimmy's eyes smouldered at him; hardly moving his lips, he said, intently: "You—well don't! You'll—well ride her to win. Never mind *him*! If you don't, I'll have you off the turf. Understand me! You'll—well ride 'er to win."

The jockey's jaw dropped.

"All right, Mr. Shrewin."

"See it is," said Jimmy with a hiss . . .

"Mount jockeys!"

He saw magenta swing into the saddle. And suddenly, as if smitten with the plague, he scuttled away.

He scuttled to where he could see them going down—seventeen. No need to search for his colours; they blazed, like George Pulcher's countenance, or a rhododendron bush in sunlight, above that bright chestnut with the white nose, curveting a little as she was led past.

Now they came cantering—Deerstalker in the lead.

"He's a hell of a horse, Deerstalker," said someone behind.

Jimmy cast a nervous glance around. No sign of George Pulcher!

One by one they cantered past, and he watched them with a cold feeling in his stomach. Still unused to sight of the creatures out of which he made his living, they *all* seemed to him hells of horses.

The same voice said:

"New colours! Well, you can see 'em, and the mare too. She's a showy one. Calliope? She's goin' back in the bettin', though."

Jimmy moved up through the Ring.

"Four to one on the field!" "Six Deerstalker!" "Sevens Magistrate!" "Ten to one Wasp!" "Ten to one Calliope!" "Four to one Diamond Stud!" "Four to one on the field!"

Steady as a rock, that horse of Jenning, and his own going back.

"Twelves Calliope!" he heard, just as he reached the stand. The telepathic genius of the Ring missed nothing— almost!

A cold shiver went through him. What had he done by his words to Docker? Spoiled the golden egg laid so carefully? But perhaps she couldn't win even if they let her! He began to mount the stand, his mind in the most acute confusion.

A voice said: "Hullo, Jimmy! Is she going to win?"

One of his young Oxford sparks was jammed against him on the stairway!

He raised his lip in a sort of snarl, and, huddling himself, slipped through and up ahead. He came out and edged in close to the stairs where he could get play for his glasses. Behind him one of those who improve the shining hour among backers cut off from opportunity, was intoning the odds a point shorter than below. "Three to one on the field." "Fives Deerstalker." "Eight to one Wasp."

"What price Calliope?" said Jimmy, sharply.

"Hundred to eight."

"Done!" Handing him the eight, he took the ticket. Behind him the man's eyes moved fishily, and he resumed his incantation.

''Three to one on the field . . . three to one on the field. Six to one Magistrate.''

On the wheeling bunch of colours at the start Jimmy trained his glasses. Something had broken clean away and come half the course—something in yellow.

''Eights Magistrate. Eight to one Magistrate,'' drifted up.

So they had spotted that! Precious little they didn't spot!

Magistrate was round again, and being ridden back. Jimmy rested his glasses a moment, and looked down. Swarms in the Cheap Ring, Tattersalls, the stands—a crowd so great you could lose George Pulcher in it. Just below a little man was making silent, frantic signals with his arms across to someone in the Cheap Ring. Jimmy raised his glasses. In line now—magenta third from the rails!

''They're off!'' The hush, you could cut it with a knife! Something in green away on the right—Wasp! What a bat they were going! And a sort of numbness in Jimmy's mind cracked suddenly; his glasses shook; his thin, weasily face became suffused and quivered. Magenta—magenta—two from the rails! He could make no story of the race such as he could read in tomorrow's paper—he could see nothing but magenta.

Out of the dip now, and coming fast—green still leading—something in violet, something in tartan, closing.

''Wasp's beat!'' ''The favourite—the favourite wins!'' ''Deerstalker—Deerstalker wins!'' ''What's that in pink on the rails?''

It was *his* in pink on the rails! Behind him a man went suddenly mad.

''Deerstalker—Come on with 'im, Stee! Deerstalker'll win—Deerstalker'll win!''

Jimmy sputtered venomously: ''Will 'e? Will 'e?''

Deerstalker and his own out from the rest—opposite the Cheap Ring—neck and neck—Docker riding like a demon.

''Deerstalker! Deerstalker!'' ''Calliope wins! She wins!''

Gawd! His horse! They flashed past—fifty yards to go, and not a head between 'em!

''Deerstalker! Deerstalker!'' ''Calliope!''

He saw his mare shoot out—she'd won!

With a little queer sound he squirmed and wriggled on to the stairs. No thoughts while he squeezed, and slid, and hurried—only emotion—out of the Ring, away to the paddock. His horse!

Docker had weighed in when he reached the mare. All right! He passed with a grin. Jimmy turned almost into the body of Polman standing like an image.

"Well, Mr. Shrewin," he said to nobody, "she's won."

Damn you! thought Jimmy. Damn the lot of you! And he went up to his mare. Quivering, streaked with sweat, impatient of the gathering crowd, she showed the whites of her eyes when he put his hand up to her nose.

"Good girl!" he said, and watched her led away.

Gawd! I want a drink! he thought.

Gingerly, keeping a sharp lookout for Pulcher, he returned to the stand to get it, and to draw his hundred. But up there by the stairs the discreet fellow was no more. On the ticket was the name O. H. Jones, and nothing else. Jimmy Shrewin had been welshed! He went down at last in bad temper. At the bottom of the staircase stood George Pulcher. The big man's face was crimson, his eyes ominous. He blocked Jimmy into a corner.

"Ah!" he said; "you little crow! What the 'ell made you speak to Docker?"

Jimmy grinned. Some new body within him stood there defiant. "She's my 'orse," he said.

"You—Gawd-forsaken rat! If I 'ad you in a quiet spot I'd shake the life out of you!"

Jimmy stared up, his little spindle legs apart, like a cock-sparrow confronting an offended pigeon.

"Go 'ome," he said, "George Pulcher; and get your mother to mend your socks. You don't know 'ow! Thought I wasn't a man, did you? Well, now you—well know I am. Keep off my 'orse in future."

Crimson rushed up on crimson in Pulcher's face; he raised his heavy fists. Jimmy stood, unmoving, his little hands in his bell-coat pockets, his withered face upraised. The big man gulped as if swallowing back the tide of blood; his fists edged forward and then—dropped.

"That's better," said Jimmy, "hit one of your own size."

Emitting a deep growl, George Pulcher walked away.

"Two to one on the field—I'll back the field—Two to one on the field." "Threes Snowdrift—Fours Iron Dook."

Jimmy stood a moment mechanically listening to the music of his life, then edging out, he took a fly and was driven to the station.

All the way up to town he sat chewing his cheroot with the glow of drink inside him, thinking of that finish, and of how he had stood up to George Pulcher. For a whole day he was lost in London, but Friday saw him once more at his seat of custom in the "Corn." Not having laid against his horse, he had had a good race in spite of everything; yet, the following week, uncertain into what quagmires of quixotry she might lead him, he sold Calliope.

But for years betting upon horses that he never saw, underground like a rat, yet never again so accessible to the kicks of fortune, or so prone before the shafts of superiority, he would think of the Downs with the blinkin' larks singin', and talk of how once he—had a horse.

THE MAJOR

Colin Davy

M Y attention to the conversation flagged, and I found myself thinking how well the name Jonathan Pluck suited the man. There was a Quakerish simplicity and good will in his smooth, round face which would have charmed the stingiest old maid of her last penny, a guileless candour which invited trust.

It was only when he smiled and his small eyes twinkled and screwed up that one sensed the mischief and adventure within bidding one beware. And as Pluck was a contradiction of Jonathan, his smart clothes and almost swashbuckling manner were a contradiction of this bucolic simplicity of expression.

Jonathan Pluck: half quaker, half laughing cavalier. A man unread, uneducated, who could hardly write his name, yet capable of devising the most intricate racing "ramp," shy and diffident with strangers, yet full of confidence in himself in his own metier; ready to give a sovereign to the most undeserving tramp, or a hundred pounds to the first "confidence man," yet a hard and implacable rival in the business of racing.

And above all, a man of indomitable courage who, on a score of occasions in a score of different countries, had seen his last penny lost in some gigantic gamble, and laughing, had battled on. . . .

My thoughts were disturbed by our companion rising.

"Looks a proper old sport," remarked Jonathan Pluck, as the stranger bade us good night and left the smoking saloon.

"He certainly is that," said I. "He was owning and riding horses when you and I were in our cradles. He rode in his last 'chase on his sixtieth birthday. He was one of the 'heads' in Roddy Owen's day."

"Was he now? And did he always wear glasses?"

"Yes, and it can't have been much fun. It was before Triplex was invented. I can't think how fellows do it. Think of a wet day with your glasses all misted over, to say nothing of the mud sticking on them. You need some guts to smack one into the last fence when you're three parts blind," said I.

"I've smacked 'em into the last when I was *more* then three parts blind," said Johnnie, with a laugh, and added, "but not blind the way you mean.

"I had an owner once wot rode in glasses," he went on. "And he was a proper sport, too. He'd ride anything, and he never knew when he was beat. He was a major in the Marines. Can you beat that, Cap? He's the only officer of Marines I've ever heard who rode anything 'cept in a cab. He was a good rider, too, and as I sez, 'e never knew when he was beat.

"Determination, that's what it was. It didn't matter whether the other jocks had knocked him rotten (and some of them were rough in those days), he'd never stop trying. He won no end of races when everyone else thought he was beat. He was a devil to scrap, too. If one of the jocks gave him any sauce or had done anything a bit tough in a race, he'd come into the jocks' room and call the feller out for a scrap, no matter who he was. I remember once down in the Isle of Wight . . ." Johnny broke off. "But you want to go to bed, Cap."

"Not until I've had one more drink," I protested. "Go on, Johnnie."

As the barman replenished our glasses Johnnie began.

"It was six or seven years ago, when I had a few jumpers at Fittleton on Salisbury Plain. Two of 'em was owned by this major of Marines. Slapstoke-Keene his name was, and his friends called him 'Slapper.' None of the horses was muchers: a selling hurdler or two, two selling 'chasers and an odd one qualified to run in hunt 'chases. I'd have been tickled to death if anyone had offered me six hundred quid for the lot. None of me owners were rich. We were all pretty much in the same boat—scratching ourselves for the next tenner.

"Sometimes the bills were paid, and more often they weren't. If one of the horses fluked a race I got the stakes to put against the training bill, and the forage merchant got a bit to be goin' on with. Often enough it was difficult to find the dibs to pay the rail fare to a meeting, and many a time I couldn't find enough for a return ticket. If the horse didn't win he had to stay on at the nearest stable to the racecourse until we scraped enough to get him back. Once I had to leave one at Tenby from Easter until the Whitsuntide meeting came round, because we couldn't find his fare back.

"Quite frequently we had to put the major up because we couldn't find the fee for a professional, and, though he was a good rider for an amateur, he was by no means first class. Well, from that you can imagine we didn't often send a horse to a meeting unless we thought he had a fair chance of winning. There wasn't any question of keeping a horse and getting his weight down for a certain race. There was usually sixty or seventy quid at the winning-post which we wanted bad, and probably five or six quid gone on the rail fair; so it wasn't often we could afford to have one stopped to have a bet another day. No. No one could have hardly said we were a betting stable in those days.

"You know, Cap, people talk a lot of nonsense about 'chasing in England being crooked. How often do you hear people talk about a horse having been kept on ice for months for a certain race? If they knew that it costs about twenty quid every time you run a horse, and if they did a bit of calculating they'd see what they were saying was all foolishness. Say one is stopped three times. Well, there's sixty quid gone. The 'oss may be dropped in the weights, but everyone else knows that as well as you.

"You find he starts at six to four or even money, and you've got to risk a hell of a lot to get even that sixty back. And say you do, you're still only left with the stake to come. Your bet has only covered out-of-pocket expenses. So you'd be just as well off if you'd won the stake the first time. No. Keeping horses in order to have a bet is no job for a poor man.

"Well, I must get on with me story. One Easter I set off for the meeting at the Isle of Wight with two 'osses. One chestnut plater called Solvent belonged to the major, and the other, an awful squib of a mare called Elsie B, belonged to me. She'd been owned by a grocer in Andover, but he hadn't been able to pay his bill and I'd took the mare in payment.

"Now Solvent was the best horse we had in the stable, a real old battler, a fine old jumper and honest as the day. He'd been a hell of a good horse in his day, but had got a bit slow. He was still a good horse for a three-mile seller or a small handicap. There was a three-mile handicap on the first day of the meeting in which there was nothing much good entered, and I thought he must have a good chance of winning it. The major had wired that he couldn't get away to ride, and we had decided we could afford to put up a good pro. I'd actually engaged Hawkey Stud to ride him. Hawkey was a real good lad and was always glad to ride as good a jumper as old Solvent.

"Well, crossing over from Southampton on the boat there was all the racin' crowd and Hawkey among them. He comes up to me in the bar and asks me about the 'osses and particular about old Solvent.

" ' 'E's top hole,' I tells Hawkey. 'If Strumper don't go, 'e's the cat's pyjamas for the three-mile chase.'

" 'Strumper *don't* go,' sez Hawkey. 'Billy told me Tuesday. He goes at Torquay.'

" 'Then you've nothing to bother about,' sez I. 'It's a moral. That's the only one I was afraid of. If only things had gone a bit better I'd have a tenner on him.'

" 'Been goin' bad?' asks Hawkey.

" 'I been scrubbing me brains out to get the rail fare for these two 'osses,' I sez.

"Hawkey looked very thoughtful for a few minutes, and

then he sez, 'I know of a job what's being worked at this meeting. I might get you into it, if you had a mind.'

" 'I wish you would,' sez I. 'I'd be more than grateful.'

" 'It's a bit difficult,' sez Hawkey, scratching his head, 'but I'll go and have a talk with Bert.'

"Now by Bert he meant Bert Scoop, a big West Country bookmaker who had a finger in every pie. There was a time when he had as many as twenty horses in training, and had S.P. offices all over the country into the bargain. It was almost impossible to work anything big in the West without him.

"When he mentioned Bert I thought to myself that the job he was talking about must be a big one. Bert wouldn't be coming to a little meeting like the Isle of Wight just for the sake of his health.

"A few minutes later Hawkey comes up with Bert, and we stroll to the back end of the ship to get a bit of fresh air and find a place where we won't be interrupted.

" 'Hawkey tells me you wouldn't mind bein' in on a job we've been thinking of,' said Bert.

" 'You've got it right there, Mr. Scoop,' I said. 'If you can let me in on it, I'd be more than obliged.'

" 'Well, it's like this,' said Scoop. 'There's an animal in one race which we're thinking of backing in an S.P. job, but we're not quite sure of the opposition. If it's done properly it ought to be returned at 100 to 6. If I can be sure of the opposition we can get five hundred on.'

" 'Five hundred,' sez I. 'Can you get all that lot on and not affect the price?'

" 'All the wires are written out now. They're Dublin, if you want to know. I've only to telegraph one word and they'll be sent off five minutes before the race. There's not a chance of the price being spoiled. And the animal *will* start at a 100 to 6. It's got no form at all and I shall be laying it at that price on me own books. You leave it to me. But it's no good talking of that yet since I haven't yet arranged about the opposition. Now, Pluck, *say you had a runner in the race*, how much would you like put on for you? What would you consider fair?'

" 'A fiver each way,' sez I, laughing. 'So long as the price was 100 to 6.'

" 'Well, you're on a fiver, each way, price guaranteed,' says he.

" 'But which race is it?' I asks, suddenly feeling that I'd spoken out of my turn.

" 'The three-mile handicap,' sez Scoop.

" 'But I've got Solvent in that,' said I. 'E's a moral to win it, now that Strumper don't go. Hawkey's booked to ride. I couldn't crook *him*. What would the major say? Why the stake's worth eighty quid.'

" 'Thought you said you'd be satisfied with a fiver each way,' said Scoop; 'but perhaps I'm getting hard of hearing.'

" 'I didn't think you were talking of that race,' I said. 'What about the others? What are they on?'

" 'Never mind the others. They're my affair. It's you and your Major Slapper we're talkin' of now,' sez Scoop. 'What do you think he'd want out of it? Would the stake be enough?'

"I thought for a bit then, Cap, and did some calculating. I knew if the major was here he wouldn't consider the thing for a moment. He'd have seen himself dead before he stopped one. He was funny that way. But if I could give him a cheque equal to the stake, and tell him his horse hadn't got a winner's penalty, I thought I could square things somehow. What the eye doesn't see the heart doesn't grieve about, and anyhow, beggars can't be choosers. In the end we settled that I should have seven quid each way at 100 to 6, and the stakes to give to the major.

"It was then Scoop told me he'd squared all the others. He didn't tell me which horse was going to win, but it was to go out in front, all the others was to lie well back, and those that hadn't fallen off was to run out at the ditch on the far side of the course the second time round. You can't see that fence from the stands: it's behind a hill, and hidden by trees and gorse bushes. Nothing was to be left to chance. Even though this job horse fell at one of the last three fences the jock must be able to remount and win. All the others had to be definitely out of the race.

"As you may imagine, Cap, I didn't sleep much. I was doing multiplication sums all night."

"Well, it never rains but it snows, Cap. Next day damned if I didn't have a hunch that that squib of mine, Elsie B, might do her stuff, and I has thirty bob on her at eights in the selling hurdle. Up she comes to win by half a length, and I'm sittin' pretty with the price of me return journey *and* a bottle o' wine.

"Then we comes to the three-mile handicap. I sees Bert Scoop just before I go to weigh out Hawkey, and he whispers 'All serene. I've sent the wire to Dublin.' Well, just as Hawkey was getting on the scale, I feel a tap on my back and looks round. And who do you think it is? With his boots and breeches and colours on, and a saddle on his arm. The major!

"I nearly dropped.

" 'Hulloa, major,' sez I. 'Where have you sprung from?'

" 'I found I could just do it,' he says with a smile. 'I got away earlier than I expected. Got a fellow to motor me to Southampton, got a motor-launch from there, and here I am. Good work, what?'

" 'Good 'evvings!' says I.

" 'I'm still in time to weigh out for Solvent,' he goes on. 'I came here because I wanted to ride. I've a hunch he's going to do the trick.'

" 'Do the trick,' says I, feeling as if someone had kicked me in the belly. 'I should think 'e is!'

" 'I'm sorry, Studd,' he says to Hawkey. 'Sorry to take you off. Of course you'll get your fee, and your present, too, if he wins.'

"Hawkey looks at me, and I looks at Hawkey. 'Major, you can't hardly do that,' says I.

" 'Of course I can. Can't I?' says he, turning to the clerk of the scales.

" 'It's quite in order as long as you weigh out now, major,' comes the reply. 'I'll send out a man to alter the board.'

"You see, Cap, it was before the days of starting declarations.

"Well, before we could think of anything to say, he's on

the scales and has passed, and 'e's off to saddle the old horse. I left Hawkey standing by the scales with his mouth wide open as if he'd seen a ghost.

"I followed the major with his saddle, and I'm thinking of a million things at once. I knew it was hopeless suggesting to him that he shouldn't have a go on the old horse. I'd tried it once before and he'd been that wild I thought he was going to knock me down. Then I thinks, I know what I can do. I'll slip enough leads out of his cloth so that even if he does win he can't draw the weight. That cheered me up a bit. We're not goosed after all, I thinks.

"So when we got to the box I says: 'I'll fix him up, major. You go and borrow a pair of spurs. It might make all the difference.'

" 'Right,' says he, and off he goes.

"And then I looks at his gear, and he's got one of those damned heavy saddles and no weight cloth at all. There was nothing I could pinch which he wouldn't notice.

"When we got into the paddock I daren't look off the ground; I'm so afraid of what Bert Scoops will be looking like—and all the others too. I tries to spin the yarn to the major that the 'oss has been off his feed and perhaps it would be better if he didn't give him too hard a race, but while I'm saying it, the old devil gives out a squeal and three kicks to show what a liar I am. Then I suggests that he should lie well back in the race, which was no way to ride the horse at all.

"The major gives me a funny look and says that he knows how to ride the horse better than anyone else, which is quite true. I couldn't think of anything else, and a minute later the bell rang and he was up in the saddle and off. I didn't know which way to turn. I couldn't think of anything but 500 quid each way, seven of which was mine, all up the spout because of a major of Marines what wouldn't see reason. Such folks never ought to be allowed on a course, Cap.

"As soon as the race started it was quite obvious which runner was the job. It was the little horse called Scollops, belonging to Percy Edward who trained down in Sussex.

"He nicked off in front straight away. Another thing was

pretty plain too. I hadn't been the only one doing some thinking since the major's name was put in the frame in place of Hawkey's. The other jocks was round the major like bees round hive, and Whip Wilson gives 'im a proper duffy-up at the second fence, in spite of the fact that it was right in front of the stands.

"At the third fence Billy Twist has a go at him. Cuts right across him, trying to put him over the wing. But the major slips him, and Billy goes over the wing instead.

"At the fourth two more have a go, but old Solvent is so clever he props and twists and gets himself out of trouble, although he damn near lost the major. Both his stirrups were gone, but the luggage was still on board. After that the major nicks off after Scollops and gets clear, but the other jocks is after him like hounds running to view.

"Cap, you never see such a race. A three-mile 'chase and they hadn't yet gone a mile. . . . Jack Trudge on Scollops going a hell of a gallop in front, then the major, and hard on his heels the rest of them, half of them with their whips out. It was so funny there were times when I forgot all the money at stake.

"Well, passing the stands the second time the order was the same. Scollops in front, the major two lengths behind, and the rest hunting the major. Going over the water they began to close up on him, and as they went out of sight down the hill by the gorse bushes I thought, this is where they'll get him.

"Poor old major, I thought. You'll get what's comin' to you now. I couldn't help but feel sorry for him, Cap.

"Well, when they come into view out of the gorse bushes there's only two in it. There's Scollops still in the lead and—well, I hadn't to use me glasses. It could only be one person. The major! He'd slipped 'em somehow.

"Three fences from home Trudge looks over his shoulder, and what he sees he doesn't like, for he draws his bat. Scollops meets the next all wrong and is down as near as a toucher. The major lands level with him.

"Then it was plain to see that Scollops was beat and that Solvent was going strong. A little fellow with a squeaky voice on the top of the stand shouts out: 'Scollops wins nothing. Fifty to one bar Solvent!'

"He wasn't far wrong.

"Now when Scollops had made that blunder he had let Solvent up on his inside, and that was how they were running as they came to the last. Trudge is riding for his life, but he glances over his left shoulder to see where the major is. Then, in the last two strides he smacks his horse straight into the left wing, right across the major. The major sees what he's after, but sets his teeth and won't pull out. They hit in mid-air with a smack you could hear right down the course.

"I can see those two chestnut horses now, and in my dreams I can hear the smack. It was the worst bump I've ever seen.

"Well, there was only one thing that could happen; they both come head over heels. It was the most horrible fall you ever did see.

"There's the crowd roaring 'emselves silly and two chestnut horses sitting up on their hunkers wondering where they was, and two jocks on their knees with their heads in their hands.

"Jack Trudge gives a kick or two, stumbles to his feet, and then falls flat on his face and stays there. The major gets up slowly, staggers about for a second, then, seeing no one coming, grabs the reins. A copper standing there gives him a leg up, and he trots down the straight to win the race. Lord, Cap, you should have heard the people cheer! I never heard anything like it, not even on Derby Day.

"Well, I runs down to meet him, and for the moment I've forgotten all about the starting price job. But as I'm leading him in I remember. And then I sees Bert Scoop, the tears running down his face and laughing fit to die.

" 'What the hell is there to laugh about?' I said to him

" 'Your governor,' he said, ' 'e got on the wrong 'oss.'

"And then I looked. And Cap, if I die today, it's the truth. The 'oss I was leading in was Scollops. The major had won on him!''

on the top of the stand above ours. Scollay's was nothing

Fifty to one, he said.

WHAT'S IT GET YOU?

J. P. Marquand

THE day had been a hard one at the Seven Oaks track. Following a custom which was invariable with him when he possessed the capital, Jack White had been betting on a series of long shots. He had not been betting blindly; instead, he had drawn upon his encyclopaedic knowledge of past performances, and of sires and dams through the equine generations. For Jack White lived from an accurate digest of facts and from the reservoir of his own personal experience derived from thirty years at the track. In speaking of the financial difficulties besetting the nation, Jack White often said that if the bankers and the brokers had known as much about their securities as he did about four-legged-prospects, there would have been no need for a New Deal.

"Furthermore," he said, "they don't take distress like gentlemen, and distress is good for the soul. That's why I've got a beautiful nature, and I have got a beautiful, even, tolerant, forgiving disposition, haven't I boys? All because I know distress."

He was right, in a way. He was a magnificent object of fortitude in his bedroom in the Hotel Dixie that evening, tilted back in his chair, his shoes off, his vest unbuttoned. He had played five of his selections to win that afternoon and had watched them good-naturedly through his nickel-rimmed spectacles as they had faded; and now he seemed oblivious of nervous strain, only gently, hospitably weary.

"It was a nice day, boys," he said; "it always is, with sun and seven good honest races. Set down on the bed, boys, and help yourselves to cigars and whisky; it's all on me." His partner, Henry Bledsoe, stirred a spoonful of bicarbonate of soda into a glass of water. It was evident that Mr. Bledsoe did not agree with Mr. White.

"Honest hell!" he said. "This track is packed with operators who ought to be in stripes. The stewards and the paddock judges are blind, and what's more—" Mr. Bledsoe groaned "—the sport is gone," he said; "there ain't no gentlemen anymore."

Jack White looked at him in mild rebuke. "Henry," he said, "don't get passionate. Henry, you've been saying the same thing for thirty years."

Mr. Bledsoe's lean jaws clamped together and he slapped a bony hand on his knee. "Well, it's true," he said. "Ain't it?"

Jack White answered with another question: "You and I've been honest, haven't we? And yet we've made a living."

"Well, it ain't your fault we have," snapped Henry.

Jack White blew a cloud of cigar smoke before him. "No, not anybody's fault," he answered. "I may be romantic, but I do like to have ideals. I like to think that the average race is straight, and I believe it is. Maybe a race is straight because a horse is straight if he has a proper family tree. He's there to run because his kind have run. He's there to run because he's honest. If he has the heart to go, he goes; and no ninety-pound boy on him is going to stop him much and no electric shocks and dope will make him go much faster. If he has the heart, he goes; if he hasn't, he fades out. No, sir, it's the horse who wins the race."

"Gentlemen," said Henry Bledsoe, "ain't it amazing that he never learns a thing?"

Jack White stared into another cloud of smoke without giving any signs of having heard. His mind was clearly back at the track again, moving pleasantly through a gallery of memories. "Henry," he said, "Honeyboy in the fifth race, did he remind you of anything? He did me, Henry."

Mr. Bledsoe scratched his chin, and the room was silent, as he thought, respectfully silent.

At any moment, in such company, a piece of information might be dropped that was as sound as a Coolidge dollar. Henry Bledsoe's slightly haggard face had brightened with understanding.

"You can't fool me on horses, Jack," he said. "I seen it in the paddock. He was like Mr. Cavanaugh's Fighting Bob, but I could tell the difference in the dark." Mr. Bledsoe glanced around the room and smiled bitterly. "And what's more, gentlemen," he said, "I can tell you just what's coming. My dear old friend, Mr. White, who would lose his shirt each meeting if it weren't for me, is going to tell you a story to back up his own convictions. He's going to tell you about Daisy Cavanaugh, who handled horses down in the state of Maryland last year; and he's going to tell you about Mr. Cavanaugh's Fighting Bob, an unlikely three-year-old, if there ever was one, in order to prove that there are still gentlemen on the track; and when he's finished, it won't mean a damn thing, that's all . . . Jack, do I have to listen? If I do, I want more soda."

Jack White blew another cloud of smoke. "Give him more soda, boys," he said. "But there's one thing, Henry: the old man was a gentleman."

Henry Bledsoe seemed refreshed by his second spoonful of bicarbonate. "Yes," he said, "old Mr. Cavanaugh, he certainly was a gentleman, and what did it get him, White?"

Gentlemen [said Jack White], I don't need to tell you about the track at Langleyville, that Mecca where sportsmen have gathered each spring and autumn to follow the vicissitudes of the running horse for over a generation. Losing or winning, I can be happy at Langleyville. The officials, right down to the gate keepers, are capital fellows, and the restaurant proprietor is very apt to trust you, if you look him in the eye. I love to look across that fine oval of green out to the rolling country beyond it. It all speaks to me of horse-flesh. Yes, and educated money, and best of all I like the air, the

spring air of the Chesapeake that is half rich land and half
salt water. . . . All right, Henry, I won't go on, but I love
artistic places.

That is why I always stop at Mrs. Griscom's boarding
house when I am down at Langleyville. The exterior of that
boarding house, two miles out of town, may not be superfi-
cially attractive, but, believe me, it has ever been a sanctuary
of the harassed racing men. Mrs. Griscom, you may recall,
is the widow of Sam Griscom, one of the most passionate
plungers in the history of the track, who shot himself at New
Orleans the day when Lightning Joe ran fourth in the Creole
Handicap. Though I do not approve personally of such
heights of feeling, that accident of Sam's, who was essen-
tially a capital fellow, did much for Mrs. Griscom's charity.
Yes, gentlemen, you can take it from me, go to Mrs. Griscom
when you are in distress. Her features may be stern, but in
her heart she knows the accidents of chance.

Accurately speaking, Henry and I were not in great throes
of distress when a kindly motorist set us down at Langleyville
one early April morning three days before the meet opened.
Personally, I should have preferred taking the train, but Henry
was holding the toll, and Henry is kind of mean with money.
Henry's got a Yankee streak that way. It was a beautiful, early
April morning, and the sun was shining on the dewy streets
of Langleyville. As we stood on the sidewalk with our suit-
cases, near the courthouse, it was like coming home. We
hadn't been in front of the courthouse half a minute before a
party I had seen near the paddock in Miami came up to us.

"Hey, Mr. White," he said, "hey, Mr. Bledsoe, will you
join me at breakfast at the Langley House?"

I did not like his looks. He was the kind who wouldn't do
something for nothing; he was youngish—which wasn't
against him—and well dressed—and that wasn't against him,
either. It was his face a pinky face with sandy eyebrows and
a round button of a nose and rosebud lips. I did not like his
face.

"That's kind of you, mister," I began.

"Greenway," he said—"Joe Greenway, to you, Mr. White. You're here early, aren't you? So am I."

Then Henry spoke up. "Thank you, Mr. Greenway," he said. "Mr. White and I have had a very hearty breakfast. We're waiting for a bus. Good morning, Mr. Greenway."

I don't know what it is about Henry, but he has no sentiment and gentle manners. "Henry," I said, "I was hungry and you took away my breakfast."

Henry only snapped his jaws together. "I'd rather go hungry," he said, "and keep my reputation. Won't you never learn to be careful who you're seen with? That boy is one of the Maxey crowd."

Now, everybody at the track has heard of Maxey. Personally, I have found him a capital fellow within limits, but everybody didn't. Jake Maxey had got into trouble at Miami, and there was a little shooting trouble in Hamilton last summer where his name was mentioned. I could see Henry's point in not wanting to be seen with one of Maxey's boys.

"What's he doing here?" I asked.

Henry clicked his teeth again. "We'll find out soon enough," he said. "You keep away from Maxey, White. Thank God I've got the roll."

"If you won't eat with Maxey's boy," I said, "let's you and me go to the hotel ourselves."

"I said," said Henry, "thank God I've got the roll. You and me are conserving capital, White, and we'll keep on conserving until we find an investment. We'll get breakfast at Mrs. Griscom's."

"Then let's hire a cab. I'm getting faint," I said.

"Hire a cab, nothing," said Henry. "We'll wait here till we get a free ride. We've only got three hundred dollars, and we don't break in until we get an investment."

It took us two hours to get to Mrs. Griscom's, but Henry was right, for we finally got set down there in front of her place for nothing. It was like being at home, once we got to Mrs. Griscom's. She took us into the parlour right away.

"You're early, boys," she said. "You wouldn't be here early, if you wasn't in distress. Well, all the rooms are taken."

"Mrs. Griscom," I said, "you come out on the front porch with me. . . . Henry, you stay here." I knew that Mrs. Griscom would be all right when we were alone. "Did you take a good look at Henry?" I asked her. "He looks just the way Sam did at New Orleans, Mrs. Griscom. You don't want Henry on your conscience, do you?"

"He's got money, and he's holding out," she said. "I know Henry."

"Yes, Mrs. Griscom, you're right," I told her. "But you know how Henry is when he gets moods. Just now he wants to feel he's getting something for nothing. When he gets it, Henry will pay for it all right."

"All right," said Mrs. Griscom, "you can have the two back rooms, and you better go into the dining room. They're having a late breakfast."

"Who?" I asked.

"The Cavanaughs," she told me. "Old Mr. Cavanaugh and his daughter Daisy."

"Not old Hendrick Cavanaugh, the owner?" I asked her. "I thought old Cavanaugh was through."

"Well, he's here," she said. "They've brought down six horses they've been boarding at Oak Hill, and the girl, she's conditioning them. She's a dear, sweet girl, too, even if she dresses like a jockey. She's going to turn the horses over to Shiny Denny."

The name made me remember Mr. Greenway by the courthouse. You have to be quick in my business in putting facts together. "I want to know," I said. "Shiny Denny was Maxey's trainer, wasn't he, back in '32?"

Mrs. Griscom understood me, and we exchanged a meaning glance. Life on the track moves as fast as the horses. I could recall the time just as well as she could when the Cavanaugh stables were known up and down the coast and when you could see the Cavanaugh colours—maroon and white and yellow—on almost any track.

"Mr. Cavanaugh needs money," she said.

"Does he own anything?" I asked.

And Mrs. Griscom sighed. "One three-year-old," she

said, "that Fighting Bob. Out of his old Daisy Dimple by Bob Bender. Maxey's trainer will saddle him in part payment for conditioning his string."

Names, as everyone must know, have a way of bobbing up and down. Horse breeding and horse sense don't often go hand in hand. In the minute, as I stood on the front porch, I was fitting together in my mind everything I had heard about old man Cavanaugh. The word was that the depression had cleaned him out. His place, Oak Hill, with its five hundred acres, its thirty-room house, its stables and its private track, had been on sale for the past five years, while the paint was peeling off it and the roofs were beginning to leak. His racing string had been sold off five years back, with the exception of two colts and his old mare, Daisy Dimple. Then he had gone in for boarding for friends and others. It was none of my business, but just the same it hurt me to think of an operator like Maxey, whose money was made from half a dozen rackets, boarding horses at Oak Hill. As I say, I was piecing the facts together, even down to this three-year-old, Fighting Bob, that was Cavanaugh's own property. Fighting Bob had performed once the previous year on the track in one of the maiden races. He had been so wild then that they couldn't get him in the starting stall. The Daisy Dimple colts were either brilliant or very wild. I looked at Mrs. Griscom and asked her a single question, purely out of curiosity:

"How does it happen Cavanaugh's staying with you?"

"Same reason as you," she said. "He was a friend of my husband's. He was awful kind to Sam." Then she looked me up and down and made a remark which I do not care to interpret:

"Mr. Cavanaugh's a real gentleman."

I sighed. "I don't like it," I said; "it don't fit right."

"What don't fit right?" she asked.

"Maxey's trainer boarding horses with a gentleman!"

I had never met Mr. Cavanaugh socially until that morning in Mrs. Griscom's dining room. He was the kind who had the same manners for everyone—elegant, fine manners. He stood up when Mrs. Griscom introduced us, a thin old man, slightly sprung in the knees. He wore a suit with small black-and-white checks that might have been smart fifteen years ago, and a pearl-gray Ascot tie. His face was lean and clean-bred like his hands. He had a snow-white moustache, waxed at the ends, and white curly hair.

"Gentlemen," he said, "I'm very greatly honoured. Though our paths have, unfortunately, never met, reputation travels far. Everyone who knows the sport of kings has seen Mr. Bledsoe at the track in the mists of early morning, and, Mr. White, I have heard you highly spoken of in many, many places. It is an honour to have you both complete our company. I look forward to happy evenings during the meeting, gentlemen. . . . Daisy, me dear, may I present Mr. Bledsoe and Mr. White?"

At first I thought it was all make-believe, but it wasn't. It was only the way he talked. His eyes were kind and steady, like his voice. He was bowing to a girl in boots and breeches standing beside him, his daughter, Daisy. Ready to ride, she would not have tipped the scales at ninety pounds. She had a figure like a boy's in the paddock; she even had that jockey slouch. She had short, yellow, curly hair and her face was as pretty as a movie queen's. Her eyes were steady like the old man's and she had a rider's mouth, firm, but not hard enough to be cruel. Daisy Cavanaugh was a lady, pants and boots and all.

"You've got nice hands, miss," I said. "I can always tell a rider as soon as I shake hands."

"Thank you," she said, "I have to have them. We've brought down Mr. Denny's horses from the farm, six of them—they're quite a handful—and one of our own, Fighting Bob."

Henry didn't say anything. Henry is never much at talking.

"Perhaps Mr. Bledsoe is surprised," Daisy Cavanaugh said. "I suppose I'm about the only girl in this business."

"Daisy," said Mr. Cavanaugh, "now, Daisy!"

"I'm sure that Shiny Denny will be very pleased when he gets here," I said. "May I ask when he arrives?"

"Sometime tomorrow morning," she told me. "He has

Stable No. 2. He's trucking down Mr. Maxey's Lighthouse. Lighthouse is entered in the South Cove Handicap next week.''

"Yes," I said. "And he will be the favourite. It's kind of hard on Mr. Maxey to run a favourite, even for a big purse." She looked at me for a second before she answered, and I looked back.

''Well,'' she said, ''what of it?''

"Nothing of it," I said, "nothing, miss. I'm acquainted with Mr. Maxey. Lighthouse is very fast."

"And may I venture to add," Mr. Cavanaugh broke in, "that I, for one, have found Mr. Maxey strictly honourable in all his dealings."

"I'm glad, sir," I said.

Daisy was still looking at me. "You know a great deal, don't you, Mr. White?" she remarked. "You follow the races, don't you?"

"Daisy," said Mr. Cavanaugh, "Daisy."

"Yes, miss," I told her. "Racing is all I know. I'm just an ordinary gambler, miss."

The hard look left her eyes. "Call me 'Daisy'; don't call me 'miss.' I'm just a common horse conditioner myself."

"Call me 'Jack,'" I said. "Every morning I'm at the track to see the exercising, I'll look forward to seeing you."

"Thanks, Jack," she said. "I'm going to breeze Fighting Bob tomorrow. We're entering him in the third race, Monday—an allowance race for three-year-olds. Will you clock him for me? I think he's ready."

"And believe me, sir," said Mr. Cavanaugh, "I should be delighted to receive your opinion as a friend and an expert."

Then Henry Bledsoe spoke up. "Mrs. Griscom," he called, "I'll trouble you for a glass of water and a spoon. I'm taking my bicarbonate now."

I liked Daisy and Mr. Cavanaugh. We had a capital time all day. We spent a long while together, running over old races and talking of this and that, and to hear him was like the fresh air from the bay. There was no hard words from Mr. Cavanaugh about anything or anybody.

"If I wager on an animal of mine, sir," he said, "I wager on him to win, and so I will do with Fighting Bob. He has the makings of a great horse, sir, and his dam's courage to run a fine race. I hope you'll agree with me, sir, when we work him out tomorrow."

Toward evening, after supper, Henry and I walked down the road a piece alone. "Old fool," Henry kept saying beneath his breath, "old fool and a tenth-rate horse."

"But, Henry," I told him, "Mr. Cavanaugh's a gentleman."

"Yes," said Henry, "and that's why he's a fool, ain't it? There's something isn't right, White; there's something isn't right."

It disturbed me to hear Henry say it, because Henry is quick that way. I knew myself that something wasn't right, but I would have bet my bottom dollar that neither Mr. Cavanaugh nor Daisy was in it.

It has been my custom for many years to rise at dawn and to proceed to the track to see the horses train. At such times, Henry would hold the watch, while I would simply sit and look and maybe walk around the stables and talk to friends. That is the time, in those early sessions, when one can learn all sorts of useful things, if one has ears and eyes. It is always a beautiful sight to me to see the horse jogging around the track, past the deserted grandstand, more beautiful than any picture.

"Believe me, sir," said Mr. Cavanaugh, "there is no Turner in the National Gallery to equal it. May I tempt you with a touch of my flask, sir? The world may change, but good horse-flesh is the same, thank God."

He said it as we stood leaning on the rail of the deserted judges' stand at the Langleyville track that next morning. Mr. Cavanaugh was wrapped in an old coaching coat that made him look like a faded sporting print on some tack-room wall. He was peering through an antiquated pair of field glasses. The sun was coming up, driving away the mist.

"Ah!" he said. "Daisy is bringing out Fighting Bob!"

Now, what I'm trying to tell you is right dramatic in its way. Take people alone, and they may have no interest, but take them in their relations to others and you can have anything from tragedy to comedy. Down by the stable then, I saw Daisy, with the sun streaking that gold hair of hers, riding a rangy bay out to the track. He was stepping soft, as though he had eggs under him.

"You like him, sir?" asked Cavanaugh, and he twisted the corner of his moustache. He was pleased to see his own horse on the track. Before I had time to think of a truthful answer—the horse's looks were good enough, but I didn't like his action—a young fellow in a leather windbreak jacket came bounding up the steps.

"Good morning, Mr. Cavanaugh," he said. "I'm glad to see you here." Mr. Cavanaugh twisted the end of his moustache again. I had known the boy since he was a kid exercising for the Whitlers. His name was Tommy Cole. As long as I had known him, he had been sober and well-behaved, and now he was training for the Huntley stables and worth all the money that they paid him.

"Morning, Mr. Bledsoe," Tom Cole said. "Miss Cavanaugh asked will you please clock Fighting Bob? She's going to turn him loose out of the six-furlong chute."

I was pleased to see that Fighting Bob had improved. He went into the stall like he was used to it, and then he came out a-roaring to a clean, fast start. Daisy Cavanaugh was riding him like a man. She was saving him till she got around the turn, and then I saw her hands move, and Fighting Bob moved with them, and then I forgot about Daisy's riding.

Tom Cole nudged me with his elbows. "Did you ever see anything so beautiful?" he asked. He was thinking of Daisy, but I was thinking of the horse. There was something in Fighting Bob's conformation that reminded me of an animal that had paid me money once. Daisy gave him his head, and he went across the line in style. Daisy eased him up and came walking back, rubbing her eyes on her sleeve, but I hardly looked at her, I was looking at the horse.

"What's the time?" she called, and Henry Bledsoe called it back.

"Mr. White, sir," said Mr. Cavanaugh, "I trust you agree with me that Fighting Bob's is a credit to the Oak Hill stock."

"He'll have mighty fine odds Monday, sir," I said. I might have added, it is one thing for a horse running by himself and another as to how he behaves in a crowd.

"Pa," called Daisy, "come on down to the stables! Shiny Denny's here. . . . And won't you gentlemen come too?"

We walked behind them slowly toward Stable No. 2, and Henry and I exchanged a glance. Henry and I may be different in some ways, but we understand each other.

"Henry," I said, "I'd kind of like to get up close to Fighting Bob. Does he remind you of anything?" There isn't much that Henry doesn't remember. He has the clocker's gift for spotting a horse in the twilight under wraps, if he has seen him as much as once.

"White," he said in my ear, "you're a born fool with money, but you're not a fool about everything. As far as my facts go, Fighting Bob might as well be Maxey's Lighthouse. Comical, ain't it, that Fighting Bob and Maxey's Lighthouse should be in the same stable? White stocking on the near foreleg, star the size of a half dollar on the forehead."

"That's the difference," I said; "Fighting Bob's forehead is plain."

"Yes," said Henry Bledsoe softly, "the difference of a white half dollar."

Then I mentioned another thought to Henry which was running in my mind: "The odds are going to be almighty heavy on Fighting Bob, third race, Monday, Henry. If ever there was a rank outsider who might start at 60 to 1, it's Fighting Bob." Henry coughed behind his hand.

"White," he asked me, "do you reckon Maxey's thought of that?"

The door to Stable No. 2 was closed. Mr. Cavanaugh and Daisy and Tom Cole were out in front of it and with them was that button-nosed Greenway and Shiny Denny. Shiny Denny was in his store clothes, polishing his nails. He was a little, leather-faced, black-eyed man, who had been a jockey when I had known him first.

"How's Lighthouse, Shiny?" I asked him. "Did he van down nice?" Shiny laughed, showing a set of yellow teeth, and jerked his thumb toward the closed door.

"Lighthouse is resting comfortably inside," he said. "Honest, boys, I wish I could take you in to see him, but now that Miss Cavanaugh's turned over to me, the stable is closed. No offence intended. Mr. Maxey's orders."

"Why, Shiny," I told him, "I always believed in quiet stables. How is Maxey? When's he coming down?"

"Mr. Maxey's coming down on Monday," Shiny said; "not that he's got anything running, you understand." Then he polished his nails again and turned to Daisy Cavanaugh. "You done a swell job on those horses, Miss," he added, "and I've got a piece of news for you that makes me kind of sick. I've got to leave for New York tonight. My old mother's dying up in the Bronx. It hurts me, because I know you're counting on me for Monday. I can't be here. I simply can't, to saddle Fighting Bob."

I saw Mr. Cavanaugh twitch his moustache and I saw Daisy's lips come tight together, and I knew the only thing they cared about was seeing Fighting Bob in that Monday's race. Furthermore in all the years I'd known him, I'd never heard Shiny speak of his mother in Bronx. I knew one thing just as sure as shooting. There was something going to happen that Monday, and Maxey was getting out from under.

"I'm very sorry, sir," I heard Mr. Cavanaugh saying. "This is a bitter blow to me, but we'll forget it. Fighting Bob can't start without a trainer."

Then I saw Daisy and young Tom Cole looking at each other, and then Tom Cole cleared his throat. "If you'll let me, Mr. Cavanaugh," he said, "I'll be proud to saddle Fighting Bob the third race Monday, and Mr. Huntley will be proud to have me. None of our own are entered. You know and I know that no horse can enter a race unless a licensed trainer saddles him."

"Why," Mr. Cavanaugh began, "that's a great kindness,

Mr. Cole." And they looked at each other for a second or two, and then Tom Cole said: "I'd do a sight more than that, you know."

Then I looked at Denny, because he interested me more than anybody else just then. It seemed to me that he was pleased—too pleased.

"That's fine," he said; "then everything's all right. You've got a great horse, Mr. Cavanaugh."

Henry Bledsoe did not have much to say that day. There wasn't much need to talk, because Henry and I understood each other. About an hour before supper, he spoke to Mrs. Griscom.

"Jack and I won't be in to supper," he said; "we're walking up to town."

It was the first I had heard that we were going into town, but I understood what Henry meant. Henry was thinking of the roll. Henry was on to something, and I knew what.

There is only one drugstore in Langleyville, and Henry and I walked in. First Henry bought a packet of cigarettes and some matches. This surprised me, because Henry thinks cigarette smoking is a sin, and he doesn't spend money without reason. Then Henry began to talk to the clerk, and talking is not in Henry's line. On the back counter of the store was a row of patent medicines, sarsaparilla, and Indian remedies. Henry is good on patent medicines, since he's tried them all, and right away the clerk knew he was talking to a master.

"Are you a salesman, mister?" the clerk said.

"No," said Henry. "Bless you, no, I've never sold the stuff. It's only I'm interested in my own insides. How's your line of hair dye?" said Henry. "Do you move much hair dye, friend?"

"Well, no sir," the clerk said; "hair dye goes mighty slow hereabouts."

"I want to know," Henry said. "You'd think somebody would buy it."

"Well," the clerk said, "now you speak of it, I did sell a bottle this afternoon."

"I want to know," said Henry. "Who bought it? An old-ish man?"

The boy in the white coat grinned. "Why, no," he said. "That's why I remember it. The party didn't look as though he needed hair dye for himself. He was a youngish fellow with a round button nose and a kind of rosebud mouth. One of the racing crowd, a stranger here like you, sir."

"Well," said Henry, "would you give me a glass of water and a spoon of bicarbonate? They tell me soda puts colour in the hair."

Once we were outside the store, Henry tapped my arm. He did not need to comment on what we had heard, because I had ears. Greenway had bought a bottle of brown hair dye, and Maxey's horse named Lighthouse had a white star on his forehead.

"Come on," said Henry; "we're going to the track."

It was pitch dark at the track by then. A light wind was blowing, sighing through the emptiness of the grandstand, and you could swear that horses' ghosts were running on the wind. There were lights in the superintendent's house; and lights in the stable tack rooms were just small dots of light in a bare black carpet. Henry tapped my arm again.

"White," he whispered, "I'm going into Stable 2. I want to look at them two horses close. Take these cigarettes. There's a pile of straw outside of Stable 3. You walk by it, light a cigarette and drop a match in the straw. And when it takes, you holler 'Fire!' That'll fetch 'em out, and all I want is half a minute."

Now, everybody knows there's nothing more serious around a track than fire. I wanted to argue with Henry, but he is hard to argue with, and I did exactly what he said. I walked over to the rubbish pie and dropped three matches in it. The straw took fire like tinder, and then I started running, shouting:

"Fire in Stable No. 3!"

The sight of the blaze brought the boys out of the stables like bees out of hives. Even when it was out, a crowd still stood around the straw pile, talking, and then Henry was back, tapping on my arm.

"All right, let's blow," he said. "Them two are alike as two peas. You go back to Griscom's, White. I want to watch that Greenway party. He'll be calling in the bank tomorrow morning or else I miss my bet."

I was tired when I got back to Griscom's, but somehow I couldn't sleep, and maybe you can't blame me, now that you see the picture as I saw it. In a sense, we were on to something good, but I was troubled by conscience just the same. The trouble was that Mr. Cavanaugh was a gentleman.

Next morning was Saturday, a bright clear day. Around noon Henry came back and we walked down the road a piece. Henry was looking pretty pleased.

"Greenway cashed a telegraph order for seventy-five hundred dollars," he said. "I guess we know where it's going, White—on Fighting Bob, third race, Monday afternoon—and our roll is going with it."

But somehow I couldn't do it quite like that.

"No, Henry," I said, "no, we don't. I'm going to tell Mr. Cavanaugh about this, Henry."

Henry's mouth fell open. Sometimes Henry is mighty ugly when he is mad. "You mind your own business," he snapped. "What are these Cavanaughs and these crooks to you and me?" I could see his point; but still, I have a conscience.

"No," I said, "Mr. Cavanaugh's a friend of mine. Mr. Cavanaugh must decide for himself." Then Henry began to swear. He turned the air sky-blue, but I knew that I was right.

"The trouble is, Henry," I said, "Mr. Cavanaugh's a gentleman."

"Well, we ain't, are we?" Henry shouted.

"No," I said, "but we've got instincts. No, Henry you leave this to me. We ought to tell Mr. Cavanaugh on Monday. It's up to him, not us."

Maybe I was a fool. I'm never wholly sure. It isn't easy, in my position, to see a sure thing tossed away, but when I think of the race track at Langleyville that Monday, maybe I was right.

We had a touch of bourbon whisky before we left for the track.

"I admire your abstemiousness, Mr. White," Mr. Cavanaugh told me, "and I honour it, but I must beg of you for once to break your invariable rule. It isn't often these days that a horse of mine is running. Maybe this will be the last time I see my colours on a track. I must beg of you, sir, to touch glasses with me. To my three-year-old, sir, Fighting Bob!"

"To Fighting Bob, sir," I said.

"Daisy," he said, "fill up my flask in case these gentlemen or I should need encouragement. . . . And, gentleman, we take our places in the clubhouse today. The admission is on me. . . . No, sir, I insist. You must gratify an old man's whim."

Once he was inside the club, Mr. Cavanaugh was bowing, smiling, talking. He knew everybody who was worthwhile there at the club. He went into one of the upper rooms and ordered a round of drinks, though I took lemonade.

"Yes, gentlemen," he kept saying, "keep your eyes on my Fighting Bob in the third race. His dam was Daisy Dimple—you remember Daisy Dimple, gentlemen."

When the horses were going to the post for the first race, Henry and I got up. "If you'll excuse us," I said, "we're going down to the stands." And then I lowered my voice and added, "Mr. Cavanaugh, I admire you very greatly; that's why I have a request to make. There's a man I want you to see in private. Could you arrange to see us in this room, alone? I want to see him before the horses are led out to the paddock for the third."

Mr. Cavanaugh's head went back. "This is most unusual," he said. "Are you insinuating that there is something wrong? If there is, I'll ask for you to kindly tell me now."

"You'll know why when I get back," I told him. "I can only say right now, I think you'll thank me, sir."

Money was going down on Fighting Bob—so much that

he had dropped from 50 to 1 to 20 on the probable-odds board.

"Jack," said Henry, "there's still time. Will you be a born fool all your life?" I knew by the odds that Maxey had placed his money, and Henry knew it too.

"No," I said, "after Mr. Cavanaugh's seen Maxey, maybe we'll bet then."

When Maxey is at the track, he always stands between races at the hotdog stand near Entrance No. 6, in case anyone should want to see him. Maxey was standing there smoking a cigarette, a broad-shoulder little man with smooth black hair and a face the colour of unbaked clay. It was the sort of face that would not change at anything. When I came up, he turned a pair of eyes on me, icy cold.

"Howdy, Jack," he said. "What's on your mind?"

And I put my arm through his and whispered in his ear:

"Maxey, you and I are walking over to the clubhouse to see Mr. Cavanaugh, unless you want for me to holler for the track detective."

I felt Maxey's arm grow stiff.

"What's your game, pal?" he asked.

"It's not my game," I said; "it's yours. We're going up to the clubhouse to talk about Fighting Bob." Maxey's eyelids fluttered, but that was the only sign he gave.

Daisy and Mr. Cavanaugh were waiting for us in the room upstairs, alone, when Henry and Maxey and I came in. I closed the door and put my back against it.

"Mr. Cavanaugh," I said, "there's something I think you ought to know. And what you do is your business, not mine. I'll never say a word, and Mr. Maxey here will tell you whether I'm right or wrong. It's my opinion that Mr. Maxey has been making use of you, Mr. Cavanaugh. Right this minute Lighthouse is in Fighting Bob's stall, with a star on his forehead painted out. He's ready to run for Fighting Bob in the third race, and I thought you ought to know."

Maxey smiled and lighted a cigarette.

"That's baloney," he said.

I looked at Daisy and Mr. Cavanaugh. Both their faces

had grown white. Mr. Cavanaugh started to speak, and stopped. "Now wait, Mr. Cavanaugh," I went on. "I'm not blaming this on you, and generally I don't go in for reform. Maxey is betting seventy-five hundred on Fighting Bob, because Lighthouse is ringing for him. If you want my opinion, Maxey has done a first-rate job. It's my honest belief that if Lighthouse runs, no one will know it. I believe that Lighthouse is a sure winner if he runs. Henry, here, is ready to go down and bet. I thought I ought to tell you first, that's all."

"Hey," said Maxey, and his voice was no longer cool, "if you know so damn much why didn't you play along and keep your mouth shut?"

"Because I've got a conscience, Maxey," I told him. "And Mr. Cavanaugh's a gentleman. I suggest we walk down to the stable right now, quick, before they lead 'em out, and see if I'm right or wrong; or maybe, Maxey, you'd like me to call for the detective. You can take your choice."

Mr. Cavanaugh stood up very straight and spoke very slowly. There was no great change in his voice, but somehow his voice was terrible.

"We'll go to the stables," he said.

Maxey licked his lips.

"Now wait a minute," he said, "wait a minute. Let's talk sense. We're all sensible here, ain't we? Sure, I had the thought two weeks ago. Lighthouse is a ringer for that dog, Fighting Bob. Listen, folks, I know when I'm licked, and now I got a business proposition. We all sit down and take it easy. We don't say a word until this race is over. I've got seventy-five hundred up on Bob and we ought to get 20 to 1. Now, come, you don't want to bust up a sure thing. Seventy-five hundred, and fifteen minutes from now it's a hundred and fifty grand." Maxey licked his lips again. "I'm being straight. I'm telling you clean truth, and here's my proposition, folks: a fifty-fifty cut, just as soon as we cash in. I'm no piker; I've never been a piker. Fifty grand for you and the little lady, Mr. Cavanaugh, and twenty-five grand split between White and Bledsoe, and that's more money than any of you folks'll see again. What do you say? Let's sit down and be sociable.''

Maxey's voice stopped, and when it did you could hear the noise from the crowd outside, a restless sound like the ocean against the rocks. It was a good quarter of a minute before anyone said a word. Mr. Cavanaugh took a cigar from his pocket, cut off the end and lighted it, but his fingers were trembling when he held the match.

"Mr. White," he said, "this is very shocking, both to me and to my daughter. I hope sincerely you feel we are in no wise connected with this, and I am very deeply grateful to you, sir. Neither my daughter nor I would have permitted a friend of hers to saddle a horse which we did not own. As for me, I want you to know that I've always raced clean. My money's down on Fighting Bob and I owe it to the public to put him on the track."

He bowed to me and turned toward Maxey. It was like a show to see it. "And as for you, you rascal," said the colonel, "I could hand you to the law, but I'm going to be the law. We're going to the stables now and my eye will be on you, Mr. Maxey. You've put your money on Fighting Bob, and if I were you, Mr. Maxey, I'd yell for Fighting Bob to win. We'll start walking to the stables, now. Mr. Maxey, you'll walk between Mr. White and me, please."

I was proud to be walking with Mr. Cavanaugh. There are not so many things that I can be proud of, but I was proud of that. He walked to Stable No. 2 not too fast, and not too slow, just as the horses were moving out from the paddock for the second race. Mr. Cavanaugh chatted to us just as though nothing were wrong. "It's a very fine day for racing, Mr. White," he said, "and the crowd is in a betting mood. Do you remember the old days at Saratoga? This is like a Saratoga day. . . . Mr. Maxey, tell your men to get outside; we shall want the stable to ourselves." We blinked, once the stable door was closed behind us, and then we were used to the fainter light. A horse was standing in the third stall on the right. His bridle was on already. I could have sworn he was Fighting Bob. Mr. Cavanaugh stood in front of him.

"White," he said, "I declare, I think you're wrong."

"Take the flask out of your pocket, Mr. Cavanaugh," I said; "wash his face for him. Whisky will take out the dye."

Mr. Cavanaugh's motions were deliberate. He drew out his flask and sopped his handkerchief with the whisky.

"Steady, boy," he said, and rubbed hard between the horse's eyes. There was a small white star between the eyes when he took his handkerchief away. Holding the handkerchief between his thumb and forefinger, he offered it to Mr. Maxey. "Take it as a souvenir," he said, "and I should keep it carefully if I were you. Where's Fighting Bob?"

"There," Daisy said, "down there on the left."

"Daisy," said Mr. Cavanaugh, "lead him out. . . . Help me to shift those horses, Maxey, if you don't want to go to prison. Then call a boy to lead my entry to the paddock."

Then, just as though nothing had happened, we walked back to the clubhouse again and stood on the terrace waiting for the start. "Yes," said Mr. Cavanaugh, "it's a nice day for a race." Maxey did not say a word.

"If you'll excuse me," said Henry, "I think I'll place a bet."

"By all means," said Mr. Cavanaugh, "and if you'll take a tip from me, I'd bet on Fighting Bob."

Then a voice shouted from the loudspeakers like a voice of doom: "The horses are now going to the post."

Maxey cleared his throat. "The betting windows are closed now," he said; "if you'll excuse me, this company is too holy. I never seen fifty grand tossed away like that. Maybe you're a gentleman, but what's it get you, Cavanaugh?"

"My dear fellow," said Mr. Cavanaugh, "it's never got me anything. It's always been a minus quality. Must you be going really? Then don't come back again." Maxey drew a deep breath that was almost like a sigh.

"Mister," he said, "you're damn well right, I won't."

Then Daisy took my hand. "Thank you," she whispered, "thank you, Mr. White."

Mr. Cavanaugh was looking through his battered glasses. "He's standing nicely, my dear," he said; "he'll start this time." And then there was a sound like waves, that sound that will make me roll over when I'm dead, a soft sound, too hushed to be a shout, and our own voices joined in it as we said, "They're off!"

Now, believe me, that first second when they're off is always just pure gold. The colour and the motion is like the sun through a stained-glass window, I sometimes think. It's a brave sight, a fine sight.

"Daisy," said Mr. Cavanaugh, "we've got a good boy up. Take the glasses, my dear. He's fourth; he's on the rail."

Then Daisy's voice was shaking. "Yes," she said, "he's going well! He's coming up! He's coming up!" I did not like to be there to see it. The boy was Jerry Hoberg, a good rider. There was a black from the Nixon stables that I had always fancied; at the halfway mark this black came out of the bunch easily. At the last turn he took second place and then he moved out ahead. Mr. Cavanaugh looked away from the track.

"A very pretty race. The Nixon black wins," he said.

"Wait a minute," I said to him—wait a minute. Bob is coming up." The crowd saw it a second later. Fighting Bob was moving as though he were pushed upon a wave. He was in third, he was in second before the boy on the black horse looked behind him. Just for an instant I thought the rush might pull him through, but the boy in front looked soon enough. Down came his whip, and the black drew off. Fighting Bob was gaining, but not enough, not enough. Daisy was holding my hand, and I saw that she was crying, and then Mr. Cavanaugh saw it too.

"Don't cry, my dear," he said. "That was a pretty challenge. He hasn't got his dam's courage, but how could we tell that?"

"Father," Daisy was sobbing, "it's my fault. I thought he was better. It was my fault to make you put up your bottom dollar." Mr. Cavanaugh patted her shoulder very gently. "My dear," he said, "others have lost with us. After all, what's racing for? It was a very pretty race."

"Yes, sir," I said, and then I saw that Henry Bledsoe was

back. Henry was beckoning to me. "White," he said, "come over here. I don't want the old man to know."

"Know what?" I asked him, and Henry looked embarrassed. "White," said Henry, "he ain't our kind. We got to keep away from sports like him. I kind of got to liking him, White, down there in the stable, and you know what I found myself doing? I found myself putting our roll on Fighting Bob to win."

I felt a little cold inside, but Henry and I have been broke before. "We're in good company," I said.

"No, we ain't," said Henry, "and that's why I'm ashamed. I been a piker, White. The last minute I put down on Fighting Bob to run second, and now he's paying 12 to 1, but don't tell the old man, will you, please? Just tell him we bet on Fighting Bob?"

HARMONY

William Fain

JOHN Stephens nodded while Auslander, the American, gave him instructions about how to ride the race. They were at St. Cloud, walking to the paddock. Stephens wished Auslander would not put his arm around his shoulder. Why did people think that because a jockey was a small man it was all right to touch him all the time? He did not much like owners, anyway. It would be a grand sport without them, he thought, and smiled; he had no sense of humour, and for him this was a pretty fair joke. Stephens did not like riding instructions much, either. Did Auslander have any idea of all the things that could happen during a race? Still, he half listened, and nodded.

"I've never run him in the mud, but I don't think he'll mind it," Auslander was saying.

When they got to the paddock, and to the horse Stephens was to ride, Auslander's trainer, Garnier, gave the jockey a leg up. Stephens didn't have much use for Garnier, but at least he offered no instructions.

The race was nothing special—a handicap at a mile and a quarter for four-year-olds and up. Stephens was on a seven-year-old bay called Pantagruel that was top weight although he had no chance of winning. He had won a couple of races the year before but would not do much that spring, even in cheap company; he was nearly burned out and had never had much heart anyway. Without thinking about it, Stephens knew what to do.

He got a good hold on Pantagruel as the tapes flew up, and took him to the rail. At the Fouilleuse, the horse had moved up on his own initiative to be about ten lengths off the leaders. Coming into the stretch, Stephens began to ride him. That is, he started scrubbing, moving with the horse, encouraging him with hands and heels but not whipping him. The horse responded pretty well; Stephens had been patient, and Pantagruel had a little run in him. He moved up to third, halfway down the stretch, and Stephens began to think the old horse might get there. He was gaining, but not fast; he could make only a little run. Then suddenly, the horse running second, an aged chestnut mare of Archer's, stopped, and Pantagruel passed her. Stephens saw it was no use whipping; the horse in front, which Dumesnil was riding, was making it all right and should win by a good four lengths. Stephens eased Pantagruel and held on to second by half a length. That was better than he had expected. Second money was seventy thousand francs; ten per cent of that was seven thousand.

Riding back to the scales, Stephens picked mud off his face. He was used to it. The waiting race was his speciality.

A man and a woman watched him ride back and talked about him; of course he didn't hear them.

"In his old age, Stephens is making combinations," the man said angrily.

"He looks terrible," the woman said. "His face looks like death. It's almost black."

"That's only mud, from being behind all the time," the man said. "The Englishman has just lost an unlosable race."

"No, under the mud he looks awful. His face looks a hundred years old."

"He must be almost fifty," the man said. "Perhaps he is senile. Really, his way of riding becomes ridiculous. He should retire. He has plenty of money. He never spends any."

Stephens was not very tired. Every race is somewhat tiring, especially at the beginning of the season, but this one had been easy. Pantagruel was a steady old horse—no good, but easy to ride.

Stephens went to the jockeys' room. Pantagruel was his only mount of the day. He was bringing himself along slowly, as he had done every spring in recent years, riding only a horse or two a day and gradually bringing his weight down and getting into form. Besides, at forty-nine, and after being fired (everyone believed) by Perrault the fall before, he was not being offered many mounts.

He didn't speak to anyone in the jockeys' room. He rarely did. He washed and dressed carefully, cleaning the mud out from under his nails and combing his heavy black hair neatly, using plenty of brilliantine. He put on clean white riding breeches, a tweed sports jacket, and well-shined black boots. If the woman who had pitied him as he rode back with mud on his face had seen him walking out of the jockeys' room, she would have been surprised. Cleaned up and dressed in fresh clothes, his binocular case slung over his shoulder, stopping to take a cigarette from his case and light it with his gold lighter, furrowing his brow as he lit it, then drawing in a good lungful of smoke with enjoyment, then letting the smoke out as the wrinkles in his brow smoothed out, he looked only about thirty-five, and quite chipper. Though he had little interest in women, he liked to be neatly dressed. He got a haircut and a manicure once a week. He was careful about money, but he liked good things—well-cut breeches, boots that cost forty thousand francs a pair, a good wrist-watch, a good cigarette-case, a good lighter, Charvet Eau de Cologne on his face after a shower. Having the best of things like that cost very little more in the long run, he reasoned. Cheap boots wore out quickly, for example.

Auslander came up as Stephens was lighting his cigarette. He was a fat man with grey hair. His face was flushed. "Nice kid, very nice," Auslander said. Stephens figured he had had a place bet. "Next time we'll do better."

"I expect that's the best he'll do," Stephens said.

"He needed a race, that's all. Don't you think?"

"He runs good when he's fresh, Mr. Auslander. That's about the best he'll do. He's getting to be an old horse."

"I liked the way you rode him, Jack," Auslander said. "You didn't take too much out of him. He'll be all the better for it. We'll win a race with him, and I'm going to put you up again, too."

Stephens looked at the tote board. Pantagruel had paid forty-three francs for a ten-franc place bet.

"Did you back him for the place, Mr. Auslander?" he asked.

"Just five hundred each way, to encourage him," Auslander said.

The stingy liar, Stephens thought. "You were lucky," he said.

"Jack, I'm going to give you a good many mounts this spring, and see how we do," Auslander said.

"What do you want with me?" Stephens said. "Garnier's got young Luzzi on contract."

"Oh, there can't be any contract," Auslander said quickly. "I don't care about the Perrault business, but—"

"I don't want a contract just now," Stephens said, just as quickly. "I'm better off on my own."

"Sure," Auslander said. "Well, I expect to use you often."

"Much obliged," Stephens said.

Stephens did not stay for the rest of the races. There was nothing of interest. As he left the racecourse, he stepped on a piece of chewing gum. Scraping the sticky pink stuff from his boot with his little gold penknife, he thought, automatically, Americans.

He went to the parking lot reserved for trainers and jockeys, unlocked his Renault *quatre-chevaux*, and drove home to Paris. He and his wife had an apartment near the Parc Monceau. During his dinner—a steak, salad without dressing, two hard, dry *biscottes*—his wife asked him, "Did it go well today?"

"Not bad," he said. "We were second."

Stephens' wife was a Frenchwoman not much younger

than he, whom he had married right after he first came out from England. She took no interest in racing. She did not think much of it as an occupation for a man to be in, and she did not realize that her husband was quite a famous man in France. Although a good deal of money came into the house, she did not believe this would continue; she never had believed so. She saved money, and hoped (without ever saying anything about it) that eventually they would buy a shop—an *épicerie*, a *charcuterie*, or a bakery. There was nothing like food, she knew; no matter what happened, people ate. Her father had been a baker in Argenteuil. She considered it a little discreditable that her husband was English, and she never brought the matter up, to him or anyone else. They spoke French to each other, though Stephens had never learned the language thoroughly.

A little later, Stephens said, "Auslander, the American, is going to give me some mounts. It was his horse I was second on today. I hear he's got a pretty fair three-year-old."

"There will be a contract?"

"No."

"Ah! Naturally! He is very glad, I'm sure, to make use of you without a contract. You should have insisted. Why do you permit this American to take advantage of you?"

"He already has a contract jockey," Stephens said. "His trainer has this young Italian, this Luzzi."

"That is to say, the American uses you when he wishes, and then puts you to the door," said his wife. "I'm sure it's very interesting for him."

Her voice was high-pitched and irascible, not because of real ill nature but because she had been brought up to believe that life was a struggle in which you must ever be on guard against being tricked. Stephens was used to her piercing voice, laden with suspicion, and it did not bother him. She was his wife, and he assumed that that was the way wives were. He and she got along well; as a matter of fact, he never thought much about whether they got along or not, though sometimes he wished he had someone to talk to about horses.

After dinner, Stephens went out to buy a *Sport Complet*.

He sat in a café and read it for half an hour, with a quarter litre of vichy in front of him. The waiter knew him but acted as if he had never seen him before; he considered Stephens a cheapskate. Stephens believed that only fools gave large tips.

When he went home, his wife told him that Garnier had called from Chantilly. She said he wanted Stephens out there at seven the next morning for the workouts. "If I were in your place, I shouldn't go," she said. "You are not under contract. He's taking advantage of you."

Stephens didn't answer.

"Well, will you go?" she asked.

"I'll decide in the morning," Stephens said.

Stephens did not go to Chantilly in the morning. He wanted to; he liked morning workouts almost more than anything else in racing. But a full-fledged jockey does not exercise horses except for the man who holds his contract, or in preparation for a classic race in which he is to ride. He could not go.

He saw Auslander at the races that afternoon, at Le Tremblay Auslander said he wanted to talk to him, and they walked through the gardens by the paddock, where flowers were planted all along the paths. Le Tremblay was so pretty that Stephens could hardly take it seriously as a racecourse.

"I was hoping you'd be out this morning," Auslander said.

"I'm not available in the mornings, Mr. Auslander," Stephens said.

"We might work out a contract later."

"I don't want a contract," Stephens told him. "How many horses have you? Ten? You don't need me."

Auslander was a man who hated to lose at anything. "I need your help, Jack," he said. "I need your advice. Why don't you come out and take a look tomorrow? I'd like your opinion on what I've got."

"No harm in that, I suppose," Stephens said.

"I've got to be getting along," Auslander said. "My sister-in-law is in the stands. You wouldn't have a winner, would you, Jack? I'd like to give her one. What do you like in the Prix Matchem? Domrémy should be able to take it, don't you think?''

''I've no idea at all, Mr. Auslander,'' Stephens said.

Auslander went back to the stands and told his sister-in-law Stephens had given him a strong tip on Domrémy. The horse finished third. ''Next time,'' Auslander said.

Stephens rode only once that day, in the last race. It was a cheap handicap at a mile and three-quarters for three-year-olds. In England, they would have thought it a long way to send three-year-olds early in the year. But these were horses of no quality, anyway.

Stephens rode a Norseman colt belonging to Médlizélatis, the Greek. As usual, Stephens waited, going along in last place for a mile. Coming into the final turn, he was next to last, and he felt then that the colt was ready to move. He had no class but he could run all day. Stephens took the colt to the far outside to make his run, but the field of twenty horses swung very wide, and the colt was carried wider still, losing half a dozen lengths.

Seeing that he was beaten, Stephens did not persevere. He galloped past the winning post in seventh or eighth position, beaten a good ten lengths. The Greek's trainer, Barsant, stopped him as he went to dress.

''Why did you go to the outside?'' he asked angrily. ''There was room for a regiment of cavalry on the rail.''

''Where were you watching from?'' Stephens asked him.

''From the top of the stands,'' Barsant said. ''There was a veritable *autostrade* on the rail for you. It appears you are too old to take chances now.''

''The race is over,'' Stephens said. He walked away from Barsant and went to the dressing-room.

It was a little race of no importance, but it annoyed him that he had made a mistake. Every jockey makes mistakes, and they do not ordinarily upset him, and no one holds them against him as long as he gets his share of winners. An apprentice that everybody's talking about may make three in one day, but if he is getting good mounts and also rides a couple of winners that day, the mistakes are forgotten. When a jockey is going down, people remember his mistakes, and he remembers them; there are not enough good mounts to blot them out. Of course, Stephens didn't think he was going down, but things were not going well at the moment.

The worst of the race just over was that it reminded him of his last ride for Perrault. Octave Perrault, the automobile man, was the biggest owner in Europe. Stephens, his contract rider, had ridden Astolat, the best three-year-old in Europe, in all his races. Astolat was second in the Guineas (the mile was too short for him) and won the Jockey-Club and the Grand Prix de Paris. In the big fall race at a mile and a half, the Prix de l'Arc de Triomphe, Stephens waited and kept Astolat far back under a tight hold as they climbed the long green hill at Longchamp, and then began moving him up as they came down the hill and into the turn. He swung Astolat to the outside on the turn, the field drifted out, and Stephens had to take him wider and wider, losing ground all the time.

Astolat was a good colt, the best in the race, a long-striding colt with stamina, and he lost no momentum in making the turn—no rhythm of his stride—but he was too far back, and as he passed the winning post, he was second, beaten a neck. He passed the winner in the next few strides, and the crowd booed Stephens back to the scales.

Perrault had been in racing a long time, and yet he believed that if you have the best bloodstock, the best trainer, the best jockey, the best lads, the best stud farm with the best grass in Normandy, one of the best biologists in France as an adviser on breeding, and the best equipment, right down to the leather in the saddles, you should never lose a race. Perrault's secretary telephoned Stephens that night and told him to come to the great man's office. Stephens went. Perrault had a whole building in the Faubourg St. Denis—a big modern thing, with lots of glass. The building was dark when Stephens arrived. A silent elevator operator took him up in a silent elevator, and he walked down the bare modern hall to Perrault's office. Perrault, a heavy, frowning man with black-rimmed glasses, sat behind his desk.

"Well, what happened, Stephens?" he asked.

On the way there, Stephens had thought he might tell Perrault that Astolat was a long-striding colt who liked to run by himself, away from other horses, and that he wouldn't have kept his stride if Stephens had squeezed him through on the rail. There was some truth in it; the horse did like to run along the outside. Stephens liked riding the Perrault horses. He liked being first jockey for the greatest stable in Europe. Perrault had, over the past twenty years, developed a breed of horses of his own—long-striding horses that never tired, that were always going on at the end. They did not have a great deal of what the French call, in racehorses, *brio*, but they had an everlasting sturdiness and gameness. Stephens liked to ride them. He believed no one suited them as he did. He could tell Perrault none of this. "I'm taking myself off all your horses, Mr. Perrault," he said.

Since then, things had gone badly. He had not had many good mounts, and he had lost some races that he might have won. The Auslander connection might help. He had had a little luck with Pantagruel. But Stephens had got the mount on Pantagruel only because Luzzi was riding another horse for Garnier. Stephens had no use for Luzzi, but the kid was riding well just now. He had had a lot of luck the past year.

At dinner, Stephens' wife said, "It went well today?"

"No luck today," Stephens said.

At six the next morning, Stephens got up and drove to Chantilly. There were no cars on the road. It had rained during the night, and everything was fresh and clean. It would be a fine day. The leaves were a little behind the leaves in Paris, but they were all coming out. He drove along slowly.

Garnier had a big place out at Chantilly, opposite the Piste de Lamorlaye, where he had Auslander's horses and those of four or five other owners. The stables were stone, forming a big square with green clipped lawn in the centre. Stephens parked his car and walked into the big courtyard. Auslander and Garnier were standing there on the grass with Jim Craye, Garnier's head lad. Stephens walked across the grass and shook hands with them.

"Mr. Auslander wants me to put you on Tekel, the Admiral Drake colt," Garnier said. "We've got him eligible for everything at Longchamp, but I don't know if he'll do anything."

Garnier spoke in English. Around a French stable, everybody can speak English; even the French grooms usually talk English to the horses. There is a theory that horses find English more soothing.

" 'E's a nice little 'orse," Jim Craye said. He was a little Cockney with bright-blue eyes and a jutting chin and no teeth, who had come from England fifty years before. He was one of the handful of Englishmen left around the stables at Chantilly. Although they were all getting to be old men, they were in great demand. Even French trainers believe that an Englishman is better than anybody else with a horse. Jim had been a good jockey, years ago.

"I could've sold him last week for two million, and bought Dupré's colt," Auslander said. "Maybe I should've done it."

"He didn't do anything last year, did he?" Stephens asked.

"I only ran him twice," Garnier said. "I didn't expect him to do anything. I'm against two-year-olds racing, on principle."

Garnier was a short, stout, sallow man with a little black moustache. He had become a trainer because his father had been one. He never expected his horses to win; he was always against racing them. And yet, because he was patient and careful, he won a lot of races for his clients.

"Tekel hasn't grown much during the winter," Auslander said. "I should've sold him and bought something else."

" 'E's a nice little 'orse," Jim Craye said. " 'E'll win 'is race."

"Bring him out, Jim," Garnier said. "Let's have a look at him."

Jim Craye went and led Tekel, a rather small, almost black colt, out of his box.

"What do you think, Jack?" Auslander asked anxiously.

"I've no idea at all, Mr. Auslander," Stephens said. "He looks all right. Bit small, but that doesn't matter."

There was the sound of a car stopping quickly, and Luzzi, the Italian jockey, came into the courtyard. He shook hands with everybody, Stephens last.

"So you going to help me, eh, old man?" Luzzi said to Stephens, smiling. Luzzi was a dark-haired kid of nineteen, with sharp dark eyes in a face still soft and without the lines and angles a jockey's face eventually gets. He looked almost girlish.

"That's right," Stephens said.

The first lot of horses was brought out of the stalls, fifteen of them, and jockeys and lads mounted them. Stephens got on Tekel's back. Jim Craye said, "Don't 'urry 'im and don't bother 'im. 'E's not mean, but 'e's got a mind of 'is own, as you might say."

The fifteen of them rode out in a long line, Luzzi first on a chestnut five-year-old, Stephens next on Tekel, and Jim Craye third, on a three-year-old bay colt. They rode to the grassy training course, the Piste de Lamorlaye, across the road. The horses walked slowly, dancing a little and stretching their necks. They were all feeling good. So were the lads. They whistled tunelessly as they rode along in the early-morning light. The sound of many birds was loud on the training course.

Garnier and Auslander walked across, and Garnier asked Stephens to work Tekel a mile. "Start off at the château," Garnier said. "Jim will get away ahead of you. Pass him after half a mile, and finish out a mile here. Let him run the last half mile, understand, but don't *ride* him."

Jim Craye started off, going ahead fifteen lengths. Stephens rode behind, taking his time. They went along that way for a while, Tekel galloping nicely. Stephens watched old Craye, riding far forward in the saddle, light and spry as a boy, coaxing the best out of a horse that would never be worth anything. Jim was closer to seventy than to sixty. It was a pleasure to watch him. After half a mile, Stephens let Tekel run a little and passed the other horse easily. Tekel had a nice run in him, Stephens found, although he had a rather short stride and Stephens could not tell whether the run would last long under pressure. At the end of the mile, he pulled Tekel up by Garnier and Auslander and slid off.

"What do you think?" Auslander asked.

"He's a very nice colt, Mr. Auslander," Stephens said, patting Tekel's muzzle. "I should think he'd do."

"Do you think he's a Poule d'Essai colt?" Auslander asked. The Poule d'Essai des Poulains is the French Two Thousand Guineas, a classic mile for three-year-olds.

"Hard to tell. I shouldn't sell him if I were you, though."

"I've got him in a mile race at Longchamp in a week," Garnier said. "I'm not sure he's ready for it."

"He's ready," Stephens said.

"You think he can win?" Auslander said. "It's the Prix St. James. There's not much in it."

"He's ready to run a good race, that's all I know," Stephens said.

"Well, anyway, one thing sure, I'm not going to sell him," Auslander said happily. Then he added, "Not right away, anyhow."

Stephens went back to the stables. He had hung his sports jacket in the tack room. He got it and put it over the grey turtleneck sweater he was wearing. As he went out again, he passed Tekel's stall. Jim Craye was standing beside it, and the colt was kicking the wooden wall. "Know what 'e wants?" Craye said. " 'E wants 'is breakfast. 'E'll kick down the barn if 'e don't get it."

Stephens had known Jim Craye for thirty-five years, off and on. In the days when Stephens was an apprentice at New-market, Craye was a jockey living in France but sometimes riding in England for a French stable.

"You've a nice berth here, Jim," Stephens said.

"Can't complain," Jim said.

"Do you ever go to the races these days?"

"I've not been on a racecourse in ten years," Jim said. "Too busy out 'ere."

Things went along pretty quietly for a while. Stephens rode better as the season wore on, but he did not win often. He won the Prix St. James—a trial for the Poule d'Essai—on Tekel, by a neck. Auslander complained that Stephens had made it too close. Stephens began to find Auslander more and more tiresome; like all owners, he was obsessed with winning.

Every morning now, Stephens went out to Chantilly to work horses for Garnier. He was happy doing this. He began to wonder if he enjoyed only practice races on the training course, where the result was decided in advance. He did not care as much as he had about winning on the racecourse. He lost some races that he could have won. Sometimes he lost because, without thinking it out, he felt that he could not win smoothly and easily, that there would be something forced and strained about winning, which was distasteful to him. He could not explain these feeling to himself, and of course he could not explain them to owners and trainers, so he did not get many good mounts. He did not mind, except for the money, he told himself, and he reminded himself now and then that he had plenty of money.

He had enjoyed being one of the great jockeys of Europe. It did not seriously occur to him now that he was ceasing to be that. His self-esteem was high still. He knew that he was as strong as ever, and that his sense of pace, his knowledge of when to move, and his understanding of a horse were as fine as ever. He told himself that he would like to ride a really great horse, like Astolat, again, one for whom everything was easy and smooth, one of those long-striding, irresistible Perrault horses. If he had a great horse, he would give him a great ride.

Stephens rode Tekel in all his workouts and became fond of the little colt. Tekel had a neat, extremely pure action, although his stride was perhaps too short for him to get a distance in good company. He was courageous; if, in training, Stephens permitted another horse to come up to him at the end of a workout, Tekel would draw away on his own courage, without urging. He had some temperament; in the morning, walking to the training course, he would shy in pretended fright at every shadow. But it was all good-natured and innocent. Stephens found that once he had called on Tekel for an effort, that was enough. The horse did not like to be reminded of what he was supposed to do when he was already doing it. Once he had begun to run, the best thing was to sit absolutely still on him. " 'E knows what 'e was put on earth for," Jim Craye said. Stephens never whipped him and did not intend to. He and Tekel went well together. He thought Tekel was good, and might be very good.

Auslander and Garnier decided to run Tekel in the Poule d'Essai, and Stephens won with him fairly easily, letting him go to the front after half a mile. Tekel was improving all the time. In Chantilly, he began to be mentioned as a horse that might be one of the good ones. Auslander got very enthusiastic and talked of the Jockey-Club and the Grand Prix.

Luzzi, Garnier's contract jockey, heard this talk and complained that Garnier should have let him ride Tekel. Garnier told him that Stephens happened to fit the colt, and that besides, it was a whim of Mr. Auslander's to have Stephens ride him. Luzzi couldn't do anything, for though Garnier had first call on Luzzi he was not obliged to use him. Still, Luzzi was resentful and talked against Stephens in the jockeys' rooms at the racecourses and in the bars of Chantilly.

One day, in a little race at St. Cloud, Stephens and Luzzi were both riding. Stephens brought his horse through on the rail and won handily, but in slipping through to take the lead near the last turn, his horse brushed against Luzzi's. After the race, walking to the jockeys' room, Luzzi said to him. "You think you're pretty hot, old man, don't you?"

"I didn't bother you," Stephens said. "You weren't going anywhere."

"You think you're hot," Luzzi said. "Sometime someone will slam you so hard you'll go down and you won't get up."

"Never mind about me," Stephens said, and walked away.

From them on, Luzzi said something unpleasant to Stephens every time he saw him. The other jockeys encouraged him and hoped that something would happen between him and Stephens. There was a feeling that because Stephens did not drink and talk with the others at the Derby, the Jockey-Club, or any of the other Chantilly bars, he was too pleased with himself. "*M. Stephens, c'est un* gentleman," they said, using the English word derisively.

Stephens paid no attention to Luzzi. He had always gone his own way. He had never been liked.

Luzzi was not popular, either. He was a foreigner. He had ridden only one other season in France. He was young and successful. Feeling unpopular and unsure of himself, Luzzi believed he could make himself liked by quarrelling with Stephens. This was only a little successful. Some of the others even resented it, feeling that, after all, they had disliked Stephens first.

Auslander decided to run Tekel in the Prix Lupin, one of the big spring tests for three-year-olds. The Lupin is at a mile and five-sixteenths. Stephens and Garnier told him this was too far.

"You mean he can't win?" Auslander asked.

"Oh, he might win," Stephens said.

"It's not his distance," Garnier said. "A mile is about his limit. He might go farther in the fall, when he's grown a little."

"God damn it," Auslander said. "I think I've got a classic colt here. I want to run him in the Jockey-Club." The Jockey-Club, at a mile and a half, is the French Derby.

"I'd much rather wait, Mr. Auslander," Garnier said. "If you give this little horse some time, he'll win plenty of nice races for you. You don't want to run him in the Jockey-Club."

"That's just what I do want," Auslander said. So it was decided to try him first in the Lupin.

The race was run on a Sunday, at Longchamp. It rained during the night and morning, but the sun came out before noon. Longchamp is the loveliest racecourse in the world, with the long sweeping green turns of the course, the speckled shade of the walking ring under the chestnut trees, and the calm, cheerful trees themselves. Fresh from the rain, the chestnut trees slick and wet, the sky a fresh light blue, and all the green a richer green, it was more beautiful than usual that day. A racecourse is at its best and happiest, Stephens thought, before the first race on an important day when the weather is fine. Then everything is clean and everything is before you. The lawns have not been littered with torn-up pari-mutuel tickets. No one has been saddened or angered by losing.

Stephens and Garnier went out on the course to see how the going was. It was heavy. Tekel had never run in the mud, and Stephens had a feeling he was too fragile to relish it. The heavy going and the distance would combine to stop him. "It's asking too much of him," Stephens said to Garnier.

"Just see that he does the best he can," Garnier said.

"He'll do that," Stephens said.

"If we can win this, it will do you a lot of good," Garnier said. "You'll be getting mounts from a lot of people."

"I'll win if I can," Stephens said. "I've won the better part of the classics in Europe. What's it matter if I win this or not?"

"They forget those other races," Garnier said.

Stephens rode in one race besides the Prix Lupin that day— a mile for three-year-old maidens that came just before the Lupin. He had taken the mount, on a big, nervous, unmanageable gelding of the Vicomtesse de Rantigny-Lazarches, because he wanted to find out ahead of the main race what the course was like. He had worked the horse once or twice at Chantilly, and did not believe he could do anything.

The field was big—twenty-five runners—and Stephens' number was 23. Luzzi, No. 24, was to start next to him on a colt of the Nawab of Bhopal. As the horses circled around behind the barrier, Stephens knew he would have trouble. His mount was in a lather, trembling and rearing, the way the ones that amount to nothing often do. At the start, when the tapes flew up, he swerved to the left and slammed into Luzzi's colt, knocking him almost to his knees. After that, there was no chance for either of them. They just galloped along behind the field.

After the race, Luzzi came up to Stephens outside the jockeys' room and said, "I don't let anybody do that to me." His lips were white and compressed, because he had decided he must hit Stephens.

"It was an accident," Stephens said.

"I don't allow that," Luzzi said, uncertain of the right words and trying to work himself into the state of fury he wished to be in.

Luzzi knew a little about boxing. He feinted low with his left hand, and then hit Stephens between the eyes with his right, knocking him down.

Stephens knew nothing of boxing. He had not been in a fight since childhood. But he had imagined being in fights, and it had never occurred to him that he could be beaten in one. He jumped up after a second and awkwardly pushed his right fist at Luzzi. Luzzi stuck his left in Stephens' face before Stephens' fist could land. The punch hit Stephens' nose, and he went down again, caught off balance. He got up quickly, and Luzzi struck him again between the eyes. As he was getting up the third time, some people grabbed Luzzi and pulled him away.

The fight had lasted only a few seconds. Not many of the big crowd had seen it, but gossip travels as quickly as tips around a racecourse, and soon everyone knew that Luzzi had beaten up the Englishman. Many people who really did not care one way or the other, but who had heard that Stephens thought he was better than anyone else, or who had at some time lost a bet on a mount of Stephens', said it was about time.

Stephens walked into the jockeys' room in a fury. He was furious partly because his nose was bleeding and the blood was dripping down over the Vicomtesse de Rantigny-Lazarches's yellow-and-white silks, which seemed to him a dirty, disgusting, and ridiculous thing to have to happen. He felt sick at his stomach. He washed and changed into Auslander's silks—grey, with red hoops on the sleeves, and black 'A's on the back and on the black cap—and as he was combing his hair, Garnier came in. The bleeding had stopped, but Stephens still felt sick. His face ached, and he would soon have two black eyes.

Garnier's pudgy, sallow, unhappy face had a look of embarrassment. "This is terrible," he said. "You understand, you don't need to ride."

Stephens, concentrating on combing his thick black hair, didn't look around. "Who will you put up?" he asked. "Luzzi?"

"Of course not," Garnier said. "I can get Kemp."

"Kemp's nearly as old as I am," Stephens said. "Do you think your horse'll do better with him?"

"You're not well," Garnier said.

"Don't be a bloody fool," Stephens said. "I'm riding him unless you order me off."

"I'm not doing that," Garnier said.

"Does Auslander order me off him? Is that it?"

"No, but he's worried. That's natural."

"Tell him to stop worrying," Stephens said. "He can buy his tickets. I expect to win this race."

Garnier walked out to the paddock with Stephens and gave him a leg up on Tekel. Everyone there looked at Stephens' battered face. He had been ready to hear them laugh, but no one did. His face hurt, though, and he felt old and sick. Auslander came up beside Garnier, smiling worriedly. He said nothing.

There was a field of eleven for the Lupin, and Stephens believed only three could trouble him: Mohilal, a good colt of the Aga Khan's that had finished well in his two races of the year; Djérama, a Boussac colt that had won his three starts; and Heronwood, a Rothschild horse that had chased Tekel in the Prix St. James and the Poule d'Essai. Boussac also had entered another three-year-old, called Phactaris, that would be sacrificed to make the pace.

The race started. The Boussac pacemaker went to the front at the signal. Stephens took up Tekel and held him in fourth position. Mohilal was second and Djérama third. They continued that way up the hill. Tekel was full of run in spite of the heavy going, and Stephens' arms ached from holding him. As they entered the little wood just below the crest of the hill, Stephens sensed that Phactaris, the Boussac flier, was having it too easy. There was not enough pace. He let out a wrap on Tekel, who bounded forward to draw even with Djérama, and an instant later the two of them went after Mohilal almost together. Tekel was running willingly, and after he and Djérama had moved past Mohilal, he gradually drew away from Djérama, and Stephens sent him after Phactaris, still four lengths in front and holding on courageously. Coming down the hill, Stephens let Tekel all the way out and clucked to him, and he moved right past Phactaris in a few bounds to take the lead. Phactaris dropped out of the race, Djérama and Mohilal stayed fairly close in second and third, and Heronwood, the Rothschild colt, began to move up.

At the bottom of the hill, Tekel faltered for an instant and seemed to flounder in the sticky mud. Stephens sat absolutely still on him, and Tekel regained his stride. Stephens knew the colt was terribly tired, though he was still going well.

Taking the last turn, Stephens sat like a rock on Tekel, not moving his hands, not looking back for fear the movement might throw Tekel off stride, though he knew the Rothschild colt would be coming at him. There was no change in Tekel's neat, flawless stride. The race was too long for him, it was beyond his powers and he was exhausted, but his heart was fine, so he kept right on, running smoothly and cleanly, with no choppiness, through the holding mud. Stephens continued to sit still. It was not his way of riding—his race was the waiting race and then the drive in the last half-mile—but this was the way to ride Tekel. The horse must do it all; Stephens' job was to make it as easy for him as possible.

At the beginning of the stretch, Heronwood came at Tekel, not with a rush but with a steady, plodding attack. Three hundred yards from the end, Heronwood's head was even with Stephens' left boot. When Heronwood was a neck behind Tekel, Tekel felt the challenge and began to fight it off, drawing away a little from the colt. Then he faltered again, and slid a little; his legs would not quite obey his heart. Heronwood gained a head on him.

Stephens had the whip in his left hand. He put it between his teeth, took the reins in his left hand without easing the slight pressure he always kept on the bit, took the whip in his right hand, and started whipping. Heronwood was so close Stephens could not whip left-handed.

Tekel floundered under the whip as if shocked. Then he straightened out and moved again. Stephens flogged him as hard as he could all the way, raising the bat high and bringing it down with a crack on Tekel's crupper again and again, even after they had passed the finish line a neck in front of Heronwood.

It was a popular win; the crowd had made Tekel the favourite, and they cheered Stephens back to the scales.

"You see," a man in the crowd said, "he can win when he wants to."

When Stephens had weighed in, he saw Auslander hurrying through the enclosure toward him. Stephens avoided him and went to the jockeys' room. He changed quickly, and got his car and drove home.

"My God, what has happened to you?" his wife said when she saw him. "Look at your face!"

Stephens looked at himself in an oak-framed mirror that hung in the dark hall. Both his eyes were black, and a band of purple-black spread across the bridge of his nose.

"Not pretty, I admit," he said.

"You've fallen off a horse!" his wife screamed.

"I have not!" Stephens said angrily. *"Ne parle pas comme une idiote."* His French tended to be a literal translation of English.

"You've fallen off a horse," his wife said. "Riding horseback may be all right for rich men. For a man in your station, it's ridiculous."

"Perhaps you're right," he said.

"Come into the kitchen and let me take care of your face," she said. "A man who is almost fifty! It's idiotic."

Like an irascible, loving mother, she took care of his face.

For a week, Stephens stayed at home. Garnier telephoned and said he would like to see him. Stephens said he wanted to rest. Garnier told him the commissioners had set down Luzzi for a month. Stephens asked him how Tekel was, and Garnier told him that the horse had limped when he was cooled out after the race, and that he had not been worked since. "His ankles look bad." Garnier said. "There may be a bowed tendon. The vet will tell me in a day or two." Garnier's voice sounded uncomfortable, as though he were trying to keep anger out of it.

"Well, I'm sorry to hear that," Stephens said.

Stephens was sure Tekel would never run with good horses again, and he believed it was his fault. He didn't blame Auslander, who was only the owner.

There is nothing wrong with whipping a horse. It doesn't hurt him much, and many won't run without it. But Stephens knew he had done something ugly when he laid the whip on Tekel. He had asked the colt for more than he could give, and Tekel, with wild generosity, had given it. Tekel had given Stephens everything he might have had in every other race he might run in his life.

Stephens stayed indoors that week, drinking coffee and reading *Sport Complet*—he sent his wife out to get it—and she began saying, "Perfect! You are in retirement, then. Do you wish me to go into service?"

But after a week, when his face looked all right, he said to her, "I'm going out to Chantilly in the morning."

"Why?"

"To ride some of Garnier's horses for him."

"The races!" she said. "I hoped you were finished with that."

"Oh, I'm through with racing," Stephens said. "Sick of it."

"So much the better. What will you do?"

"Exercise horses for Garnier."

"He'll pay you?" she asked.

"Of course."

"How much?"

"About forty thousand a month, I think lad's get," Stephens said.

"That's very good. A regular salary, even though it's smaller, is better than depending on the generosity of foreigners." She had always believed that all racehorse owners were foreigners and that jockeys were paid in tips, like waiters.

"We'd better leave Paris," Stephens said. "Too expensive. How would you like to like in Chantilly?"

"We could buy a little store there," she said. "I've always wanted a little business."

"Have you?" Stephens asked, smiling. "Well, I suppose we might. Have to look about a bit first, and go into it carefully."

"Of course," his wife said happily.

In the morning, Stephens drove out to Chantilly. It was green all along the way, now. At the village of Lamorlaye, where he turned off for Garnier's, he passed le Derby. Mme Bernard, the lean, muscular owner, was flinging water from a bucket out over the stone terrace. He thought that perhaps he'd stop and have a glass of white wine there, after the morning's work. Because he had been so serious about his profession, he had drunk almost nothing for thirty years, but now he thought with pleasure of drinking cold white wine when the workouts were over. He'd drink it out on the terrace there.

In the courtyard at Garnier's, he met Jim Craye. Garnier wasn't up. Jim showed Stephens around, talking about the horses in the slow, steady, gentle way that men have who have worked around horses all their lives. Tekel was not in his stall, and Jim explained that Auslander was selling him. Tekel had not bowed a tendon after all, Jim said, but he was finished just the same.

"You'll be out 'ere regular now?" Jim asked Stephens.

"Yes, I'm going to live out here," Stephens said.

"It's a good place. The boss is all right."

Garnier came down from his house, which was in front of the stables facing the road. He had not shaved, and was wearing carpet slippers.

"I want you to gallop a little two-year-old for me, Jack," Garnier said. He walked with Stephens to the two-year-old's box. "Take him out," Garnier said.

Stephens led the colt out.

"He's not ready for anything," Garnier said. "Maybe he never will be. Mme de Ratigny-Lazarches wants to run him at Deauville, but I'm against it. Today we'll just give him a nice gallop."

The other lads were bringing their horses out and mounting. Stephens mounted, and they all rode out across the road to the Piste de Lamorlaye and walked the horses out onto the grass.

The dewy grass, bent from being ridden over, looked blue and purple with the long morning shadows on it. The horses felt fine; they were snorting and shying. The lads felt fine, all whistling their monotonous, tuneless little tunes. Stephens, on a fresh two-year-old that had never been on a racecourse, felt fine, too. In the thickets along the sides of the training course, the birds were just tearing into their songs, as if they knew that the world had been made new that morning—a fresh, new, morning world. Stephens heard them and thought, it's all nonsense about birds singing. They don't really sing songs, they chirp. And yet—although surely no bird listened to the others—it all went fine together when they set to it early in the morning.

THE BAGMAN'S PONY

Somerville & Ross

WHEN the regiment was at Delphi, a T.G. was sent to us from the 105th Lancers, a bagman, as they call that sort of globetrotting fellow that knocks about from one place to another, and takes all the fun he can out of it at other people's expense. Scott in the 105th gave this bagman a letter of introduction to me, told me that he was bringing down a horse to run at the Delhi races; so, as a matter of course, I asked him to stop with me for the week. It was a regular understood thing in India then, this passing on the T.G. from one place to another; sometimes he was all right, and sometimes he was a good deal the reverse—in any case, you were bound to be hospitable, and afterwards you could, if you liked, tell the man that sent him that you didn't want any more from him.

The bagman arrived in due course, with a rum-looking roan horse, called the "Doctor"; a very good horse, too, but not quite so good as the bagman gave out that he was. He brought along his own grass-cutter with him, as one generally does in India, and the grass-cutter's pony, a sort of animal people get because he can carry two or three more of these beastly clods of grass they dig up for horses than a man can, and without much regard to other qualities. The bagman seemed a decentish sort of chap in his way, but, my word! he did put his foot in it the first night at mess; by George, he did! There was somehow an idea that he belonged to a wine

243

merchant business in England, and the Colonel thought we'd
better open our best cellar for the occasion, and so we did;
even got out the old Madeira, and told the usual story
about the number of times it had been round the Cape. The
bagman took everything that came his way, and held his
tongue about it, which was rather damping. At last, when it
came to dessert and the Madeira, Carew, one of our fellows,
couldn't stand it any longer—after all, it *is* aggravating if a
man won't praise your best wine, no matter how little you
care about his opinion, and the bagman was supposed to be
a *connoisseur*.

"Not a bad glass of wine that," says Carew to him; "what
do you think of it?"

"Not bad," says the bagman, sipping it. "I think I'll show
you something better in this line if you'll come and dine with
me in London when you're home next."

"Thanks," says Carew, getting as red as his own jacket,
and beginning to splutter—he always did when he got angry—"this is good enough for me, and for most people
here—"

"Oh, but nobody up here has got a palate left," says the
bagman, laughing in a very superior sort of way.

"What do you mean, sir?" shouted Carew, jumping up.
"I'll not have any d—d bagmen coming here to insult me!"

By George, if you'll believe me, Carew had a false palate,
with a little bit of sponge in the middle, and we all knew it,
except the bagman. There was a frightful shindy, Carew
wanting to have his blood, and all the rest of us trying to
prevent a row. We succeeded somehow in the end, I don't
quite know how we managed it, as the bagman was very
warlike too; but, anyhow, when I was going to bed that night
I saw them both in the billiard room, very tight, leaning up
against opposite ends of the billiard table, and making shoves
at the balls—with the wrong ends of their cues, fortunately.

"He called me a d—d bagman," says one, nearly tum-
bling down with laughter.

"Told me I'd no palate," says the other, putting his head

down on the table and giggling away there, "best thing I ever heard in my life."

Every one was as good friends as possible next day at the races, and for the whole week as well. Unfortunately for the bagman his horse didn't pull off things in the way he expected, in fact he hadn't a look in—we just killed him from first to last. As things went on the bagman began to look queer, and by the end of the week he stood to lose a pretty considerable lot of money, nearly all of it to me. The way we arranged these matters then was a general settling-up day after the races were over; every one squared up his books and planked ready money down on the nail, or if he hadn't got it he went and borrowed from someone else to do it with. The bagman paid up what he owed the others, and I began to feel a bit sorry for the fellow when he came to me that night to finish up. He hummed and hawed a bit, and then asked if I should mind taking an I.O.U. from him, as he was run out of the ready.

Of course I said, "All right, old man, certainly, just the same to me," though it's usual in such cases to put down the hard cash, but still—fellow staying in my house, you know—sent on by this pal of mine in the 11th—absolutely nothing else to be done.

Next morning I was up and out on parade as usual, and in the natural course of events began to look about for my bagman. By George, not a sign of him in his room, not a sign of him anywhere. I thought to myself, this is peculiar, and I went over to the stable to try whether there was anything to be heard of him.

The first thing I saw was that the "Doctor's" stall was empty.

"How's this?" I said to the groom; "where's Mr. Leggett's horse?"

"The sahib has taken him away this morning."

I began to have some notion then of what my I.O.U. was worth.

"The sahib has left his grass-cutter and his pony," said

the *sais*, who probably had as good a notion of what was up as I had.

"All right, send for the grass-cutter," I said.

The fellow came up, in a blue funk evidently, and I couldn't make anything of him. Sahib this, and sahib that, and sa-laaming and general idiocy—or shamming—I couldn't tell which.

This is a very fishy business, I thought to myself, and I think it's well on the cards the grass-cutter will be out of this tonight on his pony. No, by Jove, I'll see what the pony's good for before he does that. "Is the grass-cutter's pony there?" I said to the *sais*.

"He is there, sahib, but he is only *akattiawa tattoo*," which is the name for a common kind of mountain pony.

I had him out, and he certainly was a wretched-looking little brute, dun with a black stripe down his back, like all that breed, and all bony and ragged and starved.

"Indeed, he is a *gareeb kuch kam ki nahin*," said the *sais*, meaning thereby a miserable beast, in the most intensified form, "and not fit to stand in the sahib's stable."

All the same, just for the fun of the thing, I put the grass-cutter up on him, and told him to trot him up and down. By George! the pony went like a flash of lightning! I had him galloped next; same thing—fellow could hardly hold him. I opened my eyes, I can tell you, but no matter what way I looked at him I couldn't see where on earth he got his pace from. It was there anyhow, there wasn't a doubt about that. "That'll do," I said, "put him up. And you just stay here," I said to the grass-cutter; "till I hear from Mr. Leggett where you're to go to. Don't leave Delhi till you get orders from me."

It got about during the day that the bagman had disap-peared, and had had a soft thing of it as far as I was con-cerned. The 112th were dining with us that night, and they all set to work to draw me after dinner about the business— thought themselves vastly witty over it.

"Hullo Paddy, so you're the girl he left behind him!"
"Hear he went off with two suits of your clothes, one over

the other." "Cheer up, old man; he's left you the grass-cutter and the pony, and what *he* leaves must be worth having, I'll bet!" and so on.

I suppose I'd had a good deal more than my share of the champagne, but all of a sudden I began to feel pretty warm.

"You're all d—d funny," I said, "but I daresay you'll find he's left me something that *is* worth having."

"Oh, yes!" "Go on!" "Paddy's a great man when he's drunk," and a lot more of the same sort.

"I tell you what it is." said I. "I'll back the pony he's left here to trot his twelve miles an hour on the road."

"Bosh!" says Barclay of the 112th. "I've seen him, and I'll lay you a thousand rupees even he doesn't."

"Done!" said I, whacking my hand down on the table.

"And I'll lay another thousand," says another fellow.

"Done with you too," said I.

Every one began to stare a bit then.

"Go to bed, Paddy," says the Colonel, "you're making an exhibition of yourself."

"Thank you, sir; I know pretty well what I'm talking about," said I; but, by George, I began privately to think I'd better pull myself together a bit, and I got out my book and began to hedge—laid three to one on the pony to do eleven miles in the hour, and four to one on him to do ten—all the fellows delighted to get their money on. I was to choose my own ground, and to have a fortnight to train the pony, and by the time I went to bed I stood to lose about £1,000.

Somehow in the morning I didn't feel quite so cheery about things—one doesn't after a big night—one gets nasty qualms, both mental and the other kind. I went out to look after the pony, and the first thing I saw by way of an appetiser was Biddy, with a face as long as my arm. Biddy, I should explain, was a chap called Biddulph, in the Artillery; they called him Biddy for short, and partly, too, because he kept a racing stable with me in those days, I being called Paddy by every one, because I was Irish—English idea of wit—Paddy and Biddy, you see.

"Well," said he, "I hear you've about gone and done it

this time. The 112th are going about with trumpets and shawms, and looking round for ways to spend that thousand when they get it. There are to be new polo ponies, a big luncheon, and a piece of plate bought for the mess, in memory of that benefactor of the regiment, the departed bagman. Well, now, let's see the pony. That's what I've come down for.''

I'm hanged if the brute didn't look more vulgar and wretched than ever when he was brought out, and I began to feel that perhaps I was more parts of a fool than I thought I was. Biddy stood looking at him there with his underlip stuck out.

''I think you've lost your money,'' he said. That was all, but the way he said it made me feel conscious of the short-comings of every hair in the brute's ugly hide.

''Wait a bit,'' I said, ''you haven't seen him going yet. I think he has the heels of any pony in the place.''

I got a boy on to him without any more ado, thinking to myself I was going to astonish Biddy. ''You just get out of his way, that's all,'' says I, standing back to let him start.

If you'll believe it, he wouldn't budge a foot—not an inch—no amount of licking had any effect on him. He just humped his back, and tossed his head and grunted—he must have had a skin as thick as three donkeys! I got on to him myself and put the spurs in, and he went up on his hind legs and nearly came back with me—that was all the good I got of that.

''Where's the grass-cutter?'' I shouted, jumping off him in about as great a fury as I ever was in. ''I suppose *he* knows how to make this devil go!''

''Grass-cutter went away last night, sahib. Me see him try to open stable door and go away. Me see him no more.''

I used pretty well all the bad language I knew in one blast. Biddy began to walk away, laughing, till I felt as if I could kick him.

''I'm going to have a front seat for this trotting match,'' he said, stopping to get his wind. ''Spectators along the route requested to provide themselves with pitchforks and fireworks, I suppose, in case the champion pony should show

any of his engaging little temper. Never mind, old man, I'll
see you through this, there's no use in getting into a wax
about it. I'm going shares with you, the way we always do.''

I can't say I responded graciously, I rather think I cursed
him and everything else in heaps. When he was gone I began
to think of what could be done.

''Get out the dog-cart,'' I said, as a last chance. ''Perhaps
he'll go in harness.''

We wheeled the cart up to him, got him harnessed to it,
and in two minutes that pony was walking, trotting, anything
I wanted—can't explain why—one of the mysteries of horse-
flesh. I drove him out through the Cashmere gate, passing
Biddy on the way, and feeling a good deal the better for it,
and as soon as I got on to the flat stretch of road outside the
gate I tried what the pony could do. He went even better than
I thought he could, very rough and uneven, of course, but
still promising. I brought him home, and had him put into
training at once, as carefully as if he was going for the Derby.
I chose the course, took the six-mile stretch of road from the
Cashmere gate to Sufter Jung's tomb, and drove him over it
every day. It was a splendid course—level as a table, and
dead straight for the most part—and after a few days he could
do it in about forty minutes out and thirty-five back. People
began to talk then, especially as the pony's look and shape
were improving each day, and after a little time every one
was planking his money on one way or another—Biddy putting on a thousand of his own account—still, I'm bound to
say the odds were against the pony. The whole of Delhi got
into a state of excitement about it, natives and all, and every
day I got letters warning me to take care, as there might be
foul play. The stable the pony was in was a big one, and I
had a wall built across it, and put a man with a gun in the
outer compartment. I brought all his corn myself, in feeds at
a time, going here, there, and everywhere for it, never to the
same place for two days together—I thought it was better to
be sure than sorry.

The day of the match every soul in the place turned out,
such crowds that I could scarcely get the dog-cart through

when I drove to the Cashmere gate. I got down there, and was looking over the cart to see that everything was right, when a little half-caste *keranie*, a sort of low-class clerk, came up behind me and began talking to me in a mysterious kind of way, in that vile *chi-chi* accent one gets to hate so awfully.

"Look here, Sar," he said, "you take my car, Sar; it built for racing. I do much trot-racing myself"—mentioning his name—"and you go much faster my car, Sar."

I trusted nobody in those days, and thought a good deal of myself accordingly. I hadn't found out that it takes a much smarter man to know how to trust a few.

"Thank you," I said, "I think I'll keep my own, the pony's accustomed to it."

I think he understood quite well what I felt, but he didn't show any resentment.

"Well, Sar, you no trust my car, you let me see your wheels?"

"Certainly," I said, "you may look at them," determined in my own mind I should keep my eye on him while he did.

He got out a machine for propping the axle, and lifted the wheel off the ground.

"Make the wheel go round," he said.

I didn't like it much, but I gave the wheel a turn. He looked at it till it stopped.

"You lose match if you take that car," he said, "you take my car, Sar."

"What do you mean?" said I, pretty sharply.

"Look here," he said, getting the wheel going again. "You see here, Sar, it die, all in a minute, it jerk, doesn't die smooth. You see *my* wheel, Sar."

He put the lift under his own, and started the wheel revolving. It took about three times as long to die as mine, going steady and silent and stopping imperceptibly, not so much as a tremor in it.

"Now, Sar!" he said, "you see I speak true, Sar. I back you two hundred rupee, if I lose I'm ruin, and I beg you, Sar, take my car! Can no win with yours, mine match car."

"All right!" said I with a sort of impulse, "I'll take it."
And so I did.

I had to start just under the arch of the Cashmere gate, by
a pistol shot, fired from overhead. I didn't quite care for the
look of the pony's ears while I was waiting for it—the crowd
had frightened him a bit, I think. By Jove, when the bang
came he reared straight up, dropped down again and stuck
his fore-legs out, reared again when I gave him the whip,
every second of course telling against me.

"Here, let me help you," shouted Biddy, jumping into the
trap. His weight settled the business, down came the pony,
and we went away like blazes.

The three umpires rode with us, one each side and one
behind, at least that was the way at first, but I found the
clattering of their hoofs made it next to impossible to hold
the pony. I got them to keep back, and after that he went
fairly steadily, but it was anxious work. The noise and excitement had told on him a lot, he had a tendency to break
during all that six miles out, and he was in a lather before
we got to Sufter Jung's tomb. There were a lot of people
waiting for me out there, some ladies on horseback, too, and
there was a coffee-shop going, with drinks of all kinds. As I
got near they began to call out, "You're done, Paddy, thirty-
four minutes had gone already, you haven't a ghost of a
chance. Come and have a drink and look pleasant over it."

I turned the pony, and Biddy and I jumped out. I went up
to the table, snatched up a glass of brandy and filled my
mouth with it, then went back to the pony, took him by the
head, and sent a squirt of brandy up each nostril; I squirted
the rest down his throat, went back to the table, swallowed
half a tumbler of Curaçoa or something, and was into the
trap and off again, the whole thing not taking more than
twenty seconds.

The business began to be pretty exciting after that. You
can see four miles straight ahead of you on that road; and
that day the police had special orders to keep it clear, so that
it was a perfectly blank, white stretch as far as I could see.
You know how one never seems to get any nearer to things

on a road like that, and there was the clock hanging opposite to me on the splash board; I couldn't look at it, but I could hear its beastly click-click through the trotting of the pony, and that was nearly as bad as seeing the minute hand going from pip to pip. But, by George, I pretty soon heard a worse kind of noise than that. It was a case of preserve me from my friends. The people who had gone out to Sufter Jung's tomb on horseback to meet me thought it would be a capital plan to come along after me and see the fun, and encourage me a bit—so they told me afterwards. The way they encouraged me was by galloping till they picked me up, and then hammering along behind me like a troop of cavalry till it was all I could do to keep the pony from breaking.

"You've got to win, Paddy," calls out Mrs. Harry Le Bretton, galloping up alongside, "you promised you would!"

Mrs. Harry and I were great friends in those days—very sporting little woman, nearly as keen about the match as I was—but at that moment I couldn't pick my words.

"Keep back!" I shouted to her; "keep back, for pity's sake."

It was too late—the next instant the pony was galloping. The penalty is that you have to pull up, and make the wheels turn in the opposite direction, and I just threw the pony on his haunches. He nearly came back into the cart, but the tremendous jerk gave the backward turn to the wheels and I was off again. Not even that kept the people back. Mrs. Le Bretton came alongside again to say something else to me, and I suddenly felt half mad from the clatter and the frightful strain of the pony on my arms.

"D—n it all! Le Bretton!" I yelled, as the pony broke for the second time, "can't you keep your wife away!"

They did let me alone after that—turned off the road and took a scoop across the plain, so as to come up with me at the finish—and I pulled myself together to do the last couple of miles. I could see that Cashmere gate and the Delhi walls ahead of me; 'pon my soul I felt as if they were defying me and despising me, just standing waiting there under the blazing sky, and they never seemed to get any nearer. It was like the first night of a fever, the whizzing of the wheels, the ding-dong of the pony's hoofs, the silence all round, the feeling of stress and insane hurrying on, the throbbing of my head, and the scorching heat. I'll swear no fever I've ever had was worse than that last two miles.

As I reached the Delhi walls I took one look at the clock. There was barely a minute left.

"By Jove!" I gasped. "I'm done!"

I shouted and yelled to the pony like a madman, to keep up what heart was left in the wretched little brute, holding on to him for bare life, with my arms and legs straight out in front of me. The grey wall and the blinding road rushed by me like a river—I scarcely knew what happened—I couldn't think of anything but the ticking of the clock that I was some-how trying to count, till there came the bang of a pistol over my head.

It was the Cashmere gate, and I had thirteen seconds in hand.

There was never anything more heard of the bagman. He can, if he likes, soothe his conscience with the reflection that he was worth a thousand pounds to me.

But Mrs. Le Bretton never quite forgave me.

About the Authors

In addition to such enormously successful novels as *The Danger*, *Banker*, and *Bolt*, Dick Francis has written a volume of autobiography, *Sport of Queens*. His most recent bestselling novel was *Longshot*. He now divides his time between England and Florida.

Born in Wexford, John Welcome is the author of the bestselling novel *Grand National* and several acclaimed biographies: *Fred Archer*, *The Sporting Empress* (Elizabeth of Austria), and *Neck or Nothing* (Bob Sievier).